TWIN FLAMES

A LOVE STORY ACROSS TIME AND DIMENSIONS

CAROLYN R. PRESCOTT
ILLUSTRATION BY VICTOR GUIZA

outskirtspress
DENVER, COLORADO

This is a work of fiction. The events and characters described herein are imaginary and are not intended to refer to specific places or living persons. The opinions expressed in this manuscript are solely the opinions of the author and do not represent the opinions or thoughts of the publisher. The author has represented and warranted full ownership and/or legal right to publish all the materials in this book.

Twin Flames
A Love Story Across Time and Dimensions
All Rights Reserved.
Copyright © 2013 Carolyn R. Prescott
v3.0

Cover Illustration by Victor Guiza.

Novels are artistic works of fiction. Some names of towns, businesses, and buildings presented here are real, but used fictitiously to support an imaginary story. Certain incidents in these pages are similar to the author's own experiences and expounded upon within present-day scientific theory and non-fiction religious writings. Any similarity to names of living people or persona of characters is purely coincidental.

Supplemental Information

This book may not be reproduced, transmitted, or stored in whole or in part by any means, including graphic, electronic, or mechanical without the express written consent of the publisher except in the case of brief quotations embodied in critical articles and reviews.

Outskirts Press, Inc.
http://www.outskirtspress.com

ISBN: 978-1-4787-1508-5

Outskirts Press and the "OP" logo are trademarks belonging to Outskirts Press, Inc.

PRINTED IN THE UNITED STATES OF AMERICA

TABLE OF CONTENTS

The Dimensions... i

PART ONE
SINGS TO FLOWERS—LILY

Chapter One: It Hurts 3
Chapter Two: The Remembering Day. 8
Chapter Three: Strange Happenings in the Hospital.. 14
Chapter Four: Was It a Dream or Was It a Memory? 24
Chapter Five: The Wind Speaks.. 27
Chapter Six: The Announcement 30
Chapter Seven: The Arrival to a New Place 34
Chapter Eight: The First Kiss. 38
Chapter Nine: The Okan and the Purification 48
Chapter Ten: The Marriage 58
Chapter Eleven: The Hiding Place 65
Chapter Twelve: The Jump 76
Chapter Thirteen: Lily's Messed Up Escape.. 79
Chapter Fourteen: Lily's Next Adventure. 87

PART TWO
LITTLE BEAR/TWO BEARS—AHHATOME

Chapter Fifteen: Who Is Ahhatome? 99
Chapter Sixteen: The Cord that Binds. 105
Chapter Seventeen: The Hall of the Akashic Records ... 110
Chapter Eighteen: Lost in The Records 122
Chapter Nineteen: If by Any Other Name Were Called 131
Chapter Twenty: How Can Love Come to This? 135
Chapter Twenty-One: My Beloved.. 138
Chapter Twenty-Two: What Happened to Two Bears
and Sings to Flowers? 146

Chapter Twenty-Three: The Council Meets 154
Chapter Twenty-Four: Aba Ahhatome's Warning. 161
Chapter Twenty-Five: Thirty-Three Nights.. 165

PART THREE
AHHATOME—LILY
(   )
LILY—AHHATOME

Chapter Twenty-Six: The Miracle 171
Chapter Twenty-Seven: The Gift 175
Chapter Twenty-Eight: Traveling Home... 184
Chapter Twenty-Nine: Something Odd in Idaho... ... 188
Chapter Thirty: Becoming a Lucid Dreamer 199
Chapter Thirty-One: Dancing with Daemons... 203
Chapter Thirty-Two: Sammy's Secret.. 216
Chapter Thirty-Three: My Lover, My Dream 222
Chapter Thirty-Four: Kundalini Stirring 226
Chapter Thirty-Five: Back to School 239
Chapter Thirty-Six: The Shrink Is a Nice Lady 244
Chapter Thirty-Seven: Lily's Second Little Mess-Up.. ... 248
Chapter Thirty-Eight: Charlie Four Thumbs Helps Lily 252
Chapter Thirty-Nine: The Healing of Lily's Soul Pieces 259
Chapter Forty: New Confidence. 272
Chapter Forty-One: Catrina's Meltdown 281
Chapter Forty-Two: Behind the Scenes 286
Chapter Forty-Three: The Play, the End Is the Beginning... 290

Author's After Notes 305

DEDICATION

My dear mother used to tell me, "When it's your turn to go to heaven, look for me in the Shakespeare Department." We would then have a good laugh over what we thought was undoubtedly a silly concept. However, now that I'm of a "mature age," I say, "Who knows?" When it's my turn I plan to look for her and find out about any Shakespeare Department that may be "up there." After all, the smart people say, "As above, so below."

Dedicated to my mother, Janice Margaret Owens, lover of Shakespeare, and our neighbor when I was growing up, Jean McGee. Both told me to write.

A special thank you to my husband, Chris Prescott, treasured neighbors, and walking group, The Striders, who suffered through the early drafts.

Most of all, thank you to my copy editor, Melissa Breau, and the Outskirts Press team who conquered the enormous challenge that came to them in Twin Flames.

*There are more things in heaven and earth, Horatio,
Than are dreamt of in your philosophy.*
Shakespeare
"Hamlet" Act I, Scene V

The Dimensions

A part of our human soul, or a part of our light, exists in all dimensions. Within these dimensions are layers of refinement. In the human third dimensional awareness, or state of consciousness, the world appears to have distinct edges of height, width, and depth (three dimensions) of substance. It has a certain illusion of rigidity and the appearance of a period of constancy in which we are accustomed to moving in our every-day waking life where we play out our dramas.

The fourth dimension penetrates the third dimension as electrical, magnetic, and cosmic energy waves that pass through all bodies of matter and contain coded information. This dimension can be thought of as both the inside-out and outside-in, or flip-sides of the third dimension, and it functions to hold the third dimension in balance. Once 3-D particles of matter reach light-speed they jump into the fourth dimension as a wave. Without the fourth dimension "spiritual" or energy matrix of all solid forms, the more dense third dimension could not exist.

Emotions and thoughts are the instruments that humans use to bring form and shape to this fourth dimensional energy world that we visit in our dreams. It is also the meeting place of the forms made by the collective unconscious mind energies of all of us. This state of awareness is very fluid and changes shape. Skilled shamans from the past to the present have learned how to read and navigate through this world in order to help humankind understand and release the effects of trauma and assist in soul growth.

As difficult as it is to conceptualize, photons of light exist in the fourth dimension from the past, present, and even future time.

The fifth dimension has even more refined vibrations than the third and fourth, where all exists in higher octaves of light and sound. Third dimensional beings go to the fifth dimension in their thoughts to pull down energy from this level while mentally creating something. Forms in this dimensional world have no abrupt edges, where light bleeds even more easily into other forms. In the fifth dimension, time is irrelevant.

The primary temporary abode of a soul who travels through the dimensions is directly related to where he directs his consciousness, his inner perceptions, and his inner knowledge.

PART ONE
Sings to Flowers—Lily

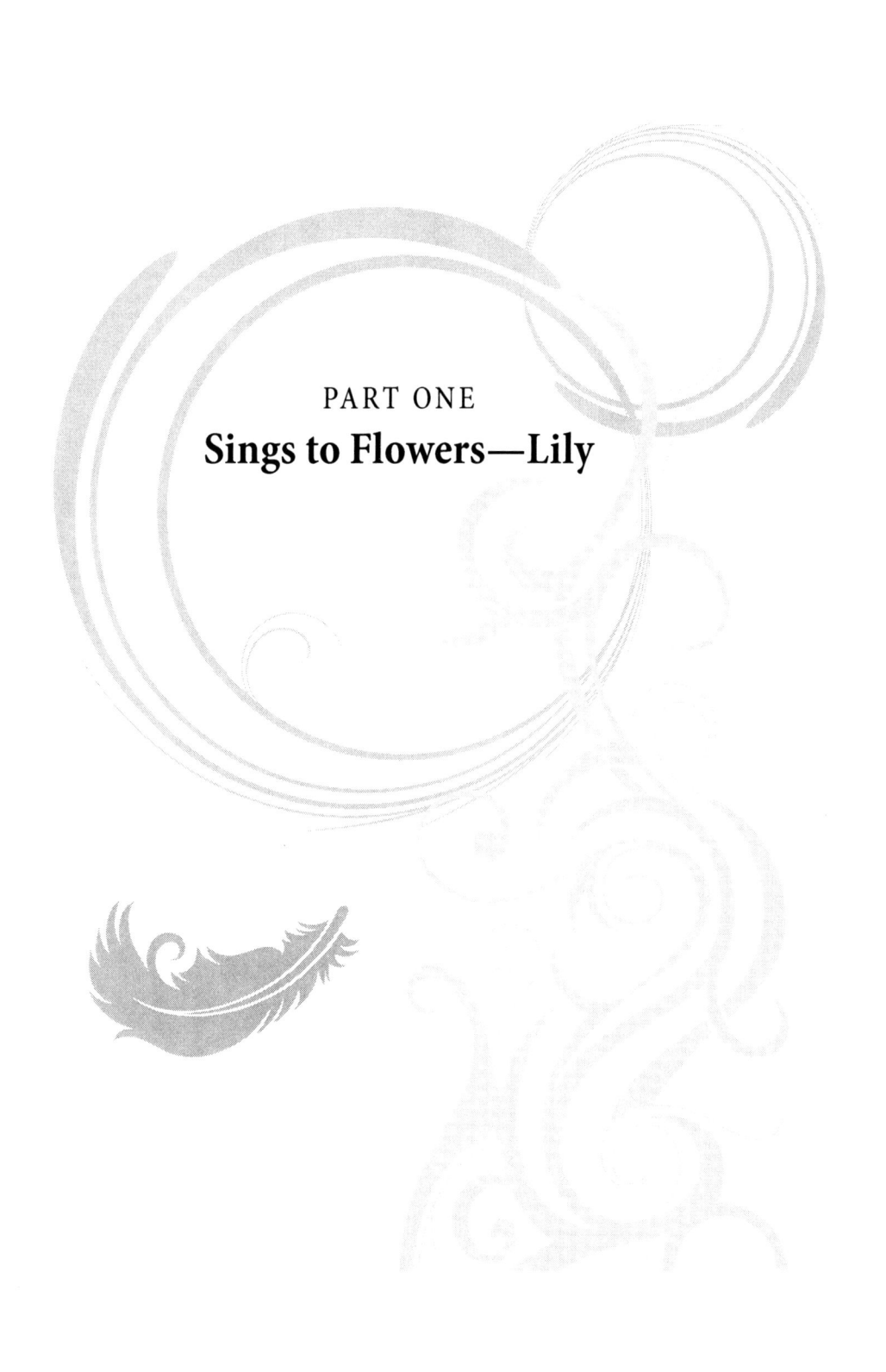

CHAPTER ONE

It Hurts

"I . . . I'm a misfit. A . . . a . . . mistake."

"Lily, sit down. Sit down here on your favorite sitting log and take a deep breath. Come on Lily, breathe. Sit down."

"Why was I made like this? . . . messed up. Maybe I didn't even have a chance. If I was a crazy Indian in my past life like No Name says, maybe the crazy from that life keeps bleeding into this one."

"Come on Lily, come on. Sit. Be still and breathe . . . Breathe deeply."

"Even my body is cross-wired . . . just a heap of tangled up broken wires . . . short circuits . . . or . . . or . . ."

She's unable to wail the next word while cascades of tears splotch up her glasses, making them useless. More wets her arms, her lap, the tops of her bare feet, and the sharp rocks mixed with broken shells and barnacles around her toes.

"Slow your breathing, Lily. I'll help. I'm right here like always, still delivering your breath like I've done for thousands of years and I'm not quitting now, but you need to do your part Lily; you need to take it in . . . a deep breath, and . . . Lily! You're bleeding! There's blood! It's on your lap!"

"I can't work a computer. I can't play a video game with my kid brother without it going berserk. I can't even work the damn toaster without it turning ballistic and cremating everything. Uhhhhhh!"

"Lily, open your hand. You're squeezing that geode so tightly that the knife-edged crystal points are stabbing you and you don't even know it. You're not paying attention. There's blood! Open your hand, Lily. Oooooh. Eeeeee. How loud do I need to howl to get you to open your hand! Even blowing your hair into a frenzy isn't getting your attention. You used to listen to me in the old days. You used to sing to me with sacred heart songs on your lips and I would tell you stories and their secrets. Remember? You used to sing to all the beautiful things around you, especially to the mountain meadow flowers for which your people named you. Have you forgotten what you learned only a few months ago? Have you forgotten your beautiful Blackfoot Indian name, Sings To Flowers? Have you forgotten how to hear me?"

"I've always called him 'The Joke.' Now the joke's on me. I made bad karma. And . . . Oh God, I long for my love . . . My love . . . My love. And . . . And I don't know if he is real or if I made him up in my head . . . If I don't know, then **I am** crazy. The White Owl, or spirit owl or whatever it was . . . and the gift feathers that came from the air . . . and the crystal geode from the Native Lady with the red paint in her hair . . . that lady said it was from him but . . . what if it's just a trick of my crossed-up brain? What if No Name isn't real, just another trick? And her telling me My Love is now in the fifth dimension and visits me? Ya sure! If she is real, then **she** must be the crazy one. Maybe we **both** have fruitcakes for brains. What if all that stuff she told me is just my **bad** brain making **bullshit**?"

"Lily, the signs you are feeling in your body and the confusion in your mind are exactly what No Name said them to be. They are the labor pains of your transformation . . . similar to what even the saints have endured, but with your own identifying mark upon them.

"I wish you could hear me. I wish you would breathe deeply. I'm trying to help you blow away the hurt! Lily. Lily. LILY, LISTEN. OPEN YOUR HAND."

There she goes, slowly rising onto her naked feet without hearing, and taking the sharp meandering path on her soft flesh without feeling, and without knowing that she causes herself to bleed.

I'm guessing she is close to another breakdown. Or is that just the outer appearance of things? Perhaps her soul is pushing her hard to grow in awareness. Maybe a complete breakdown would be her breakout of that ancient dreary self that nips at her heals. The Wind wants to know.

Now she stumbles along Puget Sound's rocky shore and weaves through the winding path where the ancient horsetail plants grow with their thin four-inch needle projections pointing in all directions and the stinging nettles wait to zap an unaware passerby. She will walk alone and with her eyes cast down the whole distance back to her home in Allyn, Washington. I will go with her, of course, while some of me remains here. I suspect she may be back again tomorrow to this buggy, rough, unfinished piece of driftwood she calls her sitting log and she will sob into me again.

I refer to myself as "The Wind" because that's what humans call me now. In ancient Greece, when they cried out to the muses, it was I who answered. Today they honor me by trusting their sails, kites, and an assortment of flying machines to my care and mostly I make myself a helpful force to humankind, but on occasion . . . I mirror . . . moments of madness and rage.

I am far more than the music that comes dancing through the treetops. I take my home in all dimensions. Wherever there is movement I am there, even inside creature's bodies.

I yearn for the days when native peoples could not only hear well the stories I carry in my songs, but would play me through their flutes and let me dance to their drums while I kept their fires glowing. I knew Lily well, or Sings To Flowers, as she was called back then.

At present she is a member of the Johantgen family. This family continues to be embroiled in love's tragedies, which have swept through them in recent centuries. And like most humans she and her not-identical twin sister have long suffered with certain typical mild afflictions.

People describe the twins as being "lovely" and "beautiful," being of the much admired blond-blue Scandinavian stock; but Lilly's sister, Catrina Johantgen—also known as Cat—has an affliction of the mind. She is obsessed with certain attributes. To that end she has mastered the art of color applications to her eyelids, lashes, and cheeks and she checks on the colors with her little pocket mirrors every few minutes to make sure they remain. Anyone or anything that comes between her and her mirrors will experience one of Cat's hissy-fit cyclones.

Lily never wears the face colors. Like her namesake, she is unusually pale. Her affliction is being stuck behind thick, monster-sized glasses in yesterday's style. They are too heavy for her delicate, petite, and perfectly shaped little nose. "Too bad, they say, "that her nose doesn't have a hump to keep those glasses in place." She props them up by wrinkling her nose or poking at them with her index finger while peering through lenses made smeary by unusually long, thick black lashes that, like windshield wipers on dry glass, leave their tracks before her eyes.

Her vision history shows her eyes changing so rapidly for the worse that even new glasses every school year have helped only for a couple of months. She hasn't seen the big class writing board for the major part of eleven years.

Lily and Cat occasionally seem to not only barely tolerate each other, but also their ten-year-old brother, who creates attention in a crowd with his red hair, his Texas-size freckles, and his tricks. He is sometimes referred to as "The Annoyance," "Bothersome Brother," or "The Joke." However, he makes The Wind laugh.

Both these girls have lost loves in their past lives. Both have howled their misery into The Wind and I have swept the face of what is now called Montana and beyond with their sad songs.

Sometimes I sang with high-pitched tones through the mountain crevasses in the west, where the Flathead Salish and the Shoshone listened, and some would weep. Men wept too, but with dry eyes.

Sometimes I chose a low-toned rumble down the mountains and over the waterfalls to those whom French trappers called the bird people, The Crow, also referred to by many as "The Enemy." But I like The Crow. They lived near a river they named after me, a branch of the Yellowstone.

Sometimes I would simply whistle and whisper the names of my heroes and heroines over and over through the prairie grasses to the east into the other enemy camps. And if a Lakota Sioux would pause in his own song long enough to wonder what magic is in the name he heard me sing, I would impart to him that song's secrets and then carry for him his own melodies.

Sometimes I would blow down over Canada to talk to the people who cook with stones, The Assiniboine. But the song that burns within me now belongs to Lily Johantgen and to The Blackfoot People.

Her recent torments in this life started during the Johantgen family's summer travel vacation. That's when the accident happened in Browning, Montana on what I call Lily's Remembering Day. I remember The Remembering Day. I can visit those memories in Lily's and my recent past and see them and feel them as though it is happening at this very moment. After all, it wasn't that long ago.

CHAPTER TWO

The Remembering Day

I can feel Lily's seventeen-year-old heart pulsing as she and her family ascend the steps and pass through the doors of the Museum of the Plains Indian in Browning, Montana. Her chest already sounds like rolling thunder stones. I'm the only one here who knows why.

The family is not noticing the stand-up sign reading "This Section Closed." Someone has pushed it aside near the entrance to a small back hallway just a few feet past the lobby, and worse, Lily is ignoring another sign in red letters plastered two inches from her nose on the glassed-in case under repair. It reads "Do Not Touch The Glass." On that sign someone has penned "GO AWAY."

Her eyes, with the help of that delicate index finger holding up her spectacles, are squinting at a worn pair of petite moccasins with a small stand-up sign that reads, "Fine Example of Quill Work—1800-1840."

I can hear Lily's thinking words wondering, *Why am I feeling a rush of tenderness toward those small porcupine quill decorated moccasins? How did I know they have dyed porcupine quills even before I read that sign? Hello there!*

Lily looks both surprised and confused. She is noticing a bulge on the outside edge of the left-foot moccasin giving it a crescent moon shape. *What happened to that left foot?*

"Ouch. A stabbing pain just zapped me on the side of my own left foot," she announces. "This is not my imagination . . . Too weird!"

No one is responding. Has her family lost their hearing? Little glistening bumps of sweat are swelling up on her upper lip and she is grabbing at her belly.

I could have predicted this moment, knowing this family's history! Maybe Mom will notice . . . Soon.

Lily's hand is pressing harder against her solar plexus. I can feel currents of nausea sweep through her stomach and up her chest causing a wretch with a gag.

"I'm going to puke."

Hey. Hey! Her body is beginning to sway and list toward that glass case! Family, wake up. Wake Up!

Her thinking feels fuzzy.

People sound like they're far away . . . leaving me . . . miles away. Is that B.B.?

"Bothersome Brother" is exclaiming, "Wow! Look at this little bow and quiver of arrows for a boy my size."

It takes Lily's careening body to spark Mom into full attention and make her soar into action.

"John! Hold Lily up! She looks like she's passing out! Lily, I have this souvenir bag if you are going to barf."

Dad is starting to get an arm around Lily's waist and it's too late for Mom to get the bag all the way open. Some vomit is landing in the bag and the rest on the floor.

I hear ringing in my ears. Or is it a few syllables that I hear? Did I hear the words "Sings To Flowers?" Is that part of a sentence or a name? Did I really hear someone say those words . . . or were they just in my own weird thoughts? And what does that phrase have to do with anything anyway?

Omygosh. My eyes are closed but I can see something. I can see exactly what Sammy is seeing, even though I am not in front of his section of the display case. My eyes are closed and I can see! I know they're closed! I know it!

I see . . . well I'm not sure . . . no, I am sure. I see three wraps of stained yellow sinew behind the arrowheads, followed by four wraps of red sinew, followed by twelve wraps of black. I see a quiver, painted with white lightning bolts, but now they are not in the glass viewing case. Jesus! These antique children's toys are in **my** hands. They're in my hands, definitely my hands, but they are small hands, like small kid's hands, but at the same time they are mine!

God! Where did this come from? Now I see two dolls and two beaver skins. My little girl hands are wrapping these things into the skins and tying them with red sinew. It's a bundle of kid's toys! And I hear singing. Is the singing in a little girl's voice coming from me? She is, I mean, I am singing a song to beavers and to flowers. This is too wild. My brain is tripping out!

The Wind knows that singing and bundle keeping were and still are at the heart of the First Nation Peoples. I remember parents who were initiated to be the keepers of a sacred bundle telling their young children, "If you touch this bundle or even cross in front of it, a ghost wolf will come at night and bite off your hands."

In Lily's vision, little Sings To Flowers, as this child is known, doesn't seem concerned about threats. This bundle may be without an official ceremony, but Sings To Flowers likes it that way. The exact bundle's contents will remain secret until the secret time runs out.

Somehow while floating in and out of semi-present awareness Lily remembers something. *How odd is this . . . remembering something that must be a part of this little Indian girl's life as if she is me.*

It was during the last full moon when I, or the little Indian girl, stumbled upon an old beaver skull wrapped inside two beaver pelts. A holy man probably dropped it. I've seen holy men use beaver skulls for rattles. I'm keeping this beaver skull, but not for a rattle. I'm keeping it to protect my bundle with its beaver power.

Her mind's pictures are over in seconds and then . . . it happens again. Lily loses the rest of her breakfast as her head bangs with a dull crunch into the museum's glass case. The fractured panel seems suspended in space before it explodes with splinters of pointed glass shards that seem for a moment to fall like slow snow before splashing on the artifacts and in the throw-up bag, while the rest go skittering across the floor in all directions up to and across the family's feet.

"There's glass sticking out!" shouts Mom, "By her eye!"

Some blood is spurting with pulsations in a thin red arc and some is trickling down over her right eye, smudging her glasses, staining her cheek, and running down her front. As her father lays her out on the cool tile floor, Lily appears to be out cold.

"Nine One One . . . Nine One One! Where's the damn phone!"

"It's in my pocket, Marge. Just grab it." Dad pulls out a crumpled handkerchief, hesitates a second or two, then applies pressure to the spot where blood spurts next to the embedded glass piece. His pressure is too timid. Blood soaks the cloth.

"It's not there!" shrieks Mom as she pulls out her husband's wallet, keys, some gum wrappers, a book of matches, even a golf ball and all the loose change in his pockets, and lets it all tumble to the floor. "I don't know why you carry around all this garbage. It's like a junk drawer in your pockets," she wails.

"Catrina! You've got it!" Dad snaps. Now he gets brave and applies more pressure to the bleeding. The blood pump slows.

Catrina, who tweets with her multiple contacts non-stop, in spite of her mother's objections, is standing wide-eyed and is stunned into finally being present. She grabs a cell phone out of her pocket and hands it to a glaring Mom. Sammy, who is observing the happenings in a state of awe, is asking, "Gee Dad, is that glass going into Lily's brain?"

"Cat, you and Sammy wait for the ambulance near the front door. Move!"

Catrina, for once in her life, does not hesitate. She grabs B.B. by the arm and quickly pulls him away. It will be a while until she stops ruminating about the glass weapon extruding from her sister's forehead and she quits touching that spot on her own forehead to feel for anything sharp and glass-like.

"What are you people doing in this area? It's closed!" A bustling bear of a woman with deep vertical creases between her flaring yellow-brown rivets for eyes is rushing up. "Oh my goodness! Oh my goodness! Our treasures! Our treasures! Is the girl hurt? This is the ss-second time this display has been ss-smashed this week. We just put this window glass here a half hour ago to keep the dussst **and the people out** while we wait for the new tempered glass. That's why this area is **closed off**! Can't you ss-see the ss-signs? There are not one but **two** ss-signs, for heaven's ss-sake." Frantically waving short stubby arms like a windmill, "Thessse old things need a ss-certain constant temperature, decreased humidity and lack of oxygen. We want it ready for the SS-Sundance festivities but the whole process has been delayed and now you people have brought even more trouble for us-ss. Thessse are delicate things!"

"I'm sorry!" shouts John, much louder than he had intended. Red-faced frustrated Dad fails to soften his remark with, "We've got an injured person here, for God sake! We didn't see your freaking signs until now. What about my daughter's vision here! Forget about blood on the damn 'treasures.'"

He cannot help being loud. Genetics gave him a barrel chest and a set of bellows that rival an opera singer's. Add adrenaline and The North Wind blows through.

Janitors are running. They are bringing tools for sweeping and mopping. The big lady is punctuating her instructions to the janitors with the pointing and waving of her fingers, while Mom is fumbling with the phone as if she has never used a cell phone before and, finally getting it right, is calling 911. "Hurry! Bring an ambulance. Our daughter is unconscious and bleeding all over the museum with glass in her eye."

The museum's lady-in-charge is rising and teetering on her tiny toes to try to dance around the smelly mess sprinkled with razor sharps. She gathers a wad of her long skirt into a knot while the fingers of her other hand continue pointing in wild circles from janitors, to floor, to clean-up equipment, and to Lily and her family. She is mumbling under her breath and through two beaver-like front teeth. "Don't try to ss-sue us-ss," she whispers too loudly to herself while narrowing her eyes and jutting out her chin. All her S's and especially her "us" hiss and linger in the air with a fine spray that squeezes out between her beaver front teeth. "Any blood anywhere mussst be removed now!" she says to the cleaning crew.

She reminds me of a hot-air balloon . . . All puffed out at the top with the pointy tied-up end at the bottom, but losing air. With one nudge I could . . . Never mind. She's blowing and whirling herself away, like one of those desert dust devils I make come from and disappear into nowhere. Perhaps she is disappearing to wait for the ambulance too . . . or to call a lawyer.

"John! You're supposed to raise the bleeding part . . . her head."

"Bleeding has almost stopped, Marge."

"Well then, you're supposed to raise the feet of someone who's fainted."

"Oh for Christ's sake, Marge! Head up or feet up? Let her lay flat then."

"Wheeeere is the ambulance?" When Marge howls her loud prolonged "where" she sounds like an ambulance siren herself.

I have never heard these two parents swear or yell at each other like this. Obviously, this is not a good day in the Johantgen family's summer trip to Glacier National Park. They had the intention of partaking in diverse new places that would spark awe and the awareness of the wonders of nature. This long-waited-for summer excursion has taken a steep and rapid downhill descent . . . in an ambulance . . . to a hospital.

I had predicted a day like this from the day Lily was born. Such a simple act it was, to climb a few steps to an ordinary-looking museum. But **these** steps into **this** museum in **this** place are more than about remembering. They are the trigger. The starting place for a wild parade of events for two souls who share the same soul essence and should have been one soul in the beginning.

CHAPTER THREE

Strange Happenings in the Hospital

Mary Tall Chief, R.N., is looking out across the hospital parking lot in anticipation of the ambulance bringing the "Bleeding Unconscious Head Injury." She is, like her name, a tall and regal looking twenty-six year old with glistening black hair tied up in a classic swirl and held in place with hand-carved bone combs. She carries her head as if presenting it like a crown of jewels atop the elongated neck of a temple column. Always she has picture-perfect posture. Her countenance is calm, as if to relax the very air around her. No wonder she is the person of choice to soothe the fearful patient and distraught family. She turns her head slowly, as if not to tip the bejeweled crown, while her body moves with graceful elegance. Her claim to fame is that she was named after a famous distant relative on her father's side, the once world-renowned prima ballerina, Elizabeth Marie Tall Chief, whose native heritage is from the oil-rich Osage tribe of Oklahoma.

Mary is checking her watch against the big clock on the emergency room wall. Just as she is starting to wonder what the problem could be with the ambulance, she sees it coming with an old blue Chevy chugging along behind. *That's probably the family in that old beater.* Then, ashamed of her judgment, *God knows there is a plethora of old beaters on the rez.*

With a long in and out breath as if preparing for a deep sea dive, she motions the orderlies to meet the ambulance, makes sure her E.R. clipboard and pen are in hand, bandage scissors in her pocket, stethoscope around her neck, and her well-practiced smile of reassurance on her face.

Presently a small, pale, and waxen figure of a lovely young girl is wheeled into the reception area. Mary notices that the girl's body barely makes a bump under the blanket. The glass piece protruding from the girl's forehead is unsettling to say the least, but Mary Tall Chief has seen worse.

"A name?" asks the receptionist.

"Lily Johantgen," Dad says, with a scratchy yet booming voice. A rare salty drop escapes down the wrinkle trench near his right eye and falls onto the papers he is given for his signature. If only Lily could see that solitary tear. She might believe her Dad loves her.

An ID band is rapidly snapped around his daughter's limp wrist and then just as quickly she is taken away, wheeled to a curtained off area, leaving Dad to manage more questions and paperwork. The rest of the family follows Lily's gurney like a row of ducklings.

Ms. Tall Chief takes Lily's carotid pulse, respiratory rate, and blood pressure, and pierces an arm vein to insert a plastic catheter for an intravenous infusion. These tasks are all accomplished with grace, a smile, and a nod to the rest of the family, who stand with wide eyes accompanied by rapid and shallow breathing, as if trying to keep the next scene from happening by not breathing their air into what may come next, which they all imagine will be something bad. Mary uses her soothing voice, and looking Mom in the eyes says, "Her vitals are very good. What time was the accident?"

"Noonish I think," says Mom. But now there is a brief family discussion bordering on argument until it is finally agreed on 12:30 pm… ish.

"So it's been approximately a half hour? Do you have an estimate of how much blood may have been lost? Tablespoons, a quarter of a cup, a cup, more? How big was the spot on the floor?"

"Blood squirted up the wall!" chimes in Sammy.

"Hush Sammy, I have to think." More family discussion is had about how much blood and a consensus is not reached.

"Well at least there does not appear to be much external bleeding at this time," says the nurse, always speaking positively with reassurance. Yet by the drained expressions on their faces they are **not** reassured. Mary remains unruffled and with her velvety voice announces, "Here comes the most excellent Dr. Jerry Dixon. He'll give you the answers you seek."

Nurse Mary doesn't need to see his face to know he is about to appear. She knows the sound of his footsteps. They are quick and precise, with purpose pushing them. Abruptly the curtains burst open as if Moses is parting the Red Sea.

"Has the glass pierced her eye?" asks Mom.

Dr. Dixon does not speak. With pen light in hand he leans over Lily and shines his light under Lily's eyelids, smells her breath, looks in her ears, checks reflexes at elbows, knees, and ankles with that familiar little doctor hammer, and scrapes the bottom of both her feet with the hammer's handle. He listens to her heart and lungs with the stethoscope that is usually flung around his neck, does a sweep of her skin looking for needle marks, even in the webs of her fingers, and toes, and under her tongue. Then, toward the end of his cursory exam, he does not answer questions, he asks them.

"Any history of diabetes, seizures, fainting or blackout episodes, unexplained severe headaches, recreational drug or alcohol use, taking any medication, her last tetanus shot was when?" Finally, for the first time he acknowledges the family, looking them in the eye with this question. "Did Lily," then briefly glancing over Nurse Mary's arm to her notes, "Yes, Lily. Did she black out before she hit her head on the glass case or did she hit her head and then black out?" Nobody can answer that last question or remember when her last tetanus shot was.

"Chief, get me the ophthalmoscope." Obviously, Dr. Dixon knows his stuff. It's all business first with him; any pleasantries come as an afterthought.

Jerry Dixon really is a nice man. It is just the way of his busy E.R., where social graces tend to slip by the wayside on occasion, especially when he is on duty. He is shorter than Mary and carries a handsome physical presence. He is wiry and fast. Mary's challenge with him is to anticipate his every move and have his equipment at hand, but sometimes she fails to keep up with him. He, like Sammy, also has red hair and freckles. He really has not lost his boyish look.

Now Cat takes notice of Dr. Jerry Dixon. In the middle of her family's tragedy, she straightens her back and puts on the pretty look she's practiced in the mirror for six years. Mind you, he is thirty-six and she is seventeen. Yet even at this tender young age she has already scanned his left hand for a wedding ring.

No ring, Cat smiles to herself.

Unsuccessfully trying to sneak a peek at herself in her pocket mirror, Cat's emergency is that she must check on herself in the ladies' restroom. Dashing away from the bedside she crashes past Dad, just coming from his paperwork duties, and turns him a quarter turn. Dad is used to this and doesn't plan to waste his energy by asking what the rush is about—if he thought about it, he would be able to guess.

"Mrrrrr. Johantgen?" Dad is nodding yes. "I'm Dr. Dixon. We are going to pull that glass weapon out of your daughter's head. There's no evidence of obvious bleeding in that right eye. Later we can dilate the eye for a better view, but I'd rather not do it now as it could cover up other important signs. The face and head are vascular areas, but it looks to me that the external bleeding is minimal," he says.

Turning now to Lily, "Is her color always so pale?" Without waiting for an answer, "Chief, order CBC, random blood glucose; do we know when she last ate? I guess she lost her breakfast at the time of the accident, right? Oh, and let's add a drug screen. Okay to screen for drugs?" he says, looking at the parents. Then without waiting for an answer he continues, while the bewildered-looking parents are nodding yes. "Chief, let's add lytes, liver and kidney function panels too. What's radiology up to, Chief? Call them and tell them we need a CAT scan."

Now Cat is re-entering from behind the curtains with her face colors in place to suit her. Teeth sparkling, no uglies caught between, V-neck tee pulled down to show just a hint of cleavage, boobs pulled front and center to make cleavage, standing tall to pull in the tummy area which never really protruded in the first place but . . . "My name is Cat. Did I hear you think I need a scan?" purrs Catrina with all the seductive power of a worshiped movie starlet.

You can feel it in the room. Behind Lily's curtain everything stands motionless, including human brainpower as all eyes turn to Cat. Dr. Dixon's organized train of analytical processes, like a well-greased mechanical device in a sandstorm, has hit grit and is thrown off track while he wonders if he has entered a time warp of inconsistency. Speechless and lost, he gazes down at baby blue eyes with half-closed eyelids and long sweeping lashes, gazing seductively at him with an upturn of her chin.

Oh for God sake, he is thinking. "N-N-N-No, no," he stammers. "No, that is not at all what I have in mind . . . or meant at all . . . no I didn't mean that." Mom has an embarrassed blotchy red neck and is giving Cat her shut-the-hell-up stare, which does not register even close to Cat's focus of awareness.

The awkward silence is broken by Sammy. "Don't ya know what a CAT scan is?" pulling on Cat's sleeve to get her attention. "He's going to check out silly Lily's brain. You know, to look for silly and whatever."

Dad grunts his annoyance through tight lips. Mom is mortified, but still manages to grab her two other children and pull them away. "You two, out in the car and stay there until we come for you." Cat takes an in-breath to object, but Mom cuts her off before a word can slide out between Cat's full and pouty lips while she pushes both her offspring toward the exit sign.

"Radiology will be ready for Lily in fifteen minutes," says Mary

Tall Chief, now returning from placing her phone orders. This pulls the doctor partly out of his bewildered state and back to directing his ship.

"Okay. Enough time to gather my wits . . . I mean . . . wheel her to the suture room and pull out that glass."

Could this be the first time that Mary Tall Chief has had to rescue him from a sidetracked moment of bewilderment? Even so, The Wind knows Dr. Dixon and Dr. Dixon's past. I confidently predict he will have several nights of recalling that lovely child-woman face with the lilting sing-song voice, asking that ridiculous question, "My name is Cat, do you need to scan me?" Then he'll wake up in a sweat from that dream of remembering Cat and think to himself, *Have I gone mad? A kid that could be my daughter has penetrated my brain! Christ Almighty!* Then he will rise from his ruffled bed for a Tylenol PM and eventually fall back into choppy slumber.

The suture room is more private, having a real door instead of a mere curtain. Everything for minor surgery is stored here and the room has an excellent adjustable overhead light that accepts a screwed-on sterile handle so that a gloved hand can move the light around to various angles.

"We'll inject first with 2% after you clean her up, Mary. It looks like a good portion of the glass has tunneled under the skin next to the bone."

Dr. Dixon uses a hard brush to scrub his hands before they disappear into the sleeves of a sterile gown, held open by Nurse Mary who then ties him up in the back. He grabs the size seven gloves already laid out for him.

Mary dips cotton balls into a sterile bowl of brown liquid which she swabs around the wound. It leaves a yellow-brown stain on Lily's ultra-white skin. Now she holds out a tiny bottle, prepared for the doctor to draw up 2% Lidocaine into a sterile syringe. The solution is injected several times around the wound.

"Oh good. She's reacting a little to the needle. Looks like she may be about to wake up. Hand me a grabber, Chief, and make sure you have a couple of mosquitos ready." He reaches his hand toward Mary for a forceps while not taking his eyes off his patient. Gently he pulls and coaxes out another inch of the glass projectile that had deposited itself against the bone and drops it into the "dirty bowl" in the corner of the sterile towel-clad instrument tray. Mary has the small clamp, called a mosquito, in the doctor's hand before he asks for it and he clamps off a small bleeding blood vessel. "We'll cauterize this little devil," he says, referring to the "bleeder," and that is deftly done.

Now he looks and probes the wound carefully for more glass and ponders a reason for the slow recovery from her fainting.

"Let's rinse this wound out with 0.9, Mary." Mary opens a fresh bottle of normal saline and pours it into another sterile bowl. The solution is drawn up in a sterile rubber bulb syringe and handed to the doctor, who floods the wound cavity.

"We'll need to put this kid on a good antibiotic and give her a tetanus shot. What have you got for suture? And by the way, for some odd reason the light in this room is bothering me. Would you turn it down please?"

"Turn it down?"

"Yes Tall Chief, Down. It's too damn bright in here and the blinding light is reflecting off the instruments."

Dr. Dixon usually calls his nurse Chief or Mary. But when he calls her Tall Chief he is getting frustrated and Mary knows not to question him and to move quickly, unless he is about to do something really stupid, which is almost never, but this request is too odd.

With a hint of irritation, "It's the same light we always have, Sir, and it doesn't turn down. I will have to search around for a lower watt bulb." Adding, "if we have any."

"Fine. Do that. In the meantime we can put a patch over the wound, send her off for her scan and sew her up after. Geez it's bright in here. If I have to I'll use my sunglasses."

What a rare spectacle! While Lily is being carted away to radiology Dr. Dixon, the Chief of E.R., is running out to the parking lot looking for his spectacles, the dark ones. He doesn't know he is being watched from another car in the lot, where Cat and Sammy sit confined to their "old beater."

The Sundance is a day or two away. Dr. Dixon will be expected at his post in the E.R., not the parking lot. He'll be needed to attend glorious sunburns, a few stumbling or immobile drunks, maybe a broken nose or two, and sometimes a more challenging catastrophe. The locals say it's the outsiders that cause the most trouble during the powwow, not only for Browning, but for Dr. Dixon. The non-Indians don't get the sacredness of the Sundance, but they do bring much-needed dollars.

While the doctor spends precious minutes searching for his best "shades" among items pulled out of his glove compartment and shuffled newspapers on the floor, the E.R. phone rings.

"Hello. This is Stu Redmond in radiology. We are sending the Johantgen concussion case back to you. Can you put Jerry Dixon on the line? He's out in the parking lot? Delivering a baby or something? Looking for sunglasses! Okaaaay, have him return my call. Speaking of sunglasses, I've noticed an extra brightness and almost an electrical feeling in the air down here. Maybe we have had a sun flare or something. Sunglasses might be what I need too," he says, while laughing. "Anyway, have him call me when he is done with his parking lot duty. This is a first!"

Returning from outside, a sweaty, scattered-looking Dr. Dixon carries not one, but two pairs of sunglasses in his hands. "Is she back yet?"

"She's on her way. Dr. Redmond called. Wants you to call back. Says he thinks there's been a sun flare."

"Oh he does? Well it feels hot enough."

"Hi. This is Dixon. How's Lily Johantgen looking?"

"Well Jerry, the pictures seem a little over-exposed, but I have confidence that I can read them well enough. I don't see anything that looks like a significant brain bleed or any other surprises. I don't understand the quality of the scans though. The equipment was working perfectly yesterday. I don't know what the deal is here. I've called the company to send a technician ASAP to have a look see. We sure don't want our equipment down during the Sundance—or any other time for that matter. You know, I may be nuts, but I could swear that Johantgen girl is glowing. She's stirring a little too. Looks like she may be waking up. She's on her way back upstairs."

"Okay Stu, thanks. I think I see her being pushed through the doors now."

The E.R. Chief looks for any change of Lily's consciousness then leans close to her ear. "Hi Lily, I'm Dr. Dixon. You are here in the hospital in Browning with your family and I am taking care of you. We are going to sew up a gash in your forehead now. You have had a concussion and we'll have you rest in the hospital overnight. Just a precaution, preliminary tests look good."

When the gurney is bumped by a fast-moving nurse chasing an alarm from a malfunctioning machine beyond, Lily moans and moves her feet. A good sign! Did Lily comprehend what the doctor has told her? It's hard to say.

"Mary, let's try the other suture room at the end of the hall for less glare."

They move to the other room but . . . "Tall Chief, I think the light here is just as bad or worse than the other. Okay, it's ridiculous but hand me a pair of those sun glasses."

"Let's try 4-0 chromic," he says as he is re-numbing the wound. "I know 4-0 thread is a little delicate, but I'm hoping with a subcutaneous stitch and some steri-strips pulling the skin edges together, it will have a good result for such a beautiful face. Brother, it is bright in here. Okay. I'm changing my mind. We will use silk interrupteds. I will at least be able to see the black thread. Something needs to be done about this light. Tall Chief, get hold of maintenance when we are through here. I need to see what I am doing, for Heaven's sake."

What should be a straight-forward stitching project is finally done with some difficulty due to the strange lighting circumstances. Lily, with Mom and Dad trailing behind, is being admitted for overnight observation and monitoring. Finally Lily cracks open her eyes and utters a few unintelligible words.

"Rest now, Dear," whispers a hovering Mom, "We'll visit again tonight and get you out of here in the morning. Sleep well, My Flower." Dad is silent.

Then Mom looks up to see the back of her disobedient daughter, who has sneaked back into the E.R. and whose eyes are looking longingly down the hall after a receding Dr. Dixon, who's about to disappear.

CHAPTER FOUR

Was It a Dream or Was It a Memory?

Lily shuts her eyes and breaths a deep sigh. Behind the liquid darkness of her heavy eyelids is a swirl of light. Around and around the glowing colors go and she has the sensation that her physical body is spinning with them. She opens her eyes to make sure that she is still in her hospital bed, but the moment she closes her eyes the spinning sensation begins again. *Open . . . still in my bed. Close . . . spinning. Open . . . body is not spinning. Close . . . spinning again and faster.* Finally Lily gives in to the sensation and lets her mind flow with it. Maybe it's the drugs doing this . . . Or? What?

The light behind my eyes feels like a whirling energy, pulling . . . Pulling . . . PULLING me into a narrower concentration of light. I'm being sucked through a brilliant tube into a narrower and tighter beam. Ahhh, I'm in something no wider than the width of a pencil lead. How can this be? What's happening to me? I'm scared. I need to try to relax. Relax Lily. Relax.

Presently, she hears, sees, and feels a sudden loud pop and her awareness is outside her body and she is looking down on herself that . . . just a minute, this is **not herself!**

I'm looking down on the same sweet little Indian girl I saw earlier in the museum visions. She is about seven summers and . . . why did I think seven summers and not seven years? Who is this little girl and am I thinking my thoughts or hers? Deciding to get a better look, Lily finds herself effortlessly drifting closer. The seven-summers girl seems to sense her presence and turns to look straight at Lily. The little girl is not afraid, but somehow just aware, as though this is a common everyday experience.

"Do you have a name?" asks Lily.

"Sings To Flowers," she says.

Intrigued, Lily thinks, *I would like to know more about you.* And before she can think another word, she is looking down at her own hands, which again have become two tiny hands. She has seen these hands before. She is inside these hands! They are her hands! She is inside the little girl's body! Is this a dream? . . . or a memory? She is a little Indian girl and she is feeling a mixture of sadness and desperation.

Oh God, I am now the little girl, little Sings To Flowers. *I feel . . . confused. Afraid.*

In the next moment Sings To Flowers is standing before her father, Hunting Elk. He is quite elderly and does not look well. His eyes are sad and there is yellowish matter collecting in the inner corners of his eyes that he tries to wipe away, but more matter soon takes the place of the previous. His thick drooping eyelids make his entire bony face sag. He is sitting, and yet bent over with the weight of his grief, crunching his shoulders. Around the bent shoulders there is no fine buffalo robe; his blanket is faded, tattered, and reeks of tobacco smoked years ago.

He musters a weak half-smile, revealing only a couple of visible teeth and reddened gums. The low light in the teepee, furnished by only a few glowing embers, casts elongated shadows that make the wrinkles and hollows of his high-boned face even more pronounced.

He speaks to Sings To Flowers with a gravelly whisper as he labors to breathe. "My daughter, know that I love you dearly and forever, even after the ravens pick for nourishment from my dead sunken eyes. All things on our Turtle Island must die in order to be reborn. I am coming close to my end time here. The Creator is calling my name in the wind, in the trees, in the grasses scraping together, in bird songs, and in the rushing waters. I hear Him calling me to return to our ancestors. If I still breathe when the snow becomes deep I will put my chilled bones down into the arms of Mother Earth and let The Wind carry my spirit to The Sun.

"I have had talks with Comes Still Alive, whose band of Blackfoot people camped with ours last summer. He will take you as his seventh wife during the celebration of the next Okan, when the serviceberries are ripe. He is a good man . . . a strong man who can keep you safe. He has many horses with which to trade for good things and many buffalo robes to keep you warm when the waters have turned to ice. His other wives can teach you women's ways.

"When your mother was alive, she was admired for her tanned deer and buffalo-calf skins. I am too old. I cannot teach you. When I am dead, since you and your brother will have no blood relatives living, Comes Still Alive may adopt your brother, Coyote Head, especially if you are an obedient wife and do not cause him trouble.

"It has been agreed upon. The elders agree also. It is final. We have smoked the pipe. You will marry Comes Still Alive."

"Can I take my toys with me?" asks Sings To Flowers.

CHAPTER FIVE
The Wind Speaks

For thousands of years the indigenous life flowed in balance with all beings who shared this planet. In the times before the white man murdered the American bison, survival dictated what was proper, including a marriage of a young girl to a much older man and husbands with more than one wife. Men were highly inclined to choose for a second wife a sister to his first wife, believing that wives who are sisters will argue less.

I, The Wind, remember the mountains and the vast northern plains when they were raw, undomesticated, and free. I also witnessed human lives that were difficult with moments terrible, there in the pristine wilds. Only the strong survived for more than a few breaths upon the ancient land. Many of the newborn babies did not live through their first winter. Women died in childbirth and by attack from their wild animal relatives who, like them, honed their survival skills too.

In harsh long winters, when the animals were starved so were the people. And this was the strategy behind the darkest deed in Native American history. I speak of the time when four million woolly Kings of the Prairie lay skinned and forsaken where they fell, precipitating over a quarter of the Piegan clan of the Blackfoot Nation to starve to death in the winter of 1883.

Therefore women, always admired for their physical loveliness, were more prized for their strength and stamina. Did a woman have enough muscle to break through four or five inches of ice for the life-giving liquid it sheltered? Or was she so weak that she might venture out too far upon weak ice, fall through, and be found when her watery tomb gave way in the spring?

Firewood gathering demanded attention and activity no matter the weather. How big a bundle could she carry through the storms?

Could she break camp and move her household at a moment's notice? Taking down and putting up teepees was women's work.

Women were especially recognized for how well they tanned hides. Were the hides soft and did they comfortably conform to the body, or were they stiff, not warm enough, and restricted movement in the hunt?

Were her senses acute enough to hear, see, and protect her baby from approaching hungry wolves?

The matter of life and death brings a totally different kind of measure of worth in determining who is a suitable mate and how many wives a man should have for the survival of his people.

Every young warrior, like the young men of today, dreamed of increasing his power. First he had to be strong and cunning. He had to be able to fight the enemy and raid the enemy's camp when duty called. He had to build strong ties within his group of men for cooperation in hunting and raiding. He had to have great command of his weapons and his horse. And if he could do all these things, he gained respect and good will.

Blackfoot raiding parties would often travel hundreds of miles to their enemies' camps, to the Crow, Sioux, Shoshone, and Flathead Salish, leaving the enemy temporarily floundering and devastated when their women and horses were stolen, but equally committed to retribution. In the fight, many men died young.

The fathers and grandfathers before them took survival cues from Mother Nature herself. They patterned themselves after the older battle-proven bull elk with his harem of wives under his watchful eye. The young males hanging in the perimeter had to prove their worth by their strength and fighting ability before they could mate and thus help preserve the strength of the species. It was not that much different for earlier humans.

A wise man was all too cognizant of the temporary status of life in general. Aware that all things grow old and feeble in time, it was sometimes prudent to add to himself and his family younger wives along the way.

When severe debilitating old age came upon him, it was common for an elder to wander off into the snow to sleep the eternal sleep rather than become too much of a burden. This especially was done for survival of the family in the winter when food was scarce.

CHAPTER SIX

The Announcement

Five native women are feeling gratitude for the early morning sun on their heads and shoulders. The last of the winter snow has left only a fast-fading trace of itself under tree shadows, making my air fresh and cool with the faint hint of pine brought to their noses in the folds of my being. The group is content, ensconced in a clearing near still-smoldering cooking fires. Their stomachs are heavy with newly killed elk, seasoned with dried flowers of wild mint and specially prepared camas roots. This is a scarce pause for sipping chokecherry twig tea from drinking bowls carved from the bark of mountain ash, before they part for their ever-present chores of water and wood gathering. The women will soon break camp for the summer grassland site, as the last of the buffalo, who usually winter amongst the trees for protection from the snows, are getting restless to join the rest of their families now feasting on the new grass shoots in the prairie.

Two Guns Buffalo Calf has just taken delight in the last drops from her buffalo-bone spoon. She takes her dainty lady's pipe and lights it with a small coal from the fire and draws a few puffs. She follows with a drawn-out drag and settles back to look at the other women. She is the first wife, or sits-beside-him woman of Comes Still Alive.

Shorter and older than the other women and with small heavily lidded black penetrating eyes, Two Guns Buffalo Calf makes up for her squat stature with a strong voice that resonates into the bones of whomever she is addressing. Her eyes can give unspoken messages and shoot riveting bolts of energy, which demand attention and respect. She is considered a holy woman, having sponsored in her lifetime two Okans, later called The Sundances. Her voice is not commanding now, but is about to impart new news to the gathering of women with a common bond—marriage to the same man. But there is a sixth wife who prefers to remain apart from the group. She drinks very little of anything, and remains alone. Her name is Stolen Lakota Woman.

The other women are waiting for sits-beside-him woman to speak, having read the signal that she is about to convey something important. The signal is that long drag on her bone pipe and then letting the breath out ever so slowly, as if in meditative contemplation, followed by looking first at one then another of her group. Two Guns Buffalo Calf relishes this moment before speaking. Her signal has ensnared their eyes. There have been whispers about an additional wife. There have been murmurs that it is true.

"There have been talks between old broken-down Hunting Elk, from the Blood People Clan up north and our husband . . . Comes Still Alive." She speaks slowly and pauses between "husband" and "Comes Still Alive," as if she momentarily had forgotten his name.

Again she is taking another long pull on her pipe. She has the other women under her spell in anticipation of a profound announcement. All but one that is, who is now looking at them, but does not come near to hear.

Even I, The Wind, could not lessen the grief in Stolen Lakota Woman with my soft blowing caresses on her cheek. It has been three circles of the four seasons since she refused to learn the Blackfoot talk.

"Comes Still Alive is taking his seventh wife and she is a child."

All eyebrows are simultaneously raised together, as if timed by beats of the drum. Being the only one who knows all the particulars, and basking in her power, Two Guns Buffalo Calf says no more. Instead, she waits for the begging to begin for more information.

"How old is the child?" asks Bird Bone Pipe Woman.

Two Guns Buffalo Calf takes another drag and a long pause, "Seven summers."

"And why one so young! He's not so young himself anymore. We will have to teach her along with our own children! My girls are already well taught and good at women's work," says Hungry Crow, trying to hide a slight edge to her voice. "I am getting too old for young children. Maybe one of you younger wives can take on that duty."

"We'll all teach," says a now glaring Two Guns Buffalo Calf. She dares to get an argument and receives none.

Somewhat relieved at this remark, one of the younger wives named Kills Many Enemies Woman, who was so named after the heroics of her now dead first husband, waits for the first wife to finally settle back again with more contemplative puffs, then in a timid voice asks, "Is he going to force himself on this seven summers child?"

Two Guns Buffalo Calf, now staring off into space says, "He will do what he will do."

"Eeeeeee. Not possible," says Hungry Crow. He cannot get it up half the time. No. He would be too nervous and with a child, he just wouldn't. He didn't take me until after my first moon."

"Can you remember that far back? Perhaps you do not want to remember," challenges Bird Bone Pipe Woman.

"He always gets it up with me," finally speaks Moon Deer Seer, the most beautiful and mother of eight children by Comes Still Alive.

Again, all eyebrows are simultaneously rising, while four sets of eyes look at Moon Deer Seer. "Well then, we will count on you to keep the Old Bear busy and exhausted every night until after her first moon," says Hungry Crow, trying to mimic the tone and intensity of gaze for which Two Guns Buffalo Calf is known.

"Eeeeeeee. We can all share in that responsibility," declares the dominant woman of the group. Now there is muffled laughter as they run private silent scenarios in their heads as to how that can be accomplished. But then, without warning, the Old Bear himself emerges from his teepee. He is going to speak.

"It is time for silence. I speak now. I am to bind for life with Sings To Flowers. The ceremony day will be chosen by the holy man Hunting Bear, during the Okan. She has no mother or aunts and no wedding costume. She will come with her father probably sometime near sundown." Looking at Stolen Lakota Woman some distance away and the circle of his other wives, "My other wives will prepare space for her and make her suitable wedding attire. Stolen Lakota Woman will be her primary teacher for this will help lift the sadness from her eyes, since her woman's parts are without fruit."

No wife speaks a word but there are many knowing looks exchanged. No more laughing. Women are taught as young girls not to giggle. Yet alone, in a group away from the male's hearing, they do laugh and joke amongst themselves like the men. All is very serious as the wives pretend to hear the news for the first time. No one speaks until Comes Still Alive, who is now departing astride his horse, is long past the hearing range of his women's talk.

Now The Wind has something to say. Comes Still Alive is mistaken. Stolen Lakota Woman's sadness has nothing to do with being childless. It is something else.

CHAPTER SEVEN

The Arrival to a New Place

The chiefs of the Blackfoot clans must demonstrate generosity by giving away their horses and other possessions almost as fast as they receive them, deliberately making themselves poor in property. By contrast, Comes Still Alive is a wealthy man. His number one lodge where he receives guests to smoke the pipe, has a central fire pit three times the average size. His handsomely decorated second lodge for sleeping, consists of forty buffalo-cow skins sewn together in ten large strips fastened together with bone skewers. His herd of horses is nearly one hundred, over which his children keep watchful eyes.

Young men anxious to prove their hunting skills will hunt for Comes Still Alive in exchange for borrowing a horse and sharing the game. If the aspiring warrior consistently brings back meat he may eventually be given a horse. However, the more a man has the more he has to guard for fear that his possessions may be stolen.

Comes Still Alive has done more than his generous share of thievery, especially in his youth. They say that he has strong medicine. He can count many coup, including horse and woman stealing, enemy killing, and scalp taking. When he wants, he can be a strong hunter and a stronger disciplinarian.

Little innocent Sings To Flowers is coming now, on a very old and very tired-looking sunken-back horse who looks as old and as tired as the old man leading it, her father, Hunting Elk. There are a few small bundles and a couple of blankets secured behind the child. Her moccasins are tied onto her feet because they would slip off otherwise. Obviously they are a discard from a bigger person. The horse is not pulling a travois, either because the two humans have nothing to add to their meager belongings or because their trusted mount does not have even a tiny measure of strength left to pull one.

The little one keeps turning to check on a particular bundle tied with red sinew as if fearful of losing it along the way. They have been walking one full day. She doesn't look particularly worried or particularly happy. She simply is doing what daughters do, obeying her father, and at age seven it is impossible to even guess the magnitude of change her life is about to undergo.

The Wind has learned through the ages that in all things there is a hidden blessing. Perhaps her youth and her innocence will help her adapt quickly to her new home as opposed to Stolen Lakota Woman's difficult adjustment.

Sizing up the girl, horse, and father, "Where are the gifts?" whispers Hungry Crow to Bird Bone Pipe Woman.

"Shush!" comes a sound from behind them. They do not need to turn to know it is Two Guns Buffalo Calf shaming them into silence.

Something isn't right. Why does the old horse lower her nose toward the ground while her head begins to slowly weave from side to side? Oh no! Without warning, the collapsing mare rolls to her side and with a long fluttering snort, breathes out her last breath. The Wind wasn't thinking about the horse . . . instead I was worried about Hunting Elk making this all day trip.

What a sight. What was to be as genteel a moment of formal greeting as could be summoned has eroded the air into awkward embarrassing discomposure. The crying little one turns to grab her watched-over bundle to her chest. Old Hunting Elk is admonishing a dead horse to get up. Two Guns Buffalo Calf is thoroughly disgusted with both Hungry Crow and her sometimes challenger, whom she secretly calls Bird Bone instead of by her full name, Bird Bone Pipe

Woman. A little boy is poking the horse's rump with a stick to test for degree of deadness. While the two-leggeds gasp and whisper, their four-legged hoofed relative remains unmoving.

Comes Still Alive is determined to bring dignity and calmness to this occasion in spite of its element of catastrophe. Wanting to offer some reassurance to his guest and soon-to-be new little bride, he raises his hand. All falls silent.

"Greetings, dear Brother and Young One. I have waited with anticipation for your arrival." Some of the women crowding around this event have wet eyes in sympathy for the girl. Others are biting their lips to keep from laughing. Still others are angry that some of the people cannot keep from stifling a chuckle. The grandmothers are embarrassed for everyone.

Comes Still Alive looks not at the dead horse or any of the activities of commotion, but looks straight ahead with eyes of respect toward Hunting Elk. He motions for the two to enter his teepee, but Hunting Elk, who finally realizes his friend has expired, insists that prayers be offered first for his dead horse.

Hunting Elk takes the free hand of Sings To Flowers, that which is not clutching her bundle, and together they kneel by the old mare. Carefully the horse's head is lifted up while Hunting Elk speaks a simple prayer. "Dear Four Legged Friend, may you run with your ancestors and with The Wind."

Comes Still Alive looks at an elder standing nearby and nods toward the dead horse. Not a single word comes from his lips, but the message is clear. Hunting Elk and Sings To Flowers are then quickly ushered inside his number one teepee and the door flap closed.

It is the elder's turn to give looks, and out of nowhere appear six young braves with a net of horsehair rope used to channel the buffalo before they are made to jump the cliff. The young men cut loose the bundles still attached to the dead horse and toss them aside. The bundles are eagerly grabbed up by Hungry Crow. It is decided that the dilapidated horse has too little meat to offer humans and would be very tough. Besides, there is plenty of freshly prepared game to be had during the days prior to celebrating the Okan. The young men roll the expired mount onto the net and drag her out of sight. A couple of dogs and some children follow to watch where they will put the dead horse, while a couple of buzzards keep it all in perspective overhead.

In the future this story will be embellished and told again and again on cold winter nights, with some lowering their heads thinking, *Eeeee. The poor little Sings To Flowers,* while others roll on their hurting sides from laughter.

At the door of the teepee, Hungry Crow, now wishing she had not judged so sharply, respectfully hands her previously snatched-up bundles to Hunting Elk. Later it will be Hungry Crow's turn to feel even more ashamed. Inside the bundles is a wonderful wedding gift for Comes Still Alive. Three bundles contain the sweeter tasting dried tobacco flowers, picked just before the first frost. They are the highly prized form of tobacco and much more difficult to obtain than the more abundant leaves and stems. These will be kept aside and saved for the pipe of the most sacred of ceremonies. What Hunting Elk's wedding gift lacks in quantity is made up for in the quality of the long-laboring work of his and little Sings To Flowers' hands.

CHAPTER EIGHT

The First Kiss

Lily is tossing and turning in her hospital bed until someone drops an instrument tray which clatters and smashes to the floor with an echoing crescendo, shaking her awake to the hospital smells and nightly din. However with Lily's sporadic waking to semi-consciousness, her dreams, the language of her unconscious, are remembered more easily. Psychologists say, "Pay attention to your dreams."

Jarred awake, Lily searches for her call-light to ask the nurse for something for a headache. After being asked a battery of questions about severity, location, and duration, and after checking too many times Lily's pupils, pulse, and blood pressure, the night nurse disappears and finally returns. She pours Lily a glass of water and presents her with medication and the note pad and pen she had requested.

"I've had such dreams . . . odd thoughts," Lily says with a groggy voice. "Memories of long ago, around here somewhere. I am sure of it."

"Really?" says the skeptical nurse.

"Yes, really," she says, pulling herself up. "It's like I'm living in two worlds. This one where I'm Plain Jane Ordinary, and another one, sort of half beyond my grasp, like it's behind a semi-transparent curtain. All I have to do to get there is just shut my eyes."

"You mean like a dream then."

"No, No. More than a dream. Way more. And behind the curtain is a world full of terror and . . . and . . . unspeakable love.

"Unspeakable?"

"Like I'm trying to say somethin' I have no words for. I want to try to write some of it down if I can."

"Sounds kind of exciting," says the nurse in a dismissive voice while turning her back to Lily and reaching for the bed lamp. Lily's eyes are cast down, as if focused on something beyond the bed sheets.

Strangers aren't going to believe me. Maybe I shouldn't even try to explain.

"Let me bring your bed light within reach so you can turn it off when you're done. It's too bright for sleeping in here," she says as she pulls the light closer to Lily. But, "Oh." The nurse realizes that the knob on the light is in the off position. She turns the light on, which seems to have little if any effect on the brightness of the room. She has a quizzical look on her face; she looks first at Lily and then back to the bed lamp. Then she decides she has too many patient call-lights blinking at her down the hall.

I need to answer those call lights without wasting a half hour to figure out this oddity. Anyway, if it becomes a problem, she'll just buzz me later. The R.N. pauses at the door to look back. *That kid seems to almost have . . . No, it can't be . . . kind of a halo? Hardly. I must be getting an aura from an oncoming migraine. Better take some preventive stuff now, before it starts to hammer me. On the other hand, I've never had a migraine aura around only one person or object. Strange.*

The Wind says, Humph. Humans do this all the time. When they are confronted with something new and even gloriously new, they have to make it fit into their notions of what they think is real in their world and miss the bigger show.

After scratching a few notes on her pad Lily turns the bed light to the off position and puts a pillow over her eyes. Soon she feels herself becoming heavy and her thinking becomes blurred. She begins to doze off, after watching a blaze of colors form and fade and form again under her closed eyelids.

Lily usually doesn't start a dream where she left the previous one, but this time is different. She feels herself shrink again into the small package of Sings To Flowers.

The dead horse incident seems to have softened the hearts of the other wives who are now committed to helping the new little stranger into the family. All the other wives but one, that is; Stolen Lakota Woman remains unmoved and distant.

A space has been made in the lodge for Sings To Flowers' and her father's first night in the new place. Comes Still Alive is pleased with his wedding gift and shares a pipe with Hunting Elk, who will be sent home after the wedding ceremony on a new live horse plus two others loaded with plenty of freshly killed buffalo and pemmican. Sings To Flowers, now with a full belly, still clutching her special bundle that is never outside her awareness, is beginning to droop her little head.

"What's in that bundle, Child?" asks Comes Still Alive.

"Toys." Her answer is surprisingly almost defiant, having snapped awake while clutching the bundle even tighter to her chest.

The majority of wives have sympathetic eyes, however Stolen Lakota Woman, who understands more Blackfoot talk than she will ever admit but will never speak it, even to the day of her death, takes a sharp in-breath and looks away. In her private thoughts she decides, *I do not want to be bound to this little child. She'll make even more trouble for me and I will never be able to escape these dog-faced people. But I swear to the moon one thing: if that child is forced onto my hip like a constant double load of wood I can't put down, I'll see to it that there will be a day for Sings To . . . What's It, to dispense with that ridiculous toy bundle.*

Sings To Flowers' sleepy wobbling head has finally found its way to the comfort of the thick shaggy buffalo robe and Lily, in her hospital bed, begins to dream within a dream. Sings To Flowers' mind races back to very recent times with a delicious cascade of flashes of sweet childhood love play.

To follow the rules of the place and time, it is imperative that young girls keep close to their family lodge, separated from boys and under the watchful eyes and tutelage of their mother, aunts, or grandmothers. In addition, all the older women are considered grandmothers to all the children of the tribe. However this motherless child has had little if any mature watchful eyes on her, hardly anything more than a sideways glance from a neighbor. By some magic Sings To Flowers has been able to run, to play, and to tag along with big brother, Coyote Head, and his constant companion, Little Bear. Both boys are three winters older than she. This is done with her tired aging father's half-hearted blessing, although a few romps in the woods are without his knowledge.

Both boys have a tolerance for the little tag-along and are protective of her, making sure that other young ruffians do not tease or otherwise torment. When they are at play they feel no need for more company than their threesome and are full of delight in everything, just as The Creator intended.

They wade and later, when it is warmer, swim naked in the high mountain lakes. They look for the pollywog people in the ponds. They look and listen for the singers of the humming music that the insect people make, the splashing music that the frog people make, and the chirping music that the winged ones that build their houses near the water make. They dash through streamlets, turn over and look under rocks for little caddis fly houses, catch for a moment the beautiful blue damsel fly to marvel at its delicateness, and revel in the perfume of the mountain blooms and berries, as well as the pungent odor of sage and waving prairie grasses.

When the boys climb the ash trees to find the perfect, strong yet supple branch for a bow, Sings To Flowers does as her name says—she sings to flowers and butterflies under the trees her playmates climb. Sometimes she climbs too. From high vantage points it seems all is perfect in the world. While the boys whittle on their bows and serviceberry shoots to make arrows, Sings To Flowers makes a family of dolls from the outer husks of the nearby cattail foliage growing at the water's edge. Sometimes she makes a family of reed ducks which skim across the water after the children blow the little floating toys away. The three are always together in play, chasing, singing, dancing, and laughing.

But there is among the childhood memories a turning point day—a day that will be called forth again and again, in both daydreams and night dreams. It is a memory that will keep Sings To Flowers both semi-sane and desperately sad and lonely during the life that follows.

Now on her buffalo robe in a new place, Sings To Flowers enters into that dream-memory. In her dream she remembers the glorious and unusually warm spring day with the sun high in the sky. Soon the camp will be moving so she and the two boys waste no time in taking full advantage of the mountain lake waters while they can.

The three children are just emerging after a naked swim in the lake. They had floated a gift of pemmican in a wooden bowl for the water people and found the bowl empty. *They must be pleased with their gift,* concludes an elated Little Bear.

"Oh!" Little Bear spies an unusual stone. It is unusual because it is almost perfectly round. It also has a deep crack. *I wonder if something's inside? I can break this open.* Without even waiting to throw on any of his coverings, he grabs a pointed stone to wedge in the crack and gives it a solid whack. The round stone falls into two pieces nearly equal in size. The rough ugliness on the outside is made up for by the beauty of the inside. Within there is a soft bluish cast from an inner family of little gray-blue crystals that sparkle with blinding light in the sun.

"The stars are in this rock! I've seen one of these before. It's a thunder egg! Old blind Crooked Tooth showed me one of these. He got it in trade. He said, 'Go find them around the fire mountains.' He said, 'There are two warrior mountains that throw these thunder eggs at each other to win looks from a beautiful lady mountain.' Crooked Tooth likes to feel them in his hand. He says even without his eyes he can feel the moonlight in them."

Little Bear looks at the shining water drops on Sings To Flowers and says, "This stone is not as beautiful as you. I want you to keep one of these pieces and I will keep the other one and when I look at it I will remember you even when I am old. And if I am blind when I am old, I will feel the sharp sparkle in the stone and remember you and this day."

For Sings To Flowers, the full impact of his words does not sink in. Not at this moment. Later she will repeat them over and over in her mind. Right now she is still in the mood of their earlier game of Chase Me-Chase You. Sings To Flowers grabs both halves from Little Bear and runs away laughing. "I want both halves, Little Bear!"

She turns to taunt and tease him into another chase. Sings To Flowers runs and hops over rivulets, barely feeling an occasional prickly stone, with Little Bear in close pursuit. Catching her several times along the way, her wet body helps her wriggle free—or does he allow that to happen just to catch her again and feel the touch of her skin?

Finally they are back running and splashing in the lake with great merriment. Sings To Flowers now pretends to throw the rock halves into the middle of the lake. This prompts Little Bear to lunge at her, sinking both of them to the bottom. Still giggling as they are rising to the surface, both faces momentarily covered by a veil of bubbles, Little Bear with Sings To Flowers in an inescapable hard embrace, rubs his lips across her cheek and ends with his lips on her lips. It is a wet kiss because, after all, they are under water.

It is the first kiss for both of them. Somewhere in the magic, the stone pieces sink to the bottom of the lake and are buried in the muddy depths. Sings To Flowers will come to this spot again and again throughout her life to search for the thunder egg halves and reminisce. She will not find them, but she will remember and replay in her mind the details of those lovely ephemeral moments . . . the moments of Sings To Flowers and Little Bear.

Sings To Flowers rolls over on her new buffalo robe and is half awakened by snoring sounds and perhaps a muffled squeal of delight. In her half-dreaming half-waking mind, she cannot quite separate what is happening in the interior of the teepee from her dream.

From the moment of their first kiss, they fall more and more into each other's lives. On hot summer nights Hunting Elk lifts the skirt of his teepee to cool down the interior with a cross draft from the welcomed night breeze. Little Bear, who after the kiss braids a small clutch of sweet grass into his hair, has made a habit of sneaking away when the moon rises high. He sneaks from his lodge to lie outside the Hunting Elk teepee with Sings To Flowers and Coyote Head, who lie with their heads poked outside while their bodies remain inside the teepee. In this way, the three spend hours in whispers and stargazing. And when the snores from Hunting Elk and Coyote Head begin, Little Bear and Sings To Flowers take more kisses before the bedazzled Little Bear must scurry back to his lodge, getting his cue to leave from the morning star that heralds the break of day.

Lily awakens, again in her hospital bed. Even in the summer she prefers soft flannel sheets to the cold, slick, antiseptic-smelling ones provided by the hospital. The night nurse is back to wake her up to ask if the headache medicine is working and check her pupils. Lily's head no longer hurts, but is full of love thoughts about Little Bear. She reaches again for her pen to write down reminders of this dream.

Now there is sleepy tossing and turning. As Lily falls back to sleep she sees Sings To Flowers is also half rousing, turning in her bed, then snuggling back again into her wonderful soft buffalo robe and falling into another dream-memory.

In her dream she is gathering many dandelions and occasionally wild marigold blossoms to add to her prairie onion skins. She will dry these and pound them into a powder for producing a yellow dye. She can use some to trade for wild iris roots or black sumac for black dye making. For red coloring she can use the roots of dandelions and if she has any rose hips left from the fall, they work for red too. Sings To Flowers is singing a very happy song these days. She is helping Little Bear decorate his first set of arrows for his newly made bow.

The dyed sinew is ready. Coyote Head and Sings To Flowers watch Little Bear wrap the shaft of his new arrows, first with three wraps of yellow. As he is doing this he proudly announces, "These three circle-wraps are for the three of us under the watch of The Creator and the nourishment of the sunlight." Next he winds four wraps of red. "These four are for the four directions. They are red, the color of blood and of power." Finally he wraps twelve wraps of black. "It is said that everything has its beginning in the dark of night. These are for the many nights we watched the hoop of star patterns through all four seasons." As Little Bear hands an arrow to his friends he says, "I want you each to have one of these arrows, for we are brother and sister forever." Little Bear is ten winters old when he makes these words. He speaks like a wise old man.

These beautiful moments come to an abrupt end when it is announced by Hunting Elk that a marriage has been arranged between Sings To Flowers and Comes Still Alive, someone whom Coyote Head remembers having seen only once at one of the big summer gatherings and whom Little Bear remembers not at all. "Can we stop this marriage?" asks Little Bear of the stars, of the trees, of anything that will listen.

The day before Sings To Flowers leaves for Comes Still Alive's lodge he meets with his love in a secret place and gives her his most treasured possessions, his bow and quiver of arrows, some stained with his blood. "You should have these, Sings To Flowers, and be the keeper of them forever because together we have made these special toys and they carry not only the spirit of the ash tree, serviceberries, deer, and the flowers you gathered, but a part of my spirit and yours." Sings To Flowers will not be able to keep them forever, but forever will treasure them in her heart and somewhere in the extended part of her mind.

In return, Sings To Flowers gives Little Bear a necklace of caddis fly casings, gathered long after the insect has gone through its metamorphosis and vacated its tiny home. Drops of her blood have dried on this necklace from accidental pricks of a sharp bone needle. "I gathered these little houses of tiny colored rocks no bigger than grains of sand at our lake where we first kissed. I had hoped someday that we could build our own lodge together. When you look upon these, remember my dream for us and that I love you forever." He will wear the necklace for many seasons until one by one, over time, the casings will be crushed or fall apart, but even then he will carry it around his neck and over his heart in his mind's eye.

Coyote Head sees pain everywhere he looks. He says to himself, *I must do something to prevent this marriage.*

It is very unusual for a son to act against his father's will. He loves the friendship of Little Bear. He loves his sister, Sings To Flowers. He reminds himself, *My name stands for being a trickster teacher . . . for being clever and sometimes just a little mean when Spirit speaks to me. What can I do? What can I do?*

Now it is known that the sour-tasting chokecherries are used to treat stomach troubles, colds, and fevers in people. It is known by some that if the leaves of chokecherries after the first frost are given to a horse even a strong trusty mount will become weak and/or agitated. Wilted leaves after a freeze makes them sweet, but it also releases a cyanide-like chemical that in larger amounts can prove fatal to horses. Coyote Head had dragged several branches high up into the mountain near the snow fields to a place where the frost hangs on everything until morning.

It was not Coyote Head's intent to exterminate his father's only horse. The idea was to squeeze out a little more time by giving the horse *just a little stomach ache for a couple of days* so it could not be coaxed to make the day's walk to Comes Still Alive's camp. This would give Coyote Head a chance to come up with another delay or even a preventive tactic. Unfortunately something went terribly wrong. The horse was too old, or perhaps the dose was too much.

Sometimes you cannot outmaneuver destiny, even if your name is Coyote Head and you have trickster powers.

CHAPTER NINE

The Okan and the Purification

For three days after his last secret meeting with Sings To Flowers, Little Bear has not been seen. The Wind knows where he is. He has taken the treacherously steep and rocky way up to the buffalo jump to be closer to The Sun. This time he does not go with Coyote Head. He goes alone. On this precipitous peak he finds a shallow depression in Mother Earth that fits him and encircles it with stones. Stones are keepers of Mother's history.

There, within his circle, he cries for The Sun to take pity on him and prevent this marriage of Sings To Flowers with Comes Still Alive. There he cries for a vision. There he lies down for three days without food or water. There, after his head for three days rests against The Mother he begins to hear her heartbeat, beat, thump, thump, thump-thump, thump-thumping faster and then thunder without lightning and then the rocks in his circle begin to jump and then roll out of place and then some tumble down the sides of his vision quest place against him and now the ground shakes and now the ground rolls. Looking up Little Bear sees a talking cloud coming for him. The cloud is loud with thumping noises inside.

Right now Little Bear makes an oath to The Sun. He vows to do the Piercing Ceremony at the Okan if Creator Sun will stop Sings To Flowers' marriage and save him from the thunder cloud. Then he sees the first buffalo face coming at him out of the dust, then a second and a third. Two-and-a-half thousand pounds of shaggy beast on four rock-sharpened hooves jump over Little Bear, who is trying to make himself small.

If I stay here I'll be ground into ground. I've got to reach the small out-cropping just over the edge of the cliff. Help me, Creator Sun! Make me invisible when I run with the herd! Little Bear leaps up just behind one of those mammoth beings and runs. Hot snorts of breath run after his heels.

And then, "Ahhhhh!" Little Bear is shoved by a grunting snout and a horn in his back and falls. He hears the pop, pop, of his own ribs a nanosecond before they explode. He finds himself witnessing the next crushing stomp on his skull from just above his rag of a body. Horrified, he watches his brains running out of his nose and eye sockets. And then no more running . . . black . . . just black . . . Nothing. Ab . . . so . . . lute . . . ly . . . Nothing . . . .

❧

Hold on. Little Bear stirs! He wanted a vision. There it was. But the ending—not pleasant. Not pleasant at all. Not a good sign. Or? Was it something that shamans go through? The dismemberment, the tearing? What kind of vision did he think he would get at the jump place where The Land holds the energy spirit of the killed buffalo?

Finally, on weak and trembling limbs he crawls down from the buffalo jump, dehydrated and gaunt. *I am going to go to The Okan. I will be near my beloved there.*

❧

People of all three Blackfoot clans are starting to trickle into the great summer gathering, the Okan. Some are arriving from many miles away, as far north as the regions of The Saskatchewan River and as far south as The Yellowstone. This is the time that has been chosen for the wedding of Comes Still Alive and Sings To Flowers.

Although wedding ceremonies for unions after the primary one are usually not very elaborate, all the wives have worked on the wedding costume for Sings To Flowers. Even Stolen Lakota Woman smiled when she saw the dress made of well-oiled white antelope skin decorated with treasured elk teeth and a fluff of ermine with an occasional black-tipped tail at the hemline. Hunting Elk had brought the elk teeth with him in a bladder bag. A well-decorated dress with elk teeth is worth two horses in trade.

Old Two Guns Buffalo Calf and Bird Bone Pipe Woman have been initiated into the Quill Society and are the only ones in their household allowed to do quill work. They have covered the new better-fitting wedding moccasins and leggings with the Blackfoot symbol of the three united tribes of the people, which is represented as a decorative three-pronged trident. The trident and five-pointed stars were made with specially selected porcupine quills that had been boiled, flattened by pulling them through the women's teeth, and colorfully dyed.

Sings To Flowers was allowed to accompany the two women on their hunt for a porcupine, but was made to stand aside when a blanket was skillfully cast and raked over the animal's body. Two Guns Buffalo Calf would not allow her to touch or gather the porcupine weaponry from the blanket. "Its spirit is too powerful," she said. Not even the initiated would try to pull quills off the back of a biting, thrashing, tail-slapping porcupine. It is said that the women who are brave enough to do quillwork will not live very long. They must make strong medicine (prayers) to prevent painful infected punctures, which can lead to intense sickness and the tragedy of death.

The Okan celebration lasts several days. It begins at sunrise with four initial days and nights of feasting and singing. Sings To Flowers has been made to help the women take the teepees down and put them up again each day in a new area for broader exposure and bonding to relations not seen for a year. The Okan is where the people learn who belongs to which clan, since the clans are constantly breaking up and reforming.

On the fifth day strong men chosen by the holy man, Running Bear, help erect the pine tree center post for the Medicine Lodge that will be built in the center of the camp. The holy man selects the tree as well as those who will prepare it.

No one but The Wind sees a determined ten-winters boy looking on from the thicket near the twelve-foot tree chosen for its straightness.

"We need a tree that has a fork near the top where we can hang the buffalo skull," reminds Running Bear. "The skull will call the buffalo spirit in to dance." Most importantly, the chosen tree is being taken from a clearing where it stands alone and has been well exposed to the sun. The men do not allow the tree to touch The Earth as it is cut down and stripped of branches.

Mothers explain with pride to their daughters that the officiator of the event will be a woman, a "holy" woman. Prior to the celebration, that special lady cries in a loud voice outside her lodge at least three times a prayer to The Sun to have pity on her, to grant her prayers for which she vows to put up the Medicine Lodge to honor The Sun and to be the Medicine Lodge Woman. "I have been at all times faithful to my husband and have lived with the highest morals," she cries. During her claims of faithfulness, if any man can prove otherwise, this is the time for him to step forward and challenge her credibility.

Perhaps she offers her services as the Medicine Lodge Woman for the protection of her husband in battle or the request for health to return to a dangerously sick child. Her intent is cried aloud within her prayer.

Sometimes the Medicine Lodge Woman has a secret. In private her husband has challenged her and now tests his wife who he suspects of the treachery of adultery, by requesting her to put up the Medicine Lodge at the Okan and be the Medicine Lodge Woman. In this position she is considered the temporary priestess of The Sun. She can only be in this exalted position if her ways have been holy her entire life. By this it is meant that she is honest and "pure," never straying from her husband. It is believed without a doubt that if she is lying about her purity her relatives will suffer and she will shortly die. Therefore, only a woman secure in her private knowledge of her own worthiness would dare step up to the challenge of being the Medicine Lodge Woman.

The Wind thinks before volunteering for this role a smart woman should make sure her next of kin are healthy, as a safeguard against the people who might suspect her of wrong doing.

During the ceremonies Sings To Flowers watches as The Medicine Lodge Woman's face, hands, and clothing are coated with paint made of red clay. She knows the color red is the holy power color that denotes The Sun and Life Force and is one of the colors on her precious gift arrows from Little Bear. She watches The Medicine Lodge Woman being given charge of all sacred bundles, of which there are about fifty in number, each cared for by various clan family "keepers" until the Okan. Everything is done with precision and ceremony, including the ceremonies of transfer. Within the bundles are skins of animals, sacred herbs, rattles, bones, scalps, and buffalo tails. But the most important bundle of all is the bundle with the Medicine Pipe.

It is in the Medicine Lodge where completion of a man's oath is performed. If he has given the oath to dance the Piercing Ceremony sometime after the last Okan, then he has agreed to have his chest flesh pierced in two places with wooden willow, bone, or animal claw skewers that will be secured with rawhide ropes. The other end of the ropes will be bound to the center post in the Medicine Lodge and pulled taut by the backward lean of his dancing until they rip through his skin. This ritual dance is promised to The Sun by the most ardent supplicant, who requests for himself or a loved one deliverance out of danger or illness.

Little Bear, at only ten-winters has made this oath. But he does not want deliverance from an illness. He wants Sings To Flowers to be delivered out of a marriage before it happens. This is not the usual prayer, certainly not from a ten-winters boy. But oaths to The Sun must be proclaimed before the people and the piercing performed before them as witnesses to his honoring his promise. If the people have not heard his oath to The Sun, will his desire be granted? No one but The Wind has heard Little Bear make his oath. Is he really obligated to do this? If he backs out there would be no shame, except maybe in his own mind. What will the holy man in charge of the ceremony think about a young boy doing the piercing?

Preparation is made for the piercing by first cleansing the body and spirit by entering the sweat lodge. It is the breath of The Creator, seen in the steam that rises when water is poured on scorched rocks, that cleans his spirit as well as his body.

Four sweat lodges have been erected for this purpose, two in front and two in back of the Medicine Lodge, in a line facing the sun. Little Bear tried to enter the one furthest away at dusk but was told, "Move away." Never mind, now Little Bear is making his own sweat lodge in a downstream hidden part of the river. He enters at night. Nobody takes notice.

He who has made the vow does not eat or drink anything from sundown before and through the day of his dancing. If the dancer has not broken free by sundown of his dancing day, the medicine man will yank on the skewers until they are torn free.

To help detract the dancer's mind from the pain, he blows with each breath into an eagle-wing bone whistle held in his teeth. Several dancers will dance at the same time, creating a cacophony of sound. The sound, the high energy of the people watching, and the lack of a full belly, help to shift him into the blessing of an altered state of consciousness.

Yet in spite of this The Wind has seen some dancers faint and some sneak away into the woods after the ceremony to cry out their pain, away from intruding judgmental eyes—but I hear them. I am acutely aware of them. Some torn dancers are aware of me as I comfort them, there alone in the woods. They are alone but for my gentle blowing on their cheeks and shoulders. I kiss their wounds softly, there in the woods where nobody sees their torments.

Sings To Flowers is watching the holy hands of the medicine lodge woman give a morsel of at least 100 buffalo tongues to every man, woman, and child, after offering the delicacy first to The Sun, and then to Ground Man who lives in Mother Earth. Sings To Flowers is overcome with awe as the offerings include over 100 memorized prayer and blessing songs.

People will attach gifts to The Sun on the Medicine Lodge's center post. These will be gifts of the best tobacco, food containing sweet, seasonal, hard-to-find berries, the highest quality quill and beadwork, fine furs, and an occasional human finger, which shows the sincerity of that person to make a powerful prayer request. The most powerful gift however, even more powerful than a finger, is a lock of hair.

The Blackfoot people say that hair is "the history of their people and the seat of the soul" and the soul protects the body. Therefore the practice of the taking of scalps, which was first introduced by European Spanish conquerors, was shockingly horrid to people who believe the soul of the scalped person to be stolen by this act. Later, when the native peoples saw their way of life being desecrated and destroyed, out of desperation and rage they performed the very same act.

Believing the soul to be in the hair is why the warrior combs a lock of his hair over his forehead for a measure of protection before battle, slices the lock short enough not to obstruct his vision, and offers the cut-off piece to The Sun. Some men do not cut their hair at all, but tie up a large knot of hair that protrudes far in front of their foreheads so that their souls will go before them and shield them from danger. Both Comes Still Alive and the holy man, Running Bear, wear the knotted frontal hair.

It is the morning of the sixth day of the gathering of the people for the Okan rituals. It has been decided that this will be a good day for the wedding. Two Guns Buffalo Calf, the sits-beside-him woman of Comes Still Alive, will be the sponsor for Sings To Flowers.

She takes the wedding child in one hand and soap made with buffalo fat in the other to a private part of the stream protected by tall cottonwoods swaying with my breath. They enter where the water takes a curve away from the view of the Okan camp.

Sings To Flowers is inching bit by bit into the water, shivering with every step, and finally her shivering amplifies into shaking, even though I pull back and blow less breeze across the water that cause ripples and goose flesh. I think she shakes more from the uncertainty of what is to come. She looks back at her bundle, having put it nearby under a tree but not out of sight.

"Your toy bundle is safe there," admonishes Two Guns Buffalo Calf. "It is time for you to think less of your toys and more about the task at hand. After today you must not think of yourself as a child, but as a wife. Come on, into the water with you. You must purify yourself for the marriage ceremony.

"Now I will tell you some things," she says with a stern and metered tone. "Do not touch turtles, frogs, or lizards, ever. They are creatures of evil. If you see one, avert your eyes and go away from it quickly.

"Speaking of eyes, make sure that you mind your own eyes. Do not be looking at the handsome young men. They will think it is an invitation. You are a married woman now. Do not ignore the fact that there will always be the eyes of others upon you . . . watching. They will see at what or at whom you are looking."

While listening to all this, Sings To Flowers' eyes widen more and more, then quickly she shuts them.

"Also remember this," continues Two Guns Buffalo Calf, not noticing the child's masked panic. "A wife follows **behind** her husband. She does not question him. She is not stubborn if he asks her to do something. He has all the power in the marriage. The wife does not involve him in gossip. She does not giggle or make a lot of noise, especially if he is with his pipe and visitors. I am telling you these things to keep you safe. Some men beat their wives. I think it is because some wives make too much noise." Sings To Flowers' eyes remain closed and she is beginning to hold her breath.

"When you are older you will know how to have more influence on your husband at night after his guests leave the lodge, but not now. In the lodge you will sit next to Stolen Lakota Woman in the position of the lowest ranking wife.

"Now get in the water and purify yourself. Hurry. Hurry! Comes Still Alive does a morning purification every single day, even when he must break through thick ice. It keeps him as strong as a bear."

Sings To Flowers' lower lip is beginning to tremble and the skin of her face is becoming tinged with blue. The Wind does not detect any breath in her nose and her heart pulsates with extreme rapid beats against and into me; she does not seem to be able to speed up her slow march into the cold waters. She holds her breath too long!

"Come now. Put your head into the water." Sings To Flowers slowly sinks to where the water can come up and over her chin, but seems stuck to go further. "Like this, Child." A powerful nudge from pure exasperation brings Two Guns Buffalo Calf's fingers to the top of Sings To Flowers' head and pushes her under. The swift current catches the two unprepared and the little girl is swiftly carried underwater downstream.

Sings To Flowers is at the edge of drowning, but finds it strangely pleasant. Her heart and mind are rehearsing beautiful memories of Little Bear and watching bubbles escape, just as they did before their first kiss. But this time the bubbles come from the end of her last breath.

She is sinking, sinking . . . sinking . . . into blackness. . . . .

Help!

From nowhere come two strong hands that pull sharply on her hair, yanking her up to the surface and into seconds of semi-consciousness before she slips back again into beautiful memories. Now two strong arms haul Sings To Flowers to the side of the stream. Two Guns Buffalo Calf, who was left far behind, is yelling and waving her arms from her position far up river. She is screaming, "Ki yo! Our child! Our child!"

Sings To Flowers is lying now by the water's edge with black lips and black nail beds and a gray-looking cold, naked body, but she doesn't feel much of anything. Her eyes are rolled up into her head. Swiftly her body is rolled over on her stomach and with a gentle but firm push on her back, water is pushed out from deep inside her. She takes a breath. Now she does not breathe.

I blow some of myself into her nostrils. I am helping. Now she takes another bubbly sounding breath, just to stop again. Finally, another breath escapes the lifeless lips.

She is still alive for Comes Still Alive.

A shaken and also out of breath Two Guns Buffalo Calf is now leaning over her. "Eeeeeee!" is all she can say. The strong arms lift Sings To Flowers up off the rocks but all that bewildered Sings To Flowers can see is the face of Two Guns Buffalo Calf inches from her face, as the helping hands and arms of a stranger deliver her into the bony arms of the old woman. Sings To Flowers is too bewildered to see or thank the helping hands that saved her. All she says is, "Where's my bundle of toys?"

CHAPTER TEN

The Marriage

Little Sings To Flowers is all decked out in her wedding finery and does look the part of a lovely bride . . . in miniature. Her hair is being wrapped into a braid by Two Guns Buffalo Calf, who cannot stop with her lectures, while Stolen Lakota Woman looks on sullenly and then finally makes a braid for Sings To Flowers on the other side. "After you become married you will always wear your hair braided. When you are old enough to have children, then you will paint the part in your hair with red clay. You will paint your part red until you are too old to have babies."

The puzzled look on Sings To Flowers' face suddenly begins to change. Her mouth is turning into the shape of a scream. Stolen Lakota Woman has snatched her bundle of toys out of her arms. The screams are so alarming, so piercing, that any person passing by would think a baby had been stolen. "You cannot take your toys to your marriage ceremony," she says in her Lakota Sioux talk that nobody understands, yet the women are shocked because this is the first time they have heard Stolen Lakota Woman speak at all.

Not too many moments of screams pass before the door flap of the teepee is flung open and in steps Comes Still Alive. He has a frown on his face. He is dressed in new deerskins with many decorations and his frontal topknot of hair has been freshly coiled and knotted. He almost looks like an Egyptian pharaoh with a snake-head crown. All falls immediately silent except for one who continues to wail.

"Silence!" comes the command. After a momentary pause that

leaves the lodge air heavy and brittle while the women silence their tongues, some of the brave women try to explain. "Speak one at a time!" he says and points to his sits-beside-him wife. Before he hears the whole story, he holds up his hand signaling, "Say no more," and swiftly solves the matter. Sings To Flowers will wear the bow and quiver of arrows over her wedding garb and the beaver skins over her shoulders. The two dolls can be tucked into her belt. Little eyes that before were spilling tears are now drying. There is peace at last for a little while.

Little Bear has heard gossip that there will be a wedding today, but he does not want to hear anything more. He is concentrating on making two willow twigs needle sharp at both ends.

The small party of wedding people move to a thicket of trees. They will take their vows in the comfort of the shade. Coyote Head, just arriving for the Okan, joins the group. He and Comes Still Alive's other wives and the father of Sings To Flowers stand in a semicircle around the group of three, the holy man and the couple to be married. Beyond the wives and father of Sings To Flowers and her brother is another semicircle where Comes Still Alive's thirteen children stand. A third semicircle of people beyond that are friends of the two families and any number of on-lookers that pass by and stop to watch.

Little Bear raises two willow skewers to the face of The Sun. "Creator Sun, I complete my vow to you today to bring Sings To Flowers back to my arms where she will dance and sing forever in my lodge and not in the lodge of Comes Still Alive. Fill these willows, gathered by the lake of our first kiss, with your fierce Sun power."

At the wedding thicket someone whispers, "He is old enough to be her grandfather." Someone else says softly, "She is very small and has a peculiar wedding costume."

The chosen willow skewers have a few knobs that Little Bear has not taken the time to smooth. Being in a hurry, he takes a big pinch of himself on the left above his heart and tries to ram a skewer through, but the knobs catch, making this maneuver incomplete. In shock from searing pain he lets go of his pinch of flesh. This is his second mistake. Unable to get the exact same degree of pull on the skin that he had before, he pushes the remainder of the skewer through a new channel. Since the skewer is relatively straight, this makes a much more painful uneven pull by that skewer.

The second skewer gets caught too, but Little Bears leans against a tree without letting go, forcing the skewer into a smooth entry and exit. At last, although his chest is bloody, his first step in the Piercing Dance is done.

Running Bear is the holy man who will marry Comes Still Alive and Sings To Flowers. He stands before the very young bride and old groom with a solemnly composed face, one half of which is painted red to represent The Sun while the other half is painted black to represent the wife of The Sun. Painted thusly, his visage represents the holiest of all unions, the marriage of The Sun and The Moon.

On Running Bear's head, behind his frontal topknot, is the upper portion of a carcass of a raven with its stuffed head looking toward the holy man's back, giving Running Bear eyes in the back of his head. He sees in all directions, the past and the future.

Through Running Bear's pierced ear lobes are slender threads of rawhide holding several ornaments, including two large shell discs taken from the body of a dead Nez Perce. The shiny pearly discs hang among tufts of white owl feathers and two golden eagle tail feathers. In his hand is a raven's wing. Around the back of his neck, like a modern doctor wears his stethoscope, is the long rope of sweet grass he will use in the ceremony.

A ten-winters boy is stepping out of the Medicine Lodge shadows, his chest covered and his legs spattered with shiny sticky-red fluid. He holds a rope, not of sweet grass, but of rawhide that has been split into four ends with each end tied securely to the willow pieces protruding from his body. Before anyone can make a move, the young boy lashes the free end of the rawhide around the center post and joins four other dancers. He leans back but the weight of his body cannot compare to that of the older men. Little Bear must jerk and jump back again and again to make any progress for tearing free. He has no whistle to hold in his teeth. His teeth are clenched and his face wears a determined frown of concentration.

It is a short wedding ceremony, consisting of a long prayer. The holy man prepares first by cutting a few inches of his sweet grass braid into a stone bowl, where he lights it with a hot coal. The perfume from the burning grass is wafted with the raven's wing over the couple standing before him. The wedding couple is asked to join hands. Little Sings To Flowers' hand completely disappears into the mountains of flesh of her soon-to-be husband. She places her other hand over her heart and the strap of her true beloved's bow.

The crowd in the Medicine Lodge is full of whispers and murmurs. "Where are that boy's parents?"

"I think he is the boy whose parents were killed by bears."

"Where is the holy man?"

"He is performing a wedding. Comes Still Alive is getting another wife."

Wedding prayers always begin with addressing The Creator. "We are gathered here to first give thanks to The Creator who gave us the sacred pipe and sacred medicine bundles, who made The Earth and The Sky and all things that live on and in the earth and all beings that live in the sky and the in-between lands. We give thanks and pray for the Naahks, those holy spirits of grandfathers and grandmothers who help The Creator. We give thanks to the spirits that have taken pity on us and hear the prayers for our people, for our families, for our health, for full bellies and strong medicine. We give thanks for the buffalo. We pray for all our relations."

Then starts a long list of specific animals, birds, plants, stones and holy places for which we are thankful and for which we pray. At the conclusion of the prayer, the holy man looks into the eyes of Sings To Flowers and says, "This marriage is seen by Our Creator as forever binding you and your two families. Even if you should marry another man someday, it is **this** marriage that The Creator honors."

Someone holds out an eagle bone whistle for Little Bear to clench in his teeth. Little Bear waves it away. He is intent on breaking free and lunges backward again and again against his tether. The less deep part of the skewer on the left side comes free. The man offering the whistle is spattered with blood and steps back.

Running Bear pauses, "Does anyone wish to speak?" He waits for a moment in case anyone has anything they wish to say. Nobody speaks, but The Wind answers with a mighty burst of my breath through the wedding thicket to which the holy man pays no attention! Since no one has spoken, you are now married," declares the holy man.

A marrow-chilling cry comes from somewhere in the camp. It hangs in the branches above the wedding couple. It drips onto all the lodges and causes the cook-fires to flare simultaneously. The Wind moans and carries the cry, spearing it into the four directions.

The Wind knows Little Bear is free. He has taken his hands and pushed on the skewers until they came through his skin, leaving a three and a four-inch gaping wound above both nipples. He is walking out of the Medicine Lodge now with an expressionless face and marches into the river for healing cold waters.

Sings To Flowers is not sure if she heard the voice of Little Bear in the crowd far behind her and wonders, *What can a ten-winters boy do to stop the action of elders anyway?*

Now she simply has no more thoughts at all. She feels smothered by some kind of a cry that fell upon her from above. Her thought energy seems . . . gone. I cannot read anything from her. She is resigned to fate.

The last half of Little Bear's prayer will be granted, but not in the way he had intended. He had prayed for Sings To Flowers to dance and sing in his, Little Bear's, lodge. This is not to be. But he also prayed that Sings To Flowers would never dance and sing within the lodge of Comes Still Alive. This will be. She will not dance in the lodge of Comes Still Alive . . . because of her great sadness.

CHAPTER ELEVEN

The Hiding Place

"Come with me," says Comes Still Alive. "We will talk now." The other six wives watch Comes Still Alive lead Sings To Flowers toward the center of the camp, which is humming with activity. He addresses the crowd.

"My friends and my relations. This is Sings To Flowers. She is my seventh wife in the eyes of The Creator. We are just married and there is a feast at my lodge." There are a few nods of approval, grunts of anticipation of pleasant wedding food, and a few whispers among the women folk. But in the shadows there is one who is in deep pain, not only from oozing chest wounds but from hearing these words. He feels his organs under his skin-rips cry out in far greater agony than mere torn flesh.

Comes Still Alive has put his hand around my heart and squeezed out the last drop. My heart is now as a small stone. My bones are crushed, but not by buffalo. My chest is without breath. I have no life. He turns away. He is going again to the river. This time he goes upstream to where the stones in the water stand tall, making their voice roar loud enough to drown out the words of Comes Still Alive and any other noise... both inside and outside his head.

Her new husband is looking down on Sings To Flowers and speaking softly, "Let's talk about Sings To Flowers as the wife of Comes Still Alive. You will see that Comes Still Alive is a good provider. You are very young and you have much to learn. You will go with Stolen Lakota Woman and she will teach you women's ways...

how to tan hides, where to gather wood and water, how to make good pemmican, and how to make the parfleche for storing it . . . how to make moccasins and many other useful things. This will be good for you. It will be good for you to learn. It will be good for Stolen Lakota Woman to be with you and to teach you."

The Wind notices that the women never stop in their work until their bones are too old and then they only pause, but when the men are in camp the men visit one another, and smoke, and move from feast to feast all day long. I must remind myself that this is necessary for building male bonds of critical cooperation in hunting and warring.

Comes Still Alive is becoming more stern in his speech. "You must always stay with another woman when you go outside the lodge. It is best to be with one of my other wives. There are dangers in the woods. At night you must be inside the lodge. There are ghosts waiting in all places outside at night. Ghosts of enemies I have killed in battle are now evil spirits. If they see you outside at night they will aim invisible darts into you and make you sick."

Doesn't he notice Sing To Flowers stopping her breath? Must he go on and on about ghosts?

"Above all, you must never be alone with another man. Never. Never. People talk and I will hear. Do you see that woman over there?" He is pointing now to a woman who holds a blanket over the lower portion of her face even during this hot day. "Her brother cut off her nose and one of her ears for being with a man who was not her husband. These things happen." Sings To Flowers does not speak, but clings to the strap of the quiver and bow that rests over her heart.

"Tomorrow I will point out the Medicine Lodge Woman to you," Comes Still Alive continues. "Only one that is the most virtuous in all her deeds can be the Medicine Lodge Woman. She also must be serious and of clean mind. Her conversation is always sober without giggling, gossiping, and especially screaming." With his last words about screaming he looks directly into the little one's eyes. "My sits-beside-me woman, Two Guns Buffalo Calf, has been the Medicine Lodge Woman twice."

Comes Still Alive has invited a crowd to his wedding feast. His wives have dutifully spread the banquet out on blankets before his lodge. There is feasting on choice huckleberries and service berries, buffalo and antelope. There is the laughter of men joking and telling their hero stories while the women scurry about, moving like darting shadows of phantoms seen in the corner of the eye. Sings To Flowers does not eat. Stolen Lakota Woman does not eat. Soon the pipe is smoked before the party breaks up and attendees move to another feast nearby. Everyone at this gathering is pleased except two.

During the feasting Sings To Flowers has a chance to slip away and hide her toy bundle from Stolen Lakota Woman, but after her new husband's lecture about not going into the woods alone she decides it's too risky. *What if I get into trouble on the very first day as a wife? What if I get my nose cut off! Coyote Head wouldn't do that. But what about my big strong husband or one of his brothers? Would they? How many brothers does he have? I don't like this. I want to play again! I want to laugh, giggle, and be silly. We had silly play. I liked silly play. Married women can't do that!* In silence she wails all these things inside her head.

Sings To Flowers is glad that she is to walk behind Comes Still Alive. That way he will not see her casting her eyes around the Okan crowd for Little Bear. But what will she do now if she sees him? She can do nothing. Not even smile.

Night is upon them. The wedding night. Comes Still Alive motions to Sings To Flowers that she is to sleep with him between layers of buffalo robes and white rabbit. Two naked bodies lie side by side. One is big and weathered. One is tiny, delicate, and smooth. Moon Dear Seer has done as promised and has taken care of Comes Still Alive's manly needs three nights in a row prior to tonight. All the women are awake with watchful eyes on the wedding bed. They have a plan of sorts if they need it, but it is far from perfect.

The air barely moves. The women all breathe silent shallow breaths and strain to hear what is happening from the deepest part of the lodge, the nuptial bed. He has an arm over the little one, no more.

If a shaft of moonlight were to enter the teepee's dark interior it would produce a glint in six pairs of wide-awake eyes peering through the black like the four-leggeds that hunt at night. Thankfully, rhythmic snores start to come from the wedding bed, allowing four sets of eyes to close for brief sleep, while two sets keep watch. When the moon is halfway to its zenith a pair of awake eyes creep over to nudge two pairs of sleeping eyes for their turn. When the moon is seen through the smoke hole of the lodge Moon Deer Seer goes to the wedding bed and lifts the sleeping Sings To Flowers away and into the bed of Two Guns Buffalo Calf. Then she takes the warm place of the child next to Comes Still Alive. She knows the old man's habits, which include the nuptial flourish almost exclusively just before the break of morning light.

This practice of watchful switching, with each wife taking her tour of duty, goes on for two cycles of the moon, until the women have peace of mind that Comes Still Alive has no intention of penetrating a child. He is aware of the switch play and allows it to continue. He never takes advantage of Sings to Flowers until well into the future after her first moon time.

In the morning, Comes Still Alive is keeping his new bride close as they walk to the Medicine Lodge. Little Sings To Flowers' feet are dutifully following behind this man called "husband" but her eyes are looking for Little Bear and something else. *Where's a good place to hide my toy bundle away from any clutching hands . . . Clutching Stolen Lakota Woman and Hungry Crow.*

Keeping her face straight ahead to his back, she glances here and there without turning her head and abruptly makes a spontaneous sharp in-breath, much louder than she would have liked it to be. She sees Little Bear standing with Coyote Head. *Why does he keep his hands on his chest? He is . . . bent over!*

Upon hearing a high-pitched intake of breath Comes Still Alive turns to look down at her. Sings To Flowers is looking up at her husband and summons a sheepish half-smile. Older age gives a distinct advantage over a youngster in this nebulous game of trial and judgment of who is righteous and who is impure.

Now comes another lecture much like the day before. "My Wife," says the towering husband, "See that woman there? She is the Medicine Lodge Woman. She always carries a sober face. She does not joke or chatter. She is never without control of her mind. She is soft spoken. She is always faithful to her husband."

Sings To Flowers feels a rush of blood coming to her cheeks and the tip of her chin. She looks at the ground. Her little hand starts to go up to her ear, but under the watchful eyes of her husband and others she thinks, *Stop. Stay still.*

Comes Still Alive is turning away now to continue his stroll. Sings To Flowers continues too, but looking at the ground. She tries to control the quivers in her lower lip. She walks right past Little Bear and Coyote Head without acknowledgment. They do not see the wet eyes or the tears trying to sneak down her left cheek.

To make matters more painful, there is no safe place that Sings To Flowers has been able to discover for hiding her toy bundle. She will have to hold it close until such a place can be found. This is proving not to be an easy task and the bundle of toys is a continuous irritation to Stolen Lakota Woman.

Even during the Okan the daily gathering of wood and water must continue. Helping the child get a load of wood on her back along with her bundle of toys is irritating. Watching the child try to fill two bladder bags while not droppings the toys in the river is even more irritating. Trying to converse in the tongue of the Lakota Sioux with a bewildered Blackfoot child is maddening.

The Wind will speak now about what the real problem is with Stolen Lakota Woman. She is not sad that she is a barren woman, as Comes Still Alive mistakenly believes. It has been three summers since Stolen Lakota Woman was taken from her family and her beloved one, Heavy Hair, so named for his luxurious long locks reaching well below his waist. Even now, as she gazes into the heavens, she can still hear in her heart the sweet notes from his flute as they came singing through the star-bright nights courting her. He had proven himself worthy of marriage, having given away many horses that he had stolen from the enemy by the means of his craftiness.

He was an excellent orator, keeping his audience spell-bound with the telling of his dangerous escapades, known as counting coups. Sometimes he told his stories with colorful masks, painted body, and pantomime. His tales contained a rich assortment of vibrant characters, some four-legged ancestors, and some winged ones who brought him messages. His stories were so mesmerizing that during the telling of them men would forget to refill their pipes, women would drop their moccasins and forget to keep sewing, and the children would forget to throw another stick on the fire until it had burned down to only a few glowing coals, requiring much stirring and blowing and fanning to renew its warmth and light.

Heavy Hair had brought to Stolen Lakota Woman's father a gift of fifteen horses for a bride gift and her father had accepted them. On the night of her capture Stolen Lakota Woman was going to give a sign to Heavy Hair that she too accepted him as her future husband.

She was waiting for his visit at the door of her father's teepee. She had wrapped herself in her beautiful wedding blanket. She was waiting, waiting, while her heart was pounding and pounding. *When would he come?*

She did not hear the muffled noise of scuffling and the cutting loose of a string of horses. She was too excited and her heart too loud in her ears. Soon he would be before her and she would wrap the two of them together, the gesture of acceptance.

And now here he was at last! Stolen Lakota Woman opened her blanket wide to bring him into her warm cocoon, not aware of the arrow protruding from his back until, while closing her blanket around them both, another airborne feathered missile found its target. It tunneled through Heavy Hair and wedged in her chest bone.

Her injury was not lethal. His was. Stolen Lakota Woman was dragged away across the prairie still pinned to her would-be husband until his larger body was stopped by a boulder, where he was ripped off of her chest, but not out of her heart. Now she secretly calls the scar between her breasts her dear-husband scar, the husband recognized by The Creator.

Why can't Comes Still Alive see what his wives plainly see? Stolen Lakota Woman is still in mourning. She has cut her hair to the length just above the shoulders. She has scarified the calves of her legs and cut off, starting at the most distal joint, pieces of her little finger of her left hand, yearly sacrificing another part of herself on what she thinks to be the anniversary of her dear one's death. Comes Still Alive had given her orders to stop mourning two summers ago. Apparently, he believes that is all that is needed to make her feel healed, which blinds him to her bloody bodily and soulful sacrifices, even when his sits-beside-him woman points the sacrifices out to him. Yet he is aware of her drooping energy, which matches the corners of her mouth, but he has jumped to the wrong conclusion about the cause of it all.

Both Sings To Flowers and Stolen Lakota Woman are suffering in their hearts for the same reason; yet though they may have suspected it, neither can be certain that the pain in the other is love-lost pain like that within themselves. You might say that they are like twins in the kind of energy they carry around their hearts and solar centers.

When the women go to gather berries or roots, they draw apart. Sometimes Stolen Lakota Woman stares at and contemplates the clouds through swollen red eyelids or climbs a hill and sings a song of deep grief. Her song is without words, but there is no question by its timbre and sad somber tone that this is a song of mourning. Sometimes Stolen Lakota Woman, while standing on the cliff edge, repeats her dead lover's name again and again. Sings To Flowers follows her example and draws apart from the group too and somewhat apart from Stolen Lakota Woman to sit or to sing out her grief into me. I take the songs of heart sufferings of both wives and give them more voice by bouncing their songs off canyon walls.

When the two return to the lodge without nearly as much bounty as the other wives, they endure looks and whispered words such as "lazy" and "worthless." But the mean words will stop in the summer to come.

Now it is fall and Sings To Flowers is working on a hide stretched out on the ground, trying to scrape off the hair with a stone knife. Her beloved toy bundle, as always, is tied to her back. The vigorous scraping activity has loosened the bundle, which swings around to her front, bumping her arm and causing her to make a small cut through the hide. After the third mistake of a cut-through where it should not be, this beautiful hide that would have made a nice tunic or skirt will now have to be used as scraps for moccasins and small medicine bags. Forgetting her sadness for a minute and overcome by her irritation, Stolen Lakota Woman loses the tight control she had on herself. She wrestles the toy bundle off the back of Sings To Flowers and throws it into the fire.

For Sings To Flowers, the world just fell away. She feels a buzzing go through her body that is at first deafening, followed by her ears coming to a point of stone silence. Dropping her knife, she grabs her bundle just seconds before the lush fur of the beaver pelt bursts into flames and snuffs the smoking end out against her body.

Now she begins to run. Her feet are running and she does not feel the ground. She does not know to where she is running. She has the vague feeling that she is running uphill and maybe, just maybe, she heard something. *The screech on an owl? Odd to here that,* she thinks. *Running now until out of breath. Stopping now. Is Stolen Lakota Woman coming after me? I don't know where I am going, I don't know where I am. Did I hear something? I better run some more, I better . . . Uphill, yes uphill, Over here, No not there, Better keep going. Got to hide my bundle. Into the woods. Yes, into the thick trees where nobody will see, where nobody will come and find. Running. Running. Running some more. This is not a good place here. Eeeeee! Creator help! Ancestors help! I cry for help! I am good. Pity me! Over there. No, not good. Where? Where? Piiiityyy Meeeee! Ki Yo! Here. Here. Maybe here. I can move it later if I need to.*

Finding a log with thick bark that is hollow at one end, she crams the bundle deep inside as far as it will go. *Now what to use to seal it up inside? Something that will not rot, perhaps some bones. If I just had a pile of old bones!* She looks around, but there are no bones on the ground. Not there!

What is she thinking! Is she thinking?

Maybe I will find some ancient bones with all the meat long gone. Something that will not attract animals. I can come back later and stuff the hole with dead bones, she says to herself, *or some stones. For now I'll use my tunic.*

As Sings To Flowers quickly removes her upper garment, on it she notices a splash of blood. *This will attract animals!* She rips and chews off the blood-tinged fringe. Hurriedly, she gathers an armload of pine branches and, stripping off the needles, she throws them by handfuls into the gaping hole at the end of the log hiding her bundle. Pine branches follow the needles, until the log can contain no more. She hopes that the strong scent of the pine will cover up her scent.

Now she stops to look at her work. *What have I forgotten? Nobody must find my precious toys given to me from My Love. Not Stolen Lakota Woman, not anybody.*

She speaks into me, The Wind, with barely audible trembling whispers as if imparting a great secret. I will keep the secret for a very long time, but even secrets die when their time is up. Putting her two little hands now on the hiding log and still in her highly emotional state and seething with raw energy, Sings To Flowers speaks to the log and makes a curse. "For all time to come, let nobody disturb your rest except me. If any intruders should do so, let their heads roll down the mountain."

Now with her toy bundle hidden, she starts to notice a throb in the outer mid-portion of her left foot. Looking down, she sees her foot is covered in blood. Sticking up through her foot and moccasin is a wicked-looking end of a torn pine bough. Its sharp point has pierced through her blood-soaked foot, breaking and pushing delicate tendon and bone through the skin. Now panic, with wave after wave of nausea, hits her. She must clean the blood away. Little Sings To Flowers desperately tries to erase any trace of it from around her hiding place with more pine boughs before she sinks to her knees and vomits; blood keeps coming. Then, rising with one foot supporting her, she spies a stout stick about two inches in diameter that she can use for a crutch and hobbles some distance downhill, really not sure where she is, and passes out.

I, The Wind, tell myself not to worry because I know that she will be found in a little while. The painful foot will heal after a bout of swelling and infection that will be treated with the same medicine Little Bear uses on his chest wound. A decoction from the pounded inner bark of the wild cherry tree and the dried herb, yellow dock, will work wonders for the physical wounds. She will always have a bulge on the outer edge of her left foot, but the foot will be functional and luckily, she will have only a barely perceptible limp. Sings To Flowers will forget her limp, but she will not forget her special toys. She believes they are safe now from thievery, or disfigurement, or burning.

What she doesn't realize is that this traumatic event will remain in her soul memory and be imprinted again at a cellular level in her next incarnation. A human body is a house of mysteries from the past and much more.

CHAPTER TWELVE

The Jump

I love the moments between daylight and dark when the mountains to the west turn purple and the cliff crags toward the east glow orange while their clefts deepen in shadow. A lone figure standing there and looking up is also washed in orange.

Why does the figure begin to climb now? Too late in the day! There's an easier way . . . a safer way . . . but a longer way . . . for another day perhaps? There is a hurry in his steps and now The Wind is curious. I will focus below on this figure.

I know this blanket, years in the making, now wrapped around those shoulders; its bottom rows were woven by child hands, the top rows woven by the long fingers of a young woman. Every thread color chosen with meaning, the pattern unmistakable just as I remember it. The pattern holds the music of dreams for a future love and for children, for wedded bliss. Angels can pluck the stings of this blanket harp that the heavens may sing of love. It is a wedding blanket . . . a wedding blanket kept hidden for four years. And now I know the figure is not a man, it is a woman.

The last orange-pink rays are sliding down the west. The mountain's shadow races upward to cover the glowing blanket with black. The woman stumbles. Hurry. Hurry. The way up is crooked with sharp surprise turns, with uneven ground; the way is confused and now the air is thick with spirits . . . Buffalo Spirits.

The woman hesitates. She is going off the path. Don't do that! It's dangerous to do that. She pays no attention to The Wind. She is climbing straight up with no path. Now she steps on a corner of her blanket. It is going to trip her! She pulls the blanket free just in time. I'll blow. I'll blow on her back and help push her up to the top.

At last. At last she is over the cliff edge just as the first stars appear.

What is she doing up here in the dark? How is she going to find her way down now? She'll have to spend the night at this place where there is a lot of spirit noise. Wild animals have been here. Many of them.

Now she is tying the wedding blanket onto her body with a rope. How odd! Oh. I recognize that purposeful rope. It's made of human hair . . . her hair. She cut her hair as mourners do, every summer for four summers on her anniversary of great loss.

How many times have I carried her grief songs and bounced them off the cliffs? But it didn't ease the pain of her internal evisceration where the hollows of her body echo his name again and again off the walls of her rib cage with each beat of her heart. "Heavy Hair. My beloved Heavy Hair. He was to be the father of my children."

Now she steps closer to the edge. The spirit noises are louder now. More stars illuminate and the moon creates lengthening shadows. Dark shadows leak even darker thoughts.

Does this same moonlight bounce off his bleached bones still lying in the prairie? Is the jawbone that once formed endearing words now separated from his skull, strewn about and picked over by wild beasts or crushed by unkind hoof? The tongue, the lips that formed those words and wrapped themselves around his courting flute, the eyes that tenderly caressed her body . . . now all dust, entrusted to the arms of The Wind. His music is gone. In its stead The Wind makes an empty monotonous moan.

Surely one of the daemons in Hell is named Grief. In that case Earthling beings, both human and nonhuman, will wander through that place from time to time. Modern counselors call Grief "a Process." Part of the process of Change.

But enough of painful thoughts.

The arms of Heavy Hair await. They are but one blessed step away.

Then it is done. Teetering a moment before taking that one step off the Buffalo Jump, Stolen Lakota Woman calls to herself her biggest change and jumps into the embrace of a different dimension's reality.

CHAPTER THIRTEEN

Lily's Messed Up Escape

"I will never make fun of puppy love again, ever," Lily declares. "Not ever again."

"What? Where did this come from, Lily?"

"Love is real, Nurse Tall Chief, no matter what your age."

"Well maybe, and please, call me Mary. I'm not that much older than you. Hey! It's time for you to get out of the confines of the hospital and spread your wings! Besides, you're not a puppy anymore. Whose puppy love are you talking about exactly?" she asks, both amused and curious while going through the checklist of items Lily brought to the hospital.

"I have had such dreams! Like they're absolutely real. Not only that, they're from around here somewhere. I know it. I just know that I know it." Lily is swinging her legs to the floor to stand up. "Ugh. My left foot is sure sore and right around my tailbone I keep getting a tingling, hot, almost burning sensation. Talk about weird. It comes and goes and creeps up my back, especially at night and it wakes me up."

"Really? Let's look at your lower back. Is the irritation on just one side?" asks Mary as she checks Lily's back. "I don't see a rash. Ever have shingles?

"No."

"I don't see a pilonidal cyst near your tail bone either. In fact, I don't see anything. You need to get out of bed before you get pressure sores on your butt. Let's look at your left foot." Then with a smile, "I don't see any blood!" Her eyes twinkle when she smiles. But there is a flash of horror on Lily's face at the mention of blood. "Just looks pretty and pink to me." Lily does not laugh. Instead she winces.

With a sigh while scooping up her notes, Lily relates to the nurse as much of her dreams as her scribbles reveal and she can remember. Mary is no longer laughing. "Lily, I have never heard such a story about those artifacts in the museum. I am deeply moved, especially if any of it is true. Jesus! Forgive me, but you're a white kid. What do you know about the Indians and their old ways?" *What do we moderns know about our own not-so-ancient ways, for that matter?* she says to herself.

"You know, there are all kinds of New Age types coming around here and claiming to be Native Americans in their past lives. Some of them are trying to use what little they know of our ceremonies and sacred teachings and are making a lot of money off what they understand only on the surface. I suppose the majority of them mean no harm, but it makes me fume. We had our land and our ways stolen and now the ancestors of those invaders are claiming our culture to make a fast buck when it was our culture that they tried to completely stamp out not that long ago. We call those New Age culture borrowers 'plastic medicine men.' Those non-Indians should butt out."

Softer now, "You do have a super absorbing story. Don't go away until we have had a chance to talk again."

On her way out the door she pauses to give Lily a smile. The R.N. notices that the light in the room, though brighter than normal, is pretty close to the usual again, not the glaring brightness like when Lily was first admitted.

Lily's family is arriving; now hugs flow all around with relief that Lily's big scare is fast becoming an incident of the past.

"Ah ha. I haven't let you out the door yet, Young Lady." Catrina brightens up. She has already done her work in front of the mirror, and smells of Mom's mother's day gift of Chanel No. 5. Alas, Jerry Dixon takes no notice of her. But maybe, just maybe he will look her way and see the beauty queen. Instead, he is pulling out his examining instruments to check Lily's eyes, ears, nose, throat, and reflexes. He has her balance on one foot, then the other, follow his finger with her eyes, point to and touch the end of her nose with the index finger of one hand then her other, and count backward as fast as she can from 100 until he stops her at number 84. Then Catrina gets a little reward. He smiles at her with his wonderful toothy smile.

Catrina's heart speeds up. The Wind marvels at his thick red hair. He looks young . . . almost Catrina's age. *I suppose she is wishing it were so. I suspect the magnetic attraction for him dwells somewhere in her past.*

"Now Miss Pretty," continues the doctor, turning to Lily, "I need your and your family's attention. You have suffered a concussion. In other words, a brain bruise. You must, I repeat, must take it easy the next couple of weeks." With a glance toward Sammy he adds, "No rough house, no pushing, no shoving, no bumping, etc. Should you suddenly have funny vision, hearing, speech, numbness, or a severe headache you will need to go to a medical facility pronto. No alcohol or recreational drugs," . . . pausing, "You don't do that stuff, right?"

"Not likely. Not Lily," chimes in Cat, trying to get another smile from the doctor; she is rewarded with one.

"Here is my card with all our numbers, including the fax should you need it for another clinic on your trip. By the way, you have been absolutely glowing. Stitches need to come out not before a week and a half and not later than two weeks."

He called her Miss Pretty. I wonder if Dr. Dixon thinks I'm glowing? After all, we are twins, speculates Catrina. *Except that, well, we don't look exactly like each other, especially with those humongous glasses.*

Catrina watches Dr. Dixon disappear into the corridors of the hospital and then out of her sight. Her shoulders slump and she has lost her general perkiness. "I wonder if I will ever see him again?" she moans quietly under her breath.

"Lily, I want to apologize." It's Mary Tall Chief coming briskly down the hall with discharge papers in hand. "I fear I was a little abrupt with my goings on about 'plastic medicine men,'" she says, handing Dad the papers. "I want to make it up to you. I have the afternoon off. My Great Great Uncle, who just turned 100, was the one who found the small bow, arrows, and dolls that are in the museum. The only thing is, it's a thirty-five mile trip to Cut Bank, out in the prairie. He's in a nursing home now and sometimes he is lucid and sometimes not. I can't guarantee anything, but it might be worth a try to find out more about those artifacts, if any of you want to come along."

"I want to go," says Lily, almost before the nurse can get her words out. She has a look in her eyes.

Cat, on the other hand, rolls her eyes. The last thing she wants to do is drive out into the windy and undoubtedly dusty prairie of dead grass. She would rather stick around here. Maybe have lunch in the hospital cafeteria. Perhaps a certain MD will be dining there too.

Dad looks more than a little concerned. "I can tell you want to go on this side-trip Lily, but the family needs to stay together. As soon as you're on the road you'll forget all about those old worn-out museum toys." Lily is putting her hand over her solar plexus while I feel her silent groan.

"What if there is another accident way out there in God Knows Where," chimes in Mom. "We've all had enough trauma. We need to stick together."

Lily's mouth is open to respond, "I'll be with a nurse!" But Sammy, not wanting a part in the discussion, has voted with his feet—they have already taken him half way down the hall to the exit sign. "Let's go. We have to catch up to that rascal," grumbles Dad.

Mary is aware of Lily's pained look. While the rest of the troops begin to run after Sammy she murmurs, "Look Lily, if your family changes their mind, I will be at the Seven Eleven near your motel at 1:00 PM. Great Great Uncle loves to gum the red licorice I get there."

I think a part of the nurse is pleased that Lily is taking a deep interest in the artifacts in spite of her lecture about "plastic medicine men." She has a kind heart and wants to please others. Besides, it has been awhile since she has made the trip to see her elderly relative.

Dad has decided. The family will stay in town for a little while after the car is packed . . . maybe go back to the museum for Lily's sake, then on to see what is happening at the Sundance site, but nobody is going off on their own with or without a guide. That's the final word.

I can't stand this, is Lily's private thought. *I'm going to Cut Bank.*

Lily looks absent . . . like a numb robot packing her suitcase slowly and saying no words, while the rest of the group chat merrily away about nothing. It's painful to watch.

*I am going to Cut Bank with or without anybody's permission. I'm practically eighteen. I **need** to go. I go or I shrivel up and die.*

Sammy is the first to have his suitcase into the car and comes back into the motel room to see what the hold-up is. "I'll help ya," he says to Lily and throws her last item into her bag and grabs it out of her hands and disappears.

Lily reluctantly descends the steps from the motel. The others are already standing near the car watching Dad wrestle and fuss over the fact that Catrina has "three times as much unnecessary stuff" as anyone else and her "bags have become progressively bigger and bulkier so they no longer fit." Lily looks across the street at the Seven Eleven store. She watches her family watching the particulars of packing the car and notices that they are not aware of her presence. This is her moment. Without hesitation she scurries across the street.

Now a little out of breath and looking out the store window, it appears that they did not see her come or go. *What time is it? Twelve-thirty. Oh gee. I have to hide in here for a half hour.*

Catrina is the one who gets away with a download of disobedience and many mixtures of mischief, not Lily. Lily doesn't upset her family ever . . . but now? Something has changed.

Sliding behind a rack of munchies, she pretends to be looking for something down every aisle in the store, while keeping an eye on the movements across the street. She is managing to look nonchalant while peeking out from behind the magazines every few seconds.

Oh God. Is that Sammy coming here from across the street? Oh Geez, it is!

"Hi," he says to the man behind the counter. "Have you seen my sister Lily? She's blond and has big glasses. She's seventeen." Lily immediately takes off her specs and puts them in her pocket, making herself nearly blind. She is holding her breath. *Did that guy see me come in?*

"There've been a lot a kids through here. Come back in a half hour and I'll let you know if I see anyone like you're talkin' 'bout. I don't have any help in here and can't be a runnin' all over town taking care of everybody's business."

"Okay, I'll just get me a candy bar," says Sammy.

"Over by the magazines," grunts the Seven Eleven man.

Whoa. Please God, don't let him see me now. And if he does come back in thirty minutes, don't let him bump into Nurse Mary.

Lily does have one small advantage. The convex mirror over the door gives Lily a view of where Sammy is moving, but only when she keeps her glasses on her nose—which she does only for a second or two when she thinks it is safe to take a quick peek. Thankfully, Sammy is too short to see the mirror when down in the aisles. The store man, however, looks up to that mirror every few minutes. But at this moment he is making change for another customer.

Lily, having stepped to the opposite side of the magazines from Sammy, stays motionless. *Please God, don't let him come around to the next aisle.*

I don't think God listens to this kind of stuff because in the next ten seconds Sammy does just that. He steps around the end of the magazine display and bumps into his sister.

"Gee Lily, did ya lose your glasses?"

"Now you listen to me good, Sammy." Lily's voice is stern as she puts her slippery glasses back on her face. "You can tell Dad where I went **after** I'm gone with Nurse Mary to Cut Bank. I'll buy you one of every candy bar in the store if you just wait to tell him in another... 15 minutes." Lily is looking at her watch. "Well let's say until Mary gets here, which should be real soon." She squeezes Sammy's shoulder, "Swear to it and don't be a creep just because you know how."

"Ouch." Sammy shrugs her hand away. "Every candy bar in this place?"

"Thirty dollars worth. That should be pretty close," she says stuffing the money in his pocket.

"Well... If that nurse shows up in a few minutes, we have a deal." Sammy's eyes are wide with anticipation as he steps around to pick out his candy. "But how do I know when I have thirty dollars worth?"

"Oh geez, Sammy. Just start picking out your favorites and tell the man at the counter that you have thirty bucks to spend. Let him figure it out."

Lily now sees that the Seven Eleven man is looking up at the mirror and then in their direction. "He's found me," Lily shouts out as she waves to the man and she is just in time for another complication. Mary is coming in the door for her licorice, Sammy has all his fingers wrapped around as much candy as they can hold, and now here comes Catrina across the street looking for Sammy.

"Don't you spoil this Sammy or I will call you The Joke in front of all your friends for the rest of your life." Lily's hand is back on Sammy's shoulder.

Mary knows exactly how much money to plunk down on the counter, having paid for licorice from the big covered glass jar many times before and she does not see them yet. In walks Catrina.

"Oh there you are," she says to Lily and Sammy who are just coming out from the back of the store. "We've been looking..."

"Just getting Sammy some candy to tide him over," says Lily before Catrina can say more.

"Tide him over until Christmas?" says Catrina.

"My goodness," says Mary, seeing Lily and Sammy for the first time and eyeing all the candy. "You have a bigger sweet tooth than me."

"Mom and Dad won't approve," says Catrina.

"Lily's going to Cut Bank with the nurse," says Sammy in spite of Lily's tightening shoulder grip.

"Mom and Dad won't approve," Catrina says again.

"Of this much candy, I know," Lily says, finishing Catrina's sentence while sliding out the door and hurrying with Mary to Mary's new red truck.

Catrina's mouth opens but is speechless. She has never seen Lily act like this.

"You didn't say I couldn't tell Catrina," Sammy shouts after the shiny truck as it pulls out. "You just said wait to tell Dad."

CHAPTER FOURTEEN

Lily's Next Adventure

The two young women drive away with the beautiful soaring mountains at their backs and enter endless rolling hills of grass and wheat fields, dotted with an occasional spruce tree. I, The Wind, am especially curious about this new adventure. Besides, I love to propel myself between the grass stems in this prairie playground. The paved road is not so much dusty as it is hot and, of course, windy. One thing is for sure. The jostling ride is starting Lily's hot tailbone irritation again. She is trying to ignore it, now that the escape has been successful, and is becoming more relaxed, but quiet.

Mary Tall Chief comments on the way, trying to keep the atmosphere light, "I've made some sandwiches Lily, help yourself. It's hot today, but Cut Bank advertises itself as 'The Coldest Spot in the Nation' and they make their point by showing off this mammoth penguin. Tourists take pictures of themselves with it.

The town takes its name from the Cut Bank River. The Blackfoot have long descriptive names for most geographical landmarks. Their name for the river is 'The River that Cuts into the White Clay Bank.' It really does make a deep cut in the land. The entire town had to be shifted to the east side of the river after they discovered that the original location on the west side was on the Blackfoot Reservation. You know about the Lewis and Clark Expedition?"

"Oh yes. We hear about them and the Oregon Trail from first grade on. Our teachers want us to remember that one or more branches of the Oregon Trail ended in the state of Washington. We even have a Lewis County next door to a Clark County in southern Washington. I'm from the Puget Sound area. We have a lot of Indian tribes around there."

"Yeah? Well here we are told that the only fight with Indians on the entire Lewis and Clark Expedition was around Cut Bank. As the story goes, Meriwether Lewis just happened to mention to the Indians he was camping with that the U.S. Calvary planned to give guns to all the Plains Indians. Lewis, not really understanding the rivalry between clans, thought that information would make his Indian guides happy. Ha! All they could think about was that their enemies would be given guns too. The Blackfoot people were and still are very territorial. Anyway, the Indians decided to steal Meriwether's guns and horses and leave him and his white buddies on foot. A fight started and two Indians were killed. But guess what? In the 1960's, a troop of boy scouts found the exact site of the fight by using Lewis' journal that talked about three lone trees and some other landmarks. We're getting close now. See that strip of green? That's the green banks of the Cut Bank River."

"I'm in love with a ten-year-old Indian."

Mary abruptly swerves off the road and applies the breaks. Her brand new slick red truck is enveloped in a cloud of side-road dust.

"I don't think I heard you right."

"I'm in love with a boy the same age as my kid brother." Lily lets tears splash on her ham sandwich with only two bites gone.

Mary doesn't know what to say. Finally, she speaks softly, "The dream you mean?"

"The nightmare! I'm a mess."

"We'll stay here until your eyes are dry and your head together. Here. Put the sandwich back in the box and grab some tissues. Here's water.

"You know, Lily, if you were thirty-seven and the young man a mature-in-the-head thirty, you would hardly know the difference. But now at almost eighteen, I just don't get it."

"In my dream or memory or whatever the hell it is, a man thirty or forty years older marries a little seven year old. A seven year old who is me!"

"Lily, it was just a bad dream! How can you be in love with a dream!? You can learn to control your nightmares, you know. Just realize that you've invented them in your subconscious and just tell the dream to fuck off. Put yourself in control. Gee whiz Lily, piss on the damn dream and its monsters. Just piss on them!"

Lily musters a half smile when hearing salty sailor talk coming from the lips of her nurse friend. "I don't think I have the right equipment for aiming my piss on anything."

Moments of silence settle over the two in the red truck, each maneuvering through their own private thoughts. Then finally, "But what if . . . what if it **wasn't** a dream? What if it was something else? You know, like a real past life memory. Like I've lived before right here in this neighborhood but, you know, it would have been more than 100 years ago or something. What if I wasn't a white girl or a 'plastic Indian' back then?"

"Reincarnation? Nobody knows about these things, Lily. My God. Can you imagine coming into this world with the memories of the traumas of a bunch of past lives? We'd all go nuts. If we've lived before on this earth, we're not supposed to remember. No. No. It has to be a dream. Just a bad dream. Like I said, piss on it."

The Wind's opinion is that the idea of reincarnation makes Mary too uncomfortable. No matter; they will both find out more once they are on the other side.

"I have another confession. I only told Sammy and Catrina that I went with you on this trip. Well, for sure Dad and Mom know by now."

"Give them a call Lily, for Pete Sake—before I get charged with kidnapping!"

"Dad? . . . I know . . . I know . . . I know . . . We'll be right back pretty soon. A couple of hours I guess. I don't know exactly. Yes, I promise. Yes, I will call. Yes ... Yes ... Yes ... I'm sorry. I said I'm real sorry. See you and Mom soon." She clicks the phone shut. "Geez. The phone vibrates when he yells at me like I'm deaf."

They rest for a half hour, speaking little, Lily still dabbing her eyes and splashing her face with cold water. After a while, "Okay Mary, let's shove off. We can't be sitting here all day."

After passing some lonely 1920's mute and hollow railroad grain elevators, it is not long before the two are pulling up to Glacier Care Center. A well-groomed middle-aged lady meets them at the door. Her outfit is a gray suit that matches her salt and pepper graying hair. Even her skin has a gray cast.

*I wonder how long it will be before that lady is a resident here, or should I say **inmate** in a place like this. All those sick old people ... It's depressing. Everything's depressing. I think it is depressing for Mary too.*

"Mary! We've not seen you for a while. I must tell you that your uncle is in and out of himself, if you know what I mean. We thought it was the end, six or seven times in the last month. It seems that he is hanging on for something, maybe for your visit. We have called his near-by family in so many times, it feels like we're crying wolf."

The gray lady bustles them down a long passageway past old people in wheelchairs. Most of the residents have blankets wrapped around them, even though it's hot. Several pairs of dimming eyes belonging to the long-time residents of Glacier Care Center are trying to focus on this uncommon scene of the gray lady with two unfamiliar people. They watch every step the trio makes down the hall. Something different for them to see is an event. Sometimes they reach out from their wheelchair cages as the little group passes by. Here and there an arm with a withered claw-like hand stretches to touch Mary or Lily, as though they can grab up for themselves a tiny measure of youthfulness.

"Here we are." The gray lady is pushing the door open and Mary and Lily step into a cave-like space. "He asks for it to be pitch-black," she whispers. All the light in the room, aside from that coming from the hallway, is coming from a crack and a couple of one centimeter-wide holes in the window shade. Mary pulls up a chair and motions for Lily to do the same.

The outline of a ghost of a man limps into focus. He is on his back. He has a prominent curved, hawk-shaped nose lit up by a skinny sliver of light passing through the torn shade.

"They like to have their own things around them in their room. He likes that old shade for some reason. We've tried to get rid of it. It looks like someone shot a bullet through it once or twice. We've asked him if there is a story behind it, but he says nothing."

She talks over him as though he is already dead. After an awkward silent pause the gray lady adds, "I'll leave you alone with him now. I'll be at the front desk."

The room has the unmistakable smell of death. Mary knows that the family has signed the **Do Not Resuscitate** paper in accordance with her great great uncle's wish. What comes to her ears sounds like an extension of the Cut Bank River, gurgling in the caverns of his chest. He labors to breathe. Mary looks at her purse.

Did I bring my stethoscope? No. Is he taking any water? There's a glass with a bent, smashed-at-the-end straw. The water pitcher's half empty. I wonder how long it's been sitting there? No I.V. Probably his wish. Just a couple of tablespoons of dark amber-colored urine in his catheter bag. How long ago was it emptied? Mary closes her eyes and puts her head back in the chair. *I've got to stop thinking like a freakin' nurse.* Two tears slide out from under an eyelid. They seem to bring her back and she remembers that Lily is patiently sitting there.

"Uncle. It's Mary. Mary Mary Quite Contrary. Remember? My garden is growing good these days." Was there a flicker of his eyelash? "I've brought a friend with me. We'd like to hear about the time you found the Indian children's toys that are in the Browning museum now. You know, the little quiver of arrows and the bow and the dolls? Remember? You were working on Going to the Sun Road."

His mouth is open. There are deep fissures in the corners. His lips look dried up and as waterless and arid as the so-called Bad Lands. There are missing teeth. All the oldsters have missing teeth. Around the few teeth that remain the gums have receded. What is holding them in place? Maybe it is because he hardly uses them anymore. His breath is fetid and it permeates the air in the room. His skin fits tightly against the bone, while folds of skin flop to the back of his neck. It appears that all the fat and muscle of his face has been digested in order to keep him alive just one more day.

Then from the bed comes a raspy whisper. "Face of Sour Spirit Who Went Back to the Sun After Work Done." Then there is a long stop in his breathing. Lily wonders if she is witnessing his last words with his last breath. Then one more whispered word. "Water."

Mary grabs the water glass with the straw, but he doesn't have the strength to bring his lips around it. She takes a washcloth from the side table and soaks it with water. He can barely suck on it but is able to dampen his parched lips.

"'Face of Sour Spirit Who Went Back to the Sun After Work Done' was the original Blackfoot name of the road," Mary explains. "It was so named after a Blackfoot legend where a spirit from the sun would descend to give a helping hand to those in trouble who cried to the sun for help."

As Mary is explaining this to Lily, it appears that there is more light in the room. Mary has seen this before, when Lily was in the hospital, but it is no less a surprise. Not only that, the horrible smell that bathed the room moments before is gone and is replaced by the aroma of wild mountain honeysuckle. Mary and Lily look at each other, but remain shocked into silence. The room definitely is becoming brighter. Then, another shockwave. Uncle Henry Tall Chief opens his eyes and sits straight up in bed; reaching for more water from his bedside table, he gulps it.

Henry looks at Lily and smiles, "You're a pretty thing." A transformation has taken place.

Mary, who never stammers or seems ruffled in any way, stammers now. "U-U-Uncle, Lily has had dreams about the toys ... or ... a ... the bundle you found that is in the museum now. Ca-Can you tell about it, please?"

"We had to hang our food high up between two trees. Sometimes them bears would git the food anyways and we had to work with no food in the belly. We had to fight them bears off all the time. One road builder, he was killed by a grizzly. We killed the grizzly after that. Now the bear spirit visits me at night and the worker man's spirit does too.

"I think there was three men killed dead on that road job. One man I was workin' with ... a French Canadian trapper turned road worker. He was called Louis DuBois. I call him Louie. He was a mean one. Always talkin' bout findin' gold and gittin' rich. I tried to tell him there was no gold in them mountains but there's no tellin' him nothin'. Heck. The government man bought them mountains from the Blackfoot Nation for its minerals and when they didn't find gold they turned the land into a National Park.

"Anyways, we was workin' real hard and payin' not much attention to the weather. It rained hard the two days before. All of a sudden, here comes a slide down the mountain. Out of nowhere it come. At first the slide is not that big and with it comes a partly hollow log and somethin' falls out of it at one end. Louie is sure it's a stash a gold that some miner has hid in that log, but it looks like a sacred beaver bundle to me. I yell, 'Louieeeee. That's an Indian bundle and you better not mess with it. It has to be handled real careful by the people that take the vow. It has to be handled right. With the prayers and songs and all.'

"Louie doesn't know nothin'. He takes out his knife and cuts clean through the bundle, hide, tie-ups, and all. When he sees it's just toys, he is real real mad and gives one of them dolls a kick and the doll's head comes clean off."

As Henry Tall Chief tells his story he is becoming more and

more animated and the room becomes ever more brilliant with light.

"That's it! Louis has angered them mountains and the Beaver People. There is a roar and the rest of the mountain slope we was workin' comes down on both of us. Rocks, trees falling from the sky, and we don't know where the other one is at. I'm on the caterpillar tractor and me and it are swept down the mountain over 200 feet. I come out alive. I'm not sure why. All 'round me are them Indian toys and I gather 'em up. Then I see Louis. I mean I see Louis' **head** right there next to them toys. The rest of him is under 400 feet of dirt 'n rock up on the ridge. He had let go of his spirit all right. The Beaver People saw to it. They finally got the body out after two days a diggin'. His neck had been skewered with a four-inch wide log, chewed into a point by beaver teeth. It went through him like butter and cut off his head clean as an axe. He wasn't a very good lookin' fella anyways.

"I keep them Indian toys for a while. Later, more and more people wants to see them toys and they gits stole a couple of times before I steal 'em back. Finally it gits so bad that I git shot at through the window," Henry is pointing to his shade with the bullet holes, "and I decide it is time to give 'em up to the museum then and there. I kept the window shade though as a reminder, and I had my daughter, Ann, bring it here. I like lookin' at it. It's like lookin' at different times."

"Wow," said Mary. "I had forgotten much of the story." Mary was looking at Lily, but Lily was shaking her head "no." At this moment the 100-year-old man owned the story. It was his. No more needed to be added. Besides, what Lily could add may have been just a dream, even if to the indigenous people dreams are another reality.

After kisses goodbye and the gift of red licorice, it's a hot ride back to Browning and the swaying of the truck causes both women to feel sleepy. They are not talking, each being again in their own thoughts. Lily's head starts to feel heavy and she is nearly asleep when a strange thing begins to happen on the road. An unusually large snowy white owl swoops down to land on the road about thirty feet in front of Mary's truck. Mary shoves her dainty feet down hard on the clutch and break. The bird does not move. "Why does this owl have his winter feathers in August?" asks Lily, after being jerked awake.

"I don't know. The Blackfoot believe that a white owl is the spirit of a deceased holy or medicine man. Why doesn't he fly away? I am going to try to maneuver around him." As she does so the owl simply flies a few feet ahead and lands again, right in their path. "Christ. This is too bizarre. I'll try to get around him again." Again, the bird flies a few feet to settle back down right on the road, in their way.

"I think this owl is trying to tell us something. Let's get out of the truck."

The two young ladies slip from Mary's vehicle and speak with soft words as they creep closer. The owl's penetrating gaze is sizing up the two two-leggeds. Then he takes flight without a sound. There is not even the rushing noise of The Wind in his wings, making Lily swallow to prove to herself that she did not go deaf. He flies directly over her head.

Gently, gently, a white feather floats to Lily's feet. She bends over to examine it. How odd is this! It has some familiar markings on its shaft and quill. There are three tiny yellow bands, followed by four red ones, followed by twelve black bands. Mary and Lily look at each other and speak together the same words, "It's a sign."

But what does it mean? Lily does not know. However, she is acutely aware that the burning tailbone feeling took a higher leap up her back the moment she touched the feather.

By the light of the next morning Mary gets the sad news from the Glacier Care Center that Great Great Uncle Henry Tall Chief has joined his dead relations. Would his death cause the owl feather sign on the road from Cut Bank? Or was it about something else?

PART TWO
Little Bear/Two Bears—Ahhatome

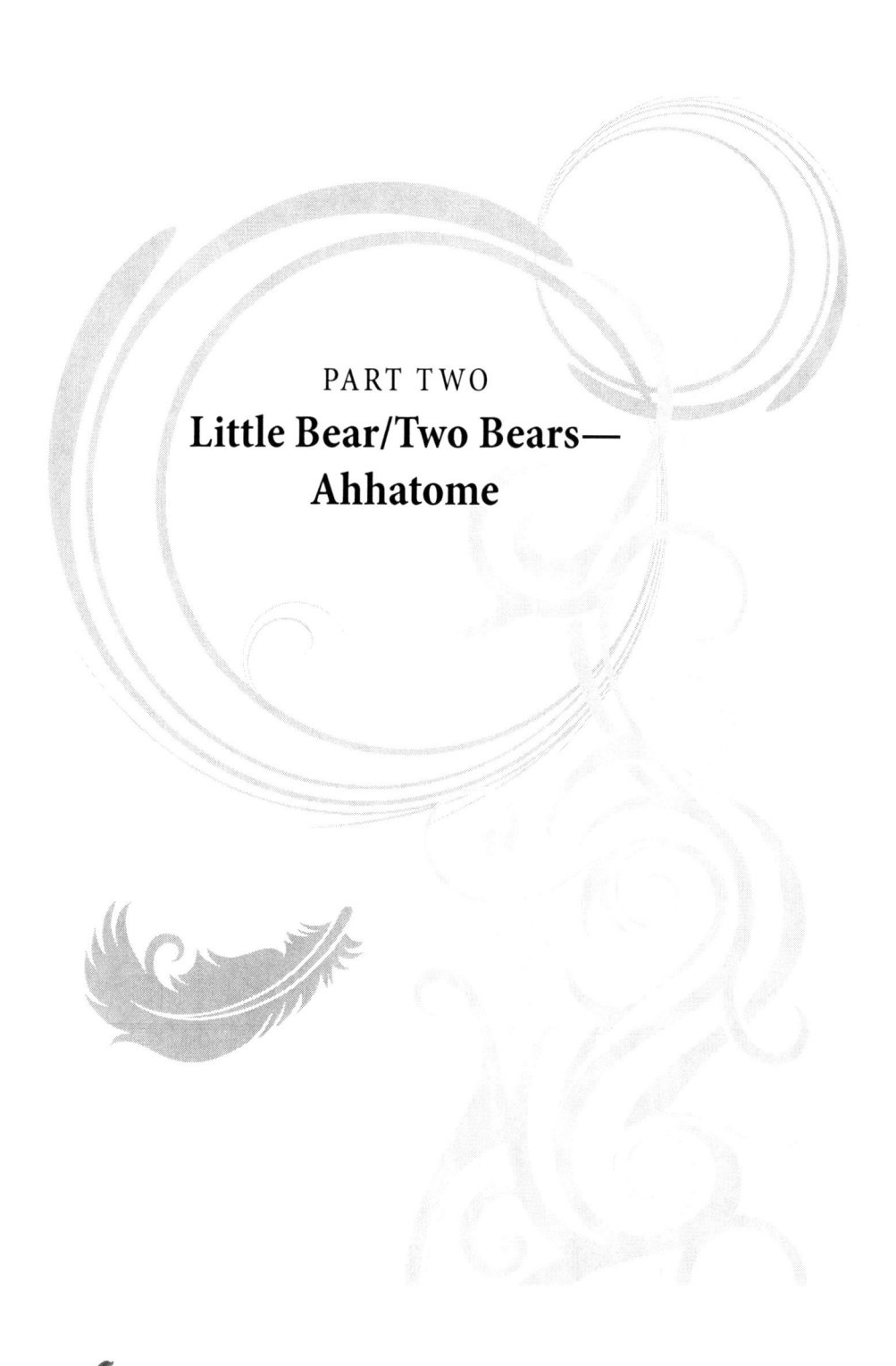

CHAPTER FIFTEEN

Who Is Ahhatome?

Little Bear died two centuries ago . . . by how Earthlings measure time. He is now very much alive beyond time, in the fifth dimension, and because he has accomplished his Earth work of developing his compassion and will he can elect to stay in the fifth dimension more permanently. The Wind is here with him, because I exist wherever there is movement and therefore I can speak about it.

5D is a world beyond the limited third dimensional physical—eyes, ears, touching, smells, and tastes. Physicality as humans know it doesn't exist here. Yet every third dimensional being has the grander part of himself living in the fifth dimension, even though he doesn't think about himself in that way. There is literally more to a human than meets the eye . . . the human eye, that is.

This place is not really a place, like a location somewhere in space. It exists everywhere there are thinking beings. Actually, everything, even a rock—a geode for instance—has an energy form in the fourth dimension and its "word" or idea in the fifth. This is the world of Mind, both individual and collective. Is a rock conscious then? In a way, yes, if a thinking mind can think of it, then it is. Consciousness is an inadequate word for little minds to try to comprehend.

What makes this world seem separate to a traveler through the fifth dimension is that the energy here is much more refined than that of the lower worlds, yet is similar to the lower worlds in that it is also a world of both the formless and the formed, the "dark" and the "light." However the so-called dark on this level is packed with power, packed with potential for all things. It is the great Mother. It is The Womb of all forms.

When an Earthling is done with his heavy energy form he leaves his body-brain complex and enters into the world of the soul-mind of expanded awareness in the fifth dimension. The soul that was called Little Bear now calls himself by a new name. He calls himself Ahhatome. He chose this name for the sound Ahh, which he made when he relaxed into this world and from the words At Home. However he is only partly relaxed because the other significant part of his soul is in and is Lily, who has most of her present awareness in the lower third dimension. This is an extraordinary case of not only separated Twin Souls, but also of dimensional consciousness separation. This presents a major challenge.

Ahhatome looks non-human to The Wind's heightened senses. He appears as a being of light around a quantity of much more refined physical substance, or ethereal substance, or thought substance, or mind substance to choose a few weak words for a great mystery.

Earthlings have light in their bodies too, but their light is stepped-down and diminished, with less activated DNA. Ahhatome's dense body, being etheric, can be made to change shape by the power of his concentrated intent and strong will.

With proper breathing, unlike most humans, he needs no solid food, but can exist solely on prana, a subtle energy form which is abundant throughout all that is or ever was and feeds everything.

There is no birthing from a womb in the fifth dimension. Beings here are mostly androgynous, except that Ahhatome is a rare exception. His soul is split. He lives here in his male fragment. He is not in near constant bliss like the others.

Ahhatome witnesses in his atmosphere something coming out of nothing, again and again. The "somethings" that Ahhatome sees appear like tiny fireflies that burst onto the scene, blinking on and off. These firefly blinks are similar to electrical nerve impulses, moving as waves over an infinite number of invisible webs on their way to and through the other dimensions as they put on more ethereal/thought substance. These waves produce instantaneous effects and therefore are considered beyond time.

Thought substance is light and sound, which hold information. Little packets of light and sound information are then called forth by a being who may live mostly in another dimension and is in the mental act of creating something.

Ahhatome and his group of beings of like frequency have chosen to create an environment that in many respects is a refined reflection of the beautiful Mother Earth domain. Colors here are more vibrant and two octaves above a third dimensional visual range.

Beings here are much more conscious of their *spirit,* to use an old word, or *energy,* to use the modern word for the same. Spirit energy displays as colors and musical notes.

Ahhatome is a light form who stays primarily in human shape because he's accustomed to it. If Earthlings could see him without being blinded, his human-like shape would show very soft edges throwing off light. He projects himself with eyes that are large and deep blue. His hair, or crown of light, is seen as golden-white, and if examined closely contains tiny filaments of all the refined higher-octave colors.

Around his form are distinct rings of colored light, emanating from his core. Descending from higher dimensions than the fifth is a ray of golden light that showers down and illuminates through him, making his heart radiant. There is light entering and leaving his feet and his hands.

If Ahhatome is near another entity that being feels lighthearted, for that is what Ahhatome is most of the time, but strangely, not quite so much at this moment. Instead, he is . . . more pensive.

Ahhatome's attention is wandering to a tugging sensation at the center of his back. It is not painful so much as it is annoying. Physical pain was left behind when his consciousness shifted. However, Ahhatome does have the memory of pain. He has, after all, lived through several third dimensional experiences on Earth.

Now Ahhatome is expecting and senses the appearance of his close light companion Horus, and turns to greet him. In comparing humanoid forms of choice, Horus chooses a shorter version than Ahhatome, with a more compact center. His light is very bright and he is also handsomely put together, with intense dark eyes. Horus named himself after the famous Egyptian god, the son of Isis and Osiris, perhaps because he particularly favors morphing or shape shifting into a falcon, or perhaps because he knows he has a gifted kind of wisdom seeing. However, Horus also has a gleeful and slightly mischievous sense of humor and has been known to delight in drawing the famous Eye of Horus with purple light into the ethers and waiting until someone in another dimension makes it heavier by their thoughts and draws it away. Sometimes it would be viewed by lower dimensional beings as a sign from God.

For this he has been warned by The High Council that his foolery is not only unbecoming behavior for a being of his caliber in an etheric galactic society, but to mess with religious symbolism often leads to misunderstandings by beings only partially conscious, and can inspire fear, controlling behavior over others, and even blood-shed amongst the more innocent and unsuspecting primitive observers.

The rules are not that hard to follow. On the 5D level the main rule is: "Do unto others as you would have them do unto you, because in the last grand analysis, the Others are You."

In the fifth dimension light beings are taught that, concerning individual contacts from a person in a lower, or better described as in a narrower dimension, it is paramount to allow the contacting entity to be his own self-teacher; to offer assistance only if requested, and then step away to allow the requester to unfold himself. Horus and Ahhatome try to go by the rules but they are both new on the learning curve of this dimension.

They enjoy flying together high over the beautiful light field in a form with wings, although they don't need wings. They both have a soul memory of being human and of being in awe of the flight of birds and wishing they could fly. And lo, that desire has been fulfilled in the fifth dimensional life where they "fly" at will in multiple choices of light forms. As they mature in this dimension they will learn how to occasionally, yet briefly, inhabit configurations of particles of more dense physical matter.

Shape shifting is not an easy thing to do for a beginner, especially to hold the shape. It takes great mental discipline. Young 5D entities who practice shape shifting have the blessing of The Order of Elders who teach it as a part of fifth dimensional development. Ahhatome particularly likes the shape of the snowy white owl. Shape shifting is fun and it is work.

"Ahhatome! Ready to fly?"

"I'm already on the move," comes his reply.

Ahhatome and Horus fly with abandonment and heavenly joy over their favorite patterns, Ahhatome in the snowy white owl form and Horus in his favorite form, the falcon. Communication between the two friends is by word-for-word mental telepathy, or by packets of information in picture-thought forms.

But now Horus turns to his dear friend. "Your light seems tight and I dare say dimmer and droopy. Something is dragging you down like an anchor pulling you backward."

"I've been feeling it. Sometimes it does not grab my attention and other times it really pulls. I believe it's a psychic hook. I have pulled it out and cut it off. However breaking the connection doesn't seem to be working. It instantly re-establishes itself."

"Well, cannot you ask for help or maybe pray it away?"

"I have asked in prayer. When I do, I notice it all the more."

"What help have you requested? Have you taken it to The Elders?"

"You know my father is an Elder. I think he'll just give me his famous knowing look that says, 'You can figure it out yourself, Son.' That seems to be his stock answer to many of my questions and his teaching strategy. Like I said, I'm pretty sure it is an unusually strong psychic cord or psychic hook. The big question is, why is it there?"

Ahhatome and Horus stop their flying and settle down on a high peak over their favorite valley. This is also their spot for philosophizing.

"It seems to me that you have two choices here," says Horus. "One, ignore it and let it continue to distract you and just let it be, even if you become known far and wide as 'The Light Being with The Hook.' Hopefully it will not grow so much that it pulls you down to a lower dimension."

"I don't think it has been growing lately, Horus."

"Or," Horus continued, "Two. Look deeply into who or what hooked you and fix the cause."

Horus' primary awareness has been in the fifth dimension a little longer than Ahhatome's and he takes a simple practical approach to problems.

"Okay Horus, I've made my decision. I'll look into what in the etheric galactic way is the cause of this thing."

CHAPTER SIXTEEN

The Cord that Binds

All new beings admitted to the fifth dimension are given a "father" mentor upon arrival. Ahhatome arrived with an additional appendage, a thick cord attached to the center of his back.

Aba Ahhatome (Aba meaning father) is a highly respected member of The Order of Elders. These radiant presences, distinguished by auras with a dazzling hue of violet rose-pearl overtones, are overseers and guides for the new entries here, where learning continues for soul development.

Auras are the divine light of the soul that shines around the being and through the veils between the dimensions of its existence. The more aware and refined both the object of observation and the observer are, the higher the color octaves reveal themselves there. Aura awareness and interpretation of auras are taught in the fifth dimension. Sometimes Earth beings are exposed to these teachings during their sleep, when they visit the fifth dimension in their dream-trance-travel bodies.

Aba Ahhatome has a gentle but penetrating gaze. His deep multicolored eyes bore through any entity he is addressing. It is common for that addressee to turn to look for who or what Aba Ahhatome sees behind him. Aba is tall, like Ahhatome. His present humanoid image is distinguished by prominent features that come with age, yet he is wrinkleless.

Members of The Order of Elders tend to dress in flowing robes that describe their office, but they are far from keeping a frozen form or specific garment of light. They are so adept at shape shifting that during their communications—which are usually by mentally projected unspoken words—they will shift into the shape of whatever subject is under discussion. This augments their conversations far beyond the eloquence of their words.

Turning his face into a softer countenance, his eyes seem to stroke his son's head while he speaks, this time not with a look, but with telepathic thought.

"Yes, my dear son, you came into this 5D world from a difficult Earth experience with an attached psychic cord. It does not appear to have increased much in size. It is quite luminous and rosy colored for the most part, but it also contains streaks of muddy gray and dark tawny yellow soot. It definitely is not a dead remnant that you can easily remove and it is not a superficial attachment, like some tend to be. It goes deep into the core of your heart through your back no matter what form you assume in your shape shifting."

Gently Aba Ahhatome continues, "You have not visited the teachings about cords or 'the ties that bind,' so let's look at a few information light bubbles about them.

"Cords are of ethereal substance, brought about by intense feelings of attachment to another more or less conscious being or object that is perceived to be both desperately needed and some distance away. It might be called an ethereal umbilical cord, considered to be a lifeline by one or both parties, who are joined together through the act of cording. In the third dimension appropriate cords are established between parents and their young children and between care givers and the fragile elderly."

Aba Ahhatome looks like he is remembering other times. "Teachers, doctors, and religious leaders are often heavily corded and feel drained of energy by certain of their pupils, patients, or followers. The emotional tone that sets a cord is an overwhelming emotional energy of neediness and the mistaken belief that one needs a particular person, or group, or what is seen by Earth eyes as a necessary thing for happiness or survival."

"Aba, did I cord someone or did they cord me?"

"Ahhatome! What a question. It is irrelevant.

"Heart and solar plexus cords suggest emotional binding . . . for example, when a lover in a new relationship about which he feels insecure, believes himself to be 'in love' and becomes 'love sick' by cording to another party from his solar plexus to the other's solar plexus. The energy records are full of examples of those who claim to be in love and, when the other party does not acknowledge them, the energy of anxiety and longing pulsate with such intensity through the cord that one or both take to their beds unable to eat or think of much else.

"To be the victim of unrequited love is in some societies considered a virtue. But in my view this requires a certain amount of stubbornness and refusal to see what other possibilities life is offering. If a very thick cord is built over a lifetime it usually means that sacrifices of other happier experiences have been made in order to feed the building of the cord.

"Most 3D humanoids are immersed in the belief of passing time and do not understand that no intense desire goes unfulfilled when it is ripe. They think they should have something immediately while simultaneously believing in linear time. All things flow from spirit, and in the world of spirit time has no significance. The fulfillment may come in the next life or the one after. But rest assured, no strong desire is denied."

"I never thought of falling in love in this way. Surely you are not saying that falling in love is a bad thing, Aba."

"No, no, not at all. What I am saying is, it just is. All things change. All experiences and happenings are, when seen in the broadest context, lessons about love. The lovers I just described bind themselves to one another by mutual consent. This is not bad or good. It just is and serves a temporary purpose. If energy flows easily back and forth between the two then the union is content. But if it becomes a one-way flow it can become a heavy drain on one party. Hopefully a lesson will be learned."

"I feel my 'temporary' cord has long run out of its 'temporary.' I would like to be a perfect lover and not tie anyone in knots. I'm not needy," whispers Ahhatome, now completely absorbed by Aba Ahhatome's story.

Aba Ahhatome is silent and looks at Ahhatome with kind knowing father's eyes. "Yes, my son. We all strive toward perfection. Your cord may not be about that kind of love. Sometimes cords are used in karmic contracts made before birth. Let's say that a family member is painfully suffering from a severe accident or illness. As you know, family members are carefully chosen with their mutual consent and agreement before birth and usually have karmic connections through cords. A situation requiring giving life energy to another, not the exact form that it takes, is often chosen by the participants before birth.

"Of course anyone is free to choose not to honor his initial intent. Nothing is ever forced. In more rare cases a highly advanced soul with little or no karmic debt may volunteer to take on some of the karmic debt of another who feels overwhelmed with the weight of it. This is a very rare act and this is the thinking behind the old custom of the sacrifice of the innocent in some religious contexts to atone for the sins of others or to please the gods with a sacrificial lamb. However it is a mistaken idea that spilling the blood of the innocent helps correct a karmic debt instead of creating more. It is entirely another matter when an advanced soul volunteers to spend helpful life force energy in service to another, for another. The point is, we should not judge our cords or those others who have been corded. Even some loving pets are corded to their masters and give of their life force and, in rare occasions, will even take on their master's illness. It is simply all about energy. How it can be modified or changed or redirected or given and received."

"This explains a lot to me, Father." After a long pause and trying to reach for the cord in the middle of his back, he says, "I wish to find the cause of this cord."

Aba Ahhatome sits down and leans back in his chair. He is gazing up upon row after row of books with their jackets of gilded letters and symbols. Aba Ahhatome does not need to open these books. He likes to have them because they give him the comfort of fond memories of learning and of favorite libraries. He says they are reminders of topics of focus.

"You have been instructed about, but I do not think you have yet experienced much if any, in the way of reading your own Akashic records."

Ahhatome leans forward, anxious to hear some new revelations. Aba Ahhatome, with his head still in a tilted back position, closes his eyes and draws in a breath as if ready to speak again. But instead, in the pause before the exhale, he tightens his light into a tiny bright pinkish dot and blinks out. This conversation is over.

CHAPTER SEVENTEEN

The Hall of the Akashic Records

No sooner had Aba Ahhatome shrunk himself down to a tiny pin point of light than, with what would have been his exhale, the dot of light starts to change color and grow into a sparking yellow-gold ball that begins to mold and shape itself, sprouting arms and legs and an unusually large head. This new presence causes Ahhatome to draw back in his chair as an entity with an enormous glistening reflective eye in the center of an expansive forehead takes shape where his aba had been sitting a moment before.

Out of this central eye comes an intense palpable beam of light. Now the rest of the configuration begins to form. "Oh, excuse me. Sometimes I forget how intense my headlight can be," comes a lilting voice filled with jolly overtones that Ahhatome receives telepathically.

"Allow me to introduce myself. I call myself Libris. I help entities discover no end to their previous personal soul adventures while I play Keeper of The Records. As you know, souls come out of Source Energy and do not die. Their temporary heavy forms die, but those old forms also have a kind of prolonged life as a recording etched on the Universal Plasma.

"You are familiar with The Akashic Records?" As Libris is altogether speaking and giggling, his central forehead eye dims as it turns a quarter turn so that the large glimmering thing now has one corner of it pointing to his nose and the other pointing toward the top of his enormous head, similar to what is seen in antique Chinese paintings. The two eyelids, now on the sides of his forehead, are halfway closed, forming a narrow up and down slit.

The being does not wait for Ahhatome to respond. "Oh, what the heck, I don't need to interfere with your light with this thing turned on." And with that the central eye vanishes. The Wind thinks he hardly needs another eye; his robe is covered with eye images. They give the robe a gold-green gleam. On closer inspection those eyes act like they are alive! Maybe all those eyes help him read The Records.

Some eyes seem to be copied from old art. His garment has lizard eyes, cat eyes, red eyes, blank eyes, even the eye on the Earthling dollar bill and a rather large Eye of Horus. They might stare at a visitor, look around as if bored, roll up or down or look at each other, sometimes in concert with Libris' feelings and sometimes not, Ahhatome cannot be sure. One thing is sure. This is an eerie robe to the uninitiated. But the creature inside projects the essence of a very happy fellow who, up to this point, doesn't seem to take too much too seriously.

"I . . . I've heard of The Records, of course," stammers Ahhatome. "But I have no recollection of visiting them. Just exactly where are they located?"

"Are you still in the third dimension, My Boy? The Records are everywhere. You are standing in them now! It's a matter of focus." Leaning an inch from Ahhatome's face, "However, it is very wise to have a guide for your first visits." He pays no attention when Ahhatome recoils.

"That's why I'm here. I heard your soul request to find the source of that thing you have attached to you. When your heart's desire aligns with your soul's purpose, then helpers arrive as well as the challenges that come with more fabulous adventure. And in case you haven't figured it out, I am your helper . . . Supreme." Libris continues while Ahhatome's aura shrinks a little.

"As you know, your greater purpose is to grow in soul knowledge, soul knowledge being quite different from, let's say, how the stock market works." Ahhatome is looking blank. "Never mind, you'll understand presently. Come."

Watching Libris as he turns, Ahhatome catches sight of a tree trunk that shines through his garment and seems within and around where Earthlings would expect Libris' spine to be. This tree has branches down Libris' arms and up into his head and roots down his legs. Tree light can be seen from his front too, but is more obvious and prominent when viewed from the back. This tree seems . . . ancient. Balls or wheels of a myriad variety of colored lights can be seen amongst its branches. *Could they be . . .*

"Yes, I like to put apples in my symbolic tree of knowledge." Laughing and turning with a wink, "Apples are the forbidden fruit you know and I love them. Or, if you read another layer to it, the Sefirot in the Kabbalah. It's about what you choose to read, so be cautious. Take those mischievous Anunnaki in the Sumerian records for instance! Now that's what I call a real read!"

What is he talking about? Libris' third eye place looks puckered up, squeezed shut.

"Yes, it's all been recorded in The Records. Everything that went down, as young Earth people sometimes say." Turning away again and motioning to Ahhatome to follow his saunter down what appears as a long tunnel, he continues in a kind of mumbling voice to himself or to anyone who might want to listen, "And, if you want to ask, 'Went down where?' In The Akashic Records, that's where . . . plus every other version and description or belief about an incident, layer after layer, stacked like onion skins around a kernel of someone's action or speaking or thinking." Turning once more to look Ahhatome in the eye, "or singing."

That "singing" comment must have been meant for The Wind. This Libris fellow certainly likes to jabber away—maybe because as one of the keepers of The Records his head is stuffed with too much knowledge for his own comfort.

"What do you mean, mischievous Anunnaki?"

"The story has a tree, apples, and a serpent. Don't forget the serpent! Look. There is so much information in The Hall that the first rule, in order not to get flattened with info or lost, is to stick to one, and I mean **one** line of questioning." While making his last statement, Libris' form changes into a growing and glowing printed number one, then back to his rounder more apple-like humanoid form.

"You ask The Records the over-all question first, then if you need more information, ask **only** for further refinement of the **first** question. Got that?

"Specific focus is the key, My Boy, **specific focus**. You will find lots of layers to your question." Libris is making his hands flutter trying to mimic "layers." "Remember, you want to focus on the cause of that snake you drag around." After a tiny moment of silence Libris cannot help but continue to fill the silence with jibber jabber.

"You asked the question concerning the Anunnaki. Now there's a story in layers. Some believe the Anunnaki are a race of serpents, some say they are the Devil and his daemons, some say they were early astronauts, others that they were 'Creator gods.' It depends on which layer is doing the talking.

"One layer shows the Anunnaki as one of several related groups who tinkered with new life forms on Earth. One record shows them using their own DNA and then disconnecting a good portion of it in an attempt to keep some of the new Earth being's lights out, to keep the modern human's brain and other systems weak and dumb. Did you know human scientists have discovered DNA that won't light up and become active like the rest of their DNA and they call it '**junk?**' That's exactly what it is. Less light for communication keeping humans isolated. Trash in the trashed. The Anunnaki and those who think they are related to them keep certain knowledge to themselves. Why you ask?" Ahhatome never asked, but he will get Libris' opinion anyway. "For the purpose of control!" Ahhatome looks unimpressed with this story. Sensing Ahhatome's boredom, Libris mumbles,

"There's more to the story, but let's not get ourselves stuck in that bog."

The Wind knows that Lebris has not studied all the layers of information about "junk DNA", or he would know that the "junk" acts like a series of switches, turning the more active light-bearing DNA on and off. The bigger question is, why do some Earthlings have more switches turned on or off than others? He needs to quit talking and look into it.

But now Libris yabbers on and on again, while Ahhatome and The Wind become restless. "Quite simply, the serpent is just another symbol for power, such as the power to heal, as suggested by the caduceus symbol that Earth doctors wear showing serpents wrapped around a staff and the awakened kundalini energies pictured as rising like serpents up a person's back. What I want you to see is how easy it is to digress and start into an off-shoot of ideas from the mere mention of the tree of knowledge, apples, and serpents.

"My good fellow, the enticement to digress and travel down off-shoots from your mission of discovery is a thousand times greater when you start exploring the Akashic Records because everything is so damn interesting. Be forewarned. You must stick to your mission and not be seduced elsewhere."

Ahhatome doesn't see a serpent around Libris' tree; or does he? He wonders, *Does Libris ever stop with his ramblings and analogies?*

"If The Hall of Records is everywhere, where are we going now?" asks Ahhatome, picking up speed while chasing after a now fast-moving-on-short-thin-legs Libris through a long energy tunnel. Here and there Ahhatome can see glints of light, perhaps from sparkling gems or luminous veins of metallic substances or, even more curious, sets of eyes up and down and overhead that watch. Somewhere within the dark is the drip-dripping sound of water echoing off the chamber walls. A breathing voice is coming from the depths. It's a blow hole where I, The Wind, come whining through.

Libris begins his program by pausing in his scurry while two large cushy chairs are summoned to materialize. *Why did he do that since we are beings of light and have no weary bones?*

"Oh, I'm sorry, I'm a bit of a forgetful librarian. You see, this is where I have some fun. The waves of information are the waves and material is the material, but because they cross between and through each other the program can be presented in as many ways as there are viewers and helpers. I love to turn a trip through The Records into an adventure. I'm doing my rabbit hole thing."

Ahhatome is not amused. With a bit of a quizzical smirk, he folds his arms across his chest while his inner light form becomes stiff and dulled down.

"Don't let your lights go out," giggles Libris. "And no, I'm not crazy! Look," he says, abruptly standing up, just after putting himself in repose. "The material you are after can be presented through many portholes." His body is gyrating with enthusiasm. "I've used the unrolling of papyrus scrolls, looking through blackened scrying mirrors, spying within crystal balls, deciphering stone and crystal tablets, surveying the sky, and divining the surface of water, even within beryl bowls." As he is talking Libris is now dancing in circles, waving his arms overhead and all around. He is like a squatty spinning top with wispy appendages.

"I've used the casting of gem stones, tea leaves, bones, the wielding of divining rods, and of course, scanning the books in the customary library with its volumes stacked to infinity. Need I go on? It's just window dressing for what we are after. I like The Way of the Rabbit Hole. It's the best. Sound waves can get us there too, you know, like the beating of the ceremonial drum or the white rabbit's ticking clock."

Libris stops spinning and addresses the rabbit hole but is really giving a message to Ahhatome. "Yes. Yes. The velvety darkness we are in now is about the psyche, the unseen behind the seen. You need to explore your whole self, the light and the dark. Now you know why I chose the dark of the rabbit hole along with that other clever fellow. What was his name?"

"Lewis Carroll," Ahhatome volunteered, having read Libris' struggling thought and becoming more sympathetic and his light more bright.

Libris looks back at his recliners, "Ahh, these two chairs are like old times. We'll relax while I give instructions." He plops himself down and Ahhatome tries to act interested. "I will be with you throughout, even though you may not see me. If you need me you must ask for me. When I present myself to you in The Records I will not be in this form. I might take the form of a tree or a rock in order to blend into the scenery. Therefore you must listen for me if you call for me.

"Remember, there are rules. We have already discussed a very important one, which is 'stay true to your mission or you will lose what you came to find out.' Also, if you meet with a door, locked gate, or other barrier do not force the door; call on me and then what did I say?" asks a squinting Libris as he peers at Ahhatome.

"Listen for you from a rock or something," replies Ahhatome.

"Good. Reading The Records requires a calm interior on your part; in other words, your emotions need to be relaxed. In the third dimension they call it a meditative or alternative state. Whatever you want to call it, the point is, if you get excited you will affect the readability of The Records. The Records will get excited to the exact proportion that you do. Therefore to maintain control, you must remind yourself to breathe deeply.

"Don't breathe like a human. When they feel disturbed in some way they breathe shallowly in the upper chest. Remember this. **Strong emotions like anger and slow deep breathing cannot exist in the same space.**

"Here is something else to think about. What we are seeking in The Records is about you, but remember that we will view you as you were in a somewhat diminished past form than what you have become now as a being of light. This unusual situation is bound to bring up emotions. Always remember, your breath is your best defense in keeping those emotions in check and in keeping your ability to read The Records."

Ahhatome has heard enough and is starting to stand up.

"We're not done. There's more." Libris is pointing at Ahhatome's chair. He wants him to sit again. "There are two main ways to view The Records. If you are observing yourself you may view your past events from behind your own eyes and inside the skin of the being that you were at that time. If you choose to view that way you will feel more like a participant.

"The other way to view is from a seemingly distant point in the scene, where you will feel more like a spectator. Either way you observe, you must observe as a spectator only. Also, at this point in your spiritual development you may not read the scene from the inside viewpoint of another person.

"There is one exception to this rule about viewing from inside another entity and that is that it may be allowed during the Life Review, immediately or soon after death of the third dimensional physical shell, when you are surrounded by guides and ascended masters. But even then it may not be allowed.

"If you chose to observe from within there is something else to bear in mind. You will **not** be able to change your previous actions or the sequence of events. Remember you are reading, not creating. This can be a cause of tremendous anxiety and frustration, no matter from where you observe. When anxiety or frustration happens, what do you do?"

"Breathe deeply," says Ahhatome, now feeling overloaded again, this time with directions. Then, somewhat sarcastically, "Is there anything else I need to know?"

"Libris is holding his head as though Ahhatome just gave him a headache. "Of course there are more detailed directions I can give you, but I see that you have allowed your irritation barrier to descend upon you. This blocks any more information I could tell you now. However, I think you have enough information to cautiously begin your search."

Libris is not talking now, but that does not last long. "What point of view have you chosen? Internal or external?"

"I think I will observe from outside, at least to start. It might be easier as a beginner."

"Good. Remember to breathe deeply; if you meet with an obstacle call me even though I may be right beside you. Never forget to set your intention first by stating firmly in your mind what you are there for, as though The Record you seek is an intelligent living being."

Libris' voice is fading, fading, and the sound of it seems to be drawing away from Ahhatome at a greater and greater distance. A swirling black hole appears where Libris was sitting just moments before. The sound of The Keeper's voice seems to have been pulled into this blackness. Ahhatome stands and steps up to the dark hole and boldly speaks his intention, hoping to follow his guide. He remembers a teaching from his father. "Let the outcome of my intention be for the greater good of all involved." Pleased with himself for remembering this teaching, he is watching the swirling blackness take on more light until a thin filmy curtain forms. *What is this? What do I do now?* Ahhatome reaches out a finger to touch the slithery curtain. He cannot pass his finger through it. Why? He is a being of light after all.

"Libris!"

"Have you forgotten your manners?" It is the curtain talking now, but it sounds like the familiar giggly voice of Libris. "Look. It's a cord that we are investigating. Right? There has to be another person or group or thing attached to the other end. Do you think it is okay to poke around into the affairs of others without first getting permission? You must ask permission from the oversoul of all the beings that will be involved in your reading. It is almost always given, but if not you must examine your motives. They must be honorable. Try again."

Ahhatome looks at the curtain and clears his voice. "Ahhm. My name is Ahhatome, and . . ."

"I know your name, to whom are you making this address?"

"Ah. Oh. I would like to ask permission of any oversoul of the people or things I may encounter to please allow me to view the history of my psychic hook which may include them . . . if it pleases Your Majesty or Majesties."

"Majesty? What majesty? No essence within a being is higher or lower than any other. There are no majesties like the kind that are in your imagination other than your own thought forms about them. We are all created from the same essence."

"Yes, well . . . er . . . ah . . ."

"You may proceed."

Ahhatome is sucked right through the curtain into moving light swirls. He is surrounded by both harmonic and dissonant sounds accompanied by a symphony of scents. He hears groups of voices laughing and sometimes yelling. He hears whispers right next to his ear. The whispers have the smell of camas root. No, it is the sweetgrass perfume. Oh, something soft has touched his lips. He reaches out for it but it is gone. What was that? Voom! A scene opens up below; Ahhatome finds himself in a tree. He has no form.

The tree speaks. "You might get more insight if you turn yourself into a bird form so you can fly around and observe from different angles," says a familiar voice. "No, not that! Too obvious!"

"I like my snowy white owl form. I use it all the time."

"You are causing a disruption in the transmission. See how the children are squinting at you in disbelief? It's summer. The snowy white owl doesn't belong in this scene. You are here only to observe, not to cause a disturbance."

Changing his form to a small unobtrusive meadow songbird, Ahhatome looks down on three beautiful Indian children, two boys and a lovely little girl. They are running and splashing at the water's edge of a small lake surrounded by a pungent cedar forest. The laughing is contagious. Ahhatome spreads his wings in preparation to fly down to join the fun, but is stopped by the unexpected movement of a single twig on the mysterious tree.

The tree speaks again. "You may choose another observation point if you wish, but keep your distance. Do you see that taller young boy near the girl? He is you in a previous third dimensional experience. Notice a pink glowing extension of light passing back and forth from heart to heart between you as the tall boy and the girl? This is a normal interaction cord. It is not dark colored and it has no hook. This simply indicates that the two of them have a healthy joyful bond, common between happy children at play."

Ahhatome stares at the handsome youngster. "That boy is or was me?" Then the sharp point of something catches his eye. The child that was pointed out to him is wearing a necklace containing a single bear claw. Ahhatome sometimes imagines that his totem power animal is a bear.

"His, or your parents in that life, were both killed by a marauding bear," speaks the tree telepathically. As this sad thought sinks in a single wave of sympathy for the boy who was himself sweeps over his little bird body. The scene before him starts to swell and flow into a wave too, then into a quivering big bubble that explodes and disappears, taking the entire scene with it.

"Oh no!" exclaims Ahhatome.

"What did I tell you?" It's Libris in his regular eyeball garment again and the two of them are standing alone in the dark. "Control your emotions or you disturb the atmosphere of The Record into the unreadable. You forgot your deep breathing!

"Now The Records have answered your question. You have witnessed the source person of your hook, but you did not yet actually see a hook, correct? So, by further refining the one question, what would your next question be for The Records?"

"Okay, I get it Libris. My next question is when and where did that happy pink cord of heart-to-heart exchange become a hook?"

"Don't ask me," says Libris, abruptly turning Ahhatome toward the swirling black energy now appearing, "Ask The Records." No sooner had Ahhatome turned toward the swiftly rotating inky hole, prepared to ask again his more specific question, when Zoom. More quickly than the first time, he is catapulted into another scene. In this new past life episode, his pretty little friend stands near him. They are at the lake, or perhaps a different one; Ahhatome cannot be sure. Ahhatome again chooses to be a little bird, this time a chickadee.

"Your name is Little Bear in this life," says a voice from the bull rush where Ahhatome's bird form sits. "Her name is Sings To Flowers." In this particular scene both the boy's and the girl's eyes are glassy and red. "A whole lot of crying is going on here," announces the bull rush. "Sings To Flowers is about to be given in marriage to an older man close to seven times her age."

Ahhatome watches as Little Bear gives Sings To Flowers his beautiful bow and arrows for her to keep as remembrances of their most happy times. There is the quiver painted with the familiar white lightning bolts and the bow. There are the arrows with the familiar wraps, three wraps of yellow, four wraps of red, and twelve wraps of black.

"There it is," says the bull rush. As Little Bear sadly and with slumped shoulders turns away from his dear beloved, Sings To Flowers' hand reaches out toward his back but cannot reach far enough to touch him. Believing that she will never see him again, a rush of energy pours forth from her heart to his heart through his back and sets the hook. As he walks away, never looking back that she might see him sobbing, the cord shimmers and shakes and stretches, but does not break.

The bull rush is saying, "Breathe. Breathe deeply."

CHAPTER EIGHTEEN

Lost in The Records

Ahhatome has his hand over his front heart-center and is breathing deeply. "Libris, there is something I do not understand. The cord with the hook that I saw placed by little Sings To Flowers was made up of bright rose-pink light with bands of pure white and gold, like the colors of a radiant sunrise. Also the light of her cord was very stretchy and elastic, whereas the cord stuck in me now seems thick and stiff and not nearly as bright. It still has the beautiful rose-pink streaks, but they seem thinner and the clear colors are accompanied by wide strips of gray and an ugly deoxygenated bloody red. In fact, the more unattractive gray tones dull down the other colors.

"I dearly loved Sings To Flowers in that life. I have passionate feelings for her still . . . even stronger. But this cord. It pulls and drags. No blame . . . I see us both as innocent."

"Sometimes we have to examine ourselves by going down into the darker colors of our being in order to ascend higher with the more refined light of compassion." While Libris speaks he sounds breathy, as though trying to breathe for Ahhatome with slow, deep breaths, perhaps hoping that Ahhatome will mimic him. I think Ahhatome will need more than deep breaths on this journey.

"Your cord is a tool for learning, a path of tenderness and knowledge expansion, but it's up to you to keep it tender. You needn't be in a quandary either. Someday you will be amused at your present thoughts about all this. So let me ask you, what would your next defining question be about the subject you have chosen to examine in The Records?"

Ahhatome sighs. "Well . . . I think I would like to see how it is from observing inside myself."

"Okaaaaay . . . This way of looking gives a different, more narrowly focused perspective; also when looking from inside it is harder to control your emotions. However you did get through this last read with minimal control. If you choose the inside-your-person way of viewing you will be privy to your private thoughts and feelings of that moment in your history, but what others are thinking may not be so clear because your own internal voice will be so loud.

"How's your proficiency in aura interpretation? That's one way where you can clearly read the emotions of another. Actually, maybe it doesn't matter. After all, you certainly weren't proficient in aura reading back then. Okay, it will be more tricky, but let's do it."

Ahhatome is overconfident. He forgets too much pride can be dangerous and figures he has the routine down. He turns, brimming with enthusiasm toward the spiraling blackness and says, "Records, I would like to view from within my previous body the point at which my heart cord became thicker and . . . well, dirtier." Then, to Libris' horror, he adds, "and you can be snappy about it."

He turns to where Libris was standing a moment ago, planning to give him the I've-got-this-game-down wink, but Libris is gone. Instead, a voice comes from inside the necklace of many bear claws he feels hanging heavily around his neck, while to his delight a new happy view opens to him. Ahhatome, now inside a beautiful well-muscled mature young body, is parting the last of a thicket of huckleberries in order to enter a small clearing where the lovely nineteen-summers Sings To Flowers is greeting him with a smile of enchantment and out-stretched arms. The bear claws around his neck are talking with Libris' voice and are saying, "Your name is no longer Little Bear. It is Two Bears."

"Two Bears? Since when?"

Immediately, over the exquisite head of Sings To Flowers appears another rotating black hole. Inside it are two bears. They are being propelled around and around by some magical force where each bear is chasing the tail of the other bear in an otherwise dark swirling void.

Too late. The warning voice from within the necklace of bear claws is yelling, "Don't go there. Off the path. Side road seducing you. Breathe," but it is being ignored. Little Bear/Two Bears and his consciousness is being shot into a side-trip about bears.

I hope Libris can bring him back. It will be difficult, especially since this is Ahhatom's first read from the internal viewing perspective, which feels so much more personal.

Being pulled down a new dark tube where he had seen the two bears, Ahhatome hears sniffing and snorting about his ears and at his back; he feels hot breath but he cannot see anything. He reminds himself to do deep breathing. He feels for his bear claws necklace from where Libris had spoken to him but moments ago. *Oh no! It's not there! Where has Libris gone?* He is telling himself to do deep breathing and is really concentrating on that now. Then all is quiet while the ride becomes silky smooth. Ahhatome tries to relax.

Ultimately he comes into more light and discovers that he is inside the skin of Little Bear of about seventeen winters, but with the necklace of only one bear claw instead of the many-claws necklace. The scene is becoming clear. He is marching off to hunt alone. He was to meet Coyote Head for this adventure, but Coyote Head has a habit of sleeping late after one of his nights of trickery.

Last night's trick included pushing a young colt who had never been separated from his mother into a teepee of sleeping Indians. The crying colt inside—hearing his braying mother outside—ran in circles, upturning everything into flying projectiles. The whole affair had created the most wonderful chaos, accompanied by women's screams, all to the delight of Coyote Head—who now is either sleeping from exhaustion or is in big trouble as usual. Little Bear did not wait to find out, but left for his adventure on his own.

Little Bear makes better bows and arrows now. He has a fine

spear made from strong dense wood. It has taken over a year to produce these hunting tools and he's ready to put them to the test. He has vowed to revenge the death of his parents, caused by the crazy marauding bear. At the same time he reminds himself that the bear people are also his brothers.

The air is clear and spicy with the smell of autumn leaves after a rain. An occasional drip is falling from the golden leaves still hanging onto their branches, down to the clouds of rustling gold on the ground. Soon the bears will be ready to hibernate. The bears should be fatter now, but a smart warrior must not trick himself into thinking that a little fat will slow a bear down. Little Bear is intent on singing his bear song to awaken The Bear Spirit. He plans to plunge his spear into the heart of the animal and then perhaps he will be honored by the dead bear's spirit as his power animal. *Wise and strong, Bear People you are wise and strong beyond other animals. I seek only to avenge my parents. Please honor me with your wisdom and strength.*

If he is successful he will be declared a great hunter and perhaps receive a new name that will proclaim him a protector of his tribe. He has no thought that he might be severely wounded, or worse, die and not return to his people. Unfortunately this sometimes happens to young men during their transformation test into full manhood. But today Little Bear's heart is filled with high expectations and song.

His goal is to climb up into the foothills in an area where he had seen the bark of cedar trees shredded by bear families in the habit of sharpening their claws there. *Evidence of Brother Bear,* he had said to himself.

Arriving and looking at the bear-marked trees, he is awestruck. They display their bear evidence, like great wounded forest beings silently crying for justice. Little Bear had forgotten how high up the tree trunks the claw marks start. Some small saplings near the larger trees have been crushed flat. *These bears are big!*

Little Bear cancels the idea of settling down under one of these scarred trees. *Too obvious. I must surprise them.*

He is considering digging a deep bear pit, cutting multiple branches with sharpened ends for stout spears and planting them in the ground at the bottom of the pit, with sharp points up. Then he will cover his deep-pit trap with cedar branches. The unwary bear who makes the mistake of stepping there will fall through to a whole lot of pain and trouble. But . . . this is a project of several day's work. *Why didn't I wait for Coyote Head?* He remembers his father's words. *Impatience is the father to rash judgments and big mistakes.*

Little Bear circles the bear-marked trees, looking for the best spot to build his trap. Everywhere looks okay, but nothing strikes him as the perfect spot. Then it dawns on him. Why not build it on the trail just as it opens out into the clearing with the bear-damaged trees? He finds the spot. Taking his spear point he marks off an elongated box at the widest part of the trail. *I don't want it too wide or too narrow,* he is thinking. *Wait.* Little Bear stands still with all his senses amplified. *It sounds like rocks sliding down and off the mountain trail . . . behind me. Are the rocks falling spontaneously or is an animal coming?* Again he hears noises. *It's a large animal!*

He jumps, trying to disappear into the bushes at the side of his marked-off rectangle, and crouches down low. Yipes! The Earth is shaking, now crashing, crunching, and more rolling stones escape down the mountain under what could be only a mighty being's feet. These Earth movements are companioned with sounds of huffing, sniffing, snorting, grunting, and groaning. Something **smells** of bear.

Whew! He is close and he smells.

Little Bear makes not a move in his hiding place and tries to be even quieter by holding his breath. "Do not hold your breath," is the silent demand heard in Ahhatome's head from Little Bear's one-claw necklace.

There he is. A gray-shouldered granddaddy of a grizzly. Now the giant rears up on his hind legs to sniff the air and is standing dead center on Little Bear's marked off box space for his planned trap. *I hope the air up there is different from where I am,* thinks Little Bear.

While not moving a muscle, he tries to determine if he is up or down wind of the big creature. He knows that bears have relatively poor eyesight, but superior smelling apparatus. The beast is two feet from Little Bear, who can plainly see the deadly hind claws that look **way too long**. While Ahhatome is trying to remember to breathe deeply, Little Bear is crying to The Sun.

Have pity on me Sun, Earth, and Moon Mother. I am good. I have danced the Piercing Ceremony in your honor when I was only ten winters. I cry now for delivery from injury and death. I am pure and have not touched deeply or slept with a woman yet. Have pity on me. Then Little Bear remembers that he has had naughty dreams about the now married Sings To Flowers. *Except that I have had one . . . or a . . . two . . . maybe just a very little more of dreams and thoughts about Sings To Flowers, but I have stopped that.*

"Leave this body. Take small bird form. Bird form now!" The command is from Libris. Two small bird forms, Libris and Ahhatome, fly out of the bushes. The rush of little wings and the rustle of leaves catch the corner of the eye of the big grizzly.

Simultaneously, a female grizzly walks into open ground around the scratching trees from the other side of the clearing. This is what the big guy was sniffing in the wind. The presence of the female bear causes just enough distracted hesitation in the male animal to give Little Bear a second or two to roll out of the way as the full weight of the mammoth bear's two front legs come crashing down, crushing the spot where moments before Little Bear lay in hiding. He misses Little Bear, all but for one claw that pierces the side of his left foot.

Ahhatome, now viewing with Libris from inside a bird form in a tree above the scene, is not sure if it is he or Little Bear that fills the air with a harrowing scream. The whole scene begins to shimmer violently and is on the verge of breaking up and disappearing until Ahhatome squeezes shut his little bird eyes and breaths deeply for several breaths.

Finally the viewing becomes stabilized, but not the scene below.

Little Bear appears out cold and has tumbled down the mountain about ten feet to where an old log has stopped his rolling. The smell of blood encourages the bear to plunge down after him, but behind the first bear comes a second one, up the trail on the scent of the female. The second bear appears younger, moves more quickly, and is leaner. The female bear appears nonchalant about the whole matter. Turning a bored shoulder to her suitors, she saunters off in the opposite direction, not wanting to be disturbed by any commotion.

The younger male challenger bear's jaws grab the first bear by his left back foot and, shaking his head violently, tears the flesh to ribbons. Bears have superior jaw power among land predators and the crunch of bones echoes through the forest. The left foot of the old grizzly is hanging by a tendon and a fight to the death begins.

The second bear rears and plunges his weight onto the first bear, who is already down on his back. More bones crush in the rib area, giving the first bear's lungs multiple punctures and causing blood to spew out his mouth. Somehow he manages to curl his back tightly and thrust his head uphill enough to grab the muzzle of the second bear and smash it to mush with all the bone-grinding strength he has left in him while he goes for the throat of his opponent with his front claws, ripping a deep gash in the carotid of the younger one. It's a lucky strike from the old grizzly, but before the young one bleeds out he is able to rip a hole in the chest of the old bear, taking fur, fat, muscle, and ribs, and exposing the beating heart.

All is quiet. Ahhatome, still with his deep breaths, opens his eyes only to two little bird slits. Even Libris' bird form has closed eyes. Little Bear begins stirring under a pile of stones, dirt, and branches that have rolled down on top of him from the desperate fight above. Nobody can believe their eyes.

After listening to the silence, with the help of his spear Little Bear struggles with his wounded foot up the mountainside to examine, as you might say, the grizzly scene. There is a lake of blood in which the two entangled bears rest. There are torn branches and uprooted small trees splattered with blood and bear tissue.

Are these bears really dead? Little Bear pokes them with his spear. Nothing moves. Wait. Something catches his eye. The dead-looking bear with an open chest has a heart still trying to beat. Without hesitation Little Bear plunges his spear into that pulsing target. It is now without motion. It will beat no more.

Next Little Bear finds a large sharp stone and asks the stone for permission to move it. He hurries too fast to wait for an answer and plunges the stone into the neck wound of the second bear, "to feed my people," he adds, then examines the carcasses.

Libris and Ahhatome are coming down out of their tree for a closer look too. Both have forgotten the concentration it takes to keep their bird forms and are accidentally relaxing into their somewhat humanoid shapes. Their shapes will not be seen well by untrained third-dimensional eyes. They will, however, be seen as two large glowing lights.

Little Bear feels the warmth of light on his shoulders, and turning sees two lights and thinks they are the spirits of the bears just killed. Falling to his knees, "Bear Spirits, you do me great honor. Your flesh will feed hungry people. Your coat will be our coat in winter. I am thankful to you and to the Sun who has delivered me from certain death. I will ask that two bear claws instead of willow twigs pierce my chest at the next Okan. Will you honor me with the power of your spirit medicine?"

Ahhatome looks at Libris and mentally asks, "How do you handle something like this? He is praying to us! He is me sometime back in a previous incarnation, and therefore he already is my spirit. He doesn't know that of course, and thinks I am a bear spirit. When he talks to me, he talks to himself in the future!"

"You cannot explain anything to him beyond his belief system. He will not hear you and the functionality of his mind is yet, dare I say it, more primitive. Not because he is a Native. No. No. In many ways these ancient ones are more enlightened than present day third dimensionals. As we have already seen, He Who Is You will learn more someday. In this scene Little Bear's perspective is too limited. And of course, there are even greater perspectives than ours."

"So what do we do? He That Is Me looks at us with beseeching eyes."

"Bow and touch the top of his head with your hand and send him a loving thought. It will make him feel better and his foot will hurt less and heal faster under his own spirit power. We must live with the fact that beliefs at this stage of development about what is presumed to be the intangible are somewhat mixed up in this world and the fact that things are not always what they seem is not always comprehended."

Who comes now? Ah, it is Coyote Head on a horse.

"You're late, Coyote Head."

"I was looking for a horse!" is his reply. "I yi yi. Did you kill two bears?"

"What does it look like?" says Little Bear. Ahhatome and Libris look at each other. They quickly retreat into small bird forms again, after giving Little Bear their blessing.

"I thought I saw two spirit ghost lights too! It looks like, by some very powerful medicine, you have killed two bears! I can hardly believe what I plainly see before my eyes."

"I can hardly believe it either, Coyote Head."

CHAPTER NINETEEN

If by Any Other Name Were Called

Never had there been such excitement as when the men from the nearest Blackfoot camp were called as witnesses to the scene where two bears were killed and to help bring the bears down from the mountain with ceremony for all to see. Around the council fires and late into the night, Little Bear is begged again and again to tell one more time how he alone had killed not one, but two bears in a mighty struggle that left the earth scarred, two bears torn apart, and the mighty hunter with only a minor wound to his left foot. Each time the story is repeated, no matter who is doing the telling, it becomes more fantastic. Now it is said that Little Bear commands The Star Bear in the night sky and that The Creator speaks to Little Bear and gives him command over all the bears walking our Earth Mother.

Soon the elders proclaim that from henceforth Little Bear shall be called by a name that such a powerful and mighty hunter deserves. He shall be called Kills Two Bears in One Day and will wear the necklace of many claws. The legend behind the name will be told amongst the people generation after generation. But Kills Two Bears in One Day, from the first moment of receiving his new name, is uncomfortable. After keeping the name for one cycle of the moon Kills Two Bears in One Day asks the elders if he can simply be called Two Bears. When the news of his new final name is spread about his fame becomes even greater. The people say, "Never will there be such a great hunter with such vast humility."

Dear God! I, The Wind, proclaim this. Some names are hard to live up to. Especially if you believe your name is famous but was bastardly begotten.

Libris and Ahhatome are sitting again on Libris' recliners—a good place to mull things over and watch the reaction of the glowing eyes in the dark from their talking.

"Who knows about the unseen forces, especially if your own awareness is diminished by observing from the third dimension," says Libris. "In the fifth dimension we know more about how energy flows and how to control it. From our perspective, Little Bear unleashed universal energies stored up from years of grieving for his killed parents. His singing and unwavering joyful attitude as he went forth to meet his destiny was his energy shield of protection. These combined energies helped design his happy outcome. So, with the energies directed thusly, who is to say he did not at that moment command the force of the bear constellation?"

"Do you think there is an entity at the highest and widest dimension that knows everything?" Ahhatome asks.

"I don't even know if there is a 'highest' or 'widest,' Ahhatome. That question is still too big for me."

Murmurs and whispers are heard in the depths of the surrounding dark. These voices talk to The Wind, who understands them. They have opinions about this conversation too. Unfortunately, because Little Bear was not aware of how energy or spirit works, he carried for the remainder of that life the burden of guilt at the mere mention of his full name, Kills Two Bears in One Day.

"It all comes back to what we talked about earlier," says Ahhatome. "Where is the truth? It depends on from what perspective you are looking. That's why one entity's truth is not the same as another one's. We in the fifth dimension see him as a hero, masterly—yet somewhat unknowingly—directing his personal energies and the laws concerning universal energies. But from the third dimension some might look at him as a liar and fabricator of stories."

Libris is laughing. "Yes. And have you forgotten that the 'him' you are speaking about is you? It points out another thing too—that from the higher perspectives there is less and less judgment. And when in a lower dimension we learn to discriminate without severe judgments and damnation; it helps us grow spiritually toward the goal of graduating to a wider field of being. Big events in your life are driven by your karma. Most people think of karma as an eye for an eye; you reap what you sow. That is the smaller vision. The law of karma is about how you handle the energy in an event driven by karma."

"There is something else I do not understand, Libris. You clearly stated that we should not interfere or interact with anything or anyone in The Records. But we did interfere when Little Bear and Coyote Head thought they saw two bear spirits. They saw us, albeit to a limited degree, and then we interacted with them after losing control of our bird forms."

"Yes we did. And here is where my own knowledge gets fuzzy, or should I say feathery? You challenge your helper/teacher/record keeper," smiles Libris. "I know of cases where a prayer made from the third dimension concerning an event that has already occurred there helps alter that past event to some degree. Whether it is a hole in the fabric of Earth time or a bleeding through from a twin or parallel universe, I do not know. I do know that such interference is the prerogative of much more advanced and expanded beings. At a higher level, the past, present and future exist even more closely than they do in the fifth dimension, but I do not yet know how to direct such an exalted energy or spirit. I do know, however, that on the trip back from the lower dimensions to the Heart of Creation it is the goal of The Universe that we become aware, expand our powers of discrimination, and master the direction we choose to send our personal inner essence.

"This is a most difficult lesson. And when slightly more aware beings impinge upon the perception of lower dimensional beings—

such as those in the third dimension—the more-asleep beings tend to externalize the miracles as outside themselves. The miracles perceived on the outside are mostly reflections generated from a programmed inside. However, I don't think we did Little Bear great harm. After all, you made it to the fifth dimension. So we helped confirm his belief in bear spirits. Well, after all, there is a little bit of the spirit of the bear in all of us. Looking at you now, I cannot say that we did you too much wrong." The heads behind the eyes in the cave are nodding in agreement.

"Before I went off on a side trip to see the bears I was about to view a romantic scene from inside my previous body when I was young and handsome and when I had my big bear necklace. I would like to go back to that record."

Libris' third eye opens a crack and snaps shut as though he was trying to view something he didn't want to see. "Getting back to the exact page is tricky," he says, rubbing his third eye place. "There are multiple scenes that can explain your request. Can you remember exactly what you asked just prior to that reading? And, by the way, I would like to suggest you don't command The Records with 'and be snappy about it.' When The Records get 'snappy,' don't expect them to give you the best scene for your mission. I always give them respect, Ahhatome, respect."

CHAPTER TWENTY

How Can Love Come to This?

"I don't think I can remember the exact words I used when I entered into that romantic love scene just beyond the berry bushes." But before Libris can tell him that he can read in The Records for the exactness of his previous request, Ahhatome is already telling the swirling darkness, "Take me to where my back heart hook cord became the thickest and darkest."

Libris' fading voice from off in the distance is saying, "I don't think those are quite the same words you used before. What is your point of viewing?" "Ahhatome!"

Too late. Ahhatome is already deep into the Akashic Records. He feels himself within a dark scene moving upward and as the scene unfolds, instead of it filling with light it remains dim. He feels for his heavy bear claws necklace, but there is nothing. Peering through the dark he realizes that he is near the top of a mountain. A skinny new moon slides out for an instant, only to disappear behind heavy soot-choked clouds from a nearby wildfire lower down.

In this record I, The Wind, and a stinging dirty rain are dancing a dark fire dance. I shove The Rain sideways while blasting the steaming smoke faster and faster across the moon's face and whipping the branches of tree after tree like the skirts of whirling dervishes. There are lightning flashes, followed by silence. Then Ahhatome realizes that the lightning flashes move and project a light on the ground exactly where and when he moves. The flashes are coming from him!

What is this? Now what?

When the light flashes he sees an old bent-over clay-colored woman with long hair escaping her braids and whipping about her by my blowing force. The crone seems unaware or unconcerned about the odd source of light, probably assuming that it is just distant flashes of lightning. Ahhatome decides to take the form of a tree in hopes that it will dim down his own light, which may be disturbing the scene. The light does dim some, but either way the withered woman pays no notice to anything. But she wails. She screams. She swears.

She is a wild vessel, completely out of control of her spirit. She does not know that her energies beckon me to blow her gray tresses straight out from her head and into twists that remind me of one of the most feared among the Greeks, the woman who suffered the wrath of the goddess Athena and was turned into the hideous gorgon, the deadly Medusa. The snake-headed Medusa delighted in turning her would-be lovers into stone.

Even if I gaze at her only briefly I begin to feel miserably locked up inside and heavy with weight, Ahhatome thinks. Now the old thing below takes out a knife and strikes the bosom of Mother Earth over and over and over, screaming, "Why, Why, Why?"

Ahhatome, who can see energetically, sees splashes of dirty brown-red muck-colored energy hit Our Mother and splash onto the crone's Medusa-like face and body. With every word she utters a slimy looking puke-green energy light drips from her mouth and from teeth whose etheric envelopes have elongated into fangs. Her breath smells of the essence of putrid decay. She does not look human after delivering those awful blows.

Now the fiend stands with her bony fist toward the sky and punches at the heavens as if she could punch out the stars, if there were any to be seen this night. Out of her head streams lightning bolts of energy, the deepest color of dead blood. She now bends to the Earth again and pulls up chunks of growing things with dirt clods attached. With these in both hands, she spins herself into a mini cyclone and hurls dirt clods, roots, stones, and plants into the air while screaming, "Two Bears, Two Bears, why have you abandoned me?"

Shocked by this loathsome display, crowned by the mention of his name, Ahhatome loses grip of his tree form and begins to slip into the formless while receiving a searing pain in his heart as the dirt clods hit him in the back, causing him to lose his concentration altogether. He is no longer joined with the tree spirit and falls to the ground. His heart cord has become thick and dirty.

Now Ahhatome groans. The Earth shutters. This scene is gone. Thank God.

CHAPTER TWENTY-ONE

My Beloved

Ahhatome is trying to stretch his mind to understand this scene when he finds himself lying on his back in the cave of many eyes. "What repugnant thing was that?" he asks of Libris, who is now hovering over him. "How did I get so far off track? What did that hideous scene have to do with me and why did I feel pain? I think I still feel it even now."

Libris helps Ahhatome stand erect and says, "Look at your cord, Ahhatome."

"Ahh! It's thicker than a two-hundred-year-old tree trunk and full of mud."

"At the time of that mad scene, you as Two Bears were already dead many Earth years. You no longer had your dense physical body, which offered a slow-down of all incoming vibrations and a slight insulating layer to electromagnetic, light, and sound energy. You see the so-called dead are more alive in their sensitivity to the energy of words spoken about them and prayers sent to and for them. Sending dark energy from the third to the fifth dimension happens all the time.

"The First Nation Peoples were aware of the impact of words upon their dead and spoke of their ancestors with only the greatest respect. They were taught to walk softly on the Earth, believing that they walk upon the faces of all their relations.

"For a First Nation woman to stab her Earth-Mother with such anger is to stab her own ancestors. Madness. And while she was stabbing and yelling out your name, she was stabbing your soul. The aged Sings To Flowers wandered the woods screaming at her hallucinations while the rest of the tribe avoided that frightening wild woman and left her to die alone not far from where you left your bones on the same mountain.

"Ahhatome, remember this. She is a part of you on the soul level. You especially made yourself vulnerable by viewing this scene without form, making yourself more susceptible to the impact of her energy. In that moment you were a naked soul. Vulnerable.

"All this 'mud' in your cord, as you call it, is augmented by your own increased attention and emotional reaction to that particular scene in The Records. But Ahhatome, do you recall what you asked for? You wanted to know the moment when your cord became the most thick and dirty.

"By the way, you can get out of a read of a bad scene instantly by saying 'cancel.' However, reading the so-called bad scenes in your lifetimes usually offers a platform for the most understanding and growth."

"It is good to know I can cancel the read of a bad scene, and I remember what I asked The Records, but I still don't believe that monster was Sings To Flowers."

"Ahhatome, think about it! Who set the hook in your back in the first place? Who has the power to thicken it beside yourself? That was her. Deranged. You read the scene where she was having one of many nights of releasing energy from years of pent up agony over what she perceived to be the permanent loss of your love."

Ahhatome is stunned into silence. Finally, after a long time, he says turning to The Records, "I want to see my beloved, Sings To Flowers, immediately."

The Records are responding, but not in the usual way where the reader can enter the scene as he reads it. The Wind wants to scream at Ahhatome that his request was again demanding of speed and not specific enough. Why cannot he remember the reading rules?

Instead of an organized scene he is presented with a dizzying array of flash pictures that seem to give background to the time from Little Bear's giving of his toy gifts to well after he becomes the holder of the new elevated name, Two Bears. One of the pictures shows Sings To Flowers' father, Hunting Elk, dying peacefully in his sleep soon after her marriage to Comes Still Alive.

The flash pictures also show how difficult it was for Sings To Flowers and Little Bear/Two Bears to communicate. The pictures leave no doubt that Sings To Flowers now belongs exclusively to the old warrior, Comes Still Alive.

It was not uncommon for new brides to become desperately homesick. At least Sings To Flowers' love-of-her-heart and her dear brother were nearby and therefore she was blessed with the knowledge that they were well, even if she could not speak to them. Also, she could hear and savor the stories of the great hunter, Two Bears.

With such tight social rules about speaking, it was common for the young men and women to contact each other with glances from their eyes. With only this means of communication, young men and women become masters of eye messages. The Wind is fascinated too by powerful human eye energy.

Little Bear/Two Bears and Sings To Flowers developed their own eye-glance language. The problem was that there were always other mature eyes watching where the young people's eyes were looking. If the people did not approve of a couple, steps were taken to separate the would-be lovers, including banishment of the male in question from the tribe.

For a married woman to take a lover was a life-threatening risk, or at the least a risk of permanent disfigurement so that any future suitors would find her unattractive. Sometimes a repentant woman would disfigure herself. There was also a psychological test of her fidelity. A wife lived under the knowledge that her husband could at any time request her to sponsor the Okan, where The Sun would punish a lying wife with death. Yet the aching of the human heart for love and the surging of the hormones of procreation allowed momentary forgetfulness of all risks.

Sings To Flowers and Little Bear/Two Bears had a secret language. It took them years to develop their language under the watchful eyes of the grandmothers. One wonders if deep down these old ones were jealous of the beauty and enthusiasm of youth while wielding their power by means of the strict enforcement of society's rules.

For the first few years after her marriage neither Little Bear nor Sings to Flowers dared to look at each other. To the advanced seer this avoidance was an obvious signal. Later, as time progressed and Sings To Flowers became more mature and relaxed in her role as a wife, she did not try to avoid a glance or two at Two Bears, especially after the saga of the killing of the bears. Everyone looked at Two Bears with adoring eyes after that and she could sneak a slightly prolonged glace at him without suspicion. However, there was only one set of eyes that ever registered with Two Bears.

Gradually, carefully, eye signals were developed between the two lovers that only they could interpret. This took great patience and was also a source of both frustration and a kind of game.

Two Bears, on the nights when the men recounted their stories around the fire, had the habit of lifting his eyes upward when he spoke the word "mountain" and at the word "valley" he would swoop his gaze from midline then down and up again. Sings To Flowers took the risk that others might see her mimic his eye movements when he spoke and suspect her of wrong doing. Two Bears tried always to avoid looking directly at Sings To Flowers. Their world seemed stuck . . . frozen until he finally caught on to her signal making.

Eventually, Two Bears realized that when Sings To Flowers made two intersecting folds with the end of her shoulder blanket, this meant, "Let's meet." Her eye movements would tell him on the mountain or in the valley, and wiping her eye as if to wipe a tear away meant by the river. He would answer back with the same eye movement and then she would stop her signaling.

But where exactly at the river or elsewhere was a problem. Finally both realized that eye movements alone were not specific enough. The next step was to bring a sprig of huckleberries or a flower from the lake's edge to pick at during story-telling—a hint as to where to meet.

"Sings To Flowers," yells old Bird Bone Pipe Woman one day over the roar of rushing river waters as they dipped their bison bladder bags into its chilly depths. "Why do you bring flowers and leaves to the lodge whenever Two Bears speaks?" The other women at the river look up to study Sings To Flowers and wait for her reply.

Splashing her face with chilly water in a desperate maneuver to fade its rushing red while thinking of something to say, Sings To Flowers finally responds, "It's my name. I am being true to my name. I was singing to the flowers and to my especially loved plants." Bird Bone Pipe Woman looks skeptical, but says no more. The other women go back to their chores. That incident effectively stopped Sings To Flowers from bringing any sprigs of anything to the lodge at story telling time, but she did not give up.

Next, Sings To Flowers tried dropping the flowers or twigs at Two Bears' feet when he was in camp. Unfortunately, the opportunity to do this was too infrequent. Once she gave a flower to a child and asked her to drop it at the feet of Two Bears. But instead of following the instructions the little girl ran up to Two Bears and gave him the flower while announcing, "Sings To Flowers wants me to give this to you." This caused Sings To Flowers' heart to pound and her breath to stop. She stayed away from anywhere those flowers grew for two full moons.

It was equally frustrating for Two Bears, who had to make sure not to have his constant companion, Coyote Head, tag along. Sometimes Two Bears would spend all day by the wrong huckleberry patch or clump of flowers at the edge of the wrong lake just to find Coyote Head looking for him there.

Ahhatome cannot take looking at these flashing pictures anymore and speaks the word "cancel." "This is just too frustrating," he says to Libris.

"Think how much more frustrating it was to be back there and living it, Ahhatome."

"I want to see the point in The Records that I was about to enter before my sidetrack into the two bears story," he says to Libris. But The Records must have thought he was speaking to it because . . . Swish.

He does not even remember the swirling lights or the unusual brightness of entering this chapter in The Records. Thankfully, he is again Two Bears and he is at last in the arms of his love in a tiny clearing in a patch of huckleberries. Neither speaks. They let their hands and the caresses of their lips do the speaking. This will be their first and only meeting where the lovers feel safe enough to express themselves to each other.

He kisses her eyes, her lips, her ears in a series of kisses from the lobe of her ear down the side of her neck and, opening her tunic, to her naked shoulder and up again to her ear and holds her head close to him and feels her breath come and go in faster little puffs against his chest. He presses with his hand on her back, bringing her bosom more tightly against him. Her breath is sweet and fragrant like the sweet honeysuckle that winds its vine around and through the huckleberry.

She clutches his back while one of her legs mimics the honeysuckle and wraps around him, causing them to tumble down, both of them giggling on the way to the soft moss under foot. Sings To Flowers is so moved that at first she is giggling, then weeping. Through tears of joy, Sings To Flowers tells him, "While bathing in preparation for my wedding I tried to drown myself."

He tells her, "I was the one who rescued you down river on that fateful day. I had just come out of the sweat lodge I had made for my piercing."

"But you were only ten winters then!" she exclaims, kissing his scars. "That was twelve summers ago when I felt big powerful arms pull me up out of the river."

"When I saw My Love about to die The Creator sent a mighty spirit to help me. I think it was the bear spirit who killed my mother and father who took pity on me that day and helped me rescue you. I had the strength of the mighty bear even though I was only ten winters. In that moment I had you to myself and in my arms again. I think, in a way, The Sun answered my cry... at least part of it."

"You still have the bear's mighty strength, My Beloved Two Bears," she murmurs as she traces her fingers over his eyebrow and down the side of his face.

Two Bears closes his eyes. "My eyes were muddied under the swirling waters. I grabbed at something down deep that kept wrapping around my wrists and thigh. At first I thought it was a whipping tangle of water plants that wouldn't let go of me. Then I saw something. It was perfect and delicate, but pale with too much blue. It looked like a beautiful shell or crescent moon when I pulled it up into the light. It transfixed me and I couldn't bring my eyes away from it until I realized that The Wind was gone from your body.

"Now when I sleep I have visions of that day when your ear showed itself to me in the wildness of your hair and I knew I had you."

To Bears leans closer to his beloved's ears and whispers to them. "You are **my** ears now. The Creator gave you to me on the day He turned you from blue back to the color of Life. No one else is allowed to touch what The Creator gave me... my two precious little moon shells."

He smiles and kisses her ears, her lips, her chin, and gives many more kisses down the front of her neck. His head goes now under her tunic while kissing, kissing, kissing in a straight line on her chest, down lower and lower as he goes to her cleavage with his tongue between two ample responding breasts.

"Two Bears. Two Bears, where are you? Are you up here picking huckleberries with the women?" comes a male voice that seems but thirty rabbit hops away.

The lovers freeze. "It's Coyote Head!" whispers the terrified Sings To Flowers. They hold their breath. Ahhatome starts to hold his breath too, until the picture begins to quiver and palpitate like Sings To Flowers' breasts—then he remembers to breathe.

Two Bears puts a finger softly over Sings To Flowers' mouth and presses his cheek next to hers. The two strain to stay motionless. "Two Bears!" cries the insistent voice, now about twenty rabbit hops away and coming straight for their little sanctuary . . . their secret, seconds from discovery!

Two Bears rises to his feet after grabbing a handful of berries out of Sings To Flowers' berry basket. Coyote Head does not see his sister lying on the mossy lover's carpet, trying to keep herself invisible. "I'm coming Coyote Head. You know I have a weakness for huckleberries, just like the bears." He is trying to smile but he has watery eyes and tries in vain to keep them hidden.

"Oh yes. A love of huckleberries," says Coyote Head, looking at and addressing the swollen lump in Two Bears' crotch.

"If you harm a woman by either your gossip speaking or your deliberate doing, I'll kill you," says Two Bears in a soft voice as he shares his handful of berries with Coyote Head.

"Any particular woman, Two Bears?"

"You hurt any woman in any way and you're dead."

CHAPTER TWENTY-TWO

What Happened to Two Bears and Sings to Flowers?

"Libris, I do not want to read anything more in The Records. My cord looks and feels even thicker and heavier than ever and I cannot figure out if I feel agitation, or despondency, or both. Where is Sings To Flowers **now**? I want to be with my beloved."

"You can answer your questions in The Records, Ahhatome."

"No, Libris. I am done with The Records. I don't want to look at any more **past** history."

I, The Wind, have watched Ahhatome since his arrival here. This is an extremely rare outburst from Ahhatome, and the emotional force of it pushes Libris back a good three feet.

"Ahhatome! Don't let an uncontrolled outburst of emotional energy smother what you want. You should know better than that as a fifth dimensional being."

"I'm sorry Libris, I'm not feeling balanced after just watching myself vow to kill my best friend and especially when, while viewing, I surprised myself by feeling justified in making that threat."

Ahhatome sits down, trying to calm his emotions with his hand over his solar plexus energy vortex and by breathing deeply. Libris is pacing back and forth in the abrupt heavy darkness enveloping them while the unblinking eyes in the cave walls follow the movements of Libris' walking. Wrinkles above The Keeper's brow are starting to form deep furrows as he stares upward at the inky ceiling. All the eyes on Libris' garment are closed, as if in deep thought.

Finally Libris begins speaking slowly as though he is reading The Records now. "After that scene in the huckleberry bushes with your lover, you never spoke to her again. You were terrified of Comes Still Alive's possible retribution upon Sings To Flowers or Coyote Head's possible acts of so-called family honor.

"An old shaman singled you out. The stories of the killing of the two bears had influenced his choice. He picked you for his shaman apprentice and you willingly went with him believing that The Creator had called you to do this work since The Creator was keeping you from the person of your obsession. You lived mostly apart from your people. You became violently ill. This near-death illness was accepted as the normal death and rebirth as a powerful shaman, which is a part of all shaman-making traditions. Through this illness it was assumed that the bear spirits had ripped the human spirit known as Two Bears into shreds until no form of that previous small self or ego remained.

"After giving in and allowing your spiritual death the power of spirit bears came forever alive in you. But there was another thing tearing at your heart that was not of any bears. It was your attachment to Sings To Flowers. That part of human yearning within you has never died.

"You developed the habit of wandering like a madman through the mountains. Sometimes you would do healing work for your people, but mostly you just wandered. One winter when there were almost daily threats of an avalanche, you climbed the drifts to purposely start a series of small ones in order to stop the mountain from burying the camp below. In so doing you were the one buried alive in a frozen white tomb. They never found your body. Your spirit wanted to be cooled off from the torment of your smoldering hot desires and you begged The Creator for rest from your anguish; and so it came to pass."

"I remember that now. I made myself miserable with longing and guilt."

"The other half of your soul was self-persecuted too. Ahhatome, I wish to show you three brief scenes."

"No. I've had enough."

"Indulge me, Ahhatome. Indulge me. Come."

Ahhatome watches Libris' breath become more visible and cloud his garment in stiff frosty film as the two are pulled, this time not into the usual darkened tunnel, but into a nose-stinging, frigid, tight, dirty-white, dense space. The walls of this cave begin to squeeze and give them the sense of being slammed through a funnel until reaching a sharp rock-hard end. Looking down they see a familiar face. The recognizable legs . . . the well-known arms are wedged in ice chunks. Two Bears has space only to move his head from side to side, but now it remains without motion.

This shadow of Ahhatome's former self has sprouted ice crystals around each nose hair and over his upper lip. Tiny beads of ice have cemented together the upper and lower eye lashes. Breath that in the past could thunder with conviction and purpose is now only visible to a seer into the fourth dimension. Only minutes ago his air had moved against the snow-wall four inches from his face, melting that rough surface, which seconds later froze again into a mirror where Two Bears could watch the formation of his own blue-gray death mask.

Ahhatome pries open a sealed lid. There is no sign of recognition in the eye. It is dull, dead, and non-functional. But as Ahhatome touches the body the last of its spirit leaps forward with talons and massive wings extended, beak open, and eyes piercing. The snowy white spirit-owl comes forward as if to melt into Ahhatome, but at the last moment it hesitates and soars through this ice sarcophagus.

"Come," says Libris, "we will follow it."

"No!"

"Ahhatome. Face this dark hour for your soul's growth." Interpreting Ahhatome's sighs for a weak yes, Libris leads on.

They follow the owl's path up into moonlight. There is a pause in several dustings of snow this night. Here it is peaceful. It is quiet. The stars twinkle and wink as stars should do. This is better.

"Where is that owl now?"

"Follow your intuition or take the easy way. Follow its light trail to that teepee yonder."

It takes no trick to ease through the skins of a teepee with a number of slumbering natives. Ahhatome's attention is drawn not to the owl spirit who is fanning a sleeping body, but to another whose teeth chatter and body shivers violently while she moans.

Two Guns Buffalo Calf awakens from the breeze of the spirit owl fanning to put fresh wood on the coals. This awakens Comes Still Alive, who pulls the shivering Sings To Flowers closer to him, but she shrugs him off. "Can't sleep," she says, rising naked from her bed after Two Guns Buffalo Calf falls back into hers. Comes Still Alive grunts and rolls over.

"I've seen this scene before," says Ahhatome.

"Well yes, you saw this scene Earth years ago as that snowy white owl-spirit hovering now over Sings To Flowers."

"She shouldn't go outside without any protection. Why is she doing that?"

"She craves for your soul."

"But . . . I am right beside her!"

"She still thinks of you as a body. Yet be assured a part of her feels your spirit around her. Her eyes are accustomed to looking for you toward the mountains." The spirit-owl sees this and is getting agitated. The more the spirit-owl is agitated, the more she becomes anxious.

Sings To Flowers is standing naked in snow to her knees. I, the Wind, try not to breathe against her goose-bumped nakedness while I feel her heart in shattered pain. She does not allow her mind to think that Two Bears may be dead even though she hears The Wind singing of it. Her eyes are following a sudden shaft of moonlight that has slipped away from a cloud to illuminate the spot on the mountain where the body of Two Bears rests in its white deathbed.

She is exhausted from her agony and her body can no longer express its tears. She is numb from feeling too much for too long and therefore is unaware of the frostbite on her toes. But worse than this, she is dis-spirited. With the longing of her heart and the looking of her eyes always to the mountains, she has cast off parts of her spirit energy to endlessly wander the mountains after Two Bears.

The soul doctors or shamans know that when a human casts off pieces of his soul openings to empty places are left in the body, making it vulnerable to invasion and mischief from lower fourth dimensional energies called elementals. Under the right circumstances they produce disorder, a plethora of diseases, and eventual death. Comes Still Alive calls the tiny spirit elementals of disintegration 'poison darts from past enemies killed,' modern man blames lack of vitamins, another energy form, and any number of reasons for the onset of disease."

"I think you are going to tell me that Sings To Flowers falls ill," sighs Ahhatome.

"Yes. Let's look at a final scene. It will be brief."

"If it is not brief I will make my visit to that scene so."

Sings To Flowers looks near death. The Wind believes that the burst of new spring energy from Mother Earth will have a healing effect. It has been two cycles of the moon since she has taken ill with fevers . . . alternating chills and sweats. She has been bathed in and made to drink a tea from juniper branches, roots, and fleshy cones. She eats little. Her face and chest energy is sunken and distorted. She labors to breathe and has a rumbling cough. Sometimes she spits sputum mixed with pus and blood.

A healer has been called many times. This night he dances in little hops, first on one foot and then on two, while a drummer strikes a monotonous rhythm. Finally, in his altered state he makes crowing noises and hammers the air with his rattles. He is calling his spirit power animal to help him. I, The Wind, see the power animal now. It is a glistening black crow who comes. The shaman's spirit and the crow dance together in circles around and around the semiconscious form of Sings To Flowers.

The shaman and his faithful helper become one entity in their swirling dance. They can see inside the body of Sings To Flowers. Ahhatome and Libris can see inside her body too. Around her heart are small moving black things. They move through her heart and her chest. They are in her veins and the smallest air pockets at the bottom of her lungs. The shaman/spirit crow comes close to Sings To Flowers and opens her tunic. He is going after those black things now. He sucks one out and spits it on the ground. It is upside down and on its belly is the unmistakable orange-tinged hourglass mark of the black widow. The shaman sucks it back up again and spits it into the fire. He sucks more this time . . . as much as his mouth can hold. He sucks and spits into the fire many black widows again and again from Sings To Flowers' front and back and from her heart. His face drips with sweat. At last he sits in a collapse. He is not happy. There remain many more spider spirits inside her. He calls out for more spirit animal healers.

A rush of wings is felt. Two beady eyes appear, then an open beak. The owl and the crow dive again and again at the spiders in Sings To Flowers' body until all fall exhausted upon Mother Earth. They are weeping in their exhaustion, while they feel their work is complete for now, until the next time. And lo, Sings To Flowers makes a recovery in her body with the return of spring but her mind does not recover.

"We will close this scene now," says Libris, "but I can tell you a little more.

"Sings To Flowers remained without child. Her heart was never in Comes Still Alive's bed and he knew it. At the hearing of Two Bears death, many days after the fact, she ran blindly into the woods as was her habit when anguished, but this time she never returned.

The timeworn and enraged Comes Still Alive stormed after her but was interrupted in the chase. A fat nest of mad hornets fell from above, splitting and spilling a swarm of tiny poison-pumping darts with wings. After feeling his anger reflected back upon him with over 100 stings, his heart stopped. I think The Wind deliberately delivered his demise. In some other reality he will learn that he was his own enemy who killed himself with poison darts. And so Sings To Flowers, like you as Two Bears, spent her last years in mindless want while wandering."

"Libris, I take it back what I said about The Records. I want to maintain my ability, such as it is, to navigate through it. I just don't wish to do it for a while. Could you check on Sings To Flowers for me? Where is she now?"

"First, you need to be the one to tell The Records you wish to become proficient and that you have no anger toward it. Speak for yourself.

"Second, during the earliest attempts at viewing, we all feel as you do. It can be overwhelming. You can see how easily someone can get caught up and lost without a guide to help navigate around the pit falls and potential traps.

"This is true of so many things in life, and it especially applies to spiritual practices where everything moves more quickly and powerfully. I have already checked on Your Love. I have steered myself around and through The Records so many times that at this point I can obtain information instantaneously. And to let you in on a secret, I myself feel the need to grow more and move on to a wider, more refined experience.

"Sings To Flowers is incarnate again in the third dimension. She is in a new body of almost eighteen summers... excuse me, eighteen Earth years, and in this incarnation she is again female. Only recently is she becoming somewhat aware of your past lives together. Her recollections are far dimmer, sometimes out of order, and as expected, not as clear as yours. Her information has been presented within dream consciousness, called by the name 'unconscious,' whereas you have the benefit of direct reading."

"How do I connect with her, Libris?"

"If you mean connect how I think you mean connect, that is impossible under the circumstances . . . not the kind of connection like humans do. No.

"Oh don't look so troubled. You might be able to connect with her here at the soul level, with permission from The Council, of course. A lot depends on how much soul energy she took with her to the third dimension this time, and the extent of her planned lessons, and how she is doing with them. Often they want the remaining soul-light left behind in the fifth dimension to be undisturbed. You can get an opinion from The Council. You can also connect briefly on the astral plane, in her dreams."

"Libris, stop! That just isn't good enough."

"Ahhatome, why do you insist on this? Such a small portion of her being is incarnate. Let her be. You don't need to confuse her natural evolution. Communicate with her on another level."

"She'll forget! The part of her that is incarnate won't remember!"

"Ahhatome, if you love her you will leave her alone. The part of her that does not die will remember. You know this!" The eyes on his garment are pinched together in a frown.

"How much torture can two separated souls take, Libris?"

Libris increases his volume, "You will not be allowed to mess up her evolution! You do not know the condition of her free will and you cannot tamper with it. You tamper with her, you tamper with yourself."

"Libris, I intend to find out, even if I have to take it to The High Council."

CHAPTER TWENTY-THREE

The Council Meets

The vast rotunda of focus where the hearings take place is concentrated in three football-field lengths in all directions with no palpable sidewalls and is completely filled with brilliant light generated by twelve Radiant Beings. The twelve elders act as a single filament for this Herculean-extended expanse. For the deliberations today the temporary arches created over the elders have a touch of familiarity to those who have walked the Earth planet. They have a hint of timeless Greco-Roman design.

Imagine such a space as this, where no microphones are needed, where no seat in the house is better than another. You can see and hear from everywhere within and the very atmosphere can act as a movie screen, but perfected to clarity beyond earthly imagination, showing objects from nanometer size without microscope to macrocosm size without telescope.

Here, feelings of those being examined can be felt and read without question of wrong interpretation. All colors, musical notes, and thought-forms from the subject are evident.

Into this arena will come pictures, records, holographs, sound waves both etheric and more substantive of all kinds, as well as visiting entities called upon to testify if need be. This is where all opinions will be considered and a recommendation finally made, but never forced upon the subject in question or any other entity.

To move against the final advice of The Council is to invite disaster, but is allowed unless it should destroy the very fabric of The

Multiverse. Personal or small group disasters would not come upon one because the council moves to punish, but simply because the All Knowing Ones can see more clearly the far-reaching effects of choosing willful disregard of their wise counsel in favor of an unwise action.

Above the head of each elder is his representative color, seen in delicate vibrations which are both one and two octaves more refined than his specific color of light. These ultra gossamer-like colors above their heads are arranged in multiple triangles, forming the sacred geometry of the star tetrahedron. The triangulation of their etheric DNA of their denser light bodies, as well as the overhead triangulated star light, provides instantaneous communication between the micro galaxies within and the macro galaxies without. Like Libris, each elder has a central eye.

Ahhatome is standing before the elders who are seated in a semicircle around him and under the etheric great arches, which reflect more light upon him. At his side is Libris, who has agreed to be his sponsor. Each Shining Elder has his compassionate eye focused on Ahhatome and Libris. They speak as one voice, while their lips remain without movement.

"We offer you compassion for the dilemma in which your divided soul finds itself, Ahhatome. We have reviewed The Records that you have read and more; we have felt the pain of your desire, and we have heard your prayers. We sent you Libris to help you remember the source of your cord and hook as a first step toward eventual removal of your suffering. There is an unrecognized part within you who wishes to keep this cord connection for now, and that is why the cord reestablishes itself after you take steps to remove it. The situation is complicated by the fact that you and your beloved are twin flames, a spiritual bond stronger than soul mates. A large part of your dear one's consciousness, which is actually a part of you, exists now in the third dimension."

"I am not sure I understand what you mean by 'twin flames,'" says Ahhatome softly with downcast eyes.

"You do not need to feel ashamed because you do not know or, more accurately, have forgotten. You are new to this experience of broader awareness. There is much for you and all of us to learn.

"Soul mates have a prearranged agreement with a member of their soul group for traveling together into a lower dimension. Soul mates have had several close relationships in previous incarnations and not necessarily as husband and wife. Their soul mate relationship could be a mother/son or a teacher/pupil relationship, where there is recognition of mutual understanding and the joy this recognition brings in the presence of the other.

"You see, speaking poetically, relationships are the alchemy and the crucible. When two souls are ready for such intense work it is one of the finest means of transmuting and burnishing the character of a third dimensional being from the proverbial base metal into gold."

"Why is that, if you do not mind me asking The Council?"

"We don't mind. Relationships are difficult because in the third dimension entities have great difficulty acting outside of their limited frame of reference and their egos create barriers. Most do not understand that one partner reflects as a mirror to the other. This brings up issues within the ego-self, which need to be healed and resolved. Simply put, this is hard work and all the meditation, chanting, and church going, though helpful in some cases, will not supplant the work that needs to be done within the self. If the one partner does not realize that the fault he sees in the other is only a reflection of his own shortcoming then problems will occur until he learns to see it as a gift of recognition as to where his own work needs to be done. The process of purification and transmutation can be lengthy and tiring.

"The genesis of twin flames came about as an experiment for more rapid soul evolution with the hope that in the final reunion of the two the Two In One could become an instrument for greater universal service. In the case of twin flames a soul chooses to divide into two parts, usually predominately male and predominately female, with the idea that the two working on the evolution of one may shorten or improve soul progress. The separated parts of the whole rarely incarnate together or on the same planet. However, should they chose to do so and should the separated parts meet while in dense physicality with their memory patterns diminished, and before each part has brought itself into balance between the male and female energies within itself—especially if the soul parts have much of the baser energies of greed, jealousy, and so forth to purge—the relationship problems between two such flames are multiplied beyond measure. Their attraction is irresistible. There will be fireworks if the two parts try to integrate prematurely while in density. In other words, to function well each part of the whole needs to be whole, as we see within the hologram format."

"So I am a part of the whole of one soul. And the other part of me feels attraction for me but has no idea how deep it goes, and only has partial memory of the whole affair while incarnate. This sounds like an impossible situation."

"Not if you do not tamper with the process and school yourself in the practice of patience. Your other half has had a difficult previous incarnation. She has tremendous work to raise her wave form to, or near, your level before you can safely meet without creating more karma that will need to be balanced. Paradoxically, the very thing that you wish to get rid of, the cord, can be used for this purpose. Send her your light of pure love. She will feel you in that energy. The conduit you use can be that cord. This will help to clean out the dark energies in it. It is the pulling hook and the weight of the dark energies that is less desirable, not the cord conduit itself. As you have been shown, the hook is set through the lower emotions of desperation, neediness, and survival fears.

"We will send your incarnate self, or Lily as she is now known, a helper should she choose to further her path of spiritual enlightenment. But we would strongly warn you to stay out of her dense space. You have not been adequately prepared to return to the third dimension while holding your wider consciousness. She has already felt a stirring of her kundalini energy, so although she is making strong forward strides in her spiritual growth, she is also very delicate. Her circuitry network is under expansion, leaving her vulnerable to harm from any sudden surges of energy.

"Again, we repeat, we do not recommend that you try to dim down your own light and reverse evolve, or try to visit your love in the third dimension even temporarily. It's too difficult and you do not have the proper training."

"What about my visiting the part of her soul light that remains here. May I at least visit that part of her?"

"The remaining part of Lily's soul light is in quietude, slumber, and rest in a purposely chosen different fifth dimension attention soul group than yours, until such time as her third dimensional "death" transformation. This is because she has a huge assignment in the third dimension of increasing her light there. Simply put, the part of her being in the fifth dimension should not be disturbed. You would serve both your purposes better by being still, quiet, and putting this whole affair to rest for now."

I wonder where her remaining soul energy is resting here? Ahhatome is asking himself in thought.

The Council answers his thought in loud unison. "Ahhatome, Be still and receive our blessing. We have given you our recommendation. This meeting has come to a close."

<hr />

"How did they know that I was planning to get myself down into the third dimension?" Ahhatome asks Libris after the meeting.

"Because they are Those Who Know. There are no secrets in the fifth dimension. It's not so bad, Ahhatome. You can watch her progress through The Records since her oversoul has given you permission to do so. I guess we know why permission was granted. Her soul and your soul are one."

Ahhatome continues to look skeptical. Obviously it was not the advice he wanted to hear. "Besides, you can talk with her in her dreams," continues Libris. "In the meantime, I suggest that you work on getting rid of your left over ego that is frustrated with the process and not enjoying the ride. In the end you will be united. It is guaranteed."

"Libris, do you know of any fifth dimensional entity that I can talk with who has had the experience of descending to lower dimensions?

"Ahhatome, please don't. It is a tricky navigation. For one thing, you must leave some of your light energy behind, and exactly how much is hard to figure out. If you take too much with you into the lower dimensions you can start fires and bleed-through holes in the delicate etheric Earth network, which at this point in time still offers a degree of protection for the Earth. That's another thing. You don't want to mess with that planet's evolution either.

"Also, if you take too little of your light with you to the lower dimensions you risk getting lost in the lower astral realm surrounding the Earth, or worse, stuck there and intimidated by beastly thought-forms that have populated that realm since any Earthling brain has been advanced enough, or maybe I should say unadvanced enough, to have fear thought-forms of one kind or another over the millennia."

"Do you know where I can get training, Libris?"

"Ahhatome, training is one thing, but there is a tendency in you, as demonstrated with your reading of The Records, that shows me that you think you know it all before you know or remember it. You must control that remaining ego fragment. There is a fine line between enthusiasm meaning to be filled with spirit and simple-minded loss of control. You need to pull back."

"You've lost the original jolly in your voice, Libris."

The Wind thinks that in every journey a man is required to play many parts, not all of them jolly.

Ahhatome is thinking to himself, *I wonder if Horus knows anything about descending or reverse evolution or whatever you label this stuff?*

"Ahhatome! Don't act like a monkey brain just because you think you remember having one!"

CHAPTER TWENTY-FOUR

Aba Ahhatome's Warning

Aba Ahhatome is looking away from Ahhatome to gaze through the portal near his favorite "thinking and creating chair," pulling on his chin and watching a star give birth to itself. "How many tormented twin-flame souls have been created?" he asks the firmament. "The torment is but a speck in the grand spectrum, but when half yourself still mostly slumbers and is only minimally aware . . . When one half sees more and the other half sees just enough to feel outside the company she keeps by believing in the illusion of separation, the more aware half feels the pain of both halves. I feel your pain too, Son. Believe me. Heaven and the angels weep for the torments of the unaware. In the darkest moment we can take comfort in the fact that nothing remains the same, not where there is Life . . . and certainly not where Life puts on the masquerade of death. I wonder if the seventh, eighth, and ninth dimension luminaries feel or even remember separation pain. As hard as it is to take, I feel that the recommendation of The Council is very wise. Earth beings are so . . . divided."

"Well, Father, I should fit right in."

Aba Ahhatome is now looking at his son as he sags into his thinking chair. "Don't joke, Son. In your case, a good part of you has evolved to the next step and the part that lags behind is making rapid progress. You do not want to interfere on Earth.

"Earth beings are such a divided house. It's not their fault. How often was the original population plan for Earth manipulated, destroyed, and rebuilt after much experimentation gone wrong? It was during those tumultuous times that humans were given the "knowledge of good and evil" . . . the belief in duality, the "us" and the "them." They see their world as left-right, up-down, under-over, male-female, you-me, good-bad, heaven-hell, rich-poor, master-slave, God-Devil. They are so emotionally attached to their belief in separation that they will fight each other to the death in order to preserve this third-dimensional belief, while not recognizing what they are really fighting about is ignorance and fear. Even within a single Earthling identity there can be a fight in the separated mind for dominance of one part of the mind over another part. Their polarized dueling dualities are endless. Even their physical brain is split in two.

"Fear is the undisputed cause of chaos, disharmony, sickness, and pain in their plane of being. Some of their leaders are mindful of this and use fear to control, manipulate, and dominate others, who, from our perspective, are the other parts of themselves. Why do they do this? Because the controllers themselves live in fear. They were created to be fearful. Fourth-dimensional low vibration entities use third-dimension fear vibration as a kind of food. It doesn't have to be that way."

Aba Ahhatome's usually smooth forehead is wrinkled with concern into a little peak of skin over his third eye, which is tightly shut as if not wanting to see further into the more primitive dimension he is discussing. "Ahhatome, can you say without hesitation that you are prepared to face third-dimensional chaotic energy and all its manifestations?"

"No, I cannot say that I am ready." Ahhatome is reaching for the star map of the dense physical plane and is sweeping his fingers across the Milky Way until his hand comes to a stop at a small blue speck, a planet with a single moon, the third from a star. "I just know where my heart is pulling me. Aba, Aba, I have memory of so much pain!" Ahhatome is striking his chest and solar plexus with his fist.

"It is that cord that pulls you. You have done good work cleaning it up with your loving energy but it is far from totally clear. It looks to me that the rest of the clearing needs to be done at her end. We have sent a teacher to guide her in this process. Luckily, she has asked for a teacher. Ahhatome, it is not too hard to loosen and stretch the cord for less pull. The cleaner it is the more it stretches. I think you can stretch it more now than before you worked on it."

Then, speaking more slowly and adding the use of his lips and tongue for more emphasis, "If you must visit Earth after much more preparation and if, and **only if** the cord has been made pure, you can use it to guide you down."

"Does this mean that I have your blessing on this adventure?"

"No. As I said before, you are not ready and she is not ready. She has more work to do, including work on this cord. Even the angels, after an enormous amount of study, cannot tolerate the third dimension with its different laws of physics for more than a few Earth minutes. The angels have far more experience and occasionally even they get into trouble. They must know exactly how much light to bring with them on each contact. Too much burns, too little makes them vulnerable to attack. And, Ahhatome, you would face multiple dangers. Never mind about the attacking thought-forms from an individual Earthling who has no understanding of who you are, not to mention your philosophy. You will **also** have to face the **collective** thought-forms created by all preceding sentient entities or daemons, as they call them, that circulate around the collective mind field surrounding that planet as you descend. Thought-forms are pretty easy to deal with once you recognize them for what they are. The trouble is, they can be clever in their deception. Son, The Council has given the best advice. Wait.

"In the meantime, I have something for you. I have the etheric blueprints of the original light matrix design of each half of the celestite crystal geode that you found in your life as Little Bear. These matrices were made of pale blue refined light. The geode halves can be reproduced in density from these. In more solid form, this gift is that which you gave to yourself and the young Sings To Flowers in your Blackfoot life. They carry the exact energy design of those that seemed forever lost in deep muck at the bottom of your special lake. When I retrieved the matrices I kept them separate and did not bind them together into the whole. I kept them just as you did when they were in their physical form, separated. I wanted to leave them as you left them, in two halves that someday you may choose to fit together seamlessly.

"The physical form of your celestite crystal geode came to rest where you found it after millions of years of being moved by fire and flood. You might say the two halves you created had already gone through trials of purification. The original volcano that birthed the geode was in Madagascar. The ancient Earthlings believed that these specific crystals helped them to connect with angelic beings. You can use them to connect with a more peaceful heart to Your Love."

CHAPTER TWENTY-FIVE

Thirty-Three Nights

Ahhatome and his close friend Horus are sitting on their "philosopher's stone," their favorite large rocky contemplation point overlooking a valley blanketed with delicate elevated vibratory colors and delicious aromas. Below lie reflections of happy places as one might see in a children's picture book, a mirror to the mind's memory of joyfulness and delight no matter what the age or dimension. Ahhatome manifests a wild rose and inhales deeply.

"Have you ever been in love, Horus?" he starts.

"Ahhatome. Do you ever think of anything else? I know your stories as you have read them with Libris in The Records. I know you've met the Emissary of Light that The Council has sent to your love as an advisor for her own light growth. I know all about how you've peeked in on Lily through The Records and I know you're sending her loving energy that shows up as your light around her, and I think your cord looks much more clear. No need to repeat the telling of it."

"I feel so much on the outside looking in. I want to be close!"

"I thought The Council warned you about getting directly involved in the third dimension. You know they called me out for meddling with the consciousness of the sleeping ones below."

"If I wanted to send her what they call 'a sign,' you know, like a love message to the third dimension, how would I do that?"

"Ahhatome, you're playing with fire and not listening. I just told you about my trouble with The Council for having fun with 'signs.' You know about my shimmering Eye of Horus in the ethers . . . my best art. That large group of people on a tour of Egypt were discussing with heart-felt passion ancient Egyptian symbolism. In an instant my art became heavy with their thought-forms and it was sucked down into their sky in the third dimension, causing all kinds of excitement."

"I don't see what the harm was in that."

"Well, to be honest, there may have been a little self-flattery involved. I think The Council was afraid other 5D beings would start having too much fun influencing lower dimensions with religious signs and maybe getting people to think it was the end of their world, among other scary ideas involving mind manipulations. So I stopped."

"Horus, I just want to send her a sign so that she knows that I am aware of her and sending her my love. How do I do that?"

"It's too bad they won't let you go with the Emissary of Light into Lily's dimension. But that is really delicate business. After all, you are not exactly an angel. I suppose you could learn angel business, but I understand it is a lot of hard work and I think you might accidentally widen the gap between the two of you even more." Horus is looking thoughtful and almost misty-eyed. "Why don't we look at the fundamentals of what I did and what we know?"

The Wind knows how hard it is to give help to someone you care about who asks for something that is potentially harmful. But in the fifth dimension if it is requested it is proper to give of your knowledge while at the same time advising of the possible risks. If a friend chooses to act against advice, ignore the risks, and put himself in a disastrous position with the knowledge given, then he makes a mistake for his own growth. One way of looking at it would be that there are no permanent mistakes. There will be growth as the outcome of all journeys. That is The Law.

Horus speaks slowly, almost groping for the right words, as if trying to figure it out in his mind as he speaks. "We know that groups of people or individuals in the third dimension who are working on the design of something such as an invention, and at the same time are excited about it, will begin by creating it in the fifth dimension with their mind work. When the ideas become more crystallized the form or design precipitates out into their third-dimensional mind extension and then materializes after some kind of active participation. That's not a mystery."

"So somebody in the lower dimension has to think about a thing or situation by using their mind power and be excited about it, which is adding emotional power," adds Ahhatome. "But all I want is for her to know that I am around. How will she know to think about a sign from me if she doesn't know I'm alive now?"

"Didn't Libris say that it was Okay for you to visit her in her dreams? I am thinking that is because in her so-called unconscious world, your strong energy will be at least one step away from her more delicate physical circuitry. Yes, I think my idea is a good one. Why don't you show up in her dreams and show her your symbols there! Maybe if you show a sign of your love night after night in the astral dimension of her dream world, then if and when she is in a relaxed state, where unconscious material bubbles up to her conscious mind, your love sign will become apparent in her third-dimensional consciousness. What do you think?"

"I am going to try it, Horus. She has been emotionally attached to those Indian toys I gave her about 200 Earth years ago. I will show her a feather in her dreams, a feather with special rings of color on its shaft that she will recognize from those toys. I will present myself in her dreams as my favorite snowy white owl form, the one I use often and the one I have materialized with etheric matter around me now. I don't think a harmless-looking owl will frighten her."

Ahhatome is doing as he promised. He is presenting himself in Lily's dream world night after night for thirty-three nights and then... Lily becomes aware of the signs that keep showing up in her dreams. By adding the weight of her intense daytime thoughts of longing onto the signs . . . lo, the owl form and the marked feather does more than show up in her thoughts. Heavy with dense thought weight, they precipitate into Lily's physical reality on the road back from Cut Bank to Browning. When this happened no one was more surprised than Ahhatome or me, The Wind. It was rare magic . . . a love letter from the fifth to the third dimension that she unknowingly helped deliver to herself.

PART THREE
Ahhatome—Lily
(   )
Lily—Ahhatome

CHAPTER TWENTY-SIX

The Miracle

"How are we going to handle this Lily situation, Marge? I'm worried as hell."

"Now John, we're going to get through this. Every parent sooner or later has to face a teen rebellion. Lily has been through a lot in the last 72 hours with a whacked-up head. At least we know where she went and who she went with and approximately when she will return, which is about now."

"Marge, don't try to use logic with me. It's not like she's a battered-up prizefighter. I feel in my bones that something's been wrong with Lily ever since we entered this town, especially that damn museum! She simply isn't herself. She doesn't act like herself. She doesn't even look like herself."

"John. Get a grip. I kind of like this town, and even the museum. I was relaxed here until . . . Listen. She called to reassure us, she promised on the phone not to pull this stunt again, and she told Sammy to tell where she went. Hey look. That's them pulling up now."

"Something could have happened out there, Marge, and we wouldn't know anything about it. The fact is she disobeyed. We had a family discussion and she disobeyed."

"I don't remember her agreeing to anything. John, tone your voice down a few decibels and play it cool, here they come."

"Lily! Your forehead wound!" exclaims Mary after bringing the truck to a stop. "I can hardly see it. The swelling is gone, the stitches are standing up, the injury is practically invisible! I can't believe my eyes. Those stitches need to come out now! I'm almost tempted to pull them myself, but Dr. Dixon is on duty tomorrow and we'll make quick work of it. We've got your phone numbers. Expect a call in the morning." Then, looking closely at the stitches, "This is one for the books. You are a fast healer, Lily."

"That's nice, but I have to make peace with my Mom and Dad now. Whatever trouble I'm in, it was worth it. I wonder what they will think about the marked feather. Anyway, I hope to convince them to stay around and visit the museum again. Sammy wanted to check out the opening of the Sundance. And Cat, I can count on her to want to go back to the hospital. She must have changed her ideal career from movie star to nurse the way she hangs on Dr. Dixon's every word." Mary can't keep from rolling her eyes.

Clutching her special feather, I see her filled with joy, even though joy for Lily is slippery. Seeing the elation on her face is causing Mom to smile and Dad to tone down the prepared speeches about family responsibility in his head. Lily promises better behavior. I'm glad tension is easing somewhat.

Sammy is excited to see the Sundance happenings and Lily was right about Cat. She is delighted with another chance to see Dr. Dixon. Dad is sighing and puffing and mumbling to himself while each family member lugs their bags and totes back up the steps to the same motel room.

It's 7:30AM when silence punctuated by snores is interrupted by the ringing motel phone. Cat sits up in bed and grabs for it, knocking it off its hook. But then, oh the sweet tones directed into the receiver. Her song is well practiced, low-pitched . . . a sleepy voice with long drawn out vowels as if she were from the South instead of the Pacific Northwest.

Cat had a plan for this early morning call from the hospital. Her suitcase and other of her paraphernalia were piled high around the perimeter of her nightstand, blocking easy phone access to all but herself. She had deliberately laid out everyone's cell phone next to the motel phone, but in the night she thought of another maneuver. The pile of cells was conveniently moved to the floor next to and almost under her side of the bed. *It could be Dr. Dixon himself who calls.* Imagine her surge of happiness, or perhaps I should say hormones, at the hearing of his voice this morning instead of Nurse Mary's. "Ohhh Yeees, Dr.Diiixon, we can come in right awaaaay. See you Soooon."

Making sure she is first in the bathroom, she leaps from bed to bath with her beforehand strategically-placed makeup case now under her arm. Sleepy Dad soon taps on the bathroom door, "Cat, was that the doctor?" He is pulling on his pants. Mom is groaning. Sammy says that he is not going anywhere as he tucks his head under the covers. Lily rolls out of bed and is thinking about the toys in the museum case.

As they arrive at the hospital a good hour and thirty minutes later, due to the bathroom monopoly by Cat, Mary greets the family minus Mom and Sammy and ushers them into the suture room. Thanks to a shuttle, the other two family members arrive just in time. Nurse Mary has already dropped the pre-sterilized suture removal instruments onto a sterile towel for the doctor.

"Do I need to wear sunglasses?" It's Dr. Dixon and Cat is all smiles. "Wow! I've never seen anything like this. When did we sew you up? Two days ago? Glory Be! I hope we can get those stitches out of there; they look pretty imbedded. Mary, those pickups are the ones with teeth?" he asks while washing his hands.

After some gentle pulling and coaxing, the sutures come free and intact. Only needlepoint pink dots remain where the sutures had been. "Well aren't you pretty. No need for steri-strips here. No need for anything. You're free to go!"

"Thaaank you, Dr. Diiixon," breathes Cat as she slides in front of the door blocking his exit.

"Thank you, Ma'am," he says looking down at her and showing his toothy smile again. "And let me add a thank you to Lily too. You are a good patient, Lily," turning to look at his handiwork, now all but invisible. "Do I need glasses or have those suture holes disappeared? This is unbelievable! Well, I like to start out my day with a miracle or two. Something to remember when it gets busy later with Sundance injuries."

"You're acting like a slut," whispers Sammy.

"Shut up, Major Annoyance," is Cat's response. This provides an opportunity for Jerry Dixon, M.D., to make his escape by reaching over Cat's head and pushing the door as wide as it will go, allowing himself to slip past her and disappear into the labyrinth of the hospital corridors and byways, never to be seen again in this life by Catrina Johantgen.

CHAPTER TWENTY-SEVEN

The Gift

Poor Cat, she is looking glum. The fantasy love affair with, sigh, "Dr. Jerry D." has ended. Unless, Oh dear, is she cording him? My prediction is that any cord she tries to establish today won't last through tomorrow. I suspect she will have many "final" loves and more than one marriage this time around. Anyway, with the excitement of school starting, I think Dr. Dixon will soon be a dim memory. Perhaps she'll remember him in her dreams, but she is not one for remembering dreams after waking up and planning her makeup and costume of the day. On the other hand, The Wind isn't always making the correct interpretation of events, and people's attitudes can change over time and sometimes instantly.

"Why don't you put that fucked-up feather in your purse, Lily. Or you could even throw it away. That's the best idea. You look stupid walking around with your tentacles wrapped around it." Attitude! At least Lily does not let herself hear Catrina's whine.

The family once again enters The Museum of the Plains Indian. The big lady with the beaver teeth is greeting them with many smiles and "so nice to see you again," which she repeats more than once. Dad has made a rather hefty "donation" and the display has been totally repaired, the Do Not Enter signs removed. Big Lady, as she is referred to amongst the family members, is pleased to show them around this time.

"Let me tell you about a happening with those toysss," she excitedly reports through her hissing teeth while almost bouncing up and down. "One of the workmen who wasss working on the Indian toy disssplay reported that at one point the toysss became brilliantly lit up with a ssstrong light and they became too warm for him to touch without dissscomfort unless he kept his hands wet. Of course I wouldn't allow that. Can't get water all over our treasures. I think he was exaggerating when he said he was afraid that the whole exhibit might burssst into flames, but I just cannot have the treasures exposed to moisture, for heaven's sake. The next day, the disssplay case had cooled down and they were able to finish their work. The workers had never experienced such a thing before."

Big Lady had never experienced anything like it either, in all the years of her work at the museum. She is looking intently and with curiosity at Lily, as if looking for a sign of the recent injury or a scar. There are no marks of any kind to suggest the injury that she had witnessed.

Lily is burning the vision of the toys, her toys she now believes, into her memory. As she does so, she feels again the strange stirring sensation of nausea and warmth around her tail bone, which is spreading slightly through her sacrum and up her lower back. "Do you ever sell any of these antiques?"

"Once in a very great while if we have a ss-surplus of a ss-certain type that has been in ss-storage for a long time and no other museum wants them. But these antiques are unique because they are children's things, which usually have sss-such a short life. We will not ever sss-sell these, I am quite ss-sure."

Lily reluctantly withdraws from her beloved glassed-in toys after she has checked her feather's markings against the arrows. The markings are the same. Three wraps of yellow, four wraps of red, and twelve wraps of black have a momentous meaning now. She vows to keep her feather until her death. Her eyes are wet and before the family leaves the museum she hugs Big Lady for a long time, while Big Lady looks sssss-surprised.

The Johantgens decide not to leave Browning without looking in on the Sundance. The August powwow is within walking distance from the museum.

The festival is arranged symbolically as circles within circles.

The Johantgens thread their way through the outer circle, consisting of parked cars, trucks of every vintage and description—the majority decorated with an odometer of high mileage. Sammy is delighted with the dream catchers dangling from rear-view mirrors, the painted symbols on the Indian vehicle's exteriors, and marvels at the high number of patched bald tires.

Crossing into the next tighter circle, Lily notices people standing around, laughing, joking, and visiting with old friends. A sadness sweeps over her as she wishes she were a part of this or that group, swallowed up by their well-worn campers, tents, teepees, cooking utensils, sacks of personal items and sleeping bags rolled out for sleeping under the stars. Walking respectfully by them, trying not to disturb those groups of close-knit alliances, they proceed into the next smaller circle, the merchant circle, with assembled makeshift stands that grab attention.

The air is heavy with the smell of "Indian tacos" being made with pan-fried bread to be wrapped around seasoned meat and other condiments, "buffalo burgers," and flat fry bread, both plain and sugared.

Cat is momentarily attracted to the brightly dyed feathers, leather moccasins, and decorated jackets—every item that can be anointed with seed-beaded Indian designs imaginable is available here for sale. Then she catches herself and decides she cannot possibly be interested in "this cut-rate junk." Who wants beaded wallets, glasses cases or, ironically, necklaces for displaying a corporation card, which are offered for sale in abundance? However, when my light breeze blows to create the tinkle of silver and turquoise jewelry hung to catch the sunlight and bring in the customer, Cat's attention is captured and she is reaching for her wallet, while Bothersome Brother eyes the dream and sun catchers of every description swaying with my controlled wind power.

The circle for walking and visiting the merchants is closer to the center. The smaller circle within the one for walking is where the Johantgens see the viewing circle for admiring the dancers. Here and there are family groups squeezed between the wooden viewing stands and personal folding chairs, treading on each other's toes to watch grandma dance. Foldout chairs sport multi-colored seat cushions, some showing many years of service and faded from the sun, others draped with brightly-colored blankets and quilts for sitting and watching the events unfold into the night.

Under a canopy of green boughs at the hub of it all is the drumming circle, consisting of young men keeping the tempo with untiring arms. They connect the crowd by magnetizing the onlookers with their beat of the drum. Women stand behind the drummers and add their voices to several songs. Everyone is dressed in their finest festival costumes that may represent birds, animals, or people. The colors delight.

At this moment ladies are dancing in a clockwise circle around the drummers in a rhythmic, bouncing shuffle. Sometimes a specific dance or an inter-tribal dance is called, where anyone can dance any dance they wish, all together at the same time. The Sundance is the Feast of the Year for the optic and olfactory nerves, taste buds, and ear drums.

The master of ceremonies is usually a middle-aged man who keeps people laughing with his jokes, explains the lessons in the coyote trickster stories, and gently admonishes the brashness of youth. The powwow is the time where the captivated and thereby gently captured young ones in the audience are persuaded to listen to their elders. Sammy especially loves the trickster stories.

It is here where cohesion is felt after the rendering apart of a culture, and where the First Nation Peoples are given a renewed sense of solidarity by reminding them of their roots and the important contribution they have to give to the world as teachers by example and stewards of our Earth Mother. Each member of the Johantgen family is privately wondering why all this feels familiar.

Lily keeps telling herself that she is being completely irrational as she searches through the throng of the faces of young men looking for, of all people, Two Bears. It's just that these faces seem so recognizable in many ways. She reminds herself that *it's just the genetics. If he was alive today he would be over 200. Even too old to be dying in the room next to Henry Tall Chief.*

The rest of the family is totally engaged in the wares showcased in the souvenir stands. She is stopping now and staring at the ground, telling herself, *I'm stupid.* Then she reaches for her feather, safely tucked into her large knot of blond hair, and sighs.

She feels happier to be amongst what feels to be her people, yet deeply sad that they do not recognize her as such. While she has been searching the faces for her beloved, she is met with sets of vacant unresponsive eyes, one after another, after another, after another. *They will never see me as one of them,* she thinks, *especially with my extra whiter-than-white skin, definitely whiter than that of the normal white person. With Crazy Horse living in their marrow, I might as well be Colonel Custer's great great granddaughter.*

"Lily."

Huh? Did I hear my name? The family is way down around the circle and they all have their backs to me. Who else knows my name from around here? It's not Mary's voice . . . certainly not Dr. Dixon's. It's a lady's voice, but I can't place it. Is my wanting Two Bears causing me to hear things now? Help. I'm losing it."

A woman is motioning to Lily to come to her jewelry stand between a booth with leather goods on one side and a display of Native American art on the other side. She is an attractive lady of about thirty-five and, strangely, her lovely smooth and wrinkle-free face seems familiar. The lady stands out from the other women in that she has painted the part between her braids a bright red. Her costume, though definitely authentic, is made of deer hide and decorated with a few elk teeth, but is not nearly as colorful as most of the other costumes here. It doesn't have any fancy dyed feathers.

As Lily comes closer she is struck by a warm glowing light that fills the jewelry stand and, at the same time, she is more aware of her tailbone sensation. "How did you know my name?"

"This is going to surprise you, but I will answer your question honestly. I read your aura where I saw the familiar thought form of Two Bears."

Lily is speechless. Finally she says, "What? You saw who? You saw Two Bears?"

"No, I saw a thought-form of Two Bears in your aura. The aura is the egg-shaped open-ended space around the physical body that is filled with divine light and is readable to some."

"I don't know what you mean by 'thought-form.'"

"Well, to try to answer your question, if a person entertains a thought or group of thoughts either consciously or unconsciously about something or someone repeatedly, the energy of those thoughts imprint their aura, that's all. It's like putting some information in a file that you intend to use again in the near future. The thought-form gets more or less stuck for a while in the aura, until it is released or incoming thought-forms released from other people come in to join it and make the form stronger. Like thought-forms attract like and stick together.

"As a matter of fact that is why inventions that are similar or almost identical, as in books or pieces of music, may be created around the same time by two different people on opposite sides of the world. That is also why people who think alike or have been persuaded about something by a strong charismatic speaker seek each other out. They are stuck in each other's aura imprinting until they consciously release or dissolve their thought-forms."

"I've never heard of such a thing in all my life! But how do you know the name Two Bears? Are written words stuck in my aura too?"

"Some people have them. Yours is more a picture in your mind. I know Two Bears from more expanded reasons. Now is not the time or the place to get into that subject. I may or may not explain later someday."

Lily is having trouble comprehending all this. The lovely Indian woman is reaching under the counter and she brings both her closed hands out from underneath. "This gift is for you. I think you will recognize them as a lost gift that you had at one time until you threw them away." Slowly opening her hands she reveals the two halves of the beautiful thunder egg with its center of pale blue crystals. "The crystals within your stone are also known as Angel Communication Crystals."

"Where did you get them?" stammers Lily.

"There's more than one way to go fishing, Lily. Their energy matrices were reproduced in the fifth dimension and subtle substance allowed to accumulate on them until they were heavy enough to precipitate back into the third dimension by drawing in the denser matter, atom by atom, molecule by molecule, from the originals in the lake. It's a fairly simple matter."

Now excited and not fully comprehending, "What is the name of that lake? I would like to go there."

"There are many small unnamed lakes at the bottom of hundreds of little basins tucked amongst the mountains, but the geode halves are not there now, Lily. Both halves are there in your hands. When the original energy pattern or spirit of the rock is pulled out the dense form of it temporarily falls into dust. The spirit or energy pattern can then be used to reproduce the form in density exactly as it was anywhere you choose. Keep the two halves of the rock close. It will help you feel close to Two Bears. He gave me the geode matrix for each half, knowing that in my travels to your dimension they would put on more density and could be given back to you."

Lily looks dumbfounded as she strains to comprehend by examining and recognizing her precious thunder egg halves.

"This should not be thought of as a miracle, as some people choose to do. It is just a little more science than you are aware of at your present time. By the way, Two Bears has a new name now. He is called Ahhatome."

"Ahh... What? He is alive?"

"Ahhatome, and yes he is alive. Ah-(like awesome), ha-(like hot), tome (like home). You have much to learn. Even just the basics," she says softly. "Hold out your left hand Lily, and keep the stone halves in your hand for a while." She is placing the crystal half-orbs in Lily's hand.

"Oh, they are very warm in my hand... And..." Her right hand is reaching around to her sacrum where there is a strong feeling of bubbly warmth.

"Not to worry, Lily. You are feeling an awakening within your denser body. We can talk about that later too, if you like." The Indian lady turns her head and sees the rest of the Johantgen family at a far distance. They have just turned around and are looking right and left with an anxious expression. Dad especially has a wrinkled brow, concerned that they have lost Lily again.

"Lily! Lily!" Many heads are turning toward the voice with the booming bark.

Lily wastes no time in rushing to catch her family's attention, calm her parent's anxious faces, and show them the beautiful stone halves. She leads them back to... but she is gone!

"She was right here! Her stand was between this leather stand and this art stand that are now next to each other, I swear it's the truth! I swear it! I know these are the stands on either side of the jewelry stand where I received my blue crystal stones. I recognize the art and this jacket here. It has an eagle with a feather on the back all done in beads." She turns the jacket over and indeed, it does have a beaded eagle carrying a feather.

"What happened to the jewelry booth that was between your two stands?" she asks of the leather and the art merchants. The merchants are looking at each other in bewilderment. They say they do not know of any such jewelry stand or merchant in old traditional dress with red paint in the part of her hair or anything about any of Lily's story. They are assuring everyone that they were next to each other from the start of the festival until now.

Dad says, "Lily, you could have remembered this jacket from before you came upon the stand where you were given the rocks and…"

"Let's get Lily out of the sun and get her a cool drink," interrupts Mom. Mom and Dad are looking at each other and giving each other signals with their eyes.

Sammy joins in with, "I think it's the bump on the head. Now Silly Lily is even more silly." "Silly Lilly" is Sammy's favorite rhyme and he thinks this is his opportunity to sing it.

> "Silly Silly, Lily Lily
> won't be kissed by Billy or Willy
> 'cause she's such a chilly nilly."

"Enough, Sammy!"

Catrina says nothing. I think she is trying to mull it all over, but the whole thing is too much. She decides that if she thinks about this anymore she will have a worse headache than when she saw her sister fall into the glass display case. With a grunt or two, Catrina releases those complicated thought-forms and lets them go out of her aura.

CHAPTER TWENTY-EIGHT
Traveling Home

Lily is only half listening to the Glacier Park guide drone on and on about a series of important dates in the park's history and the history of Going to The Sun Road. She always carries with her the stone halves with the pale blue crystals and keeps her special feather close. *I swear on the love of Little Bear or Ahha . . . to keep my feather until death do us part. It will always be in my hair or over my heart in my bra.* Sometimes she just admires it in her hands.

"Lily, you look screwier than a fruit loop with that ridiculous thing, the way you keep drooling over it. Disgusting," snorts Catrina out of the corners of her nose and mouth. Then she adds, while pointing to Lily's head, "I don't know what wanders through your little box of insanities and imaginary miracles, but I do know I don't want to be bothered with it or you, especially with weird feathers or any other weirdness sticking out of your head!"

Lily says nothing. Instead she straightens her back and looks at her sister with calm eyes until Catrina turns away. *I'm witnessing something I never thought I'd see; Catrina shriveling from a look . . . especially a look from Lily.*

For some reason the stone halves are always warm. "Whoa. I hope those things aren't radioactive," Sammy comments.

"Get real, Sammy. Why would anyone cart around something radioactive? The lady that gave them to me was holding them too, you know. It's just a broken thunder egg."

"Well I never saw your lady with the red in her hair. Maybe you just dreamed that silly stuff up."

"There is evidence of human use of the trails within the park going back about 10,000 years," explains the park guide. He is a handsome youth and by his looks could be a younger brother of Dr. Dixon. This fact is not missed by Cat.

"In the 1800's, English, French, and Spanish trappers combed the mountain valleys for beaver pelts. The Great Northern Railroad built a line over Manias Pass, which was completed in 1891. In 1895, miners acquired mountains east of The Continental Divide from the Blackfoot Nation. Only tiny amounts of copper and gold were ever found. In 1910, President Taft declared this land, which had been called a Forest Preserve since 1900, a National Park.

"The Going to The Sun Road, which goes for fifty miles east to west, took thirty years to complete and opened in 1932. The most difficult part was the construction over the mountains at Logan Pass. The grade is only 6% because the 1930's car had to shift down to second gear. There are two tunnels and in those days they could only bore through the mountain five feet in a day. The east tunnel is 408 feet and the west is 192 feet. Three men died during construction. In 1931, a caterpillar rolled down 200 feet off the roadbed."

Lily snaps awake. She is raising her hand, ready to fill in more details between this monotonous reciting of dates. When the handsome youth, probably from some nearby high school, looks at her with knitted eyebrows, Catrina growls, "Put your hand down. Whatever you do, do not embarrass me." Catrina now steps in front of Lily, trying to cover her up. Rude!

Lily refuses to hear her. She is thinking, *He has his little story memorized, but doesn't want me to intrude. Probably afraid I will ask him a question. What the heck, I'm going for it.*

"The man who fell with his caterpillar was Henry Tall Chief. He was working on the road with Louis DuBois, a French trapper who got his head sliced off by the Beaver People for disturbing a sacred Blackfoot beaver bundle that had a curse on it."

There is dead silence. Every one of the twelve sightseers in this little group is turning to look at Lily, who has now a face tinged with pink. Sammy is delighted with this revelation, but Cat, who wanted better eye contact with the guide, turns to speak in hushed but forced tones, "Now all these people know for sure you're whacko. If you're walking next to me they'll think I am too, so don't! . . . Unless you want those retro-glasses knocked off your face." Lily is not listening.

"Let it rest, you two," says Dad, who tries but cannot quiet his voice. Mom is nodding her head and looking intense. Now I see Mom and Dad pass that special look between them again. The rest of the audience, realizing that Lily is not going to say more, turns back to the original speaker who was shocked into silence but now has mostly recovered with only a slight stammer to his memorized speech. He has no idea how to comment on Lily's comment, so he just valiantly forges ahead.

"The the t-two lane road is open only from June to October. In the spring, it is one of the most difficult roads to pow, I mean plow. The biggest snow field is just east of the pass. It is called the 'The Big Shit,' Oh God, 'The Big Drift.'"

Now, with a face red enough to match Lily's, "Even now when we can move 4,000 tons of snow an hour, it takes ten weeks to clear the . . . it off the road. You will notice that there are few guardrails. This is because the late winter avalanches repeatedly destroy every protective barrier ever constructed." With his speech done, the young man sighs and rolls his eyes up to God.

In spite of all this, just one word from the guide is making the hair on the back of Lily's neck stand up and her arms have chills. That word is "avalanches." *Why?* She is wondering and thinking of Two Bears. *Could he have died years ago somewhere in "The Big Drift?"*

The Wind answers "yes," but she can no longer hear me. He was pushed many miles down the mountain during snowmelt . . . miles away from any search party and the wild wanderings of Sings To Flowers.

Why do I think he has anything to do with an avalanche? What's the matter with me? Am I going bananas? Why did I have to open my big mouth just now? Cat's right, I probably sounded like a total idiot. I want to get outta here. This place creeps me out.

CHAPTER TWENTY-NINE

Something Odd in Idaho

Catrina wants to stay longer at Glacier Park. What other reason could it be than something to do with the young guide who looks like a younger Dr. Dixon? She also does not want her sister standing next to her. But much to Lily's relief the family votes to continue their trip, while Catrina's lower lip pouts even more.

"More days and nights have already been spent on this trip than intended," says Dad. Everyone is piling back into the car with their "treasures."

Lily has her thunder egg halves and a new jacket with pockets with a gathered edge that will keep the crystal half-orbs from falling out. Cat has a new pocket mirror that magnifies on the opposite side of the regular mirror, even though she already has several of this type, and a new jacket with a pocket to hold it. Mom has not one, but two new floppy sun hats for herself, but will plant them on the girls' heads if she thinks they are too exposed to the sun, and Sammy... What is that? His pockets are bulging with stuff and I detect what looks like the butt end of a slingshot sticking out of one pocket. Probably a good bit of "ammo" in one of the other pockets.

"I'll be ready for any bear," Sammy proudly announces, but nobody pays attention to him. He is also clutching something in a brown paper bag tightly to his chest; he purchased it from one of those knick-knack-paddy-whack stores. He won't let anybody see what it is. All we know is, "It cost twelve bucks." Sammy, still trying to get somebody's attention, yells, "Did ya know a grizzly bear can run the length of a football field in six seconds?" At last everyone is looking at Sammy. However Mom, eyeing Sammy's fat pockets, comments, "Really Sammy, I'm glad you are protecting us but please go easy on the sweets."

"Oh Marge, it's the kid's vacation." Dad's take-home prize is a flatter wallet, but he's happy about the trip. Everyone seems okay now and the family has certainly seen some sights. However The Wind detects something more creeping up on the horizon. I am starting to feel sparks and a stronger-than-normal electric feeling. I suspect it has something to do with Lily.

The family has been alternating between moseying and hustling around the mountains and through the valleys on US Highway 2 to Kalispell, where they'll turn south to Lolo Pass to follow Lewis and Clark's trek west through the Bitterroot Mountains on that historic route to the Pacific. The Northwest Passage Scenic Byway is thickly forested with many miles of windings and turns and no gas stations. Sammy's candy-filled stomach has felt better days. Dad hopes the old car will make it and that there is a gas station soon.

If it were not for the Lochsa River, which means "rough water," by the side of the highway, the sun would not find its way to the road through the dark blanket of trees. The Sun is almost down and with relief the Johantgens see more patchy open places, smell randomly placed ponderosas, and spy the lights of the little town of Syringa, Idaho. There, on the Middle Fork of the Clearwater River, not far from where Lewis and Clark camped for six weeks while the Nez Perce instructed them in the art of pine tree canoe making, the Johantgen car sputters on its last drops and rolls up to River Dance Lodge.

"Wow," says Mom, "I think that's a famous place."

"Looks like an expensive place, Marge."

"Can't we stay?" whines Cat.

Lily doesn't speak and Sammy is asleep.

Then, turning to one another, the parents say simultaneously, "Let's stay here."

In no time every corner of their delightful log cabin is humming with the noises of peaceful sleep, lots of snoring on the part of Mom and Dad, augmented by a few squeaks and groans rising up from their room on the main floor. But there is one upstairs in the loft who is only sleeping in short little spurts, with long wakeful periods in between.

Lily is awake again, feeling restless and sweaty. There have been lightning-like flashes outside the windows, which illuminate the interior of the cabin for a second. She is listening for a clap of thunder, but there is none. *That's odd,* she thinks as she leans against the slick hand-hewn railing above the main floor to peer out toward the river. *I'm going to check out that light.*

She grabs her new jacket and is surprised to find that the pockets containing her crystals are warmer than usual, as though recently touched by a hot iron. She smells the jacket pockets. There is no burn smell. On the lower floor, there is still light from the fire's last dying embers. She checks there for scorch marks. *I'm getting so I don't trust my own judgment. Nothing's wrong.* Squeaking the door open, she steps outside into the dark.

Away from the cabin it is a pleasantly cool night with a gentle breeze that ruffles the back of Lily's hair. *Hmm. Those intense flashes seem even more pronounced down by the river. It's only a short walk.* The bumpy path down to the water continues to be lit every few seconds, but no thunder. *How odd. These lightning flashes are closer together than I'm used to. Maybe it's not lightning. A search light? No, that's crazy.*

My feet really like the feel of forest trails better than city concrete.

The aromas of the woods, with wild roses and a rare whiff of native blackberries, brings with them a feeling of longing and ... there is a strong smell of ... wood smoke. *What? A campfire at 3:00AM?*

Squinting into the dark in the direction her nose suggests she sees the glint of flickering light between the trees and bushes. It is magnified by big flashes reflecting off the ground. When she finds her way out onto the rocky shoreline she sees an old woman hunched over a crackling fire about fifty feet upriver. Lily turns to retreat to the cabin. *All she needs is a big black kettle, and she can pass for a . . .*

"Lily, come sit with me; there are no witches here." The voice calling out seems familiar.

Didn't I just go through something like this with that Indian lady? Lily hesitates, then decides to approach.

"You need not be afraid of those who call themselves Wiccan. Most of them are harmless nature lovers trying to do good deeds. And for the few who try the black arts, if you can call it that, they teach themselves a tough lesson around the next corner. You are well protected with light, Lily, energetically speaking. Come sit."

She sounds like the woman who gave me the crystal thunder egg halves, but this cannot be her because this lady has deep lines in her face like the skinned apple I left out for a year. The lightning flashes show her gray hair and a hump in her upper back. Her dress is . . . unfamiliar.

"You know my name!" says Lily. "Who are you?"

"I am to you exactly what you decide to perceive me to be." The voice was not only familiar, but gentle and reassuring, almost laughing. The deepest lines in the old face are smile lines.

Feeling a bit braver, Lily asks, "Well who do **you** perceive yourself to be?"

"I give myself no labels, I have no name."

"No Name? Then may I call you No Name? Are you a teacher?"

"You may. I like that. And yes, I can be your teacher if you request that of me. But know that I can show you only that which you are open to contain and eventually a teacher wears out its welcome in order to open the way for the student to move on."

"You called yourself and teachers an 'it.'"

"My dear, a teacher does not have to be a person."

"Okay," taking a gulp and feeling even more brave, "I would like you to teach me. What about this big flashing light, for starters," Lily says, sitting down on a log next to the old woman's fire and at the same time wondering why she is not afraid.

"I'm glad you have decided to sit. If I told you that the flashes are from someone thinking longingly for you and trying to get your attention, you might have a problem with that idea."

"Ha! You're right! I thought maybe they were some strange northern lights."

"You can put any label on this phenomenon you would like. Who can argue?

Lily, do you remember when I gave you the two halves of the celestite crystal geode that are now warming your pockets?"

"*Ahh . . . Well . . . The lady that gave me the stone parts was, ah . . . young . . .*"

Turning to Lily and looking her in the eyes, the old lady transforms herself into the young Indian woman in native dress, red part in the hair, same face and same smile. "Human eyes live under a cloud of illusion. Not only that, they choose their illusions and their delusions."

"How did you do that?"

"It's called shape shifting and it is only a minor distraction from what is important in life and why we are meeting, yet on occasion it is a useful tool. Lily, I have witnessed your dreams and your desire to be with Ahhatome, or Two Bears as you remember him."

"Yes. I want to be with Two Bears again." There is a huge flash in the sky after Lily makes this declaration. "But how would this be possible?"

No Name rises to her feet and shakes a finger at the stars and addresses the heavens, "Be careful you don't start any fires with your misguided enthusiasm." Then, putting her hands on her hips and looking up, she continues, "Just because one lives primarily in the fifth dimension does not mean that he is perfect. Far from it. He may have mastered some things, like survival fears and self-doubt. He may have developed his will to a higher degree, but that does not mean that he is finished or done with his unfoldment." She sits again and whispers to herself, "Incorrigible." Then turning to Lily with a softer voice, "You must always stand in your own truth as you understand it, always."

"Who are you speaking to, No Name?"

"Whoever or whatever may be listening," she says, glancing up.

"Lily, people are constantly changing, redirecting, and altering the outcome of their lives. You have made the first step. You have declared your intention. But there is something holding you back and making you struggle against yourself."

No Name looks into the fire. "Fire is the electric energy of passion and being brave enough to leave the old ways behind for good."

"Like burning your bridges?"

"That's one way of putting it." No Name picks up a pebble and throws it into the river. "Water shows us our emotions. Humans try to change the course of the river by throwing a few stones into it. They need to change themselves before their river will permanently change course." No Name looks back into the flames for a minute before she speaks again.

"Lily, you have corded not only to another being, but to certain places."

"Corded?"

"Yes, corded. Allowed yourself, to your detriment, to become overly attached. People in this dimension do this to each other and to places and even to things. It is not a completely bad thing. But when a cord of attachment is deeply entrenched you can lose a part of your being, a soul fragment."

"That sounds really creepy," Lily says, shivering even though the temperature is comfortable on her skin.

"By the time Earthlings have lived several decades, almost every one of them has a piece of themselves missing. To my eyes people with missing parts look like wandering ghosts, almost as much as their missing parts do. When you are ready, you can bring the lost pieces of yourself back. In so doing you might see and experience the circumstance of the emotional pain and suffering that caused the fragment of yourself to break away. If you wish to continue on this path, you must consciously allow that missing fragment to speak to you by opening your mind and heart, examining it from every angle, and healing it with the power of love and forgiveness."

"If it hurts so much, why would I want to do that?"

"If you want to join with Ahhatome, you must prepare yourself to handle more energy. You will not understand much of this advice, but trust me. You first must make yourself whole and more balanced and not so needy. He needs to do the same."

No Name is rising and looking into the river. This night Clearwater River seems faster and deeper but highlighted with glints from the stars, the moon, and the fire. No Name sees more in its depths than humans or even The Wind can see. "Water reflects back emotional information for those who can read her," she sighs. "You can do this in meditation; you can do it here after stilling the surface water of your mind.

"I am seeing you as a young beautiful Blackfoot Indian maiden," she continues, "desperately in love with the shaman apprentice named Two Bears. Two Bears loses his body in an avalanche."

"Avalanche! Oh God. I knew that to be true somehow!"

"They never find his body. You are Sings To Flowers and you are searching from late spring to early fall every peak and cranny of the mountain area where he disappeared, looking for a piece of something that is his . . . something of him you can hold. Late in life you find what could be a part of a medicine bag, but you are not sure if it is his."

There is an uncomfortable dead silence. Smoke is rising from the fire and becoming thickened, as though something is snuffing the life out of it.

Lily has teary eyes from stinging smoke. She moans in a cracking voice, "I threw the medicine bag down in disgust. After all, if it was his, his medicine was no good. It didn't protect him. I threw myself on the ground and gave Mother Earth a pounding. I stabbed her. How dare Our Mother cover him in snow and choke his air and snuff him out like the last dying ember of the fire that warms us in winter? How dare the old dead shaman take my beloved from me? How dare The Great Spirit allow this when my love was so pure?"

Lily shrieks, "How could they? How could they rip my heart into pieces? And they wouldn't even tell me if the medicine bag was his? Why didn't the spirits take pity on me and reward my searches year after year after year and give me even a little token of him to hold close to my heart for the rest of my life? God Damn!" There was another display of lightning and then the first far away roll of thunder.

No Name speaks gently, "You have your lovely crystals from him now." Lily takes them out of her pockets. They are very warm and she trades them back and forth between her hands and examines them closely as if trying to see Two Bears in the crystals. After all, No Name demonstrated she could see him in the fire and in the water. But Lily does not see.

No Name continues, "And at your death when you were an old crone, your thoughts of grief returned again to the mountains. You lamented and did not forgive the old shaman, Mother Earth, Two Bears, or yourself. You blamed all of them and yourself for your lost love. It was at this time that you reinforced a splitting apart, a fragment of your soul to wander the mountains still looking for Two Bears and I might add, if you are twin flames, then you can think of it as a part of **his** soul wandering too.

"Now when other people, perhaps on a hike, visit that area it does not matter if a gentle breeze blows the scent of wild flowers while the sun is sweetly warm on their heads and shoulders. Instead of feeling the joy of that beauty they will sense the energy of your grief which remains sobbing and beating your fists there. Most of these visitors to your 'haunting' will wonder why they feel sad. A few others will know it is not their grief that they feel, but grief belonging to another. And a fewer still will feel the loss of love and the Native American story that precipitated there. And this is how we haunt places and affect others.

"It was also at the time of your passing from that life that you darkened the cord even more and deepened the hook in the solar plexus and heart-gate entrance of the soul then known as Two Bears. This soul remains tormented by your hook until you release him and call back your soul fragment from the mountains."

"I had no idea that such things were possible." Lily sobs, overcome with this realization. "Oh please God, help me, help me."

With a gentle hand No Name caresses her hair, lifts up her face and wipes away tears. "Most people in the third dimension are unaware. It is what it is. Trust me, Lily. The Universe hears the prayers of your heart and forces are set in motion to answer them even before you ask verbally as you did just now. But you need to help yourself too. When you are ready you can relieve the all-around suffering by calling that soul fragment back to yourself and releasing the hook in Two Bear's soul.

"Lily, unconditional love is not about hooking, binding, or clutching. It is not about tying up another, no matter how sweetly done. No, that is definitely not about love. Hooking and clutching is about trying to serve what the small unaware self thinks it needs for happiness. Real love lets go . . . lets the beloved fly to where the beloved needs to go and is secure in the knowledge that in so doing the beloved has been served well by Love. And because Love is the uniting force of the universe, the glue, so to speak, real lovers are secure in the fact that all Love returns to Itself again on the roads of Life."

"You mean that the beloved ones will be with each other again?"

"If they create it that way, absolutely."

"How do I do that, No Name?"

"Move into and play the part of Great Love and you will become It. Removing the hook and calling back your mountain wandering soul fragment would be a good beginning."

"I hate to sound like a broken record, No Name, but how would that be done?"

"Lily, I have given you the starting information. You need to design the rest of the retrieval yourself. But I will give you a hint. You want to engage your whole self, including your whole mind in this work. When I say the whole mind I mean both the conscious and the unconscious mind. One of the things that will impress your unconscious mind is ceremony."

With those parting words No Name begins to shrink into a dot of pink light; the fire also shrinks before Lily's eyes into a dot of yellow-orange light and together they both blink out. Lily feels the spot of rocks where she was just speaking to No Name. There is not a trace of her or a fire. The rocks are all cool. There is no smoke. There are no coals. There are no cinders. There are no pieces of burned wood anywhere.

Lily is feeling like a fledgling that has just been kicked out of the nest. Not only that, she is suddenly aware it has started to drizzle. She shivers. She wraps her jacket tightly and heads back to the cabin. No one is stirring. This gives Lily a measure of, but not complete, relief while she sinks into her bed with wet clothes, sleeping for a minute or two and then awakening to stare at the ceiling trying to recall Two Bears' face . . . and the things No Name told her . . . and to wonder again what he looks like now.

But now there is a huge flash of lightning, accompanied by a loud crash of thunder that is immediately behind it or simultaneously with it, it is hard to tell. There is also a kind of electrical fire odor that permeates the room and lingers in the air. Everyone jolts awake and is shaken when they discover that the tall cottonwood outside Lily's window is split in two.

Was that a white owl flying away just now? Against everyone's protests, Lily runs outside. She sees and picks up another white feather, which she finds under a sizzling, hissing, and smoking overhead wire. On its quill the feather has mysterious bands of yellow, red, and black. *It's a sign for me. It's a sign for me. I know it is a sign just for me from him.* She is aware in the knowing part of herself when she thinks these thoughts.

After listening and waiting for more thunder and lightning, all is quiet. When the unnerved family eventually pulls itself together enough to check themselves out of the lodge another peculiar thing happens.

This morning there is a young smiling lady behind the desk. As they are almost out the door this happy person calls Lily back.

"I have something for you Lily. An old woman brought this here early this morning and told me that she thought you would be interested in this."

"Did she leave a name?"

"That's the odd thing. I asked her for a name, but she said that she has no name! And if that wasn't odd enough, there was another odd thing. She said, 'Tell Lily to keep the crystal geode halves on her bedside stand at night and that you would know why.'"

Lily is handed a small thin book. *I will definitely keep the crystals near. Wow! This is great,* she thinks. *I'll have something to read on the way home.* She opens it and reads, "How to Become a Lucid Dreamer."

CHAPTER THIRTY

Becoming a Lucid Dreamer

Lily is opening the book from No Name, determined to read it with the help of her forefinger holding up those heavy glasses in spite of a jiggling car ride over the Cascade Mountains. From time to time she looks up from her book to wonder what Ahhatome looks like. *Does he look like Two Bears? No Name described him as a being of light. What's that? Does he have a face? Does he have, you know, other parts? Is he an angel? It's hard to know how this book can help, but it is from No Name after all, and if anyone knows my situation, she's it.*

Lily reads, "A lucid dream is a dream in which the dreamer becomes aware that he is dreaming. With practice, some people are able to go to bed with the intent of becoming awake in their dreams. Once a person is aware he is dreaming it is possible to learn how to control the dream to a certain extent. He may choose to fly to Paris, breathe underwater, or banish any monster that may be unlucky enough to appear, simply by speaking to the frightening thing with firmness and authority."

The book about lucid dreaming also states, "Experiencing a lucid dream is not the same as an OBE, or Out of Body Experience. A dream is a travel within the so-called unconscious mind and is considered not real by today's modern people." To The Wind the dream is an extension into another reality, the reality of the mental energy world, which connects with our physical world and connects us to each other.

Lily reads, "In an OBE the traveler practices moving his consciousness to a more confined space within the etheric double of his physical body and, after becoming skilled, can visit actual physical places in this world. Some people have experienced an Out of Body situation during severe illness or a near death happening.

"In some indigenous cultures being near death or having a severe illness was a sign and almost a requirement for the making of a shaman. The Out of Body Experience, because of its close tie to the physical reality, is more easily remembered. The lucid dream on the other hand, where the traveler enters a much broader field of consciousness, is more slippery to hold in memory."

Ahhatome is not enthusiastic about meeting his beloved in the dream world for that very reason. He wants Lily to remember their meetings now, while she is still incarnate. Will Ahhatome ever learn patience?

The way The Wind sees his position, since he knows Lily is not likely to fall in love with an owl, he wants to present himself to her as himself. As for Lily's position, I think it is Lily who pulls the owl form the rest of the way down into her reality, not Ahhatome. Ahhatome merely provided the opportunity by showing his snowy white owl for thirty-three nights in her fourth-dimensional dream world. But Lily draws the owl form to herself, in her third-dimensional consciousness by repeatedly dwelling on the owl in her daydreams. It's a sign, but hardly enough to ease her aching desire for him.

Ahhatome has already come into her third dimension with too much light and has even caused a lightning strike. If he could manage to do what he has not been able to do yet, come into her world with less of his light, he might be nearly invisible to most people and it is uncertain if Lily would be able to see him. With too little light he could even get hung up in a different reality. That leaves him with only one other choice for now due to his inexperience. Meet her in a dream. In a lucid dream she could participate more. As for his part, even in a dream he must keep the meeting brief like the angels do when they visit.

Lily is determined to give the ideas in her book a try in spite of the fact that Catrina calls her book a "fantasy trip" and refuses to read past paragraph two. "You're already weirded-out Lily; the last thing you need is this trippy book for your messed up head."

Lily attempts with some difficulty to ignore her sibling and tries to forget that even ten-year-old Sammy calls her Silly Lily. From Lily's reading she wonders, *perhaps I can see Ahhatome in a dream.* She is not telling anyone her thoughts on this, especially Catrina, and is going to follow some of the suggestions in the book, even now as she is riding home in the car.

Three times a day, while awake, she secretly does what the book calls a "reality check." She asks herself if she is awake or dreaming. There are many ways to do this. She has chosen to look at her hands and pinch the end of her little finger when she thinks no one is watching. She has remembered the expression, "I had to pinch myself to make sure I was awake."

In a lucid dream people do not feel pain unless it is coming from the physical body as they are awakening and their consciousness is shifting back into the body. Often in a dream the hand may have not five, but four or six fingers. The purpose of doing a reality check in the daytime is to get the brain in the habit of doing this, in the hopes that a reality check will be done in dream time too, helping the person become aware he is dreaming.

She is learning other checks she can do while dreaming, including something as simple as leaning against a wall. In dreams a person will feel himself fall right through a wall because his awareness is, after all, not in his dense physical vehicle but in an energy world. Also, mechanical things in a dream, such as light switches, do not respond normally as they do in the physical reality.

Lily writes inside her book's back cover, "Write the dreams down immediately in order to help remember them."

Lily repeats in her mind, *Set the alarm for one hour earlier, state the intent to be lucid in the next dream, then go back to sleep. Sounds pretty easy. Oh, and Be Persistent and Patient.*

She reads that once she is awake in her dream she can control it with commands, so if the picture gets dim or shaky she can command more light and tell it to stabilize.

I, The Wind, plan to whisper this thought as a reminder as she sleeps. Sometimes my whispers can help things along, but mostly I can only observe and help record what comes down. In the third dimension it can take quite some time to train the brain. I wonder. Who exactly is training it? Humans must be a whole lot more than just brain.

CHAPTER THIRTY-ONE

Dancing with Daemons

"Horus," asks Aba Ahhatome, "Do you know the whereabouts of Ahhatome?"

"No. He told me that he is going on a mission. He did not want to fly with me as usual," replies Ahhatome's friend.

"That confirms what I didn't want to know. It's an old habit of mine not to focus on unwelcome news, but there comes a point when it's important to do just that," declares Ahhatome's father. "My son has taken only two classes in reducing and controlling his light for entering other dimensions safely, and already he is trying out what takes the average new light-being many intensive classes to learn, not to mention a good bit of personal instruction from knowledgeable guides. I know where he is headed, even though he has closed off any viewing of his recently created Akashic Records, even to his aba.

"He has left an enormous amount of his light here in the fifth dimension. He is unprepared for what he may face on his way through the lower subdivision of the Earthling emotional field around that planet.

"If he goes down by following that attached energy cord he drags around, it might not be quite so risky, but the last I focused on Ahhatome his cord still had dark areas so the ride would be far from smooth. My hunch is he is going to try a direct descent. That was the subject under discussion in the few classes he has taken. His desire has taken over his reason. He is not listening to the advice of The Council or me. He acts just like an Earthling! I'll follow his light."

All beings leave a light trail behind them as they go about their business, which gradually dissipates by the various universal currents and The Wind. Fortunately, it is much easier to follow the trail of a light-being than the much dimmer ethereal light trail of a human.

The now-worried Aba Ahhatome is trying to send Ahhatome telepathic information but he can tell that his thought messages have been interrupted by thick and sticky density. *It is my prayer that Ahhatome has taken enough light to pass straight through the overpopulated lower-astral emotional dimension. But if he gets hung up there and encounters frightening ethereal beings, then let him at least have enough light so they will shrink back. Will he recognize those monsters for what they are . . . just the Earth's collective thought-forms of the so-called "seven deadly sins" currently in vogue? Ahhatome, if you can hear me, are you remembering your classes?*

Aba Ahhatome quickly reads in The Records the class material recently offered to fifth-dimensional newcomers. *I see a class has been given about the ugly thought-forms having no life of their own. The class covered the fact that the beings in that realm are only grotesque illusions of the mind and are fed by sentient beings who either excessively fear or desire what is perceived to be a sin.* But alas, Aba Ahhatome does not see his son present in the class that is making that important point.

With great circumspect Aba Ahhatome, following Ahhatome's light trail, sinks into density. He too must leave some of his light behind him, but he is much more skilled at judging the correct amount and will retreat should he have difficulty pulling down more light as needed. Beginners in this endeavor are often not cautious enough and sink themselves down like a stone thrown into gravity.

At first as he enters Earth atmosphere he encounters the higher levels of the collective Earthling mind. All this is easily revealed to the soul who is out of body, but is beyond the veil for most humans who are still attached to the density of their physical vehicle or host, as it is sometimes called.

The upper or outer etheric layers around Earth Mother are exquisite to behold. They contain musical harmonics in mathematical formulas and geometric designs with many octaves of color. Who ever thought of math as music? Some know. But Aba Ahhatome does not linger at the higher levels. He sees his son's light trail heading straight into the dense emotional fields. Lower and lower the trail goes, through darker and darker emotional storm clouds with heavier and heavier hail stones with sharper and sharper cutting edges, until he arrives at the lowest astral level and the very gates of Hell.

Two grotesque gargoyles guard the barred entrance to Hell. They look just like the stone gargoyles guarding the great buildings of European money, except these here move and have power. Their eyes are sunken black holes that consume light, which is one of several methods by which entities who present themselves at the gates are sucked into Hell at the discretion of the beasts. Aba Ahhatome begins pulling down more light from above before he goes one centimeter closer.

"What comes to the gates of Hell?" asks the first gargoyle of Aba Ahhatome. "Not another being of light!"

"It's Armageddon!" shrieks the second gargoyle and they nearly fall off their perches with a torrent of cackles and guffaws that shake the ethereal ground.

"I come to retrieve my son. Stand aside," announces Aba Ahhatome, growing himself into a tower of light.

"You're a misfit. There is no place for you here."

"You'll be eaten alive in minutes."

Immediately Aba Ahhatome focuses himself into a thin laser beam and cuts through the bars into Hell. It makes no sense to try to reason with the unreasonable. Off in the distance behind him he hears, "Oh My. I do believe my whiskers have been singed!" and more laughter, if you can call their snorting grunts and squeals a kind of laughter.

Aba Ahhatome puts his hand through Ahhatome's light trail. It is thin and weak. He gathers up just a little. Yes, this light definitely belongs to Ahhatome. Being back in the dimension of Earth time, he knows he has little of it to waste as the trail is beginning to break up and dissipate already.

Growling . . .Yes growling and a touch of groveling sounds are seeping through the cracks of a wall in front of Aba Ahhatome. The light trail seems to disappear into the wall. Fortunately walls are not a big problem for Aba, who lasers himself through them. It is too late to wish he hadn't.

Behind the wall lurks a furious fiend about ten feet tall with green eyes as large as grapefruits bulging out of inadequate eye sockets. *Oh God! Ahhatome's light trail seems to go into the monster. Did this thing devour my son?*

It has gigantic claws three inches wide and fifteen inches long that curl and hook downward so that if the wrists of the monster are not held constantly in an extreme flexed-back position its claws tear at its own flesh. This explains why the tips are covered with dark black-red blood. The upper jaw fangs do the same thing. They dig into the grotesque thing's neck, also drawing its own blood unless it tips its head all the way back and opens its mouth wide. With its head and wrists cocked back, when it comes straight at you it looks like a giant eating machine. It cannot speak with such massive fangs, but can only growl and groan from deep within its throat.

Coming in to attach to the monster are millions of bug-like creatures who have tiny hooks themselves that they use to latch onto the hide of the beast. When the monster groans and growls, a swarm of the hook-bugs fly out of its mouth at Aba Ahhatome, but his light zaps and sizzles them.

"What in Hell are you?" asks Aba Ahhatome by mental telepathy. "Never mind. I am going to guess that you are the green-eyed monster called Jealousy. Have you eaten my son?"

"And why would I do that?"

Good. The monster has telepathic communication. That makes sense since he has been around for millions of years.

"I am constantly fed and nourished by the insane overly-jealous wishes and thoughts of all the Earthlings who can create them. Since like thoughts attract like, those nasty thoughts collect and create me.

"Don't you see those little hook-bugs? Those are trillions of jealous desires and thoughts sent out from Earth. Things sometimes go the opposite way here in Hell. Those little darlings are not drawing blood from me. Oh no. They are feeding me. They give me the blood or life energy of angry jealous Earthlings. I am very strong as long as anyone is very jealous or angry."

It shakes its fist in the air to show its strength. Several hook-bugs fall off and immediately reattach themselves. The fiend then goes into a fit of fury. Hook-bugs fly everywhere and try to cover Aba Ahhatome. The strong rancid bitter smell of fried hook-bugs offends the nose as the little shriveled carcasses pile up around Aba's feet.

"Calm down. I want my son back!"

"Your son? Did he recently die, perhaps by heart attack while in a rage of jealousy? Then he would be delivered directly to me for him to examine his own mean energy. It scares the hell out of them until they wake up."

It tries to laugh but chokes on the hook-bugs that feed it deep in its throat. Finally it communicates, "Your son must be the other light-being that visited me. I explained to him how I loathe my job. The extreme positions of my neck and wrists are painful. I dwell always in the same despicable jealous position. I long for variety of thought and better movement. If I ever evolve into something better than this, I swear, I will never have a jealous inclination."

"Where is my son?"

"Your son felt sorry for me and gave me a kind thought. It felt like a blessing to me as it sunk into my back." The monster turns to show Aba Ahhatome his back. There is a baseball-sized glowing orb deep in the base of the spine just above the mammoth tail. "Go ahead and take the light. Any dignified monster wouldn't display it and it made a part of me disappear!"

As Aba reaches for the light and pulls it out, a cavity is left in the monster that quickly fills with hook-bugs. The monster moans. Aba Ahhatome throws the light orb toward what little is left of Ahhatome's light trail and it immediately blends into what can barely be seen of his trail and makes it brighter. Aba Ahhatome mumbles, "Thank you and God bless you," giving him just a little pinch of his own personal light, and hurries on.

A newer higher-pitched groan . . . then a Moan and then a WAIL slices the dark from where Ahhatome's light is leading his aba. These unholy sounds would cause the insides of all Earthlings to shrivel into knots, electrify the hair on their forearms, and dry up the spit in their mouths.

Others have come here before me, Aba Ahhatome is thinking to encourage himself to keep going. Without warning the toes of his left foot find themselves hovering over a darker space and he retreats quickly from the edge of a deep pit. Below and in front of him his son's light disappears into a scene of great commotion. The wailing noise is shivering and shaking the walls of this blackened cavity and loosening stones.

Within it is a strange breed of little spiny moles that can be identified by three concentric circles of needle-teeth that rapidly repair themselves and are powered by a mouth that rotates three chisel turns one way and then back again in the opposite direction. Aba's light brings clarity to the scene but causes these spiny little ones, called pit-diggers, along with other rat-like creatures, to race up the sides of the pit, pushing, shoving, tumbling over each other, and backsliding, while some are able to jump off a body part of their comrades and scurry up and over the edge. Aba peers gingerly down into the depths. The escaping pit-diggers are darting into the dark.

The pit absorbs much of Aba Ahhatome's light but even with it dimmed down another grotesque shape comes into view . . . a spirit being of uncertain lineage . . . with bird feet too huge for his bony humanoid body. The creature is disarranged with eyes in the back of his head. Sometimes the fiend's head snaps 180 degrees around to his back. His steps forward are faulty and he falls several times with his feet tangled in each other. Most remarkable of all, he shimmies and shakes so violently that there is little if any meaty flesh on his bones and his colorless skin falls like loose drapery over his gaunt frame. The fingers of the spirit are five times the length of a human hand. Their joints are bumpy knobs the size of small apples separated by long stretches of thin twiggy bones crowned by even longer curly dirt-filled fingernails. The creature, while always looking behind himself, raises a shaking hand forward as if to point to an unseen form, while his apple joints rattle. Sometimes he tries to scratch a picture on the wall of his pit, but alas, the unsteady hand brings forth ill-defined markings of indeterminable picture pieces. He or It, it's hard to say, is becoming more and more frustrated, wailing while trying to wipe the half-made picture away, then twirling around as if he hears or smells an intruder.

"I smell your sweat!" wails the jittering thing as it grows three feet taller than its original twelve feet height and points a trembling finger at its miserable cave drawings. "I can predict your future and it is a catastrophe! There is no hope. Who will take care of your son after you die? What if he becomes ill? Who will look after him? Without you he constantly falls into trouble."

"Beings of light do not sweat and do not die. I do not know of whom you speak."

"The walls of my pit sweat." Soon several pools begin to form in the bottom of the pit as the monster screeches in knowing delight while scenes, pictures of Ahhatome's and Aba Ahhatome's past, begin reflecting in the pools of "sweat."

"Look, look, LOOK and see your miserable future!" screams the beast. "Look into your future and weep." Pictures of Sings To Flowers and Little Bear being pulled apart with much agony is one scene among many others, all being played out upon the agitated murky reflection pools in the fiend's pit.

"I know exactly who you are," says Aba Ahhatome with a steady voice. "You are the well-known Worry Monster, who cannot relax into the present moment. You look constantly behind you at unpleasant memories of the past and use those to predict the future. You need to look to your future when your emotions are calmed, or into smooth clear waters to see for yourself a happy truth. Your predictions for me are not real unless I start to believe them and add my own personal worry energy to them. Now what have you done with my son?"

"Done with your son? What would I do with a light being? Do you think a light being would join me for one moment in my pit? I believe he circled around the edge of it and went that way." His shaking finger moves so wildly that he covers over 90 degrees of the circle around him. Because Worry Monsters are always looking behind and can never see clearly the way to a happy future, or sometimes even any future, Aba Ahhatome goes the opposite way than that indicated by the miserable thing and luckily soon picks up the trail his son left behind.

Strangely, instead of hideous groans, growls, and grunts from where the light trail leads next, Aba Ahhatome hears singing arising from a beautiful meadow surrounding a lovely lake. There are frogs sitting on lily pads, singing a chorus to the dragonflies. The nearby cedars are swaying to the music and whispering melodies to the winged ones in their arms and the winged ones are answering back with song. All seems in perfect harmony. *How can this be? Did I slip out of Hell somehow?* Aba wonders.

Even the green grasses are singing and flowing with delight in wave after wave. Aba watches the dancing heads of the daisies, corn flowers, and chamomile buds nodding and bowing toward the lake, so Aba Ahhatome's eyes follow the direction of their nods and he looks out across the water ripples to see a figure in a canoe. *Is that real or just a reflection?*

Then a profound thought comes to the surface of his mind . . . something a master told him once about the third dimension. *Pleasure and displeasure float together in the same boat for balance. If you remove either part, the boat will sink. Could this be about that? What place does a calm canoe, a pleasant activity, have in Hell? Yet, my son's light, though what remains of it is very dim now, is around that canoe.*

Aba Ahhatome has no time to reflect any longer, for before him now comes floating across the water, without the use of a paddle, a breath-taking beautiful sweet fawn standing in the middle of the boat. *What extraordinary apparition is this?* The fawn induces in Aba all the gentle mother/father care-giving feelings that nature intended for baby creatures and now the fawn is beginning to change shape.

The long deer face is beginning to flatten and round out into the face of an exquisite woman. When her entire body is transformed Aba Ahhatome is transfixed in awe by the spectacle that embraces his senses. The woman is stepping gracefully from the boat and with a sweeping motion of her arm and long neck, invites him to join her in the canoe. By identification of the light trail present, there is no question that Ahhatome has been in that canoe, so his aba has no excuse not to go there also.

Her movements remind him of the Snow Swan. Her skin and eyes glow with an irresistible refined radiance and Aba Ahhatome dares not to look long into the green reflecting pools above her dainty nose for fear of losing himself. He feels pulsations of energy surge against his eardrums like crashing waves. His knees are weak as he strides down the beach to meet this princess.

Flopping himself down in the boat, he is glad to sit. At least now there is little chance of falling down from the sight of her and looking completely foolish in her eyes. The maiden sweeps herself into the canoe and sits facing forward directly in front of him. For this Aba Ahhatome is also thankful, for now he can admire her from behind without her knowing, or so he thinks. Her glimmering long black hair defies the laws of gravity and floats about her head and face as though she were under water. Thin strands of seaweed studded with pearls adorn her crown. Aba Ahhatome admires her long straight but supple back. Her garment consists of fine mists, the edges of which are outlined in rain droplets that reflect his light like glittering diamonds and tiny stars. Every movement of her raiment brings a burst of flower fragrance and Aba Ahhatome is floated out across the lake thoroughly intoxicated.

Wait a minute. Pleasure and displeasure float together in the same boat. Something is wrong with this picture, thinks Aba Ahhatome. *What is this lovely creature's name and why is she in Hell? And above all, where is my son?*

"Where is my son?" he asks the lovely graceful one.

She speaks not a word but floats the boat without effort to the center of the lake. The canoe comes to a stop there, as the beautiful woman stretches out her arms over the waters bringing them to a motionless clarity. The breezes stop their gentle sighing and the frogs stop their song. Not a leaf moves. Not a single bird note comes singing. M-o-v-e-m-e-n-t - s-t-o-p-s. The... Wind... is... as... if... frozen.

Aba Ahhatome does not move either but feels pregnant with expectation. Should he shift his gaze up he would see movement... fast movement. I am blowing and swirling clouds around a central opening of calm positioned directly above the woman's watercraft and its occupants. Like the eye of a hurricane, which often forms over bodies of water, a portal is opening between heaven and hell. When a ray of light through the parted clouds falls upon her, she lurches back.

Presently a single drop of crimson-colored light falls from the end of the finger of the beauty's divine hand and drops into the depths. The stunned aba recognizes that light as belonging to his son, Ahhatome. *How does this woman discard in the lake my son's Life Force? Could it be that he shape-shifted into this woman? Why?*

Why in Hell? No. He would not treat his aba so. Yet, we are in Hell, . . . No. That's not it. Besides, it takes a lot of energy and concentration to shape-shift and I can tell by his trail that he has little light left. It has to be something else going on here. Something else. But what?

"Where in Hell is my son?"

For a moment, Aba Ahhatome thought he saw his son's face, stiff and looking like a mask, deep down within the lake. But no, if he was there, he is not there now. Aba Ahhatome pulls his eyes back from the water to look at the beautiful maiden, the princess of any man's heart. But . . . where is she and who or what is this?

The thing before him seems to be woman, but more like a living sexless carcass of slime. The translucent scales of its back show red underneath and it is speckled with oozing boils. *If it were not for my son, I would take leave of this place,* he thinks to himself.

"NOT POSSIBLE!" comes a rasping voice. The maker of the voice turns to look him in the eye. "You are in MY boat now."

Before him glares a welted up face, covered with disease. The eyelids are swollen almost shut, barely showing two angry red slits. The blood vessels on what was, just moments before, her swan-like neck are bulging and heaving. Three welts between her eyebrows pull the leathery skin there into two deep furrows making a perpetual frown that not even a lethal dose of Botox could soften. Her breath smells of sulfur-laced rotting death and Aba Ahhatome, who is shaken into awareness that his light is dulling down, hopes she will not speak again.

"It is obvious that you are angry. Perhaps your name is Anger, but I've already found the Anger Monster previously in Jealousy. There's more about you than what I can plainly see. If I can call you by your true name and see you for what you are, I will get back some of my power, my light. Is it Lust? Is it Seduction? Is it Theft? Is it Greed?" At the words Theft and Greed the monster barely flinches, yet that is at least some reaction. "I feel that I am close, but not right onto your game. Those names must be component parts of something bigger."

Aba Ahhatome closes his eyes and asks the heavens for help. He sits in silence. He sits and sits. Then, when he is about to give up and blink out, it comes to him. It comes to him from above, right through the opening into Hell and into his mind.

Sitting taller and squaring with the monster he announces, "Your first name is Deliberate Deception and your last name is User of the Innocent and I demand that you return my light and that of my son.

"Every Ponzi scheme, every corporate manipulation to fleece the public, every broken promise, every fraudulent advertisement of self or other, every bait and switch deal that Earthlings make, has made you. You create a trap for others, but in so doing you trap yourself because you live in fear. You fear being found out. You fear you will run out of suckers. You fear that your scheme will dry up and not work anymore. You live in the trap of your own making, your 'boat' as you call it. No wonder you live in Hell. If the devil by any other name were called, it would be FEAR. You are in business with all the other monsters in Hell."

Aba Ahhatome has nailed her (or it) on the cross of truth. She is giving Aba Ahhatome an icy stare; then she turns into an ice sculpture that melts in seconds from the power of Aba's returned light. Deliberate Deception User of the Innocent is flowing to the bottom of the boat making it list to one side while something else begins to stir . . . something that Deliberate Deception had covered up.

Pulling away the tarp that hid him, Aba Ahhatome finds his son, weakened but still alive. He gathers Ahhatome in his arms just before the boat groans onto its side and the lake swallows it and Deliberate Deception User of the Innocent. As far as Aba Ahhatome is concerned, she's gone. Dissolved by truth. Aba fills this empty space with joyful words, "Come Son, we are going home."

"Aba, I learned something on my trip down here. Some Earthlings say when they are ready to leave, 'Let's blow this Popsicle Stand' and 'Let's get the hell out of Hell.'"

"To 5D beings Hell appears as easily broken spindly sticks that support monsters that melt like popsicles. But there is more to those hook bugs than they pretend to show. On the surface they are weak creatures with a short life span. Their power comes from their massive numbers. When one blinks out, others take its place. Yet on the inside they're not so grotesque and being close to these Hell creatures has given me insight into their creators."

"I think the fear-based brains of humans create the monsters in Hell."

"Yes. The Hell Creators not only have a limited perception of light in only a tiny narrow beam of their reality, but in addition to their light-holding incompleteness, what they think they see holds a great deal of distortion. Remember, light is coded information that their brains need to decode properly. Even our fifth-dimensional light bathes the third dimension, but it is as though our gift-light is being twisted and mostly covered up."

"Aba, my beloved is among them! She is cut off from the rest of the universal inhabitants and its wonders . . . She's behind prison bars! I believe human DNA, the carrier of human light, has been tampered with."

"I agree, yet in spite of this, here and there some have been able to break out of their diminished selves and perform feats outside their usual norm only to be labeled heretics, lunatics, and witches, and be burned at the stake . . . or the opposite, be known as saints or even prayed to as gods."

"At least there is hope and even proof of breaking free. Half of me has escaped this 3D prison. I want to bring the rest of me home."

"I know Son, I know. And let's not forget that fifth-dimensional beings also evolve to higher dimensions. But for now, 'Let's get the hell out of Hell.'"

CHAPTER THIRTY-TWO

Sammy's Secret

Sometimes you just get tired of your trip and want to get home. Home for the Johantgens is in Allyn, Washington, a quaint and quiet community located near the tip of one of Puget Sound's many fingers of salty water, which dominate the western part of the state. Nearby loom the Olympic Mountains brushed with broad strokes of white. But the Johantgens belong to the water, The Sound, the lakes, waterfalls, and the many ponds choked with water lilies for which Lily was named.

Dad drove with determination from Syringa in Idaho following route 12, over White Pass in the Cascade Mountains to Interstate 5, north to the turn off at Olympia, then toward the Olympic Mountains through Shelton and home, all in one day. Ah, home at last and the taste of Big Bubba's Burgers and Lily's longtime favorite, Montana Bison Burger at Lennard K's Boat House.

The girls' birthday is in one week and, from Mom's point of view, there is always too much preparation to be done. However, this time there is a twist. Catrina and Lily will triumphantly reach the coveted age of 18. And there is more—Cat has a date! It will be her first date, as far as her parents know.

The Wind knows that is not altogether true since she has already had mixed dates on the sly, supposedly just with girlfriends, where boys appear from nowhere. Lily is not interested in dating right now and that suits Mom and Dad just fine. Cat however, has a different view.

Lily just better stay out of my way when my date arrives. "Keep those nasty bird feathers in your room," she says, dripping with ice sickles "He'll think I live in a chicken coop."

Dad has had a sour stomach ever since he found out about The Date, and he is secretly writing down for the third time a list of things he wants to check out concerning this young man. First of all, he must not only come to the door to meet Cat's parents, he must sit down with the rest of the family at the table and have birthday cake. When he is trapped in the family fold, even ever so briefly, he can be plied with questions. The questions have to be subtle, yet telling. Dad has to be able to read between the lines accurately and, at the same time, not scare the youth into silence. *If you lay one finger on my daughter I will blow your head off,* is *not the right approach, but that kid better get the message.*

Dad goes over his list.

1. Cat needs to give us his first, middle, and last name, address and phone number.

He crosses off middle name; after all, since he works up the hill at the post office he has a great deal of information at his fingertips. Maybe he will even know the parents. Believe me, anything coming through the Allyn P.O. with that kid's last name will be under scrutiny from now on. *Maybe the kid's house is on my mail route. In that case, if any "smut" goes to their home, I will know it. There better not be anything in brown wrapping paper with this kid's name on it. Then again, they hardly wrap magazines in brown paper anymore.* There have been big changes since he was a kid and got a few brown-papered girly magazines until his parents intercepted them. He can still hear their displeasure after forty years.

2. Drive by the kid's home.

If it's neat and tidy, I'll feel a little better. If not, well then what? He doesn't want to break Cat's heart, but well, let's say he will at least start to feed the Worry Monster even more.

3. Check out his clothes and his haircut.

How obvious is that. Dad cannot stand kids walking around with shredded holes in their pants, not to mention wearing pants that are practically falling off. *Shoes untied or without laces? Good God. Such a kid will never be in charge of anything, and since he looks the part, will be penniless. How will he support a wife and family if he cannot buy decent pants?*

I wouldn't mind a look inside the boy's wallet. He better have a valid driver's license. How old is this kid anyway? I wonder if I could check out his wallet and what if I find a c-----? I can't even say the word. What if I don't find one? Jesus! What am I thinking! It's just a simple date. Harmless. Not to worry. Much.

Dad cannot take it any longer. He has a headache; he feels weak and in need of a nap. He crumples up his third list and tosses it with the first two wadded-up notes in the bucket under his desk. He has fed the Worry Monster enough. He has to stop.

The day is here. It's party time! The table is set. Grandma and Grandpa Johantgen from Poulsbo arrived last night. Lilly and Cat have blue and white streamers, their high school colors, hanging from the light over the table and looping around the room. Huckleberry upside down cake is ready with eighteen candles times two. Normally the room would be filled with girlfriends, but that will come tomorrow—a sleepover is planned after the grandparents leave.

Today a quiet cake and coffee/punch affair is planned where Cat can have her young man mostly to herself and Dad can ask his questions if he can remember them. Lily does not know who the guy is and is only mildly interested. After all, she has her own mysterious happenings on her mind and her more numerous tailbone-to-waist "hot flashes" as she calls them.

"Don't worry, Dad. I'll test out The Creep for ya."

"Creep?" Looking down, he notices that Sammy is holding the crumpled up list he had thrown away under his desk.

"Give me that, Son." He grabs the wad and tosses it into the kitchen trash, forgetting to ask Sammy about the exact nature of his test.

The doorbell rings. For a couple of seconds everyone freezes and looks at one another to see who will move first. "Cat, it's your date. Get the door," says a slightly nervous-looking mom. You can almost hear a simultaneous intake of breath as everyone waits to see who the young man is on the other side of the door. Psychology books tell us family members will size him up within two minutes. Poor lad. The unsuspecting innocent has entered the lair.

Holy Smoke he's short! At least a foot shorter than Cat. He cannot be older, thank God. He has a baby face without any fuzz and thick glasses. Dad has a softness in his heart for anyone stuck behind thick lenses. He wears a pocket protector sans pens. He is only an inch taller than ten-year-old Sammy. Even Sammy is surprised by the sight of him.

Maybe his voice hasn't dropped yet—or his testicles, Dad thinks to himself and almost laughs out loud. The boy's hand is small in Dad's, trembly, and moist.

"Have you got a driver's license, Young Man?" What an opening statement. Where is his, pleased-to-meet-you?

"I have had a license for a week, Sir."

"It's not a learner's permit? It's the real deal?"

"Oh yes Sir." The proud fellow pulls out his glossy fresh license with a broad smile, showing white but crooked front teeth, framed by deep dimples in his cheeks, and two rather large stick-out ears. He is really quite cute when he smiles, in an impish kind of way. Dad's heart is softening more.

"But how far are you going with this new license? Did I hear you're going to the movies in Port Orchard?" Cat is now sending her Dad daggers and the rest of the family is lining up mentally behind this young man in his defense.

"I've driven there six times already, Sir." The young man has practiced the drive over and over so he can ferry his queen to the movies with ease and finesse.

"Why don't you show this young man to his seat at the table next to you, Dear," Mom says to Cat while cutting off her husband's line of questioning. "John!" she whispers sharply, "Give it a rest."

The tension in the room relaxes. People are starting to have a good time. There is laughter around the table and people try not to notice the huckleberry skin plastered on the guest's front tooth. Dad is now totally disarmed and has forgotten about his list, when Sammy decides, *It's time to test this guy's metal with my trick gizmo.*

Everyone except Sammy had just filled their mouths and there is a lull in the conversation. Sammy has slipped his hand into his pocket and is fishing for a remote control device. Poof—pst-pst-st-st-st. It comes from under Mom's chair. Mom looks around. There is a startled, somewhat bewildered look on her face. Everyone else is looking at their plates. Lily starts to choke and has to leave the table. Grandma and Grandpa smile at each other. "What's a little gas among friends," announces Dad to Mom, trying to make light of the embarrassing situation.

Grandma says to Mom, "You must be getting old, Dear."

No one is more shook up than Sammy. He thought he had taped his new fart machine under the chair of the kid taking out his sister. Unknown to him, Mom had moved the chairs around in a way she thought would provide more room at the table.

There are five different sounding farts in his new machine from the curio store in Montana. Sammy had practiced behind closed doors, having set the machine to go off at his favorite two or three. *What a great idea. What a superior test.* But the last person he wanted to embarrass was his mother and he did not press the remote button again to get the other two *good sounding ones.* Not this time.

The front door is finally safely closed behind the exiting Cat and her new beau. "You didn't even ask for his name!" Mom scolds her husband.

"Well neither did you," he replies, "and besides, I already know his name: Timothy Wilson. And I know his address and his parent's names too, and their phone numbers. I know he is in the same class as the twins and he is seventeen years old and that he is driving his parent's car and the license plate is . . . ah, I have it written down somewhere."

Sammy is dashing to pull off the fart machine from under his mother's chair and stuffs it under his shirt to disappear into his room. *My perfect test backfired.* Backfired indeed, in more ways than one.

A couple of minutes later when he appears again he sees his mother running her hand under her chair and finding nothing. She gives a sigh and starts to gather up the dishes while Lily stands looking out the window . . . seeing nothing.

Lily is lost in her own thoughts and daydreams. This time, Sammy decides to keep mum about his sins.

CHAPTER THIRTY-THREE

My Lover, My Dream

Day after day and into the nights Lily practices her lucid dreaming exercises. Several times she remembers upon awakening that No Name has visited her in a dream to tell her to, "Relax into it." "You're trying too hard." "You are too tense." "You're breathing too shallowly." Lily keeps on working. She is driven to become a lucid dreamer by her determined and dedicated will. She doesn't know it, but this is also soul development work. No Name has additional unspoken motives.

At first her little bedside notebook fills with just a few words, then paragraphs, then several pages, and even sketches. Every night she places her celestite crystal geode pieces and her "miracle feathers" next to her bed. Sometimes in her dreams she sees brilliant colors, geometric forms, tunnels of light, even The Eye of Horus once in a while. Yet there is nothing she recognizes as Two Bears or what or who might present himself as Ahhatome, and she cannot say with certainty that she is awake and able to direct her dreams. She continues to do her reality checks and sometimes pushes herself beyond the recommended three times a day.

One night, Lily dreams of walking in a place she has walked hundreds of times, the long public dock in town that juts out into the North Bay. She marvels at the clarity of the water and the plumage of the sea gulls. She is also noticing a tiny spider floating in the air about twenty feet away. Without warning it is swooped up by a saucy black raven that comes careening down over her head. The water seems more bright than usual and Lily brings her left hand up to shade her eyes.

Wait a minute! She cannot feel her . . . She is not wearing her glasses, yet her vision has never been this clear, ever! Is this her accustomed reality? No, it is not. She must be dreaming and she knows she is in the dream world. She knows she is awake in her dream!

Lily is filled with excitement. Finally! Finally! But . . . now her dream picture is shaking and beginning to dim and a second later Lily is awake, but in her bed at home in her customary visual haze.

Never mind. She takes the crystals in her hand and holds them over her heart. The crystals speak to her with warmth. Lily tells herself that she will learn to control her dream the next time.

The clock says three in the morning. *Plenty of time to dream again.* She decides to prop herself up and puts the geode halves back in their place to read a little in her book.

She learns that for thousands of years Tibetan Monks practiced "dream yoga" and have developed complete mastery of their dreams. She also discovers the very thing I, The Wind, was trying to whisper in her ears. She can command her dream to "even out" if it gets wobbly, and she can ask it to "brighten" if it becomes dull, and "darken" if too bright.

Feeling drowsy. She does a reality check by looking at her hands and pinching her little finger. *Yes, I'm awake.* Now speaking out loud to her precious crystal half-orbs, "I want to go back to the dock by the gazebo." The bedside light is turned off. Lily deliberately slows and deepens her breath. She closes her eyes, but tries to stay awake within and looks up inside her head toward her mystical third eye.

It works! She is back on the dock and she is awake and she knows she is dreaming. She continues to breathe slowly and deeply into her diaphragm. "I demand to see Ahhatome," she says and is controlling her dream.

The light in the sky, a star perhaps or a meteor, is very bright but somehow it does not hurt Lily's eyes even as it comes closer. The light approaches slowly . . . sometimes it seems hesitant. It skims across the water without any noise. It appears now as a column of whitish gold and there seems to be a stream of light that stretches up-up-up into infinity. Faintly at first, and then more definitely, Lily can see an outline of a youngish man within the light column. Most remarkable is a pulsating star burst within him, sending a radiation of pale pink and white gold expanding halos from his heart center in all directions. *Whoa! Is this Two Bears or Ahhatome? Ohmygosh!*

No more thoughts come. She simply feels the glory of his presence. Finally she lifts her eyes to his and feels his energy fill her. He comes closer and wraps his spirit around and through her. It is as though they are linked, cell to cell, corpuscle to corpuscle, while every fiber and thread of her being becomes gently glowing, warm, and expanded.

Her identity is becoming lost. Now she is no more. She is beyond this universe. She is more than the multiverse. She stretches beyond time. She is everything and she is nothing. The fusion lasts for seconds—or was it an eternity?

Next a sensation of pulling, tearing, and shredding consumes them both. They cannot stay locked in a dream embrace for long. Ahhatome especially must be careful not to prolong his visit to this Earthling mental world of the dream for fear of causing Lily's human brain to become erratic and misfire. She simply cannot assimilate the refined energy for very long without becoming greatly disoriented and eventually nerve damaged.

Reluctantly, Ahhatome must turn away from his beloved, a part of himself. He must end the contact. It feels to him like a repeat performance of the episode in the huckleberry patch but with even more mental pain than before. He has to allow himself to be severed into two again. As he turns away, Lily reaches for him before she sees the cord and hook that was placed years ago through his back and into his heart. With her desperate reach now, she inadvertently deepens his hook. Before she can try to pull it out she wakes up back in her bed, paralyzed with grief. She will not try lucid dreaming again. To reach ecstasy and then be yanked back to her old reality is too painful. Lily must deal now with deep sadness. "Why did No Name let me go through this?"

Lily hears in her mind, "You have experienced only a small segment of the journey you have chosen. Be glad." The voice she hears belongs to No Name. Is this tough love or the work of tough rules? It's painful.

If joining just to separate again is this bad for Lily and Ahhatome in the dream world, I cannot imagine what joining might be like with one of them in and the other out of the dense physical world, or even if it's possible. I, The Wind can't begin to think about it.

CHAPTER THIRTY-FOUR

Kundalini Stirring

The Friday before Labor Day weekend is here. Being true Northwesterners, the Johantgen family has a camping weekend planned to celebrate the holiday at one of their adored places, Lake Crescent, in the northern part of the Olympic range.

However today Lily is looking through the big glasses in the optometrist's office. This is a yearly ritual in preparation for school, and right now Dr. Peterson is shaking his head in total amazement. "Lily, I have checked your records from last year and the two preceding. My notes show that your vision has been stable but severely nearsighted at minus eight diopters with significant astigmatism. Yet today, after triple checking, I can find no astigmatism and you are at minus five diopters. You are still nearsighted, but there has been a huge reversal. I have never seen anything like it in my thirty years of practice.

"Essentially, your eye balls, which were overly large or deep, have become shorter and your corneas have taken a new shape without laser treatment! I can hardly believe my own eyes. It gives me great pleasure to give you a new prescription with weaker glasses for your myopia."

"Would glasses that are too strong for me give me headaches in the spot right between my eyebrows and make me see bright-colored flashes and especially a lot of blue lights?"

"Talk with your medical doctor."

One more stop is left before getting ready for Lake Crescent. Her family doctor is to check out Lily's tailbone and lower back. She decides not to mention flashing lights.

"It's perfect," he announces. "No numbness, no inflammation, coccyx joint not calcified . . . it still wiggles," he smiles. "Get out of here and go to the mountains."

On the way to Lake Crescent Lily looks buried in thoughts not of this world. She finally revealed the No Name visits. Dad had hinted about "a trip to a shrink." Mom said, "Let's not rush things." Sammy's comment was, "Lily has always been silly." And Cat's thoughts about what to wear on the first day of school leave no room for Lily's problems.

When Lily told her dad that asking every new person she meets for a full name and address is "beyond snoopy," the final outcome of that conversation was, "No more speaking to strangers then, especially if they give you **no name**." The Wind tried to warn Lily to go easy on her dad, that it's a postman's job to dwell in names and addresses, but lately she can get bold and blunt and doesn't hear me.

Lake Crescent has a row of charming little cabins for rent near the lake's edge. Mom likes the fact that there is an even more charming lodge with delicious meals, giving her a rest from the kitchen and recovery from the slumber party. Sammy likes the two huge stuffed elk heads with expansive antlers on each side of the stone fireplace and the walk to the nearby ranger station where he plies the rangers for bear and cougar stories. Dad likes the fishing and the girls like to tan, or at least Cat still does. Lily is full of sighs and just sits at the edge of the pier looking into the water. She doesn't seem to care that she will soon be showing off a fashionable new pair of specs. If this were Cat she would be jumping for joy to get rid of the glasses that look more like binoculars.

It is hard for the family to know what Lily is thinking these days, but The Wind sees her emotions and thought-form energies. She suffers. She sometimes cries to me when we are alone. Now, as she sits slumped over at the end of the dock staring into the water, she is trying to visualize what to do for a ceremony to call back the lost part of her wandering spirit in the mountains of Montana, and how to pull the hook out of Two Bears, and she is trying to remember his new hard-to-remember name, Ahh . . .

"Are you going to mope all day? You're a real fine example of fun for everyone in this family." Dad is standing at the other end of the dock. His large bellows put force behind his fire that startles Lily and almost blows her into the water.

At dinner Mom gets stern. "We're all going hiking tomorrow, period. Lily, cheer up. You are bringing everyone down on this trip. It's the end of summer. Let's try to enjoy what's left of it, please." Dad's jaw is set; he gives a single nod of approval at his wife's command.

"Can we take the hike to Pyramid Peak? The rangers say we might see a bear," pipes up Sammy. At the mention of "bear" two of the three women cringe, however Lily comes more alive and out of her doldrums for a few breaths of brighter air. "The rangers say all you have to do is make a lot of noise, like pounding on a tin cup with a spoon and singing Yankee Doodle, and the bears will leave you alone."

Cheered by a substantial breakfast, the Johantgens are ready for a morning adventure on Pyramid Mountain near the lake's north shore. It's a seven mile trip from the trailhead up and back, winding to an elevation of 3,000 feet. At the summit is an old 1942 WWII look-out cabin built to spot feared enemy airplanes coming from Japan down Puget Sound to bomb Seattle, Tacoma, Fort Lewis, and McChord Air Force Base. Thirteen of these wooden cabins were built on various prominent mountain peaks throughout the Olympics. There are only two now, left to rot and sink back into the bosom of Mother Earth.

Lily seems to have come to life and is leading the pack up the trail with Mom coming last. After trudging about forty-five minutes past the almost dried up June Creek, the family comes to a large slide area several hundred feet across. The path lies naked to the elements there with no vegetation and it becomes so narrow that the hikers have to place one foot in front of the other. One false step and it's a long way down the mountain.

Dad is now coming to the slide and waits for Mom. The children have already crossed this treacherous spot.

"Come on back, kids. Too dangerous," he yells.

"Lily is already way up the trail and she can't hear me!" Sammy shouts back.

"Okay then, Mom and I will turn around and wait below. I don't think your cell will work in these mountains. If you're not back in reasonable time, we will contact the rangers. Don't go any further than the spotter-cabin. Keep together."

"Dad, nobody has their cell on this hike anyway!"

A mere half hour later comes The Rain. Just a little at first, then a torrent, making the trail muddy and the chance of more slides increase. The teenagers hear falling rocks off and on, both in front and behind them. Then Lily spots something. It's in the mud. Fresh bear tracks going their direction up the trail.

"Yankee Doodle now!" Lily is yelling back behind her. "Yankee Doodle went to town a riding on a . . ." Three kids are slushing up the trail pushing their lungs into urgent robust song. The trail begins a snake-like weave with the bear definitely staying on their path. After about 100 yards of switching and singing Lily starts to wonder, *Maybe we should not walk so fast. What if we actually catch up to the bear?*

Lily slows her pace to think about a retreat when just around the next bend the bear prints veer off the path and head straight down the side of the mountain. *What a relief,* she thinks—until looking below Lily sees something big and black eating huckleberries. It's about 200 feet away. The bear senses the intruders and is growing taller, rising up on his back legs while looking up at them and sniffing the air. *Omigosh. A bear can cover a 300-foot span in six seconds.*

The Wind does the calculation. If this bear wants to charge they have approximately four seconds to live—unless he is slowed down by the uphill climb; that gives them what, five seconds?

"BEAR! BEAR!" Screams Lily. "Look big." "Scream." "Make noise!"

Sammy, who had earlier picked a walking stick with green growth, frantically waves and shakes his leafy baton overhead, then drops it and reaches for his back pocket. The ten year old is growling loudly and showing his teeth, looking more pathetic than ferocious, but the missal from his slingshot parts the bear's hair. The bear looks at Sammy while Cat picks up stones and throws them at the beast, missing by several feet but making a distraction. Lily jumps up and down yelling at the beast, "Suck eggs." What? Suck eggs?

Sammy screams, "You mean, Fuck eggs!" Lily and Cat momentarily forget their fear and look at Sammy with widened eyes and dropped jaws.

The bear looks perplexed. He's fat. Maybe he's full and maybe he doesn't like the taste of kids. Maybe he can't decide which one to eat first.

Now he is looking up and up, gazing at a spot above the young people where I blow the vegetation with my furious gusts then blast him in his face. The bear grunts, turns, and runs his six seconds down, instead of up the mountain. Whew. The kids sink down right in the mud, exhausted but glad they were not the big brute's lunch.

"Let's not tell Mom and Dad about this," sighs Lily. "Why not?" cries Sammy. "Because." is the short terse reply. "Because then I would have to tell about your dirty mouth."

Sammy whines, "I want to go back down."

"Fine!" says Cat. "You want to go back down to where the bear could be waiting for you? Or do you think you can talk to that bear with all that growling and swearing? I vote we stay here for a while."

"Look, we are only a few feet from the top and the rain has stopped. Let's at least go to the lookout cabin and then turn around. Agreed?"

The other two look dubious, but nod their heads in agreement and begin to trudge on. They are now above the rain clouds and watch long vertical cloud wisps blown by The Wind swirl and twist like dancing ghosts. Lily is putting her hand over her solar plexus.

For the last half hour, even before she saw the bear, she has felt discomfort. *It feels like a piano wire being pulled and twisted, tighter and tighter. Sitting and resting gives no relief.*

At last there is no more uphill climb. They have reached the ridge and more evidence of bears greet them. The pathway leads along the spine of the mountain where there is a forest of trees with deep claw marks. *Bears or cougars?* Sammy wonders. They will walk quickly through this part of the forest until they come to the lookout. They'd rather be looking out at the scenery than looking out for bears. They soon see something just ten feet away. A peak stands apart from the main body of the mountain, cradling something wooden at its center.

What a very old and dilapidated wreck of a building it is. Long buffeted over the years by my howling winter dances and heavy snows, there's not much left.

"Gee!" Sammy speaks for all three.

To get to it you have to walk out on a narrow bridge of land, approximately fifteen feet long and one-and-a-half feet wide with a drop-off straight down on both sides.

"They should have roped this place off." The stand-apart peak is about thirty-five feet wide in all directions.

"Do we really want to visit that old rotting thing missing its roof?"

"We can do it."

"Let's take the easy way across the land bridge on all fours." While Lily is moving along the land bridge on her hands and knees she remembers what No Name had told her in a recent dream about ceremony and being reborn.

"In the most sacred of our ceremonies we are reborn. We enter the sweat lodge naked, as we were in our mother's womb, and we enter with humility by bending and entering like our four-legged relatives who were also made by Heavenly Creator."

I, The Wind, will make a song now. In the song I will sing out a little of what I and the other elements have witnessed. Not everyone will hear me. I hope Lily will. I sing that the theme of being reborn to a more elevated state of awareness than the previous one is the major theme of The Universe. The flow of Life Force is from the lesser to the greater, from the simple to the more complex. Being born again in this context simply means coming into greater knowledge, knowledge that is profound enough to cause a change that is actively demonstrated in an individual's behavior. This majestic theme is far greater than any single philosophy can contain, religious or otherwise.

I sing about ceremony. Done in a group or alone, ceremony is a powerful tool to direct subtle personal energy. Ceremony brings separated parts of the psyche into a more unified whole by bringing focus to an intent. The unconscious part of humans is more open and susceptible to the language of ceremony because the huge sea of both individual and collective unconscious "thinks" and communicates in pictures. It is dream language.

Not only can the conscious mind communicate with the unconscious by the powerful means of ceremony but the reverse is also true. The unconscious part of ourselves can communicate with our conscious mind through meditation, through the remembrance and correct interpretation of our dreams, and through the shaman's healing ceremonies. This is the song I am singing today through the trees above Lake Crescent and I am whistling it through the cracks in the old lookout for those who can hear me.

Lily, Cat, and Sammy successfully transit the land bridge. They are walking now on level ground around the skirt of what was once a cabin. This strip of ground is not any more than five feet wide before it drops straight down. Soon the clouds separate enough to see Lake Crescent, a sparkling sapphire snuggled in a nest of green far below to the south. To the east the smaller Lake Southerland reveals herself. And to the north they can see the salty Strait of Juan de Fuca, where the Pacific Ocean enters Puget Sound.

The scene before them is mesmerizing and transforms their awareness as they gaze below from their high perch. They rest there and watch the spiraling columns of fog drift and glide on the swirls of The Wind. However, there is one particular gathering of vertical mist that is beginning to take on a shape. This one has a violet hue and is taking the form of a woman.

Lily becomes aware that the pain in her solar plexus has vanished. Gone. As though the piano wire around her midriff had been sliced apart. She looks around at her siblings to find both of them asleep! *What's going on? My brother and sister do not sleep on hikes. Who or what is causing this? Is that No Name in the fog?*

She does not take solid shape but stays looking like a violet-tinged fog lady. A shaft of light hits her now and then, making her sparkle. She does not come upon the land, but stays suspended about ten feet out from the cliff edge in midair. She speaks.

"Sweet Child, it is imperative that you do not dally longer in removing your hook and calling back your soul fragments. There is a moving current stirring and wanting to rise within your body. This is a normal happening in an Earthling's experience at some unknown point in their future. Your time is beginning now. But your past hurts and traumas are like beaver dams against the flow of this energy that wants to rise higher in your body and open for you doors of compassion and knowledge. When the energy is backed up it begins to flow into other smaller channels, causing the pain of too much pressure. This force comes like labor pains, rising and falling, as in giving birth. You are in labor of birthing a new you and, like all births, no two are the same in all details."

"You mean giving birth to a baby? No Name, I'm a virgin. This can't be."

"Lily, **you** are the baby. This information in centuries past was kept secret and in the hands of a few and told to the so-called common people in the form of myths, legends, metaphors, parables, and allegories. Eventually with this energy comes an increase in power and some have misused it and caused harm to themselves and others. Today, with the tremendous increase in fourth-dimensional energy, cell phones, remote controls, and computers, stress has been put upon the human body to physically change as these energies penetrate and pass through the physical.

"There are also cosmic energy fluctuations that pass through the body as the Earth changes in position on her journeying toward the center of the Milky Way galaxy and the so-called 'dark rift' as it appears through the telescope. Lily, you and other humans need to prepare the channels within the body to be able to handle this new energy increase as well as the potential awakening of the latent stored energy within the sacred sacrum bone above the coccyx, referred to in some texts as kundalini."

"Kundaaaa . . . lini?"

"The name is not important. As you might expect, it has different names in different cultures. It is important to understand what exactly this energy does when it becomes active. There are etheric openings along the human spine that, to those lucky enough to be clairvoyant, look like whirling funnels. These protrude from the body at certain levels from the tailbone to the crown of the head. In most literature the major ones are seven to ten in number. Actually there are many more, smaller, swirling etheric openings, such as at the palms of the hands and the soles of the feet.

"In those beings where the special kundalini energy yet sleeps, which is the case of most Earthlings, these charkas, as some call them, are working only to a minimum and are covered with an etheric veil or filter. When those filters, or 'seals' as they are known in the west, are opened by the rise of the kundalini energy, it allows for more light and sound energy to activate the body. The chakra systems of children are more open. As humans mature and begin their journey into various emotional and mental traumas the spinning of the openings slow and the veils thicken. Emotional or physical trauma causes partial blockages. That is why it is important to clear those blockages before the awakening of the kundalini energy."

"How does one prepare the channels, No Name?"

"We have already touched on the most important aspect, forgiveness, which is only the first step in the active form of love which prepares the channels and opens the heart. The heart is the 'narrow way,' and I might add the only safe way, for the rising kundalini to activate the higher energy centers above the heart, including the etheric energy center at the crown of the head.

"Usually people think of forgiveness in terms of forgiving others. It is also important to forgive the small self, the ego self who lives in fear and is lost in survival issues and all its ramifications. At one point, when the soul has matured further, it sees nothing to forgive."

"No Name! How can this be when there is so much terrible in the world?"

"As the soul develops compassion he begins to understand that an Earthling's point of view is too limited to judge others. And when he remembers that all beings move according to their understanding of their world judgment begins to fall away even more."

"Are you saying that when people do evil things they should go unpunished?"

"No, the world does not work that way. There are always consequences for any action. But in your own personal world you must decide where or to what to give your energy. In a world of evildoers and horrible deeds there will be a whole system for dealing with that. The wrong doers and the punishers are but flip sides of the same coin, as your people are fond of saying.

"Calming down judgment frees up energy for something else and relaxes the subtle energy meridians of the body-mind and, by the way, makes you more pleasant to be around. The sins of others are not looked upon as okay, but actions of humans confused and just falling short and missing the mark of their contract with themselves."

"What about this kundalini?"

"Kundalini energy has been referred to in ancient times as goddess or Mother Earth energy. It rises through the part of the body that touches the Earth, the soles of the feet, to combine with the descending energy some call the masculine aspect, through the crown. The marriage of these two primary cosmic energies takes place in the heart. This teaching is worldwide but encrypted in major religions.

"The marriage of the opposites, dissolves and releases the tremendous force of previous polarization for the final realization of the divine called 'enlightenment.'

"Lily, anyone experiencing kindalini energy needs to follow the rules of moderation in all aspects of physical life. The body is the vessel, the container, the 'holy grail' among many others for the Life Force and is Spirit in crystallized form.

"Lily, you can find certain yoga classes dedicated solely to the purpose of making the kundalini energy rise with certain postures, breathing techniques, and other practices. It is good for you to stretch your body to keep it supple and to breathe deeply. But overdoing the deliberate awakening techniques before the body's subtle energy conduits have been developed through compassion and forgiveness is dangerous. It literally is playing with the fire, the creative force of the universe through your body. There are protective etheric veils at certain levels along the central spinal canal to keep the rise of the potential "fire" in check, but if they are ripped open prematurely there is potential for imbalance and damage to underlying organs, including the brain.

"Lily, the pain you are feeling at your solar plexus is a blockage you must remove. Remove that hook in Ahhatome or Two Bears. The two of you are one. To complicate matters, you are now on a large cone-shaped Earth body, a pyramid-shaped mountain. A large body like this mountain in this shape will concentrate its own kundalini force at its apex, which you are now sitting upon. Right now I am diverting the mountain energy into myself for your protection. In your fragile state of the stirring sacral energy with uncleared channels, you need to get off this mountain, which is part of the cause of your pain, and mentally ground yourself every day or even more often.

"Imagine in your mind energy from your tailbone sliding back down into the ground and being reabsorbed. Lean back against a tree and mentally send the energy down by way of its roots. Hug a tree once in a while."

"They make jokes about 'Tree Huggers' in Shelton. They just don't like 'em."

No Name smiles, "If you do not imagine the flow going down you will be more susceptible to the natural upflow of this energy, which in your present state augments your pain. Remember, your imagination directs the force, so use this knowledge to your advantage."

"No Name, I want to clean out my channels. I want to remove Ahhatome's hook now."

Lily frantically searches around for something that looks like a hook. There is a small thin delicate twig on the ground with just the right shape. She is going to the very center of the cabin, which is the center of the strong rising energy field of this mountain peak. She is raising the hooked twig into the air and, since the cabin has no roof, into a moment of sunlight. Three times. Three times she yells with conviction, "Universe, Mother-Father God, I remove the hook I placed long ago into the heart and solar plexus of my love, Two Bears Ahhatome." Then she says, "It is done."

Now Lily is taking the hook-shaped twig and breaking the slender thing into as many tiny pieces as possible and is dropping the crumb-like sections one by one in a straight line through the space between two slats of the floor. There they will be, undisturbed in a straight row without a hook, even until they rot into dust. Lily has finally made her hook removal ceremony. It is followed by a flash of light.

The Wind is giving this monumental moment such a sigh of relief that I blow myself into the fifth dimension. At last . . . at last . . . I see that the psychic energy hook of emotional desperation placed in Ahhatome's heart almost 200 years ago is released. There will always be an energy cord between these two lovers as long as they are separated, but the dragging hook that weighed him down and pulled him backward is gone. Ahhatome and Lily are now more "enlightened."

Lily's sleeping siblings are beginning to move slightly and become restless. "No Name, did you put my brother and sister to sleep?"

"Lily, you are also asleep, just not as deeply. However, you are stirring in your slumber."

CHAPTER THIRTY-FIVE
Back to School

Lily is known as "the quiet one" and is called "Four Eyes" by some schoolmates who prefer to wear a mean spirit. This label, better meant for a monster, has jumped with her from grade to grade, needling her more in high school. After a week of school nobody but her sister has noticed her new look behind fashionable glasses and Catrina is silent about the matter. That Four Eyes name won't die. No one sees that Lily no longer has to push her glasses up or hold them on her nose and she doesn't hear The Wind whispering, "You're a blossoming beauty."

Heaping on more unpleasantness is the fact that even though she has had less upper abdominal pain than before her ceremony for releasing Ahhatome's psychic hook, the pain did return. She is more remote and doesn't speak at all about her summer vacation and nobody asks about it. Even Catrina's rants don't irritate anymore. *It's just noise.*

I wonder. Is this a sign of spiritual growth or is she becoming more depressed and beginning to slip over the edge?

Lily can still be drawn to the beauty of nature outside the classroom window and the internal landscape of her mind, but not the teacher's latest chemistry scribbles accompanied by *that long-winded monotone voice that doesn't know when to stop.*

She goes into nature more often now and cries out her secret agonies into The Wind. She has a special log by the water where she goes almost daily. She takes her shoes off to mentally send some of her energy back down from her tailbone through the soles of her feet into the receptive Earth as No Name has instructed. I too am sad. She no longer remembers how to hear me.

Catrina is her twin's opposite, an extroverted showoff. Like a wound-up chatterbox she overflows while telling her friends about The Dr. Dixon. "When I fluttered my eyelashes he became splayed out like fresh meat. It wasn't as though I was naked, but that's how he was looking at me." And then she says, "I almost got cut to ribbons when the glass shattered in the museum." Come on. Her spin to Lily's stolen story.

In school Catrina is seen in the largest and the loudest group that transverses the hallways, always making sure that envious eyes are on her as being a part of the in-group. She and her friends are admired by all except for a few "dead heads" and "dweebs" not worth consideration or the time of day. The Wind remembers a time in the distant past where she always drew apart from the group.

Cat's group is constantly on display. And as such, while eyes are on them, her group's eyes scan the admiring crowd of "wannabes" for any reaction to their parade of beauty queens, cheerleaders, class president, class treasurer or class something-or-other who travel together, eat together in the cafeteria, and are seen together at the movies or paintball park.

In their imaginations and daydreams they are the future movie starlets, brain surgeons, C.E.O.s of Fortune 500's, or whatever the latest "cool" thing is to be. Each of the Chosen Ones also emboldens the other members of their stellar pod. For certain they are a loud crowd that sweeps aside others as they approach, like a gaggle of geese, picking and eating morsels of this thing or that thing on their way.

Catrina has informed Lily not to walk the school halls next to her in her "wigged out" condition or bring those "filthy feathers" around her and especially around "my friends." "You look like some kind of train wreck and it's absolutely embarrassing."

Only once have I heard Lily verbally stand up to Catrina. "If you think there's something wrong with **my** mind, you need to know you're **way more mindless** than me," she said. "You don't have an independent thought separate from that group of tootie toot snobs you travel with. And you're bitter. Bitter. Bitter. Bitter."

After that rare defensive attack, Lily doesn't seem to care, while doodles of bows and arrows, buffalo skulls, beaver faces, the letters T.B. and Ahh, stars, and butterflies collect in the margins of her notebooks. She is distracted by remembering small flashes of light she thinks she sees some nights in the corner of her bedroom or larger ones off in the distance when gazing out the window. Nobody else seems to see them and she dares not speak about the thunder-less light flashes too often and never mentions the appearance of No Name anymore to anyone.

The bell rings and what follows is that dreaded computer practice lab, an elective Lily signed up for to get out of music. She thought of skipping it, because last Saturday night she had another night-flash incident and this is only Monday . . . not enough time for the effects to wear off.

Lily slides into her chair in front of the computer monster. Sure enough, within five minutes the computer is going haywire. It scrolls on its own. The last half of a sentence jumps back into a paragraph written at the top of the page.

Don't you dare go black on me, she is thinking, and so it does.

"Reboot it, Lily," the teacher says. So she does. And does. And does again.

Damn.

"Take another seat, Lily." The bad behavior of the machines follows her around the room from machine to machine while every kid in the room is snickering and watching her instead of their own computers. "Try this new keyboard, Lily."

Why don't they just send the new keyboard back to the factory before they even open the box?

They bring in a line of computer geeks and gurus who try to fix the problems, but the more tinkering they do to solve the cause of the mishaps, the worse they get. And now Lily has been dubbed "The Computer Hexer" by a couple of new students. This new name, "Hexer," follows her around the school and makes her afraid to tell the lab teacher that sometimes just waving her hand over the keyboard or mouse makes it react, or that the toaster at home overheats in her presence and burns the toast at every setting, or that the lights and T.V. sometimes switch on by themselves.

It's a lonely world when you cannot talk about the bizarre things that happen to you except to some kind of a spirit or angel that comes around when least expected to give you a lecture about something weird. And speaking of weird, how would anybody feel if their mom and dad thought them weird in the head and were thinking about packing their kid off to a shrink? What if the other kids in school find out about that when they already think you are overly strange? What if the kids that call you "Four Eyes" or "The Hexer" find out and blab all over school about Lily being crazy and being sent to a psychiatrist or maybe even needing to be locked up?

Mom is suggesting to Lily, "Try out for some extracurricular activities like the school play. You know, Lily, to lift you out of the dumps."

Lily objects by saying that Cat's the movie star of the family, but Mom is arguing that she should try out with Catrina for a part anyway. "If you won't try out for the play they're working on now, at least consider this year's Shakespeare play in the spring. You think about it, Lily." Lily will have none of it. She's not about to get up on stage in front of those name-calling kids for anything.

Finally the day comes when the dam breaks and Lily gushes out upon her stunned mother all of her held-back stories through heart-wrenching sobs. "I had no idea. Just no idea," her mom keeps repeating.

"And on top of this," Lily is saying, "Dad doesn't yell at his other kids like he does me. His eardrum-splitting words feel like a thousand needles. I'm afraid of him."

"He worries about you more, Lily. Catrina is tough. Sammy is just . . . Sammy. You're easily bruised, like the petals of a lily. When he's anxious his voice increases volume and I too hear the lack of softness, but he loves you, Honey, honest. He does."

Lily mouths words without sound, "I'll try to remember that. But it's hard."

After the deluge of fantastic revelations and the crush of her feelings, they sit for a long time in silence. Then, slowly, painfully, Mom rises out of her chair, pats and gives Lily a kiss on the head and says, "We'll get to the bottom of this," and leaves Lily to sit with herself, a mere husk, a hull of a person.

The Wind thinks that as agonizing as it was, the fallout was a good thing. Keeping things locked up inside soaks up a lot of a person's energy and can lead to wrongful rumination and depression. Lily's husk now has huge cracks in it. I think a new Lily is going to break out.

CHAPTER THIRTY-SIX

The Shrink Is a Nice Lady

Dr. Caroline Snipes is looking at Lily over the rim of her tortoise-shell half glasses. She is listening intently. She already has extensive notes about the family and "the difficulties" from her mother's perspective. Today is Lily's first exposure to the doctor over the circumference of a cup of peppermint tea, known to calm the stomach. Dr. Snipes has quite a stash of teas that she shares with her clients. The individually silk-wrapped tea bags are nestled in a beautiful wooden box with a large butterfly of hammered brass imbedded in its lid. Next to the elaborate tea box is a round cut-crystal vase filled with exactly twelve perfect pink rosebuds. From a suitor perhaps? A rose for every month of the year? There are no ashtrays. There is a tiny eye-catching brass standard with tiny lion-clawed legs for her professional cards.

Her fancy Seattle Fifth Avenue office is on the 22nd floor of the tall building, boasting floor to ceiling windows, with their natural light and stunning views of Puget Sound and the Olympic Mountains in the distance. The plush rug, of a violet-gray hue, bounces your steps up to an equally cushy rose-colored couch with fluffy flowery embroidered pillows. The doctor likes color. Mixed with the smell of her roses her visitors might detect a faint whiff of furniture polish in the air that has brought the gleam of perfection to her majestic handworked mahogany desk, where her yellow paper pad and shining silver pen have been resting the last half hour. At first Dr. Snipes had been taking copious notes. But now she has leaned back in her chair, absorbed in Lily's story.

Caroline Snipes is what some call "well put together." Not only are her clothes and accessories coordinated, but every wisp of blond hair is caught up just so in a slick up-do, her red painted nails freshly done without flaw, her make-up applied with an artist's touch that Cat would envy if she were here. Envious associates whisper that, "The lady looks as though she just fell out of a fancy magazine ad." Her business suit is, well, businessy. It has enough padding to square her shoulders and make them look bigger than her hips, instead of the other way around. She has a little dainty sparkly pin on her jacket lapel, it looks like the letter 'C.' But I think all this controlled mannish suit look is covering for a very soft-hearted interior. I would guess her to be about thirty-five years, give or take.

"This is quite a story, Lily. When your mother first told me about your alleged past-life experiences as Sings To Flowers I thought it might be a variation of one of the dissociative disorders, where the little Indian girl is really a part of your present-day self. To be honest, I am not so sure that I believe in reincarnation, although there are plenty of my professional colleagues who do believe in it and practice past life regression hypnotherapy.

"What I find so interesting is your remembering such details of the Blackfoot culture. You are sure that you have never studied any of it in school?"

"No Ma'am. We made maps of the location of the local tribes, the Makah, the Chimakum, the Klallum, the Quinault, the Quileute, and the Twana, around where I live. Mostly we just learned the names and where they lived and where they fished."

"Between your mother's visit and yours, I did some study about the Blackfoot people. I could find some, but not all the details you provided. To be honest, it makes me wonder about reincarnation, even though I cannot accept it totally as fact. However I am the first to admit that the field of psychiatry is young and growing and learning every day as we speak.

"Certainly little Sings To Flowers, as I know her through your telling, had childhood trauma worthy of dissociation. Dissociation is a defense mechanism for dealing with the physical, mental, or social trauma or abuse. Psychologically, a part of the traumatized mind runs for cover and hides, causing dissociation of some kind, often—but not always—with amnesia. However the good news is the Sings To Flowers part of you is remembering the trauma, which actually is the first step of healing. I will be frank. I have never tried to help someone in the healing process of a past life dissociation.

"As far as this business about kundalini, there is a mention of such in the DMS IV, or the Diagnostic and Statistical Manual of Mental Disorders, fourth edition, describing 'Spiritual Crisis' as one of the disorders and kundalini is cited there. The manual also describes 'Mystical Psychosis,' which is a much more serious condition, which raises the question of possible relationship of one to the other. The so-called kundalini manifestation is also acknowledged in literature concerning some of the Christian saints who practiced persistent long hours of contemplative prayer. So it is not completely unknown to Western studies, while it has widespread acceptance in the East. With our shrinking world, some of the East-West ideas are starting to blend more and more." She pauses to chuckle a little to herself about The Shrink, talking about a shrinking world.

"We have two foci of interest here then," she continues. "I have found in my practice that often by focusing and bringing a resolution to one situation that the other sometimes spontaneously resolves. I am going to suggest that we focus on one problem at a time. I am going to prescribe some medication as well."

"I don't want medication!" Lily proclaims.

"With the proper medication we can expect some relief from your depression. Maybe take it for just six months?"

"No way!"

"Alright. Just know that it is available to you should you change your mind and if you become worse I will be very firm about recommending it. In the meantime I am going to suggest something that I only suggest to a very few of the kind of patients I usually see. I am bringing it up for your consideration because of your strong orientation to the Native American culture.

"There is a psychotherapist who lives near you on Case Inlet and has an office in Shelton. He treats many of the Native Americans there according to their tradition. He is Cherokee by orientation, but has been received well by the Pacific Northwest tribes. He does what is called a 'soul retrieval ceremony.' The few who have participated in his ceremony therapy have had, quite remarkably, a very rapid recovery. Actually, they often feel better more quickly than those who go through the traditional long-talk therapy for certain dissociation disorders. The problem for most of us non-hippie types is that few are comfortable with the ceremony. There are drumming and animal sounds involved. But this may be just your cup of tea," she smiles while lifting her teacup to her lips. "If this sounds helpful to you, I can arrange it."

"Yes. I would like to try it. No Name told me to call back the part of my soul that I left in the mountains of Montana."

"Lily, have you ever considered the fact that No Name may be the part of your wise self that has separated from you in your mind?"

"Nope."

CHAPTER THIRTY-SEVEN

Lily's Second Little Mess-Up

"No, no, no. It was all that Indian stuff that got your head turned around in the first place."

"But Dad! Dr. Snipes thinks it's a good idea to look at the problems head-on. The shaman's treatment would help me do that better than anything. I already have an appointment."

"Cancel it. Lily, you need to stay in reality with a board-certified psychiatrist, not some Half Crazy who's probably fooled around with mind-altering drugs."

"You mean like the ones I refused from Dr. Snipes?"

The Wind wishes Dad could remember that he himself was Native American in a past life or even a person of color before that.

"Lily, Shamanism is a booby trap for the mind. You are to stay out of it."

A week passes, but Lily does not cancel. On top of that, she and her mother have been up to something. They've been driving off to somewhere, just the two of them, every afternoon. When they return Lily's eyes have a gleam.

Then one Saturday Dad comes home for lunch to find Cat tweeting and laughing into her phone. That's usual. Sammy is throwing his basketball against the garage door, having missed the hoop five out of six times. That's usual. It's also usual that Mom is pouring warmed-up soup into four bowls. Wait a minute. There should be five bowls. Dad sees it.

"Where's Lily?"

"She went to her appointment."

"That shaman guy? Who's driving her?"

"She is."

"Marge! She needs a license!"

Mom is pulling a paper out of the kitchen junk-drawer and waves a learner permit in front of Dad's face. "She wouldn't wait for lunch and was afraid you'd try to stop her. She just wouldn't wait for me; she grabbed the keys and took off."

"Give me that. What's the address in Shelton?" Tearing the paper from her hand, he does not wait for an answer. The screen door bangs on his way out as he jumps back in his mail truck, leaving evidence of the relationship between the application of gas and the rotation of tires stamped in the driveway.

There's a speed trap between Allyn and Shelton. In fact there's more than one. Usually mail trucks are slow pokes. Dad's truck is flying and is way outside his route. Is this because he is concerned for Lily or concerned that his authority has been challenged?

Dad rounds the corner to the speed trap well known by local drivers. There's Lily, pulled off to the side of the road, and sitting behind her is that familiar black and white car with powerful twinkling colored lights.

"Now we're in for it!"

He's right. When Dad pulls his mail truck to a stop behind the cop another flashing light pulls up behind him. People are gawking as they drive by two cops, a mail truck, and a car with a very young driver. Perhaps it's gang related or a sting?

"John! I thought someone had stolen your mail truck!" says the sheriff after emerging from behind.

"Oh, good. It's you Henry. Maybe you'll go easy on me. It's kind of an emergency."

"Oh? Somebody sick?"

"You could say that. We're going to a doctor's appointment."

"We? Is that one of your girls up there in front? Well, I guess it is.

Why the parade? She up there and you back here in your mail truck? And isn't town behind you?"

"Well we're late. The appointment is in Shelton. We got confused."

"Well I guess so! You can't be going this fast John; you know that. Almost 50 in a 35. You're not a tourist."

The policeman in front of the mail truck is walking back. "Hi Henry," he says to the other cop. "The young lady up front says she has a learner permit but it's not with her. To top it off, there is no adult in the car."

"Yes, well I'm the dad, following close behind to watch her every move and monitor her driving. Here's her permit." Dad is waving it. The Wind is blowing on it to make it flutter.

"Sir, the adult needs to be **inside** the car, not following. As a public servant you should know that." Shoving the paper back in front of Dad's nose, "It spells it out right here in black and white."

"Well yes." Dad is thinking, *black and white is my problem today.* "I was just going to tell my daughter that I plan to pull the mail truck up to the gas station that's right up ahead, leave it there and join her in the car."

"It's Okay, Steve," says Officer Henry. "I'll take it from here. We've known each other since grade school. This was an emergency. John doesn't plan on this happening again—do you John?"

"No Sir."

The cop from the police car behind Lily is folding up his ticket book. He's getting back into his flashing black and white and sits there while Dad drives his mail truck to the gas station and walks back and gets into Lily's car. Eventually both cops pull away.

"You're one lucky young lady, Young Lady," Dad booms.

"Yes I know, I'm sorry Dad, but I'm going to my appointment. You know what? I'm the one in the driver seat."

"I can see that. But the only reason we're heading to Shelton is because I told the cops that's where we're going. Here's the deal. One more driving mistake and I am taking over, we are forgetting any appointment and turning around, cops or no cops."

The Wind thinks they got off easy. It's a good thing that mail delivery people and cops take coffee and donuts at the same place in Allyn.

CHAPTER THIRTY-EIGHT
Charlie Four Thumbs Helps Lily

Lily is parking the family car in front of the shaman's office. She had already practiced this trip with Mom. Dad is thinking he's just going to trade places with Lily and head straight back to Allyn. But not so fast—across the street is the same police officer that stopped Lily earlier. He's looking at them over the top of his reflective sunglasses.

"Well Dad, if we are putting on a show for that cop, we better go into the building."

"Five minutes. That's it . . . or until the policeman leaves."

Charlie Four Thumbs has a Masters Degree in Mental Health from the prestigious Columbia University. He also has been called a shaman, a label derived from the steppes of Asia, at least from an anthropologic point of view. However, many First Peoples do not accept the idea that their ancestors originally came over the land bridge in the Bering Strait. Therefore, he does not call himself a shaman and winces if he hears another refer to him as such. He considers his therapy a blend of indigenous spiritual healing traditions. The word is out about his "cures" and he is well known amongst the tribes of the Pacific Northwest. If he has to refer to himself as anything, he uses the words indigenous healer, and then only rarely.

When he was a little boy at the mission school he told the other kids that when he was born his mother bit off his extra thumbs, and proudly displayed his scars to prove the validity of his story. This was, however, a partly made-up story that gave him special standing among his classmates and he has been, well, special ever since. The truth is, he **was** born with extra digits, an extra thumb on each hand. But they were removed under sterile conditions by a board-certified surgeon in a North Carolina county hospital.

The Shelton building is a two story old brick, lath-and-plaster structure that looks to be of 1920's vintage, but has been neglected over the years. Begrudgingly, Dad enters with a nervous looking Lily and climbs well-worn steps. There is no name on Charlie's office door, like all the other office doors in the narrow hall lit by a single shade-less light bulb. Clients just learn where to go and if a stranger accidentally picks the wrong door and blunders into a private conversation, in this town people just go with the flow.

They pause in the hallway, wondering which door to knock on first, but before they do the door at the end of the hall opens wide.

"Lily and Lily's Dad? Enter." A man of average build, a face with plenty of laugh lines and no frown creases, greets them with a broad smile. He steps aside and motions for them to take a seat in a room lit with a single old scratched-up desk lamp and a small, high-up, divided single-paned window. Dad takes note that he will not be able to check on the policeman across the street from here. He's stuck. They take seats on two of the only three chairs in the room, all rolling naugahyde office-type.

Lily is wondering what Dr. Caroline Snipes would think of the dust bunnies in the corners, the spilled coffee stains on important-looking papers, and piles of disarranged professional magazines that cover the top of his desk, which is a piece of plywood supported by two saw horses pushed against the back wall. Above his head is a large poster, bulging in the center and held up with thumbtacks displaying a picture of a bear adorned with long claws and longer teeth. At the sight of this sagging poster Lily begins to relax. Underneath the poster is a large abalone shell containing a small bundle of sage wrapped with a red cloth and burnt at one end.

He is dressed in a bright orange-red shirt, a black bolero-style vest, jeans, and cowboy boots. His long hair is braided neatly and his hands have two large silver and turquoise rings that distract you from the scars on the thumb side of his hands, which are hardly noticeable anyway. For some reason Lily notices that his fingernails are clean. Everything about him is clean actually and very picturesque, down to his silver feather earring. Lily likes him instantly. Dad withholds his opinion. When he opens his mouth to speak his words and the timber of his voice seem filled with magic and strong medicine.

"Dr. Snipes has sent me your information. You have quite a story to tell. Your journey in your last physical life or the one you are remembering actually brought back some pleasant memories for me of my grandmother. So I thank you for that.

"As Dr. Snipes has explained to you, I use ceremony as a treatment therapy to reach your subconscious mind. Mind is to brain as soul is to body. Mind and soul cannot be separated. When incarnate, the mind/soul energy field surrounds and penetrates the dense physical vehicle even at the cellular level. Severe trauma in a past incarnation can carry over as 'cellular memory' because the mind and soul live on after the brain and body are gone."

I wonder if that is why I became so ill at the sight of the deformed moccasin in the museum. Maybe I have soul memory around the stick going through my left foot.

"Mind and soul are energy that takes form in other realities too. An experienced traveler through the other realities can find what we call broken-off soul pieces and help them rejoin the main soul body, which helps the client become more whole, the personality more stable."

Dad, who at the beginning was shifting around in his chair, is starting to look interested. His chair isn't squeaking as much.

"I would like to explain to you a fundamental difference between modern psychotherapy and the beliefs of most indigenous peoples that have been handed down by oral tradition for many generations and in all parts of the world.

"The current belief taught today in schools of psychology is that in times when a person believes there is a threat to his safety, a part of his psyche or mind can split off, causing the person's personality to become fragmented and weakened. We are taught in school that this split is an illusion. People particularly vulnerable to this phenomenon are little children with stern or harsh parenting or a grown person under a rigid authoritative individual or group.

"Part of the parents' and teachers' job is to help the children adjust and conform to the standard norms of their society or 'domesticate' the wild untamed behavior in order to help the child become a 'successful' contributing citizen. Depending on the inner strength of the one being tamed, anything from outright physical abuse to a simple comment like, 'You'll never be good at that,' can send a soul piece fleeing for safety.

"Sometimes parents or religious teachings use shame to control whatever behaviors they feel are misfit. In the worst cases the behavior that is a misfit becomes confused with **who** is a misfit, or the person doing the action rather than the action being the problem, and a child can be unwisely and unhappily labeled in his own mind for life.

"In the native tradition these broken away fragments of self are viewed as actual parts of the soul or the spirit of the person, in flight to a different reality for the same reasons as modern psychology states, but that this reality where the soul piece is hiding is far from an illusion.

"Specialized native spirit healers have learned how to travel in the other realities. In the tradition I use there are three worlds, the lower, middle, and the upper worlds. In other traditions this is called the divisions of the astral world. We have all traveled to the other realities many times in dreams. A part of the life force or soul remains connected to the sleeping body while the rest of the spirit travels. However the healer is trained to travel between and through other realities with a more awake and aware consciousness and can travel with purpose and do work in the other realities."

"How is this possible?" asks Lily.

"We have spirit or totem helpers. Because we native people are close to our Mother Earth, and because we honor all plants, animals, and birds as our brothers, or relatives, they come to us when asked. Our spirit blends with theirs in the other worlds and we take on some of their powers to accomplish tasks. For instance, the spirit animals that often come to me are the bear who lends me his strength, the raven who is one of the smartest of the bird people, for his intelligence, or the eagle for his excellent sight. Things look differently in other realities. It takes a lot of practice and a good measure of courage."

"Once you get to another reality, what do you do there?"

"Our animal helpers search out and find the split off pieces of a client's soul energy and we tell those pieces that it is safe to come back to this reality. If the spirit piece is ready to come home it will then be blown back into the client's body."

"Wait a minute. What do you mean by that?"

"There are doorways into your body. Your mouth and nose are obvious ones and I sometimes use one of those, depending. But there are also spiritual doorways and if the trauma or pain is in a particular location, then I will use the corresponding spirit doorway along the spine or top of the head and blow the missing part back into your body with a sound. I know this may seem very strange to your ears.

"When these doorways remain tight in fear of trauma they can cause pain, just as the inability to release a traumatic event memory can cause the damming up of Life Force, which also translates into physical pain."

"I have heard of this explanation before from No Name. Do I have to do anything special to get ready for the ceremony?"

"First, I need your permission to do this work. Second, your being here today with your parent is for the purpose of explanation and preparation. I ask that you bathe before you come and that you do eat meat. This surprises some people, but the purpose of eating the meat is to help keep you grounded in this reality. You will lie down on a mat and be in a mentally receptive mode, by doing as much nothing as you can." Charlie Four Thumbs is smiling.

"There is one more important preparatory exercise I would like you to do before your ceremony appointment. I would like you to have a small notebook and pen by your bedside and to carry it with you throughout the day for the next two weeks. Before you go to sleep at night ask your unconscious mind to remind you of any uncomfortable incidences with another individual or group from your past where strong unpleasant feelings around that situation remain.

"When a memory bubbles up, write it down with a few words, but it needs to be about a specific situation. Write it in the past tense such as, 'I felt anger in the mountains of Montana when I was an old woman in my life as Sings To Flowers.' Anger is part of the human condition in this dimension. You cannot stamp it out of yourself. The important thing is whether you have learned to transmute the energy of it or whether it is stuck in your craw. Please bring the small notebook with you when you come to ceremony.

"We do not do the ceremony work here in Shelton. You need to come to my place near Case Inlet if you choose to pursue this. I have prepared a small sanctuary there in nature. It is away from traffic noises and other modern day intrusions. There will be another two-legged helper present, a human drummer, a lady, although traditionally it is a man who drums, but she has been drumming with me for years. Spirit healers use the sound of the drum or rattles to enter into a trance and be carried to other realities to do their work. Some healers take plant drugs for altered states of consciousness, but I do not do that nor do I recommend it for anyone as it is hard to work well under its influence and can open doorways to other more serious problems."

Dad is strangely silent on the way home. He even forgets to see if the cop is still across the street. Finally he says, "I cannot for the life of me know why, but that Four Thumbs fellow made sense to me when I should be thinking he's full of shit."

"I think you love me after all Dad." Dad smiles a yes, then turns away to hide a tear.

CHAPTER THIRTY-NINE

The Healing of Lily's Soul Pieces

The sacred space around the simple one-story three-bedroom home with a separate one-car garage belonging to Charlie Four Thumbs far exceeds expectations. His two acres of Mother Nature are on the waters of the ever-changing Puget Sound and face the orange-pink of morning. Every tree has a bird, bat, or butterfly house. The red-bellied Douglas squirrels, chipmunks, and raccoons are daily visitors who come to feed on the sunflower seeds that the birds purposefully drop under their feeding stations. A 2,000 pound eagle's nest sits near the top of an old Sitka spruce at the edge of a thirty-foot cliff overlooking the water. When the tide is out several families of deer wander through and take the path down to the water to lick salt off the wave-smoothed rocks. Later in the season Mrs. Four Thumbs will feed clouds of petite darting humming birds.

At this moment a blue heron is performing as a motionless living statue on the lower sunken part of a large crustacean-crusted boulder. He stands on one foot buffeted by the lap, lap, lap of the water. Earlier this morning three seals were competing for attention by slapping their flippers on the water's surface to stir up a boil of herring.

Lily has her assignment, the notebook where she's written unpleasant memories, in her hands. She was surprised that, as she remembered them, their memory still irritated her even if the incident was long ago. She is following Charlie and Sarah Williams, the drummer, along a meandering path through woods of fir, madrona, cedar, and spruce. Here and there are clumps of budding salmonberry, wild rose bushes, and salal.

They step in time to the drumbeats, letting the toes of their bare feet caress the moss on the trail. They have been reminded that they are walking upon the face of Mother Earth and the dead ancestors of all peoples. Here and there Lily is surprised by the intense unblinking gaze of a carved wooden totem animal.

Now and then the forest hush is pierced by distant calls from a seagull or a chirping eagle. Then, with a rush of wings, a raven, black from beak tip to tail feathers and glistening in the sun, glides over their heads leading the little group as if on cue. The bird makes no noise but lands daintily on the roof of a low round hut constructed of cedar within a clearing rimmed with large barnacle-marked sea rocks. His eyes carefully consider the approaching two-leggeds. He stays motionless except for his eyes and does not fly even when the three humans begin their slow rhythmic clock-wise march around the hut with Charlie's singing prayers, burning sweet grass, and drum music. Four times they circle before bending low and entering through a small enigmatic door that, like Charlie's home, faces sunrise. Their clockwise walk continues inside with bowed heads.

At the top of the domed roof is a twelve-inch hole that lets in sunlight by day and starlight by night. Directly under it in the earthen floor is a fire pit with five large white flickering candles placed closely to one another, one at the center and one at each of the four direction points within the circle. They cast eerie dancing shadows against the curved walls, which represent the roundness of Mother Earth, the hoop of the stars, and the circle of our lives.

Charlie will sit or lie opposite the door in the west. Drummer Sarah will sit in the south. Between them and the candle fire is an altar in the shape of a half-moon that is curved around the fire pit with the thickest part in front of the spirit healer.

Upon the altar sits a vase of assorted feathers—that of the eagle, the raven, the jay, and the white owl reveal themselves in the dim light. A duck feather sits next to a bowl of water. There are several rattles on the altar in front of the drummer.

The four basic elements, fire, water, earth, and air are represented within this sacred space. No one walks between the fire and the altar. Lily makes out a turtle shell, an abalone shell with cedar shavings and sage bundles for smudging. Lily will lie down in the wisdom position, the north, on a thick bed of sage which, when crushed by Lily's body, fills the space with its organic aroma, thought to bring in the spirits through the dome's overhead opening.

Charlie instructs Lily that she is to treat her little papers of unreleased angers and fears by burning the papers and purifying the disquieting energy they represent in the fire. He explains that the release of the angers, resentments, and fears will create vacancies in her body, which will be filled with her missing soul parts.

That being done, the medicine man begins smudging Lily, after lighting the cedar in the abalone shell and fanning the smoke in her direction with the eagle feather. Next he takes the duck feather, dips it in the water, and sprinkles a few drops on the top of her head. He then motions for Lily to lie down on the sage mat, which is surprisingly soft. The aroma becomes strong and heady to the point of near intoxication. Charlie instructs, "Lily, take slow breaths deep into your abdomen and in your mind let your muscles dissolve and your bones become hollow and receptive. That is all. I will do all the work. You will just be."

"Rrrumph . . . Rrrumph . . . Haaa," Charlie makes low guttural sounds in his throat as he shakes his rattles, one in each hand, while he moves about the interior of this sacred space. "Eeeeek . . . Whip . . . Whip," Bird-like noises are heard while Charlie shakes his rattles directly over Lily.

Soon all is still within the walls except for the steady beat of the drum that initially was quite slow, but now has quickened. Lily notices that her heart has become synchronized with the drum, three beats of the drum between every beat of her heart. Soon it feels as though she is both the drum and inside her own heart. She cannot help but think of Ahhatome and the white owl feather she just saw on the altar, the strange white owl she met on the road from Cut Bank, and the marked feather that was laid at her feet there and in Idaho. Beat . . . Beat . . . beat . . . Deeper . . . Deeper . . . dee . . .

Whoosh, is the feeling and then a soft popping sound. Lily isn't sure if she has opened her eyes because her vision is fuzzy. The colors are muted, not as much as a black and white movie, but blurry. *Maybe it's because I lay my glasses aside.* Reaching for her glasses she notices something else. Her hand will not open or close or clutch anything. Her hand creates a silent breeze when she moves her arm. *Omygosh. I do not have a hand or arm. I have a wing!*

Realizing this, Lily is jumping to her feet. But she doesn't have any feet! Her vision is now clear. Lily looks down on two big thick-toed bird feet with talons peeking out below her legs encased in feathered pantaloons! Her eyes pierce through fluff and are fixed in their sockets, yet more aware of the tiniest twitch of mouse or lemming, while her head swivels effortlessly right and left as though on a greased ball bearing.

"Jesus! Jesus!" This is more an expletive than a call for The Master. Instead of a holy savior, as one might hope for, she looks up at two coal-black eyes set deeply in the head of an equally black massively-beaked gigantic raven.

"What are you doing! You need to be in your receptive state back in the ceremony lodge," says the raven by mental telepathy. Lily hears every word perfectly.

"Okay. Okay. But I do not know how I got here and I have no clue how to get back, and believe me, I am more than happy to go." She is speaking without speaking. She is mentally speaking and the bird seems to get her words.

"Come on, I'll take you back, but you need to stay put. All these reality shifts take my energy and I have a lot to do for you. No guilt intended. You simply follow the drumbeats back. The drum sent you out by coordinating your own brain/body rhythm with it. You just follow that process again to get back into the body. You're not out too far, it should be easy."

Abruptly, Lily is waking up back in the ceremony hut. Spirit healer Charlie is leaning over her. On his head is the raven . . . the real raven or . . . the other real raven.

"I'll be back soon. Stay here." He goes back to his place to lie down. Within three beats of the drum, his consciousness flies away on black wings.

Lily is trying to relax. She is looking at her hands. *Yes, they are fingers not feathers.* She closes her eyes and takes a deep breath of relief. Beat . . . Beat . . . Beat . . . Relax . . . Relax . . . Re . . .

Whoosh . . . . Pop. "Oh no! Please, not again! Where's Charlie or that black bird! Ahhhhh, I'm a pile of white feathers! Okay, Okay. Just follow the drumbeat back. Okay."

Splat. It was like hitting an invisible shield. Splat. SPLAT. SPLAT—THUMP. "CHARLIE! Where are you?"

Whoosh. *OOooooooooh. Am I falling or flying? Vision is again a blur.* Not because Lily in her owl form cannot see—it's that she moves faster than the speed of light in this reality layer. *Where am I going? I am stopping! Help!* The white owl is looking down with precision vision on a strange scene. There is Charlie, or Charlie's raven form, just below. He sees her.

"I couldn't help it," Lily's owl is telling the raven. "It just happened by accident and I cannot get back. Something keeps stopping me."

"If you have mixed intentions and if you were out of synchronicity with the drum you can get temporarily blocked. You must have become frightened and that sped up your heart, forcing you out of the vehicle of the drum's vibrational waves. Perhaps you have done shaman work before in another life, but you are, as they say, rusty. You have forgotten a lot," he says, adding, "If you ever knew it. Okay. You can go with me, but stay out of the way. If you get frightened all hell breaks loose. If the scene is disturbing shut your eyes, breathe deeply, and say to yourself, 'Stay with Charlie.' Now fly into that tree and stay there until I tell you differently."

Lily is not sure how to fly. "You flew here, Lily. Just think yourself into that tree." Lily sees a tree that she swears was not there a second before. She is looking at it and then suddenly she is in it. She still is not sure if she actually flew there. She is wondering if Two Bears' days as a shaman have anything to do with her newly found awkward ability to cross over into this place.

What a strange sight! Looking closer, there is a fuzzy, blurry-looking replica of Lily, pretty much as she is in high school now, but she is sitting behind bars in some kind of cage. As if this is not strange enough, the door to the cage is swinging loosely back and forth in The Wind and has no latch. It can be pushed open or shut with a puff of breath, but the girl doesn't want to come out. The young girl is wearing a T-shirt with some letters on the front and back. On the front is printed the words "Four Eyes." On the back is printed "Computer Hexer." Perched on the very tip of her nose, putting the viewing areas in front of her cheekbones instead of her eyes, is a pair of glasses a good half an inch thick. Someone has taken a black marking pen and has drawn eyes on the glass, so indeed, it looks like she has four eyes. In both back corners of her jail are heaps of broken computer parts. *What in the world? Or, What in this world, reality, or dream, or hallucination is this?* Suddenly Lily knows the answer. *It is a **recently** lost soul piece.*

How is Charlie going to retrieve this soul piece who does not want to come out from behind her bars but stays huddled up, sitting on the floor with her hands wrapped around her knees? This scene is depressing. Everything about her is gray. Gray shirt, gray sunken eyes. Good grief, she looks like a cartoon, complete with a little gray cloud above her head that pours down rain now and again, just on her. "How can you let yourself get so upset over nothing?" Lily shouts out telepathically from her owl form.

"Keep still," it's Charlie or Raven, or Charlie as Raven talking to her owl now. He turns back to the gray girl and speaks softly and gently.

"You need not be disturbed by the ignorance of others. Remember, those that call you names, that try to make you look less than you are, do so because they themselves are insecure. They feel puffed up and important when they belittle others, but only for a moment. In the eyes of onlookers, they look smaller, not bigger. Remember hearing as we judge others, we are judged? Here is the important lesson to know from your experience. It is such a simple thing really. But when others around you seem to forget it, their forgetting helps to make you forget it too. Here it is.

"You are not a pair of glasses. You are not ever what you wear. You are not a designer label, the car you drive, the house you live in, the color of your skin, or the pimples on your face, which by the way, you don't have. You are something far, far greater. You are Divine Spirit as are all things. You, like others, are spirit that was never born and will never die. You clothe yourself temporarily in flesh from time to time to have certain kinds of experiences. But you are not your experiences, or how you think you look, and you are certainly not the judgments of others.

"Now that you know this truth you can come back and enjoy the physical life you are in now, even if others do not yet have the grasp of your truth. Come now. Let's go back to your Earth experience. Standing in your truth will give you inner strength of character."

Lily is reminded of what No Name once said. "Standing in your truth does not necessarily mean arguing with others who have a different point of view. Someday you will allow the others to stand in their truth, even if you don't like it. Arguing just helps to put the other person in a defensive posture and hardens his belief. If you feel like it, simply state what you believe and that should be enough. You don't even have to do that much. Standing in your own truth is an internal knowledge and an internal experience. It is an internal posture of mind rather than the creation of arguments that can split friendships. It is an internal shield to your psychic doorways and it makes you very strong. But remember, at the highest level on your journey, eventually all dogmas and postures of truth dissolve into the Great Oneness."

Is there a half smile on the young girl's face? I believe so. And more is happening. The raven is stepping aside and holding the cage door open. She is stepping outside. Her form is becoming more difficult to see. As the details of her form become more faint, the raven is growing larger, until he is the size of the girl. Then it is clear what just happened. The soul piece turned into a fog and was sucked up through the breathing holes in the raven's beak.

I didn't even know that I lost a soul piece so recently, Lily mused.

The raven heard her musings. "You are young. When you are old and have lost quite a few soul pieces along the way, you feel the loss of each and every one, but sadly, few know what it is about. You've heard the saying, 'It takes a village to raise a child?' Well, the fact is, each person **is** a village. In a healthy person, it is a well-integrated village. It is so well integrated it feels like one being."

"What did you do to that little girl? Is she now inside you?" asked Lily.

"Yes. She is the energy of your sad self released from the prison of her sad and depressing thoughts. After our talk, she is now hopeful and almost joyful. In this state she was not hard for me to swallow. I will be blowing her into your body when we get back. I want to put her in the main vehicle of your current awareness, rather than this flighty owl dream form you have chosen."

"I don't remember choosing it."

"Come on. We are going to visit the heaviest astral-ethereal layer of the Montana mountains where you demonstrated your rage as the old woman, Sings To Flowers. I'm bringing you with me because your consciousness doesn't seem to be able to stay in your physical vehicle during this ceremony. But I am warning you—what you see may not be pretty. Since it is old energy it may be breaking up, but you can never tell for sure until you get there. It was powerful energy and that can stick around, sometimes for centuries. You must, I repeat, you **must** stay calm. Do you think you can do that? If not, we will have to quit right here."

Lily, or Lily in ethereal owl form, is nodding her head in agreement. In the split of a second they come upon a place that I can only describe as grotesque. There is a ghostly form of an old woman who has lost her head and both her arms. "This is a good sign," explains the raven, trying to keep Lily calm. "The old angry energy is breaking up."

Lily is taking deep breaths and periodically shutting her owl eyes, but so far she is staying calm enough. The headless, armless ghost body is running around in circles. The hem of her skirt is on fire. Her head, partly eaten away by fire, is screeching, "I'm on fire! I'm on fire! Get me out of here!"

The trees in the etheric layer are a little further ahead in time than the dense physical layer and have now lost all of their leaves. The Wind blows with such strength that the naked branches toss, turn, and bow, while the specter's head is bounced from one branch to the next as though The Wind is trying to break up the bodiless head into a thousand pieces. Here and there her wild wind-blown hair gets caught in the tree branches making the degenerate's head scream louder and curse. A strand of hair catches on fire and the phantom head smashes itself against the trunk of the tree in an effort to put the fire out.

Opening her eyes again to the headless wound-up apparition body, Lily notices an unmistakable bitter burned-body stench that is explained by thousands and thousands of hook-bug carcasses scattered about the fiery terrain. They had been attached to our Earth mother on the etheric level in this small, secluded area of beautiful Glacier Park for over two centuries. Some are still smoking, some are already burnt to a crisp, and some are just now caught by leaping tongues of flame. Two ghost arms are moaning and trying desperately to sweep up what they can of the old spirit crone's hook-bugs who are still living and running around, trying to hide under hot rocks or run for the hills. The arm pieces are trying to force the bugs into a ghost sac to be moved to a safer place, which is hard to do because the hook-bugs are frightened and try to escape the sac when at the next moment the entire clutch of bugs explodes into fire. The arms and the bugs are screaming. But more than screaming, the hook-bugs are making a popping noise and jumping like popcorn as their hard exoskeletons burst when on fire. But lo, what is this that Lily sees?

When the hook-bugs burst open, spirit butterflies of every description, soft colored with silvery glittering overtones, escape from their previous bug form. What was the hard covering of ugly hook-bugs hiding from the casual observer who may enter this reality? It was the potential of butterflies, the symbol of transformed energy.

The raven wastes no time in sucking up the butterflies. As he does so he grows bigger and taller yet. He is now so large that he can look the bodiless head, still caught in the branches, straight into those blood-shot eyes. He then carefully untangles a swatch of that knotted-up hair, and speaks softly.

"We have heard your painful cries for help and have come to assist you. There is one here who has lived your agonies as you." The eyes of the spirit are looking around, but do not recognize the owl as herself. "We acknowledge your suffering and we honor your humanity. You are now in transformation and you are in evolution of your soul. The pain and the fires of alchemy will stay with you as long as you try to cling to your old form. It is time for you to surrender this way of being and go home. If you choose to remain here you will continue separated from yourself, miserable, and in pain."

All the parts of the disassembled spirit are stopping to listen and considering the words of the gentle and wise spirit healer. Then, slowly, the spirit parts of the old Sings To Flowers come together to make a whole. The fire still licks at the hem of her garment and leaps to wisps of her hair, but she does not cry out or seem to feel the flames. Her eyes are softening and looking younger and more vibrant. The outline of her reassembled body becomes fuzzy, but at the same time it is infused with bright golden light where moments earlier there was but fire. Now the light is beginning to condense into a brilliant orb the size of a Ping-Pong ball, which is swallowed by the raven in one gulp. Not even a smoldering ash remains on the ground for I, The Wind, have just blown them into the air and forever away from this beautiful, holy, and previously haunted spot.

"We have one more stop on our way back," said the raven. "Come."

"Where are we now?" asks Lily.

"Look and see."

Are those three objects ghosts, or pillars of salt, or perhaps pillars of white ashes? They are so old and stiff and barely holding together that one dare not sneeze for fear of blowing them apart. "Am I supposed to know who or what these stiff things are?"

"Look again, Lily. You know these shadows very well."

"I think not. I do not know them at all. They don't even look real."

"I know," sighs Charlie's raven. "That's what most humans say about this reality except those who know how to work in it. Look up close."

"I don't know these stern, unmoving, rigid, taut-looking people. Do they ever smile?"

"Oh yes, they do or did, just not when you were around. You do not recognize three teachers from your life as Sings To Flowers? They stole your childhood. Unknowingly, of course, which is most always the case. Don't get too close. I want you to recognize them before they fall into dust, which they are about to do."

"Holy Ashes! Oh . . . My . . . Gosh!" Lily now knows, without knowing how she knows, that these three lifeless forms standing with folded arms across their chests all tightly wrapped in shredded blankets are . . . Comes Still Alive, Two Guns Buffalo Calf, and Stolen Lakota Woman. "Yipes, how do they look so old!"

"So joyless, you mean? All teachers are a reflection of self. Did you know that? So they are a reflection of you at that time, aged before you were meant to age. You wanted to play, run, laugh, swim naked, be noisy, and be **silly, Lily.** In that culture it was thought unbecoming for a bride to be as a child, even if you were one. To be so would cast a bad reflection on your husband and the rest of the clan.

"Lily, I am going to tell you what one of my spiritual teachers told me many years ago. Have you heard the phrase, 'And the child will lead you home?' It means never throw away the attitude of the heart of a child, to be in awe, to be delighted with the discovery of each new thing. Look. We live in such a beautiful part of the world, rich in water, mountains, valleys, and wild life. Go daily, even if it is for a few minutes, to sit and do nothing but enjoy nature. Nature nurtures and keeps the child in you alive. Nature raises your vibrations and when that happens you nurture nature as well as the child within.

"Water is affected by your childhood joy and visa versa. No wonder you wanted to swim naked in the lakes with your Love. After all, humans are mostly water. There is more communication in our bodies than that which communicates by way of our nervous system and the meridian energy system recognized in Chinese Medicine. Water is a vehicle of communication, carrying vibrations from cell to cell within the dense physical body. When your vibrations are high, like a child in awe, at peace, and in the state of expanded or "altered consciousness," as some say, you may be surprised to see that if you are sitting by a lake it will be calmed and it will also reflect to you its deepest secrets. I tell you this only because you have the ability to slip into another reality. This would not be useful information for where the majority of people are today on their soul journeys.

"Above all, try to see the world through the eyes of an innocent child. To repeat myself, because it is so important, be in awe and aware of the splendor around you. You can consciously cultivate the attitude of thankfulness for being the recipient of splendor and, more than that, this attitude of heart is critical for the manifestation of anything you may desire. Be aware of the splendor. Never fall asleep to this attitude. Be in awe. This is a great secret."

"I'll try to remember that always," Lily says softly.

"Now, let's blow down these old worn out joyless husks of what once contained robust Life. They are of no use to the vital living now."

So Charlie, the spiritual healer and Lily's teacher, along with Lily, who is both his client and **his** teacher, are together huffing and puffing and blowing down three old worn out houses. Houses that are mere shadows of what once were houses of and for Living Spirit. Lily sneezes a few times, having caught some of the dust in her owl eyes and beak, but I, The Wind, am quick to blow the rest away. Little particles, etheric dust of Lily's former teachers, will settle back into the ethereal layer of Mother Earth. The spirits of those old relics live in new houses now.

The Owl and the Raven return to the ceremony hut. Lily's solid human body appears to be asleep. The Wind hears her murmur, *I am not myself, but whatever I am is wonderfully made.*

Then Charlie, with the help of his spirit animal, blows new life into the empty spaces in Lily's solar plexus and her heart.

CHAPTER FORTY

New Confidence

As the pages of the school calendar are turned, Lily's eyes have more light, her face more smiles. She has had follow-up visits with both Dr. Snipes and Charlie Four Thumbs. Charlie has encouraged Lily to mentally speak to her returned soul pieces before falling asleep. She is telling them, "Thank you for returning" and reassuring them that she is watching over and caring for them.

The Wind has witnessed the cord between Ahhatome and Lily lose its muddy colors; it is refined, more elastic, and without its deep hook. As she makes spiritual advancements, so does he. People affect one another, especially twin flames.

It is now early March and time for this year's auditions for the last school play of the year, the tragic love story of *Romeo and Juliet*. Lily is thinking that it might be fun after all to have a bit part in this year's grand finale, or perhaps help with the scenery, even though, *It's Cat who lets it be known that she is the real movie star in town and 'the natural choice for Juliet.'* After all, it's Cat's senior year. There can be no question that the role of Juliet will be hers.

Lily comforts herself with the thought that she may feel closer to Ahhatome while working on this most famous play about love, but then dismisses that idea as foolishness.

Mr. Heartwood, teacher of composition, English literature, and head of the drama department, has a favorite Shakespeare play that he cycles every four years so that every student that graduates from North Mason High will have had a chance to be a part of it, even if just as an audience participant. The other teachers have long ago guessed his favorite, having seen it recycled again and again with a new set of faces and new paint applied to old scenery props.

Mr. Heartwood could be Danny DeVito's identical twin, even down to his five-foot frame, bald head fringed with dark hair, chocolate-brown eyes, and exuberant personality magnified by waving arms. But that is where the similarity ends; for it is also rumored in whispers in the hallways, accompanied by giggles and guffaws behind his back, that Mr. Heartwood has never had a lover. They say that, "He lives vicariously through the Shakespeare characters in his classes and his productions on stage." The rumor is only partly true. He does have a love life, but that is none of anybody's business. It is also true that Mr. Heartwood, like many people, is in love with the works of Shakespeare.

"Shakespeare reaches beyond the mere depths of character in his plays," Mr. Heartwood is telling his literature class. His students will study *Romeo and Juliet* through the spring until it is presented on stage and he especially encourages his students to try out for parts since they will be well prepared by him, he believes, for understanding the depths of it. Both Lily and Cat are in his class.

"Shakespeare also touches the mystery and the majesty of being, by his genius choice of words," continues Mr. Heartwood. "A Shakespeare phrase can be studied and re-studied and still leave us with multiple choices of interpretation. Truly he was, and is, one of the greatest playwrights of the English language. He was not only a master of words, he was a master of showing humans to themselves through his history plays, his tragedies, and his comedies. He reveals to us the history of human intellect and emotions, and the results of playing one against the other."

Some of the students are starting to nod off. Mr. Heartwood seems to have that effect on all but a few of his students when he begins to wax in eloquent speech. Perhaps those who do not sigh and shut their eyes with drooping heads have their inner eyes set on stage or movie stardom. It is clear that one of those is Catrina Johantgen, future movie star, or so she writes in any student yearbook offered to her, as well as on the cover of all her personal notebooks.

"Who can tell me what the story of *Romeo and Juliet* is about?"

There is silence. The students' nervous eyes dart around the room from one to the other, while some shrink down in their chairs, trying to become invisible.

Finally, a hesitant hand is raised to half-mast and quickly pulled down again, but too late. It is not missed by eagle-eye Heartwood. "Timothy Wilson. What can you tell us about *Romeo and Juliet*?"

"Well, ah, Well I guess everyone knows it's about a dude that falls for a hot chick and they're like really in love, and they get it on . . . and everything like that."

Mr. Heartwood is trying not to roll his eyes, which is part of a teacher's skill with his students. *So much to teach. So much to learn. So little time to get them on the right path. Will these kids ever make it in the world? Will the thick scales ever fall off their eyes?* Mr. Heartwood is thinking all of this in the flash of a second.

"Yes, Tim, but what is the tragedy of the story?"

"Ah, well. It's ah . . ." It's clear that Timothy Wilson is fishing for an answer. "It's that when you fall in love, a . . . well, ah . . ." Mr. Heartwood is nodding his head in the affirmative to encourage the boy to continue. ". . . It's not worth all the trouble you have to go through."

Some students are trying not to laugh but cannot hold back and are doing it with a closed mouth while laughing through the nose. Other heads are nodding in agreement. As Tim looks at his classmates he sees that he has made points, but Cat, who sits directly behind him and refers to him as her "personal set of wheels" is sending him looks that, if he takes notice, could suck the juice out of him. And if he doesn't take notice? He's beginning to flinch from an unexplained sudden stiff neck and upper back. The Wind speaks into Catrina's deaf ears, "Watch out! Bad Karma."

Mr. Heartwood on the other hand feels a kinship with Tim. They both have suffered the indignity of being judged unusually short for a man.

Okay then, the drama teacher thinks. *It's clear to me that I will have to give a short synopsis of the story, as I have had to do for the last fifteen years. Why do I keep expecting something different . . . like perhaps one of them has actually read the play? Half of them wander the halls like lovesick fools. You'd think they would be interested.*

"Do any of you know how old Juliet was?" There is no response. Most of the students are looking at their feet. "She was not quite fourteen years old! Not only that, Juliet's nurse tries to convince Juliet's mother, Lady Capulet, by swearing on her 'maidenhead at twelve years old,' that Juliet is not yet fourteen. This is critical because age fourteen was considered the marriageable age in the Middle Ages. The nurse does not want Juliet, whom she loves as her own child, to be whisked away from her.

"Does anyone know what is meant by or why she swears 'by my maidenhead at twelve years old?'" There is a pause. The students look like a blank sheet of paper with no pen and empty heads.

"Virgin!" shouts Mr. Heartwood. Every eye in the room pops open. No slumbering eyes now. Mr. Heartwood has used this technique to awaken his students before. He goes on to explain further, "A young girl before first intercourse was considered pure. The nurse is simply stating that she swears that her statement is pure and true. Truly, Juliet is not fourteen.

"In the early 1300's, the wealthy people had nurses to suckle their children. Breast feeding was considered by the highly respected ladies of society to be a messy business that interfered with their lavish parties and more lavish gowns. The nurse was usually a servant who was also nursing her own baby when she was needed for this duty by her mistress." There is a muffled snicker in the room and some of the boys are shifting nervously in their chairs. Mr. Heartwood cannot hide his annoyance with an obvious change in the volume of his voice, but he perseveres.

"In the case of our Shakespeare story, Juliet's nurse has had a baby that recently died at the time when Juliet was born and needed to be breast fed." There are a few more snorts in the class. Mr. Heartwood's eyebrows tighten but he does not acknowledge the disturbance. "In general, the nurse would then be expected to live with the family and raise the child. As such, she would become fiercely loyal to the child and child's family. From the child's view her nurse was a second mother and later, the older child's confidant.

"In *Romeo and Juliet*, Juliet's nurse was not convincing in her argument with Juliet's mother, that Juliet was younger than fourteen years, and Juliet is immediately betrothed by her parent's will to the Count Paris. Her mother argues that she knows wealthy citizens in town whose daughters are younger than Juliet and who already have children.

"The theme of the story is about love and hate. Two families, like the Hatfields and the McCoys, are bitter enemies. Even the servants of the opposing families cannot stand their servant counterparts of the rival family. Juliet is a Capulet and therefore by the accident of birth, is the destined enemy of Romeo of the Montague family. Is there anyone who can tell me what happens next?"

Not a student moves a muscle. Mr. Heartwood, on the other hand, is in control of himself again and does not appear to be perturbed, as he is now capturing himself by the lure of the story. "The Capulets are giving a masked ball for their friends and of course, no Montagues are invited. Romeo, a daring fellow, upon the risk of death, sneaks into the Capulet party where he sees the beautiful Juliet. It is mutual love at first sight behind their party masks." Half the students, who had fallen asleep again after the use of his usually successful Virgin Strategy, are now starting to come back alive as Mr. Heartwood continues to weave the famous story.

"After the guests leave the Capulet's home, Romeo, now drunk on love, decides to scale the wall into the Capulet's orchard where Juliet has come to her bedroom balcony in her night clothes to cry to the moon that she has fallen in love with the enemy of her household. There, in the famous balcony scene, the lovers pledge undying love and plan to meet the very next day to be secretly married by Friar Laurence. If Juliet were alive today she would not even be in high school yet when she married Romeo!" Suddenly everyone is sitting up straighter in their chairs. Mr. Heartwood has the room's attention at last. It is about time.

"And here is where the story takes a turn for the worse. Juliet is secretly married to Romeo, and at the same time, betrothed to The Count. She runs to Friar Laurence for help. He gives her a potion that makes all her vital signs disappear, but only temporarily, causing even her doctor to think she is dead. She takes the concoction on the morning of her planned wedding to Count Paris.

"The bereaved family, instead of watching the lovely Juliet walk down the aisle at her wedding, is now laying her out in the Capulet family crypt on a cold slab. Romeo gets news of Juliet's death, but not the news from Friar Laurence that she is only temporary without signs of life and will wake up after several hours. Romeo, stricken with grief, buys potent poison which he plans to take himself and die next to the body of his beloved."

Mr. Heartwood pauses for a moment, considering if he should continue with the rest of his speech. He sees this class as barely awake, but then he decides to give it a shot even though he may be talking to the air.

"Shakespeare is a metaphysician." The eyes in the room are starting to turn dull, just as Mr. Heartwood predicted. Trying to recapture his audience, "Shakespeare stories are allegories." The eyes are turning duller yet. "Shakespeare explains a deeper spiritual truth through his stories, if . . . if you have the wisdom to hear and to recognize it. Is there anyone in this room who thinks they know what the deeper truth is here?"

Lily raises her hand. Mr. Heartwood is shocked. He has asked this question every year for fifteen years. He has a respondent. His first!

"If you repeatedly think or speak poisonous thoughts or poisonous words toward certain others, especially over generations, and add the power of a group, the result will be powerful bad news for both sides. You actually poison yourself, for we are all one." Lily is speaking with confidence, remembering the teachings of No Name.

There is silence in the room. Everyone, including Mr. Heartwood, is looking at Lily as if they have seen her for the first time. Mr. Heartwood is holding onto his desk. He cannot believe his ears. Out of the mouth of babes sometimes comes a new or old truth, depending on how you look at it.

Mr. Heartwood is now speaking very softly. "Yes, yes Lily, and next Romeo kills Paris, who has come to Juliet's tomb to mourn, and then commits suicide by drinking the poison he purchased from an apothecary. Juliet awakes to find her beloved next to her, dead. Despondent, she takes Romeo's dagger and kills herself. The families are so saddened by this tragic outcome of their years of petty bickering that they swear never to fight again. They both have paid a terrible price for their hatred. One has to believe that the lovers are together in heaven."

Mr. Heartwood is more cheerful after the insight from one of his students. Maybe this class has a future after all. "Students," he says, "I want some volunteers to read Juliet's lament on the balcony. I want you to read it now to yourself, on page 325, Act II, scene II, starting with O Romeo, Romeo and think about what is being said here. What exactly was Shakespeare saying? Is there more than one way to interpret the first line? I would then like volunteers to read eleven lines out loud.

Catrina Johantgen's hand is the first to be enthusiastically raised.

> *O Romeo, Romeo! Wherefore art thou Romeo?*
> *Deny thy father and refuse thy name;*
> *Or, if thou wilt not, be but sworn my love*
> *And I'll no longer be a Capulet.*

> *'Tis but thy name that is my enemy;*
> *Thou art thyself, though not a Montague.*
> *What's Montague? It is nor hand, nor foot,*
> *Nor arm, nor face, nor any other part*
> *Belonging to a man. O be some other name!*
> *What's in a name? That which we call a rose*
> *By any other name would smell as sweet;*
> *So Romeo would, were he not Romeo call'd,*
> *Retain that dear perfection which he owns*
> *Without that title. Romeo, doff thy name,*
> *And for thy name, which is no part of thee,*
> *Take all myself.*
> Act II, Scene II

"And what, Catrina Johantgen, is your interpretation of the first line?"

"Well, I think she is saying, Romeo, Romeo, where are you?" says Cat.

"All right, who else will read these lines and tell me what they think the first line means?" Four more girls read and give the identical interpretation as Cat. Why do they do that? Is it to reinforce each other? After all, Cat is a member of "the group." To oppose her interpretation is not a way to win a popularity contest.

"Lily, I want you to read." Lily had not planned on reading, but Mr. Heartwood has put her under the spotlight. She reads.

"And what do you think the first lines mean Lily, in context with the rest of the passage?"

"I do not think it means, Romeo where are you? I think it means, Why is your name Romeo?"

"And why do you think that, Lily?"

"Because, Juliet has been raised to think that any first name attached to the last name, Montague, is the name of evil. To her, because she is a Capulet, the name Romeo Montague should mean

The Enemy. She's having a hard time with that idea after meeting him and falling in love."

Mr. Heartwood has a poorly disguised pleased look on his face, but says nothing about Lily's interpretation. He says, "Sign up now for try outs for parts in the play. Try outs will be this Saturday in the cafeteria. The assignment of character parts to those who have tried out will be announced then. After the choice has been made about who gets which part we will have costumes there and seamstresses to measure and alter costumes as needed. Lily, come see me after class."

After class, Mr. Heartwood tells Lily he wants her to try out for the play. I think he wants her to be Juliet. I also think Catrina is going to have a "freakin' fit."

CHAPTER FORTY-ONE

Catrina's Meltdown

"The Nurse? The Nurse? He expects me to be the Nurse! And to wear that?!" Catrina is pointing to the fat suit undergarment laid out on one of the cafeteria tables for her to try on for her costume fitting. "Nooooo Waaaaay! And what is this piece of garbage? It's all shit!" She is picking up a plain brown dress of nubby, coarse, loosely-woven itchy fabric with long sleeves and a high collar, along with a starched white apron that complements an even more starched-up long white head piece with wings like that of a centuries-old style for nuns.

"I am **not** going to play this part!" She is throwing down the garments and preparing to thunder out of the room. As she departs down the aisle made between two long rows of cafeteria tables festooned with costumes, swords, feathered and sequined materials, she creates a mini tornado-like wind that knocks several items to the floor and renders the laid-out goods all cockeyed.

Mr. Heartwood was expecting a little resistance from Catrina, but not such a theatrical display. If she ever makes it in Hollywood she will be one of those temperamental volatile types that nobody wants to put up with. Mr. Heartwood is not going to put up with it either. He is going to save her movie career. Now. He has placed himself at the exit door, spread eagle. He is stretched to his absolute maximum and then some, width wise. Any extraneous movement in the room may have the power to topple this man in his precarious position, on his face or on his back. His arms and legs are over-extended out to his sides where the tips of his middle fingers barely meet the vertical up-right parts of the double door casings, making him appear about four feet tall and making his eyes at the level of the approaching Fury's bosom. All the other eyes in the cafeteria, which were previously on Catrina, are now on Mr. Heartwood.

Catrina is caught up short by Mr. Heartwood's blockade. He looks absolutely ridiculous, but the seriousness on his face and the graveness of the situation keeps the room quiet but expectant. What is to happen next?

"You and I are going to have a talk," he says with tightened-up neck muscles and semi-clenched teeth. His fiery eyes meet with equal force the fire from the eyes of Catrina. The situation has come to the boiling point of this most serious situation because Mr. Heartwood is stuck. He cannot move of his own accord, even if he wants to. He has pulled the muscles in his groin. His thigh adductor muscles are screaming in agony and he cannot bring his legs together.

Dear God, now what? "I'm stuck!" yells Heartwood. "Uah…Uah." One of the big football guys, who gets a silent part in the play as a guard, is coming. He lifts the yelping Heartwood into the air. Gravity swings his legs together as Mr. Heartwood screeches his agony. The football guy is gently placing Mr. Heartwood back on his feet, but he can barely walk. He is holding onto Willie's, the football guy's arm, and with his other arm he reaches out for Catrina who was effectively stopped in her tracks and even now has a slight look of pity mixed in with the intensity in her eyes.

"We are going across the hall," says Mr. Heartwood, and the two help the hobbling man to a vacant classroom where Cat and her teacher each take a seat after Mr. Heartwood says, "Sit."

"I'll call you," he says to the young man, "when I need to stand up again." Next he turns his attention to Catrina. "I'm going to save your neck for your Hollywood career, so listen up." Brave Mr. Heartwood, he is going to valiantly deliver a long speech from his tortured body while ignoring intense groin discomfort, at least for now.

"Gone are the days of making someone a star on the big screen by looks alone. Today stars must have talent. They must be able to play a variety of roles if they're going to have any staying power. A movie career used to be called the heartbreak career, because once the fancy camera filters could no longer hide the wrinkles and other imperfections of age a leading lady, especially, was done. The world has changed since those days. Now we have people who truly understand the art of the industry. Look at Dustin Hoffman in Rain Man, Meryl Streep in Julie and Julia. And of course, Danny DeVito isn't so bad either." Catrina is actually cracking a half smirk and half smile.

"That is what acting is in the 21st century. Those now-famous actors are not just about the beauty queen's or the leading man's look, and they are the actors that people want to see. Also, a nasty attitude begets nasty attitude back at ya and will ruin your career faster than anything. Be forewarned.

"The part of the nurse, in my opinion, is the best role for showing talent. Any actress or actor can be a leading lady or leading man with good lighting and good camera angles. But not everybody can be a good supporting character actor because the actor needs to be so much more versatile. Those are the roles you want in the beginning of your career before the casting people pigeon hole you for just one type of character and your talent, demonstrated very narrowly, becomes less and less in demand as tastes in movies change."

Catrina is sighing. It is not clear if she believes what Mr. Heartwood is telling her.

"There is a long passage given to Juliet's nurse in Act I, Scene III, where the nurse desperately tries to save Juliet from marriage and knows that she is failing to convince the Powers That Be that Juliet is less than fourteen. The nurse therefore becomes even more desperate and rambles on and on, making little sense. It is the most difficult speech in the entire play. Few can do it convincingly. I believe you can do it."

With this last comment the pout on Catrina's face is turning into a small smile. Mr. Heartwood is in great pain. He is trying not to show it, being like some of Shakespeare's characters, who deliver long speeches just before they die.

"There is one more thing, Catrina. The keys to success are as follows. First, use the force of your mind and your intellect. Think about your desire and picture it in your mind. Second, engage the force of your emotions, but be careful in choosing your emotions, lest they cause others harm. Know and be aware that the power of your emotions will trump the power of your intellect every time.

"There is not a warring nation's general, a political leader, a revival tent preacher, a football coach, who does not use inflammatory rhetoric, either positive or negative, to stir up the emotions of the people he believes he can inspire to accomplish a goal. For success, the first and second powers must be in agreement. And you must inspire the most important person. Yourself.

"Finally, the power that trumps the other two powers is the power of your will or your intent. Whatever you do, do not give up. Every day state your intent out loud. Then let it go. Be ready to receive the opportunities the Universe sends your way and move on those opportunities, as long as it is in alignment with your goal, even if you judge them as small and unworthy of you, such as the part of Juliet's nurse."

"Why do I need to state my intent out loud?"

"I read it in a book and then tested it myself. Teachers are forever students. Your unconscious mind hears it best out loud or something like that. I don't remember exactly. They say you can be even more convincing to yourself by stating it to your mirror."

The Wind whispers, "There's a lot more to Catrina than what she thinks she sees in the mirror. The mirror emphasizes the less of her." But Mr. Heartwood cannot hear The Wind through his pain and Catrina cannot hear through her mad anger.

Mr. Heartwood is tired and looks the part. *Will any of this sink into Catrina's brain?* He wonders. *Will she remember a single word of this talk ten years from now or even tomorrow? Is my effort even worth it? I know as a teacher in the teaching moment I can never be sure what the final effect will be, if any,* he sighs.

He may not know what effect he is having, but he knows this. *I have done the best damn job I can with this kid.* He is satisfied with himself, even if nobody else will ever sing his praises. This makes him feel good inside, while his inner thighs feel like hell lit them on fire.

CHAPTER FORTY-TWO

Behind the Scenes

Mr. Heartwood has not been seen in school for a week. Without Heartwood, the air in his homeroom was as flat and sagging as a week-old helium balloon, but today he's back. He's also brought back with him his enthusiasm.

The young substitute teacher, a new graduate from Teacher's College who goes by the name Miss Higgby, was there in body, but not in spirit. She had the students read from *Romeo and Juliet*, but it was obvious that she was not paying attention. Her mind had to be on something else or someone else, because she would often lose her place or be unaware that the student currently reading had come to the end of his assigned passage. *Romeo and Juliet* sometimes has a strange effect on people, perhaps triggering the memory of a distant or current love.

Before his return Mr. Heartwood's entire domain had slumped. But in spite of the fact that he is confined to a walker with little wheels for the next two weeks, the preparations for the play have come magically alive.

Seamstresses and mothers are sewing and altering costumes. Some of the old scenery is being discarded. Dads are helping with the redesign and the fortifying of old props to look new. The odor of fresh paint permeates the atmosphere. Three girls assigned as make-up artists are practicing on their families and even on kid brothers and sisters. Ticket sellers are counting bleacher spaces and chairs and trying different configurations of them in the gym. A stage is being put together on risers that can be taken up and down in an hour. Two student musicians, one who plays the oboe and one who plays the flute, will provide Elizabethan music for the Capulet ball scene as well as a sad refrain at the end of the play where the two lovers die in each other's arms.

Practices for the school play are every Monday, Wednesday, and Friday nights, as well as Saturday afternoons. There is a sense of urgency as Mr. Heartwood tells everyone that, "We are a week behind," "Listen up people," "We have lost a week," and "Let's get cracking." Seeing Mr. Heartwood struggle with his walker, trying to maneuver around folding chairs and over extension cords, is making the cast and crew push themselves 110%.

Cat does not whine that she, not Lily, should play Juliet. At home they recite their parts in the shower and at the dinner table, much to Sammy's consternation. There has been so much reciting that even Sammy, as well as Mom and Dad, have Cat's difficult speech memorized. It is a long recitation where the nurse proclaims that Juliet will not be fourteen years old until the next Lammas-Eve, for it was on the eve before Lammas when Juliet was born. The discourse begins:

Even or odd, of all days in the year,
Come Lammas-eve at night shall she be fourteen.

Mr. Heartwood explains "Lammas Day, sometimes called Lammas-tide, was originally a pagan Celtic harvest feast day celebrated from sundown August 1 to sundown August 2. It was later adopted by the Catholic Church as Loaf Mass Day, where the people would bring a loaf of bread to the church that was made from the first harvest. In the Middle Ages it was indeed a reason for celebration after the first wheat and corn harvest, for it meant that the crops were safely gathered and stored for the next year, and this meant that their crops had escaped the blight and therefore the people had escaped a shortage of food, or worse, a famine.

"When Shakespeare tells us that Juliet was born on Lammas-eve, he is speaking to us as he often does, through the use of allegory. Juliet's life was cut short, on the eve of when she could enjoy the harvest or fruits (consummation) of her love with Romeo," says Heartwood.

On Tuesdays and Thursdays Lily and Cat take the bus back to Allyn from their school in Belfair as usual, but they're sure to include a stop at Big Bubba's Burgers, then munch their way down East Drum Street to the community gazebo where they'll practice the lines exchanged between Juliet and her nurse.

They try hiding their French fries from winged French fry eaters who keep a constant vigil on customers with a white sack in hand coming from Big Bubba's. Once the girls duck into the gazebo the birds will stop swooping at them and they can rehearse their parts without interruptions from crows, gulls, Sammy's silly comments, and his sillier antics. And he calls Lily "The Silly."

Sometimes after church Lily and Cat hike up to Lake Devereaux just past the entrance to St. Albans Girl Scout camp to the boat-launch parking lot, where the boys lucky enough to have access to a car sometimes park with their girlfriends after nightfall. But in the daylight of Sunday afternoons the boat launch site is unusually deserted and is another good place to practice.

The result of all this is that Cat and Lily are feeling closer, even though Cat is constantly teasing Lily about "carting those two rocks and dirty feathers around everywhere we go." Forgotten are the differences in their temperaments, their styles of make-up and dress, the groups they hang out with or, in Lily's case, the absence of a group. They have actually been seen laughing together.

It has been several weeks since Lily has seen the flashing lights around her anywhere. People are getting used to the electrical misfires around Lily and she and others are learning to live with them.

However, recently the flashing lights have reappeared and Lily catches herself thinking about Two Bears and Ahhatome. *Maybe it was all a dream*, but when she thinks that it feels wrong. It especially feels real when she has one of her tailbone "hot flashes."

No Name has not been around lately. Perhaps she is simply aware that Lily is in a whirl of preparation activity. Sometimes Lily wonders where No Name is and where she goes.

Practicing for the play is a long process. Little by little there is better timing of the lines. People are forgetting their parts less and less. The musicians are more together and in tune and hit a screeching note only on rare occasion. The electrical devices have been fine-tuned many times. It is not known how much of Lily's energy field is having an effect on them, if any, but they have needed more fussing with than usual.

Either Mom or Dad has brought the girls, and Sammy, to every nightly rehearsal without fail. Sammy sometimes listens, sometimes fidgets, or sometimes he is allowed to wander back stage and help out with the preparations there. Dad proudly comments that Sammy loves the electrical accompaniment for the play, both back and front stage. "It is a sign that someday he could be a successful electrical engineer!"

Two days before opening night a strange and eerie calm descends on the school and the participants in Shakespeare's play. Even the weather has stopped raining, and The Wind is no longer blowing, and the water on The Sound is without a ripple. In fact the water has been like glass for two straight days and nights. This is not normal. Is it partly due to the fact that everyone in the play has practiced until they are saying their lines in their sleep and can not bear the thought of repeating their parts one more time and are walking around with a dazed look? Or . . . Is something else about to happen?

CHAPTER FORTY-THREE

The Play, the End Is the Beginning

*All the world's a stage,
And all the men and women merely players:
They have their exits and their entrances;
And one man in his time plays many parts.*
Shakespeare
"As You Like IT" Act II, Scene VII

The big night has come. Friends and families have greeted one another and found their seats. The programs explaining the story of *Romeo and Juliet* have been read and re-read. The parents of cast and stage assistants have found their children's names and are pleased that the spelling of them is correct. The programs will be used as fans, saved to be pressed into scrapbooks and diaries, pinned to bulletin boards, or even framed. Mr. Heartwood has never looked so dapper in his black tie and black patent leather shoes, smelling of men's cologne. He is also without his walker. Yesterday he left his cane in the back of his closet and today has only an almost imperceptible limp. The lights are being turned down low and a hush descends upon the audience.

The play opens with a fight scene in the streets of Verona between cocky young men of the House of Capulet and the House of Montague. The lights flash on their swinging swords, every move having been previously rehearsed at least a hundred times. The heated words of the actors are being projected well, even to the last row of the listeners. The dramatic physical, as well as verbal, dueling between the two feuding families, including the heads of both houses who come to see what the latest squabble is about, draws the spectators into the story just as it was hoped.

Mr. Heartwood is pleased. But, Oh my! Am I seeing what I think I am seeing? There is a little buzz between the students in the audience when one by one they notice who is sitting next to Mr. Heartwood. Their drama coach and the mystery woman sitting next to him have shoulders that are touching as they are leaning into each other. Sometimes they turn toward each other and they smile a special smile. Why, it is none other than Miss Higgby! Among the students I am hearing, "Could it be?" "Oh Wow!" "Could it be that old Heartwood has a love life after all?" So there are two love stories to watch tonight and most of the students are watching both . . . the story of *Romeo and Juliet* and the story of Mr. Heartwood and Miss Higgby.

Presently Romeo makes his appearance. This coveted role was awarded to none other than Timothy Wilson. He appears a good sight taller with platform soles and one-and-a-half inch heels. Mr. Heartwood has also seen to it that Timothy stands slightly more downstage, closer to the audience, which will give the illusion of more height, and that he address any person he speaks to by looking above the other's downstage shoulder, rather than directly at the person's face. It's working. Not only that, it seems to me that Timothy's voice has dropped an octave since the time he was at Cat's birthday party.

Timothy has found his inner strength. He has endured the teasing and whistles from the other boys for winning this role and he has held his own. All mockery and joking has stopped now and Tim is delivering a superb performance tonight. Mr. Heartwood is not the only one who is admiring Tim's performance. Catrina Johantgen, watching from the wings, is deciding that Tim makes a rather fine figure of a young man and, in spite of his somewhat squatty stature, his tights show off a well-turned calf muscle. She is deciding to drop the cruel reference to him as "my personal wheels."

Now it is Cat's turn to make her entrance on stage, but no Cat or Catrina is present. Catrina Johantgen is gone. Instead is a very portly, doddering, middle-aged woman. "Her apron strings are tied high," a metaphor for pregnancy as they used to say in the old days, but in this case the apron strings are tied high because her fat-suit makes her rotund in both her front and her rear. Even her voice is different—lower, more even, not the soaring flighty teen talk. Her gestures are a little halting, as though she suffers from rheumatism in her hip joints, elbows, and neck, and she appears as though she might topple over any minute from her top heavy mid-section, balanced precariously on unusually trim and dainty ankles. This is going to be a great presentation of Juliet's nurse.

Lily enters a few seconds after Cat as the young beautiful Juliet, looking not a day past thirteen or fourteen. Her long hair is caught up behind her head and cascades loosely down to the middle of her back in gentle undulations that catch the overhead lights. She will wear her hair up in a bun with a sparkling tiara for the ball scene. There is some color on her cheeks, and lips, and mascara!

She has a green velvety sleeveless outer garment decorated with gold braid and dotted with sewn-on small crystal beads that flash here and there with her movements like tiny dewdrops. The outer garment is tied under her bosom and when costume change is needed the outer garment can be turned inside out, revealing a gold interior with even more decoration of bead work for the Capulet ball scene. The undergarment that covers her arms is a soft, filmy, puffy long-sleeved white gown that will serve as her diaphanous nightdress after swiftly removing the top garment. Hidden within the folds of the pockets of the reversible top dress are the pale blue celestite crystal clusters, Lily's "lucky pieces," as she calls them. Hidden also within one of the pockets are her two magical feathers.

Most remarkably of all, Lily wears no glasses, which gives her a fresh new astonishingly exquisite face. Her eyes without glasses show very much larger pools of blue than when viewed through the concave lenses for the extremely near-sighted. Her vision is blurry, but she can make do without them. It bothers her not that she cannot see the faces in the audience. She just needs to be able to exit upstage without falling off the platform's edge. So far, so good.

Cat has only a few sentences to utter as a kind of a brief warm-up before she must give "her difficult speech." Her lines being so early in the play sharpens their difficulty. As she begins the three remaining members of her nuclear family and even grandma and grandpa begin to mouth the words, as if they can help with the delivery of it.

Even or odd, of all days in the year,
Come Lammas-eve at night shall she be fourteen.
Susan and she (**psssst-st-st-st-pop**) *God rest all Christian souls!*
(**pssssp-psp-pssp**)
Were of an age; well, Susan is with God;
She was too good for me: (**srrrrp-rp-rrs-s-s-s**) *but as I said,*
On Lammas-eve at night shall she be fourteen;

Mother is horrified. Father looks confused. Where were those supplementary sounds coming from? Sammy is trying to hold back his glee and trying unsuccessfully to stifle his giggling. His eyes are watery and he is blowing snot out his nose. He is also trying to shrink in his seat. Mother has just spied a suspicious hand moving in Sammy's pocket. She grabs his wrist and pulls it out. Sammy's hand is clutching a remote control device.

"Don't you dare!" she says with a locked-up jaw. "Drop it!" The offending mechanism is dropped into Mom's hand. Mom is afraid to handle it. Being careful not to touch any of the buttons, she gingerly lays it inside her purse. *At intermission I will throw it in the trash in the ladies room,* she thinks. Then, after rethinking her plan, *No, too risky. What if someone throws a heavy object on top of it, making it fire off again?*

Grandma and Grandpa are not catching on to any of this. Perhaps they are hard of hearing. Dad is just now getting the whole picture. He is giving Sammy that look and whispers, "Son, my father would have taken me to the wood shed. Thank your lucky stars I'm not him. But you and I are going to have a serious discussion at intermission."

Although there were a few delighted snickers and chuckles among the audience Catrina took no notice of it. The very nerves in her lips and tongue and the well-worn synapses of her brain are so wired to keep going after weeks of practice that it is uncertain if she even heard the fart machine taped near the microphone above her head. The stage hands were not so oblivious however, and the apparatus is quickly discovered and removed at intermission, handed to an embarrassed dad who. back stage with his son in hand, ceremoniously smashes it with the heel of his shoe, never to be heard from again.

At the intermission between Act II and Act III Mr. Heartwood hears nothing but positive responses to the delightful interpretation with sound effects, by the nurse. "It added just the right touch to that long-winded speech by the nurse," is a common comment. "Heartwood! A daring do! But it went over well." "I don't know if Shakespeare included that in the script, but it added the right touch."

Mr. Heartwood is going back stage to find his movie star, Catrina. "Catrina," he says, "the audience loved your interpretation of your long dissertation in Act I. But next time, please run any additional sound effects through me." He then pauses, "unless they're accidental."

I don't know what makes young boys act out in such a publicly disgraceful way. He was brought up under every social decorum. Perhaps it is an attempt to get a little recognition, even if a negative one, when so much attention was being paid to the girls and the play, the play, the play—the only topic of conversation for weeks by not only Mom and Dad, but also Grandma and Grandpa. Personally, I think it comes from his past history and it is just in his genes. But from whom in his current family tree? Nobody can decipher.

As the play continues, all goes perfectly without a hitch. No lines are forgotten. Nobody falls off the stage. The hastily repaired ladder on the backside of the prop for the balcony scene did not collapse. Mr. Heartwood is starting to relax and enjoy the performance of his young charges as well as the company of his Somebody Special, snuggling close and mentally hugging him on his right side.

It is Act V, scene III. Romeo has taken all his poison and is dead. Juliet is awake now and finds his lifeless body. She says:

> *What's here? A cup, closed in my true love's hand?*
> *Poison, I see, hath been his timeless end:*
> *O churl! drunk all, and left no friendly drop*
> *To help me after? I will kiss thy lips;*
> *Haply some poison yet doth hang on them,*
> *To make me die with a restorative.   (kisses him)*
> *Thy lips are warm.*

Juliet hears a noise . . .

> *Yea, noise? Then I'll be brief. O happy dagger!*
> *(snatching Romeo's dagger)*
> *This is thy sheath (stabs herself); there rust and let*
> *Me die.*

Oh my. Oh my. I did not expect this! My thoughts have fallen silent. I will remain quieted while I orient myself to what I have just witnessed.

I've seen this before . . . Way in the past . . . Wind, why are you surprised? This is not new. I remember it now.

On the surface of it, it may seem too horrible to tell. Let me think. To third-dimensional creatures it will be unexplainable . . . cause anguish.

Why now? Things were going so well. Why in the middle or end of a play? It shouldn't be anywhere in any play, and in front of an audience!

Maybe I should remain silent. Yet, nothing expressed does not allow for soothing, and too upsetting if allowed to stay stuck in the caverns of the mind—needling while it grows until it bursts with fury upon hastily built emotional walls. This time the walls are too weak. I will speak then as I continue, probably for weeks, to absorb the series of shock waves from all the witnesses.

There was a flash of sorts. No experts could agree as to what the flash was or what followed after. They say, "What you see is what you get." What you get is not only what you see with your physical eyes from where your awareness sits at that moment, but what you see in your mind or self-imposed interpretations, and those two together make your perception. It is your perception that you live with all your days.

It made all the papers and the teleprompters and the talk radio shows, but no late night jokes. No. They thought, "Too awful to make a joke out of it."

Juliet, or Lily, just disappeared. Everyone saw the flash. Some said that there was a flash earlier in the play too, during the balcony scene. They said it was high and over the left part of the stage. Others said no, that was not where it was. They could not be sure because it had momentarily blinded them, like flash cameras used to do. At first, some thought a bunch of people disregarded the rules and were taking pictures.

But then the heat came . . . so intense that it melted the paint off the scenery, but strangely, only in a very small circumscribed spot. Within that spot, even the glass melted. The tiara placed on Juliet's head when she was laid to rest in the Capulet tomb and which was later found ten feet from the spot of her last moment on stage, contained glass and crystal beads. The metal of this crowning headdress was twisted and scorched and the glass was mostly melted away.

Glass becomes liquid at 2,000 degrees Fahrenheit. When the scene had cooled enough for inspection, they found drops of congealed globs of glass and metal combined. What was left, or what could be found, was analyzed at more than one prestigious lab.

Some swore they saw, but not everyone saw, flames shooting from Juliet's mouth. Some said she was aflame like a "**human candle**" before she "vaporized." Others said it was not a flame—it was a light. Still others said it was two flames that became one flame.

As for Romeo, there was a miracle. He was found unharmed but shaken through his bones and somehow flung clear across the stage a good fifteen feet, thereby protecting him from the intense concentration of scorching heat.

There was only one burned area in the entire room and that was where people last saw Lily. The burn was only two feet wide, but like a laser it went clean through the stage, the gym floor, the sub floor, a heating conduit beneath that, and some water pipes.

That's it, a laser! Coherent light waves . . . like that which can come from a higher dimension . . . or, within a whirling vortex in this dimension . . . or mechanically produced down here. Ahhatome. He had something to do with this! Or, I remember in ancient stories told, the rise of the two snakes, the kundalini energy finally merging with the pineal gland in the brain, the so-called third eye where one can see into the fourth dimension. Could Lily have burst open her pineal third eye with such unusual intensity that it created a vortex of photons within her own body's atoms to reach the speed of light, which then caused her anatomy to jump into the fourth dimension or higher?

Nothing was left where Lily was last seen except one shoe, like in the Cinderella story, and a small pile of ashes from an undetermined source found in the crawl space under the building. However, one other item was discovered there: the celestite geode. It no longer was in halves but perfectly round and whole. It was fused into the original piece without so much as a hairline where the fusion had taken place.

Why didn't it melt like the glass and other crystals? The experts say that if it were on her person, as Catrina Johantgen claimed, it should have melted, producing a red flame. Nobody saw a red flame and neither did I. Some said, "The geode was left as a sign" . . . "a token" . . . "a reminder that we aren't as smart as we think we are." "There are some things that happen that just cannot be figured out down here."

Catrina said, "Lily left it for us on purpose." To me, it is obvious what the fusion of the geode meant.

Everybody hates unsolved mysteries. And although the physical signs of burning were erased after the fire marshal's and expert's thorough investigations and analyses, the mental and emotional fallout has not cleared. I suspect it will never completely clear until more humans evolve their spirit, which evolves their understanding.

Some say it was yet another case of spontaneous human combustion. The opposition to that theory says that spontaneous human combustion is not a theory recognized by any hard proof demanded by sound science. Even so, along with my, The Wind's observations, there have been other eyewitnesses to a few cases of people suddenly bursting into flames.

Every theory imaginable has been visited upon the Johantgens, including that presented by a visitation from a spiritual man from India. He suggested that Lily was in a state of imbalance. He tried to explain that too much of the universal prana energy shot up the right side or Pingala (masculine channel) of Lily's back instead of the appropriate one, which is the central Sushumna channel, due to some blockages in the Sushumna and Ida (feminine channel). This eastern explanation, though interesting, sent the Johantgens to their computers to look up "premature kundalini awakening," but did not answer all their questions or make them feel the slightest bit better.

Another group of New Age Christians said that Lily simply ascended, like the rest of us will do at some future time. The intense light around her body was similar to the transfiguration of Christ and other saints seen prior to their ascent. They use as a partial support for their argument the fact that when a body is cremated at somewhere between 1400 and 2100 degrees Fahrenheit, it takes an hour to burn the first 100 pounds. Lily was gone in what seemed only seconds.

Was it an early example of the Evangelical Christian "rapture" some wondered? Others said, "No, that is not how the rapture is supposed to start; in that case all Christians will just be gone, taken up, no burning of anyone or anything even similar."

Was it Ahhatome, having tried before to come into the third dimension with too little light energy, with the result of his being stuck in the Earth's lower astral plane? Did he come again, this time with too much light . . . light that burned a hole through the etheric dimension veils right above his beloved, as a strong cutting laser might do? Maybe it was a plasma beam.

In fact, I suspect he had a role in this happening. He demonstrated time and again a disregard for the recommendations and advice of The Keeper of the Akashic Records, The Council of Elders, The Emissary of Light called No Name, his friend Horus, and even his father, Aba Ahhatome. I believe his love for Lily and perhaps his watching the Juliet drama unfold, blinded him into a headlong precipitous action.

In an effort to confirm my strong suspicions and understand more, I took a journey to other dimensions to see if the answer was there. I went to the fourth, fifth, and sixth dimensions, but I did not find the lovers. I could not help but wonder, even with my access to other dimensions, if they are truly twin flames now permanently fused would I or anyone else be able to distinguish one from the other within the new combined fused-together one? The entities I encountered in the higher dimensions only looked up when I questioned them. After my fruitless search I came to an understanding that fits for me at this point in my own developing journey.

I noticed that, as I rose to the sixth dimension, I began to lose my old sense of self. I felt myself blending with other natural forces and expanding into the great potential of being with my individualized energy melting and spreading out into more. In the highest realm I was able to reach there were no vibrations, no identifying frequencies, no division of light and dark, only stillness in The All Encompassing Oneness. I was not able to stay there as just The Wind. I began to wonder if, in the great Life drama, The Creating Force breaths out energy that becomes a multitude of individualized forms over millions of Earth-time years whereby this is followed by a great in-breath. Perhaps the "big bang" was the out-breath and the in-breath will draw us all up to be out breathed again into something new. I began to think that Lily and Ahhatome have melted into a higher dimension and are on the cusp of a great in-breath for the rest of us. Yet, in that high dimension there seemed . . . no breath at all. It is a great mystery.

Mr. Heartwood's eyes herald a new nightly routine. They open precisely three seconds before the cuckoo clock in Heartwood's dining room chirps three times. Even while nestled in the tender arms of Miss. Higgby, his thoughts begin to churn and confirm to himself again his final decision.

Henceforth, never will the characters in Romeo and Juliet march across the stage of North Mason High. Not while I'm Director of Drama.

Next his mind will plumb the depths and semi-comfort of familiar words:

Tomorrow, and tomorrow, and tomorrow
Creeps in this petty pace from day to day,
To the last syllable of recorded time;
And all our yesterdays have lighted fools
The way to dusty death. Out, out, brief candle!
Life's but a walking shadow, a poor player
That struts and frets his hour upon the stage
And then is heard no more. It is a tale
Signifying nothing.
Shakespeare
"Macbeth" Act V, Scene V

Many years later, an older lady, covered from head to toe in black and her face heavily veiled by a tight weave of fabric that hangs down over the broad brim of her hat, is entering the Museum of the Plains Indian, in Browning, Montana. There had been many pre-arranged meetings with the museum's curator and a famous trial lawyer from Seattle, who now accompanies the mystery woman. He helps her out of the car and holds her arm when going up or down steps. The lawyer's name is Samuel Johantgen. He has a reputation that follows him as being clever, almost too clever. If you are a witness in a trial, you do not want to be cross-examined by this man. He knows all the tricks. They say that, if need be, "He can pull the rabbit out of the hat and the wool over the jury's eyes faster than anyone." Nobody can remember if or when he ever lost a case.

The morning of the day before, the mystery lady stopped at the local hospital and presented a bronze-engraved plaque, "To the Memory of Dr. Jerry Dixon." After her donation of five million dollars, an entire wing of the hospital will be added onto the existing hospital and be named after him. The Dixon Wing will be designated for reconstructive surgery, specializing in facial reconstruction after severe accidents. There will be an additional stipend of one million dollars every year to help those who need but cannot afford this surgery. The money will come from The Jerry Dixon Foundation, established in his name by the mystery woman.

In the afternoon of the previous day, she paid a long visit to another more elderly and regal lady, now living in Cut Bank. This lady was invited to go with the lady in black and her lawyer to the museum, but instead, though truly grateful for the invitation, she explained that her older tired body doesn't travel well anymore. She simply gave them her blessing. Together the three of them remembered and told their stories of years ago, and laughed and cried. The lady in Cut Bank is Mary Tall Chief who reported to her two visiting friends that Jerry Dixon was killed years ago in an auto accident. He had endured severe trauma to his head. His face was unrecognizable. The lady in black already knew about this, but let Mary tell the story in her way. The veiled lady will see to it that Mary will want for nothing in her old age.

Today is an important day for the secretive lady and her lawyer. The rumors flying around and between the museum employees is that the lady dressed in black is a very famous movie star who wants her identity kept quiet.

The two visitors to the museum are now returning to their car with a special bundle. Inside are some toys; two are dolls, one doll has a body that has been separated from its head. There is a small quiver decorated with white lightning bolts appropriately sized for a child, a bow and a few arrows wrapped in sinew with three wraps of yellow, four of red, and twelve of black. They are being carried in a small oxygen-free display case.

Papers have been signed to the affect that these two people and their heirs will be the assigned trustees of these items for the museum, and they may be returned to the museum at a later time, should the condition of the items or their care become in question by either party. The museum has also received a healthy donation of two million dollars.

I know that you know who the lady in black is. But, since I am The Wind and can slide easily between the threads of the veil that covers her face, I'll check on her identity for you. Yes, you are 100% correct. It is she.

Author's After Notes

As you have seen in the story, Ahhatome was both Little Bear and Two Bears in his previous life with Lily. Lily was Sings To Flowers. Were you able to determine who else may have shared a life with them in their First Nation experience?

It was not intended for you to be able to determine all of them, because when we meet others in our present lives, it is not known from what other lives they may have come, or what parts they played in the past, or even if they had a past life the way we think of it.

Catrina Johantgen (Cat) was **Stolen Lakota Woman** in her previous life.

We have a hint in chapter eleven when we read:

"Both Sings To Flowers and Stolen Lakota Woman are suffering in their hearts for the same reason, yet though they may have suspected it, neither can be certain that the pain in the other is love-lost pain, like it is within themselves. You might say that they are like **twins** in the kind of energy they carry around their hearts and their solar centers."

In the previous life, they would not have shared their mutual agony due to the age difference and they were not close. In this life they are again twins in experience, having shared the same womb at the same time, and have been given another chance to care for one another.

Old habits are hard to break. Stolen Lakota Woman constantly chided Sings To Flowers for carrying her toy bundle everywhere she went. Catrina could not help pester Lily about "the rocks" and the "dirty feathers" her twin carried.

There is another hint in chapter thirty-five. When speaking about Catrina being solidly in the "in-group" at school, "The Wind remembers a time in the distant past where she always drew apart from the group."

Dr. Jerry Dixon was **Heavy Hair** in his previous life, the love of Stolen Lakota Woman.

In chapter three, after he notices Cat for the first time, there is a word clue:

"Dr. Dixon's organized train of analytical process, like a well-greased mechanical device in a sand storm, has hit grit and been thrown off track while he wonders if he has not entered into a **time warp** of inconsistency." Why this choice of words in his thought process?

In Chapter three we read:

"... he (Dr. Dixon) will have several nights of recalling that lovely child-woman face with the lilting sing-song voice ... He'll ... think to himself, *Have I gone mad? A kid that could be my daughter has penetrated my brain.*"

We are challenged in this story about how we think about age. The obvious examples are the jarring age difference between Comes Still Alive and Sings To Flowers and the age disparity between Catrina and Dr. Dixon, as well as the big fuss over Juliet's appropriate age for marriage. Cat, in her youth, is quick to act on her feelings. But the more mature and sophisticated Dr. Dixon, has had more time to be "domesticated," as Charlie Four Thumbs would say. He does not act on his soul impulses of recognition, which cause him nights of sweats and sleeplessness.

Sammy Johantgen is again the brother of the same soul, Sings To Flowers, now known as Lily.

He was Sings To Flowers' brother, **Coyote Head,** in their Indian lives. They are very close in both lives, in spite of his nick names, "Bothersome Brother," "The Joke," and "Major Annoyance," given to him by his sisters. He continues to carry over his trickster behavior from his previous life into this one and on into maturity, where it is shown that a negative thing can transform into a positive thing. His belief in his ability to trick people helped him to become a sly and tricky trial lawyer, after justice. He is the one you want on your side in the courtroom.

Comes Still Alive and **Two Guns Buffalo Calf,** his sits-beside-him woman, or number one wife, have been soul mates for many incarnations.

Both have chosen to be the opposite sex in this life. This time around, Comes Still Alive is Mom, **Marge Johantgen**, while Two Guns Buffalo Calf is Dad, **John Johantgen**.

It was Two Guns Buffalo Calf who nearly drowned Sings To Flowers when in her exasperation she pushed the child's head under water in an area of swift current. This helps to explain why in this life as her father he over does it in trying to keep his children safe, wanting to know not only who their friends are, but as much other information as possible, even to the point of being a snoop in his children's eyes.

Lily's mother was Sings to Flowers' husband, "Comes Still Alive." This man unknowingly stole from Sings To Flowers (now Lily) her joyful childhood soul piece. In this life, as Mom, she is very concerned that her children are having fun. She does not worry so much if Sammy is having fun, because he seems to make his own fun.

She worries more about her girls. She wants Cat to stop her tweeting and "be present" during their trip to Montana in order not to miss the new sights and what's happening. She wants Lily to stop being depressed and go on the family hike at Lake Crescent. She wants them both to be in a play, because she wants them to play. "Play" is the key idea here, a small hint as to who she was in her past life, the husband who stole child's play.

Lesser characters we know also had a former life. In chapter ten, the holy man **Running Bear**, who has the stuffed head of a raven in his hair looking behind him and who officiated at the marriage of Comes Still Alive and Sings To Flowers, is **Charlie Four Thumbs** now. He has the same totem animal, the raven, in both lives. He wore the carcass of a raven in his former life and in this life he has a live raven and "another reality raven" in his shaman work.

The very timid wife of Comes Still Alive in spite of her name, **Kills Many Enemies Woman,** is practicing inner strength and authority in this life as the psychiatrist, **Dr. Caroline Snipes.**

It is hoped that this story has touched upon these parting thoughts:

Spirit is energy, is Life Force, is Light, is Knowledge. The nature of our being is thought on the wings of perception. The substance of our being is light in various gradations of density, even to crystallization, the carbon ring molecule of physical life as we experience it in the third dimension. One follows the other. The driver behind any movement and materialization is intent. Life flows more easily by acknowledging The Divine in all things, keeping the wonder alive, and loving our neighbors in spite of our perceptions.

It is my sincere wish that you have enjoyed with me, our story making. A story without a listener is not alive. An unread book languishing on a shelf is not whole. It's only half. The reader completes it, gives it life, and makes it whole. Thank you.

Subjects ever so briefly touched upon in this book:
1. Akashic Field
2. Celestite Crystal
3. Chi Sickness
4. Christian Contemplative Prayer of the Saints
5. Etheric Hooks
6. Kundalini, premature awakening
7. Lucid Dreaming
8. The Pineal Gland, The Third Eye
9. Soul Retrieval
10. The Source Field
11. Spiritual Crises

CPSIA information can be obtained at www.ICGtesting.com
Printed in the USA
BVOW030942160413

318060BV00004B/148/P